JUDGMENT OF DRAGONS

Kriku was standing below her on hind feet, holding the flame-ball in his seven-digit hands, eyes on fire. Prandra scrambled away from the heat. Kriku opened his great fanged jaws, tipped the white fury into them, closed his mouth. It glared for a moment through the ivory bars of his teeth: the sound of a bubble popping, the hiss of flesh on fire, and it was gone. The gates of his eyes opened into the nothingness of space beyond cosmos....

"Qumedni," Prandra said, "you are better looking as a Solthree."

**A starcat and rabbi tale, with dragons, by
PHYLLIS GOTLIEB**

Berkley Books by Phyllis Gotlieb

A JUDGMENT OF DRAGONS
SUNBURST

A JUDGMENT of DRAGONS

PHYLLIS GOTLIEB

BERKLEY BOOKS, NEW YORK

A JUDGMENT OF DRAGONS

A Berkley Book / published by arrangement with
the author

PRINTING HISTORY
Berkley edition / April 1980

ISBN: 0-425-04631-1

A BERKLEY BOOK ® TM 757,375
PRINTED IN THE UNITED STATES OF AMERICA

Contents

1

SON OF THE MORNING

BY THE TIME KHRENG AND PRANDRA CAME OUT OF
deepsleep the ship was in Solthree orbit. Lights warmed around
them, the deep yellow of their sun; they slipped the clasps of their
webbing, leaped out snarling and yawning hugely, stretched to
the limit the hinges of their fanged jaws.

Khreng was a seasoned traveler; he had been twice to the
system called the Center of Worlds, where Galactic Federation
was based, and once to Sol III. Prandra had never before lifted
off Ungruwarkh, but her mind broadcast no complaints, and he
asked for none.

The ship was wakening, systems quickened from mainte-
nance level, Khreng's blood rose with the heat, and he wrapped
his tail round Prandra's waist; she tapped his nose lightly with
the pads of her hand. "Food first."

He growled without malice and dug in the food locker. "Dog
food!" That's what it was. Meat for cats was as scarce in the
Center as it was on Ungruwarkh, but colonists demanded and
got amenities for their dogs.

"Wuff, wuff!" said Prandra. "I can eat dogs too. Little things
you say they are? Why do I leave Ungruwarkh?"

"On Sol III you get meat."

Nice fat people, she thought slyly.

"Then you get killed. They have death bullets there," he
pointed through the viewer to the blue-brown globe stippled
with white, "not stunners like the GalFeds'."

She spat.

They ate and got full but not satisfied; then they coupled,
combed each other, and bathed. "Now the ESP."

3

He picked up a small blunt rod and pushed a button. Their fingers were too broad and padded and their prehensile tails too thick to handle the controls designed for humans and many other life-forms, but they had a multitude of small implements, some they had made, others had been made for them; no task they were determined to perform was impossible for them.

At the press of the button the ESP's case opened slowly to the warmed air, and the ESP began to waken.

His name was Espinoza, but he refused to be called ESPinoza, said it was too robotic. He was a brain in a midnight-blue glasstex globe, three hundred years old, and he had spent seventy-seven of them as a man. His self-image was this: a man thirty-eight years old, of medium height, brown-skinned and wiry, black hair and mustache, deep brown eyes, white even teeth. Scarce as ESPs were, even good second-graders, over two hundred years was a long time to spend as a brain in an upside-down fishbowl; he often said he was tired. "How can you feel tired?" his superiors asked with unconscious cruelty. :*Believe me, I know when I'm tired.*: Brain cells number in the trillions, but they die eventually without regrowing, and he knew he was raveling around the edges.

His thoughts gathered:

A string of onions hanging on the wall, my mother's house...like everyone else's his oldest memories were the strongest.

Diego! Diego, it's morning and he had grown up in a slum in Sao Paulo, what was there to wake up for?

Dvora, will you

"Espinoza," Khreng said. "We're in orbit."

:*Present and accounted for,*: said Espinoza. :*Home already?*: A thought shaped like a sigh.

"What next?" Prandra asked. She too was an ESP and she would also become a brain in a globe; it was part of the price for the ship, the instruments, the meat. Her eyes were wide apart, bad for close work, and she peered with difficulty through the blue glass, wanting to see what she would become.

The brain, freed of its skull plates and suspended in the nutrient bath, had become smooth and spherical, anchored by the pink cables of the vertebral and carotid arteries leading down into the pump that fed them with blood. It was not a dramatic brain, it did not throb, bubble or blurp, but the pump hummed steadily, or it would have died.

"What's next, Espinoza?"

:Pick up the radio messages, eisenkop!:

Khreng grinned. He was not hungry enough to eat a three-hundred-year-old brain. He turned a knob.

The computer rattled, squawked and said:

GALFED RELAY STATION OF FIJI TO SHIPS IN SOLTHREE ORBIT:

THE FOLLOWING SHIPS ARE IN SOLTHREE ORBIT, DATE 7572/58/186/1132:

ANDROMEDA STAR, ORE CARRIER FROM SOLNINE. MESSAGE TO JOE WISNICKI OF WARSAW, SOLTHREE, IT'S A BOY, CONGRATULATIONS, MOTHER AND CHILD WELL—

"How long does this go on?"

:Be patient.:

YSKELADAR RUXCIMI, QUARANTINED HOSPITAL SHIP CARRYING 172 CASES FUNGUS PLAGUE, STAYING THREE MONTHS.

Khreng yawned.

ZARANDU OF THANAMAR VI, BENGTVADI SECTOR 221-278, SUPERFAST CRUISER, RELAYS MESSAGE TO *GALFED SURVEYOR 668X327* FROM GALFED CENTRAL—

"That's us!"

—ORIGINATING FELDFAR 553, ANAX II, LOCALLY UNGRUWARKH, TO KHRENG AND PRANDRA FROM GALFED OBSERVER STATION. MESSAGE: ALL IS WELL, THE (WORD UNCLEAR—KITS, KATS OR KIDS) THE KITS, KATS OR KIDS IN GOOD HEALTH, TUGRIK HAS HIS SECOND TEETH—

All those light-years for this? Prandra wondered.

"Be quiet, that is my son," Khreng said.

—AND EMERALD LOOKS LIKE A FIRST GRADE ESP.

"Ha." Prandra grinned. "And that is *our* daughter."

"It's time for a male to have the ESP." He raised his hand over the switch.

:Wait—:

WARNING TO ALL SHIPS IN SOLTHREE ORBIT. QUMEDNI SHIP TENTATIVE IDENTIFICATION: *AMHIBFA'S DAUGHTER OF KWEMEDN,* IS STILL ORBITING BEYOND GALFED LANES, EXACT WHEREABOUTS UNKNOWN. DO' NOT ON ANY ACCOUNT REPEAT DO NOT ON ANY ACCOUNT TRY TO CONTACT THIS SHIP: THE *RUXCIMI* TRIED CONTACT AND BURNT OUT A FIVE-STAR ESP. REPEAT—

:Switch off.:

"What is that about?"

:With luck we won't have to find out. If you have messages home, send them now. We go down in two hours twelve minutes.:

"First I want to see what is in this place once more," Prandra said. "There is not enough time before lift-off."

:Don't be long.: They left him, but his mind whispered behind them: *Burnt out the ESP? lucky devil . . . the shape of a sigh hung like a raindrop from a branch. . . .*

GalFed Surveyor 668X327 was a good used ship with a second-grade ESP, a new hypnoformer, and a late-model computer; and it belonged to Khreng and Prandra for as long as they wished to use it.

Khreng and Prandra were a pair of big crimson cats weighing about a hundred kilos each, Khreng slightly heavier, Prandra's fur a little darker. Digits rather more elongated than those of Earth cats gave them almost plantigrade feet and, with the help of the prehensile tail, fairly manipulative hands. They could walk on their hind legs with some discomfort, preferred to go on all fours and squat on their haunches to free their hands. It was hard to estimate their intelligence since no Ungrukh had ever agreed to be tested and there was no arguing with their fangs, claws, and muscle.

The first GalFed surveyor team to touch down on

Ungruwarkh stepped out on the barren plains, sniffed the air and coughed, and declared it a poverty planet. Their ESP had reported traces of primitive civilization, but they did not expect to find much.

While they were unloading, a big red cat appeared half a kilometer distant and loped quietly toward them.

:He likes your smell, he's hungry,: the ESP said, and they stiffened. :But relax, he's much more curious... his name is Khreng.:

He stood among them very still, and a cat-fancier from Sol III slowly put a hand on the massive head. A comparative anatomist from Sirius V considered bone structure and had a stray thought of a lab and dissecting-table; Khreng grinned, and within fifteen seconds seventy-five cats, claws out and fangs bared, appeared from behind boulders and out of fissures and cracks, and ten minutes later truce terms were arranged. The ESP had been working so hard on the receiving end that he had not given thought to the possibility of telepathy in Earth-like jungle cats.

The planet, out on the tip of a Galactic arm, was a bit smaller than Sol III and a bit denser; it had a distant yellow sun, rarefied air, and was half covered in water. Life spread thinly over a great chain of archipelagos spiraling from pole to pole; the climate ranged from semitropic at the equator to cold plains of red lava in the temperate zones; the cat-civilization, numbering about a million, lived in tribal units wherever food and water were available; competition for them was intense. They had never been threatened by larger predators—the meat animals, now near extinction, ran to pig and rodent types—and they had made few local adaptations except for the red fur with which they blended into the red of the sparse soil and the lava on the plains, and the big black chevron running from the crown of the head down either flank, much like deeply shadowed fissures in lava, centered with a thin white stripe resembling the salt and snow crystals that sifted into the cracks. They did not need weapons for the few animals they hunted, but they had developed sophisticated builders' tools for their shelters against the treeless cold of the plains, and for the flotillas of rafts they used for fishing. They hated the fish, which harbored parasites that gave them enteritis, but they were starving.

Fortunately, GalFed was happy with the Ungrukh. (a) About a third of them were telepathic, most often the females, and many of these at least second-grade; ESPs are rare, particularly where language is advanced, and for Galactic liaison and socio-biological sciences they are invaluable; (b) they were an evolutionary puzzle: very nearly Solthree cats with big brains, language, and a civilization only a few thousand years old and no relatives to evolve from or with on the planet.

So GalFed got their proto-ESPs and Khreng and Prandra their ship with its ESP and equipment, and they were coming to be educated, like cat-Candides, in the ways of the world, the enriching and sowing of their meager soil with grain for fodder, the raising of cattle from stocks of frozen embryos.

:*Time to go,*: said Espinoza.

They wheeled him into the shuttle on a dolly and bolted him in. Khreng checked the ship once again. Everything was neat and tight. He stepped into the shuttle and pulled the switch for the lock-doors. Then he strapped himself down alongside Prandra.

:*This boat's very light and it might yaw,*: Espinoza said. :*Don't be nervous.*:

"Why are we nervous? There's nothing fearful here."

:*I wish you people would learn to use something beside the present tense.*:

"Why must we?" Prandra asked. "It always is the present."

The radio beeped and said:

GALFED   SURVEYOR, YOUR CHANNEL RE-QUIRED FOR EMERGENCY LANDING WILL YOU ACCEPT COURSE CHANGE OR WAIT ONE ORBIT?

ACCEPT COURSE CHANGE, Khreng answered. The last landing had given him a terrific case of motion sickness, and he wanted to get it over with.

Then for half an hour they spiraled downward. There was no yaw, no nausea. "This is much bet—" Khreng began, and Prandra screamed.

Something was going round and ringing. Them? Over and

over and over. Warped, they elongated. Transparent, they contracted. Star-spirals ever-which-way. Nothing to them, not a sound or thought, and the planet below them and above a cloudy rope. Then they went everywhere. And all black.

Still.

Khreng snarled, "That is something new GalFed does not trouble to inform us ignorant Ungrukh."

They were landed, evening sky in the viewer.

"No," Prandra said. "The ESP is unconscious. Something is wrong."

"Dead?"

"No. The blood supply is cut off and comes back."

"That is much quicker than the other landings and much more unpleasant."

"I tell you something is wrong! Espinoza!"

:What? what?:

"What is happening?"

:You're asking me?:

"Who else do we ask? You are the ESP. Are you hurt?"

:What have I got to hurt? If I had a head I'd have a headache.:

"Espinoza! What is happening?"

:Something picked us up and put us down. You tell me.:

"I look and you esp," said Prandra.

:Trees, land, sky . . . that's good to know. We seem to be in a blackberry patch. Give me latitude and longitude.:

"51′30″ N, 20′17″ E. Where is that?"

Espinoza considered. *:About halfway between Lublin and Warsaw . . . :*

"But what does that mean, Espinoza?"

:We're in Poland, not far from Warsaw, where Joe Wisnicki comes from, and mother and child are doing well, with congratulations. Only half a world off course.:

"You are making some kind of game."

:No, I'm not. It's nothing serious, we're down safely, we just went off course.:

Khreng said, "The course record is the same as on the indicator." He played the taped directions from Fiji Station. "I make no mistakes."

:Raise them on Fiji then, nudnik!:

After a moment, Khreng said, "There is nothing anywhere on the band. Static only. No disrepair indicated."

:Try the ship computer.:

"There is no answer, Espinoza."

It was growing dark. The evening star rose in the viewer.

We are on Earth . . . the thought was a whisper, a mutter . . . finally he said, *:Hypnoform the shuttle compatible with surroundings—if it's working.:*

The hypnoformer was not exactly a cloak of invisibility; it generated a hypnotic field around a person or object that convinced the viewer that he was seeing something else entirely, and it was useful for contact with fearful or suspicious aliens. Khreng set dials, knobs, switches. The machine was built into the bulkhead; a growl began in its base, rose gradually to a whine and then a sound beyond hearing; in the distance, dogs were barking . . . "It's working," Khreng said. The barking stopped; the sound had reached its peak of silence.

:With our luck it could just be pretending to work.:

With real luck the shuttle had blended into its surroundings and was invisible to all external eyes. "You expect enemies?"

:No . . . not yet.:

"Then let's go out and greet the friendly natives." Khreng didn't mean that literally but as a gesture of solidarity with an ally, a custom of his tribe, to show that he had no fear, and he made it because he sensed fear in Espinoza. A brain in a bowl is not supposed to be able to feel or fear, but a glandular body might impose certain ineradicable habits on its brain over seventy-seven years of existence.

"You say the Solthrees have death bullets," Prandra said.

:Children, it's more complicated than that . . . :

"What then?"

:We'll scan and find out.:

No person lives in this thicket, hermit or woodcutter; there is not enough for him, nothing to attract even Khreng and Prandra, hungry as they are for meat. But there are many small animals: birds above, then squirrels, chipmunks, a few pheasants and rabbits, a bat swooping, flittering moths; and below, moles, grubs, worms. And insects, smaller and smaller sparks of life, each emits its own whisper. Life proliferates helplessly wherever it touches, and even on Ungruwarkh, where it has to make an effort, there are many forms beyond the microscope. But on Solthree, officially designated a Mother of Worlds by GalFed, the noise of life currents is almost deafening to a telepath.

"I don't know that I like it here," Prandra said.

:And I can't promise you will, either.:

Beyond the woods a stream with a few unremarkable fish; beyond that a village....

:No power, they aren't using power...:

"If there is no radio working—"

:There can't be a power blackout over the whole—no planes in the sky, no—check radiation.:

"Nothing beyond normal."

:Then it's not a war...:

Prandra's fur stood on end, and Khreng said, "Stop that. You are making me feel ill."

"I am not as brave as you, big man," Prandra said and pulled her mind away.

"What you are thinking...," Khreng said to Espinoza, and his voice lowered till he sounded like a tiger with bronchitis, "...at GalFed Central they tell me there is no such thing as time travel..."

Three hundred and twenty-four people live in the village. Two will soon die and three more hope to be born; the rest are making a tremendous earthly din: to the Ungrukh, who don't talk much and have fine-tuned ears, it is fearsome, even strained through Espinoza's mind. Women are banging pots, yelling at quarreling children; merchants bargain with farmers, all weary now, they want to go home to supper; boys fight in the dusty streets, are pulled apart and slapped; in the House of Prayer forty-odd men and boys are making extravagant promises to God and demanding Heaven and Earth in return; at the village's northern rim, farthest away, the blacksmith is shoeing the last mare of the day—there's a piece of meat for you!—and the distant *tink* of his hammer is almost peaceful....

"What language are they speaking?"

:Yiddish, mostly.:

"I am told nothing of that one. Is it spoken by many?"

:Nobody. It died almost a hundred years before I was born ... I took my Hebrew lessons from the grandson of the last Yiddish scholar ...:

"But just for this reason you cannot be sure—"

:Let me tell you ...: Espinoza pulled his mind back into the silent boundary of the little ship. *:At GalFed you heard that we don't use time travel, not that we don't have it. There was a device built right on Solthree: a fifty-two-year-old man was sent back fifty years. They brought him forward again well enough, in good shape—except that he had a bad case of diaper rash, a compulsion to suck his thumb, and no memory of anything that happened.:*

"Then it is useless," Khreng said.

:It is to us.:

"But there is somebody else that uses it," Prandra said. "You are thinking of the Qumedni ... and of the Qumedon ship in orbit, the one that burnt out the ESP."

:That's right.:

"You cannot be sure of that."

:Not until we find out much more. Just the same, I think they may have set up a time-vortex here.:

The Qumedni make their home in the Galaxy, but they don't belong to GalFed. They don't need to; they have so many talents, powers and dominions that they hardly know what to do with them, and sometimes they make mischief. Most of the time they coexist peacefully with GalFed and occasionally even make contact, trade bits of information and warnings of local conditions for small souvenir items they consider quaint. No one has ever seen a Qumedni or wants to; perhaps they are pure energy forms: they surely have a repellent field about them, and their powers are so supremely discomfiting that the more one knows about them the less one wants to know.

They travel back and forth in time as they please, shape the worlds of their dominions to their fancy, set up their time-vortices where they choose. One concession GalFed managed to wring from them was an agreement to set up a warning signal around every vortex.

"There is no warning," said Prandra. "We come straight down without even stirring the leaves."

"And in one-tenth the time," Khreng added. "That at least is good."

:... And a Qumedon ship burning out an ESP, behaving like an enemy—though they've never exactly been friends. Perhaps some kind of renegade ... :

"Tell us what to do, then Espinoza, and what time we are in."

:Listen ... listen to the people ... :

Ten zlotys is nine zlotys too many for such; what did you expect, gold with bells around it? didn't I tell you (slap) not to (slap) climb trees? what can I help it if, leave off already, how can I study when, where did you put, I told him and told him and he went, tell me what do you want from my grey hairs, hah? tell me? *oy Zevi, oy Zevi, what did you do that you should die?*

"This is a hard place, it's hard," Prandra whispered. "Everyone here is hurt and bent, even the children ... except for that blacksmith, maybe."

:And he's a bit of a simpleton.:

"Like the people of Ungruwarkh, Espinoza?" Khreng asked with a fanged grin. He was neither hurt nor bent.

:I'll tell you, if the Ungrukh break off relations with GalFed and stay on Ungruwarkh and starve, they might possibly escape getting bent.:

They waited, crouching like hearth cats in their small space.

Among the people of the village no one clear voice rises to describe itself in terms of time and the world. But it is night, they close their mouths, bite their tongues if they have to, fold away their grievances. *Tomorrow is erev Shabbas, tomorrow, tomorrow* ... A few students read by candlelight, the black letters shimmer on the white paper like the flames of their candles, the rest lie down on beds, cots, feather tickings, most of them trembling with weariness, and sleep. Rats and mice scuttle among the weathered timbers of the houses; a stray pig grunts in the street (and Prandra's ears twitch, her eyes sparkle . . .)

A voice, in a small tuneless song, quavers on the light wind:

> *Chava, shtel' dem samovar, ai lyu lyu, ai lyu lyu;*
> *Chava, shtel' dem samovar, ai lyu, lyu!*

The rabbi is sweeping the synagogue. He is thinking of hot tea with lemon, his wife's hands around the samovar, her family's treasure. . . .

Espinoza fishes deftly, not to disturb, comes up with a name: Eliohu ben Shmuel Greenblatt, big name for a thin little man, about forty, looks much older, thick grey in the hair and beard—so call me Reb' Elya, everybody else does, I'm not proud! He sings:

> *Come children, drink the Rabbi's grace*
> *and eat his Sabbath bread;*
> *the wisdom shining in his face*
> *will multiply in light and place*
> *its crown on every head!*

That's not me! I'm not wise, and my beard is full of sweat.

All right, but why is the rabbi sweeping up?

Espinoza gave Reb' Elya's neural connections a nudge. Even a humble village like—what's it called? Kostopol?—even Kostopol should be able to afford a shammis to take care of the shul.

Reb' Elya turned silent, rested chin on hands clasped around the broom handle and watched the lamplight flickering on the walls. An uneasiness which the merchants, scholars, workaday people had managed to push down below the level of consciousness rose in him like a bloated thing surfacing out of the depths of a pond.

The shammis is dead, that's why! Dead for no reason. Zevi-Hirsch Dorfman, a little sour apple of a man who never opened his mouth except to curse his life and the lives of his wife and children, had flown into a fury at Janchik, the big peasant boy who helped the blacksmith. For what? Janchik, a sleepy good-humored farmer's son who had drunk tea often enough at Reb' Elya's table, and who hardly ever got drunk—liquor made him even sleepier—had started shouting in the middle of the street, things about poisoned wells and Christian blood used in Jewish rituals, things no one would have suspected seeping into his mind let alone coming from his mouth. And Zevi, with Passover coming in midweek, had opened up a mouth back at him; and Janchik had clenched his huge fist and killed him with a blow. Last night, at the end of the evening....

The street had cleared like dust beneath a broom, and when they had all crept back an hour later in the silence, the darkness, the body was lying there in the mud, flat as it had fallen, a pig rooting in its belly....

Even for Kostopol it was not a pogrom, but—

Reb' Elya shook his head, swept and sang:

> *For all of time you long to fly,*
> *you build a pair of wings;*
> *and in one teardrop of his eye*
> *the Rabbi sails across the sky*
> *to meet the King of Kings...*

Reb' Elya giggled. "Wings, wings! Sweep, wings!" he told the flying broom. Dust obeyed him.

The shul is a small humble place, dusty, the windows are dim, and there is no obligation to make it a shining Temple when you can never own the land it rests on, but Passover begins Tuesday night, there is no time to elect another shammis with the usual politicking, and Zevi had a habit of hoarding cheese rinds and bread crusts in the cupboards and on the shelves behind the volumes of the Talmud; Passover uses no bread. Besides, Rabbi Yaakov Yitzhak of Lublin, the great Seer, will be staying over this Sabbath on his way home from visiting disciples all around the country....

Espinoza said, :*Early nineteenth century Poland, things were fairly quiet, maybe early Alexander the First...*:

*   *   *

"Explain, Espinoza, what is this?"

:*A village of Jewish merchants and traders surrounded by Polish farms. Look, I was a Solthree historian, but I don't know everything that happened on Earth, and I was a Jew, am a Jew, so you know something of what that is—but these are Eastern European Jews and my ancestors were from Spain; I don't know everything that's going on here because the speech and customs are not all the same as I learned.*:

Prandra said, "They are disagreeable people. I think they are screaming prayers even in their dreams."

:*They think they have a direct line to God and they want to keep it open.*:

Prandra sniffed. The Ungrukh living on the temperate plains were very possessive about their volcanoes, where the Firemasters they worshipped had their dwelling places.

Now the shul was clean for the demons and dybbuks who slept there after midnight. Reb' Elya flung his broom in the corner and listened, half fearful, for the whisper of Lilith on the wind, for ghosts scuttling in the beams, chirping and scampering in the rafters. The dogs had set up a furious barking a short time before, and he wondered what wandering soul had aroused them. Oy, Zevi-Hirsch...he sighed and sang again:

> *Whatever price the Czars may claim*
> *he praises One alone;*
> *the Rabbi sings the Holy Name*
> *and laughing, climbs the steps of flame*
> *to sit beside God's throne ...*

Ai, ai! He sang:

> *You, Reb' Elya, know no Names*
> *you, Reb' Elya, are an ignoramus*
> *you have your Rebbetsin,*
> *and your Rebbelach,*
> *and your samovar, bim, bam!*

He blew out the lamp, closed and locked the door behind him, and went home to Rebbetsin, rosy-cheeked Chava, and to the Rebbelach, four little boys who slept tumbled together on the bed in the corner, side curls tossed out over the featherbed or lying along their cheeks and trembling with their breaths.

And to the samovar, bim, bam!

A weary thought: sleep/home/twilight from Espinoza. He gathered, directed himself to the matter at hand:

:I think we've been sent backward about seven hundred and fifty years. I take the number from local conditions, and from Reb' Elya's thought of the Lubliner Rabbi who was well known around here in the early nineteenth century ... :

"Could all this be something like the 'plains-companion'?" Prandra asked; she was thinking of the hallucinations that sometimes plagued lonely hunters on Ungruwarkh.

:Not with three hundred and twenty-four complete and distinct people, as well as all the animal life ... and a natural time-warp only turns up in deep space under conditions that are extreme and peculiar. No, I think the Qumedni has set up a time-vortex, and it's pulled us in. He may be some kind of renegade or criminal among his own people; the hostility and the lack of warning seem to go together. Sometimes a Qumedon ship won't answer a message, but it almost never attacks the sender.:

"You think the Qumedni is down here?"

:We got dumped here. If there's a Qumedni, I don't know where else he'd be.:

"Do you really believe in that Qumedni, Espinoza?" Khreng asked quietly. "I think you are only trying to give us hope where there is none."

:What can I say? Assume there's a Qumedni and a vortex. If we came down in it, we have to go up in it. I don't think his shuttle would have enough power; it's probably generated by the mother ship—and he could go off with his vortex and leave us. Or he's gone. So much for hope.:

"There is no sign of aliens here."

:Except us ... still, the shammis and the blacksmith's boy behaved out of character, and that's typical of Qumedon mischief.:

"It is also typical of many peoples in every time and place," Khreng said dryly.

:Yes, but it's really odd that Zevi-Hirsch went into such a rage.:

"What is strange about a man fighting back?"

:When your method of survival among hostile and suspicious people is to keep the peace at all costs—it's lethal—but so are Qumedni.:

"All right, Espinoza," Prandra said. "You convince us we must look for a Qumedni. Or more than one."

:You realize that if he's here he's hostile, and he can esp you but you can't esp him. He may have taken on the shape of a Solthree.:

"I go scouting and find that out."

"No, you do not," said Khreng. "I am the one to go out, and you can read me back here."

"You know that's not close enough for good cross-readings."

"I am going! Otherwise you are giving me hell and blazes for bringing you across the Galaxy for nothing."

"Oh, you always think you must be the big man just because you are first out to meet the GalFed surveyor team."

"That's right," said Khreng. "And it goes very well, too."

"Because the rest of the tribe is together waiting to jump out!"

"You are only thinking of that pig running around the streets!"

"Of course. I come here with the promise of meat and a great deal of knowledge from wise teachers, and I am stuck in an iron box with death and dog food!" She lashed her tail, endangering everything in the vicinity. "I must get out!"

"See? Here are the hell and blazes already."

:Oh for God's sake be quiet, you pair of actors! You're sending my blood pressure up.:

"The pump is working perfectly," said Khreng.

Prandra said, "Look, Khreng, on Ungruwarkh I am your choice because I am a good ESP and know where to hunt. You are mine because you are clever and strong and a fine tracker. Here it is a case of being an ESP and knowing where to hunt when there is no track."

"You cannot esp a Qumedni."

"When the valley people come to raid us with that spy who cannot be esped, do I find him or not?"

Khreng grunted.

:You cross-checked...:

"Only go round them, I can shield a little, and make a network because each is known to so many others, and finally there is one the others know whom I cannot esp. I must be out near them; I cannot do that from this place."

:A Qumedni can take almost any shape.:

"If it is not a Solthree, we find that out and try something else."

"I wait for you outside the ship," Khreng said, determined to salvage something. "If you are in trouble, I am not wasting time fiddling with lock-doors to come after you."

"I am always grateful for help," Prandra said complacently.

:And luck,: said Espinoza.

The planet teemed with strange odors. Khreng's and Prandra's were not among them; they had decontaminated and deodorized so that the local animals wouldn't jump in the air at one sniff of them. They had nose filters to lower the oxygen to its level on their own planet, but there was more life there, more to smell: earth, air, water, animals, men....

Espinoza had said; *:You should hypnoform into a Solthree, or at least a blackberry bush, make yourself inconspicuous...:*

"Espinoza, as a Solthree I must go on two legs and I get nowhere; in my own shape, if someone sees me—well, the people here believe in demons, and whatever they are, I am not far from what they look like—so they say, 'Oh, God help me, there goes a demon!' and shiver and say their prayers. If they see a blackberry bush running by in the street, they think they are going crazy and start screaming. Forget it!"

She left Khreng hidden in the shadows; opened her mind, her senses; padded easily among the thickets, tail curled around her rump to avoid breaking branches, could feel her shoulder blades, her haunch bones working freely under her skin in the cool air.

She crossed the stream and the dirty road and went up the village street. Houses clustered at either side, and it widened at midpoint into the marketplace; the synagogue was here, and it sheltered bats and mice; if there were demons, she missed them.

The pig was here too, grunting among the burdock, thinking of sleep. In a while it would get more than it wanted; she passed it without a glance. She was not wearing her harness with its civilized implements, only a belt with a pouch and a knife.

Back on Ungruwarkh the thought of coming across the Galaxy had not dismayed her, but she had been disturbed at the prospect of going among so many beings, not of her species, who had so much flesh on them. Down among them she found it was not their flesh that disturbed her but their noisy heads. Being with Espinoza had prepared her for complex multilayered minds; now she was surrounded by hundreds of them, dreaming and weeping; their bodies were only unregarded appendages. She thought it might be more pleasant to make the acquaintance of some of Solthree's big cats, even if they were a bit backward.

She went round the houses, silent, twitching her tail, not understanding all she picked up, leaving Espinoza to sort and collate; plucked out one thread of identity and another, tying knots of relationship in them.

A thin current of odor from dough for the Sabbath bread, rising on warm stoves, flowed about her; one more strange smell among thousands for an Ungrukh who knew nothing of cooking except sometimes to roast those detestable fish.

Fish and edible birds were being stored here too, in cool places...there was a lot of food in the little house of Zevi-Hirsch's widow Tsippe, whose neighbors had provided for her: she was asleep, salt crust on her cheeks;

(What is that?) *(tears: weeping/grief)* (for that mean little man? does he leave her then without provision?) *(she helps support the family taking in sewing—make-and-mend-clothing—because the sexton gets more honor than pay)* she sniffed (what an honor)

The one whose helper started it all, Shloimeh the blacksmith, sometimes called King Solomon, Shloimeh-ha-Melech, because he was a bit of a fool: snoring happily beside his wife (bleeding? blood?) *(she's menstruating, too bad, so he's—hoo, what a sinner!—dreaming of dancing a kazatzka with)* the servant girl who worked for

Reb' Zalman Dorfman *(the Rich Man, cousin to Zevi-Hirsch*

Dorfman the poor man) who was taking in the Lubliner Rebbeh for the Sabbath; wondering how to impress him, for a rich man in Kostopol was not much better than a poor man in Lublin...turning his mind away from the death, the funeral, the weeping widow (fear, discomfort—don't be scared, big man, she's not planning to beg). Prandra passed him by with a last wisp of thought: idiot rabbi...still, the cantor (prayer-singer? oh, like the rabbi in the synagogue—not much better than an Ungrukh)...the cantor

Nachman Klein, had a fine voice, doubled as (slitting throat of an animal? blood again?) *(ritual slaughter)* (don't bother explaining), was dreaming of singing in a fine synagogue in Warsaw (wearing no clothes?) *(typical Solthree dream)* (if you say so)...his demon daughter Sheyndl, a tough little girl, wakeful, sucked her braid and planned to drive a goat into shul one Sabbath in the middle of the most tearful and dramatic part of *Ribono shel olom*...(poor man)...and

Reb' Elya, the innocent dream rising from him in a perfect sphere of light, wearing a white silk caftan and embroidered yarmulkeh, broke the Sabbath bread at the table of the wise and the holy...

(nothing here...tomorrow three boys come home for Sabbath from the yeshiva, and some others...)

:All right,: said Espinoza. *:Come back.:*

:About that pig...: she had a sting of conscience. *:Does it belong to someone here?:*

:Jews don't eat it. It does belong to someone, but I guess it could drop dead anytime from disease or old age. Give it a merciful end and hurry back. Don't eat any till it's irradiated.:

She found the pig drinking from the stream, stunned it with a blow of her tail before it could squeal, dragged it through the water into the thicket, dug a pit with her claws, used the knife to slash its throat; the blood sprang into the pit—

:You'd also make a good kosher butcher,: said Espinoza.

—And the entrails followed; she covered them over, stamped down the earth, took a film sack from her pouch and packed the meat in, sealed it...

And felt a most peculiar sensation at the back of her neck. The fur rose.

Espinoza asked, :*What's that?*:

:*I don't know.*: She put down the package and stood still. Nothing but the night and its small noises. Her pulse was steady... and a little tingling went along her nerves, a physical sensation raising her hairs of their own will.

:*Some kind of radiation?... a force field?*:

:*I go look.*:

:*Take care,*: said Khreng.

:*No!*: Espinoza called. :*Come back!*:

She disregarded them, crossed the stream, and stood at the edge of the road. This way Lublin? That way Warsaw? She didn't know which. She chose a direction and walked, meter by meter; early spring night, branches studded with leaf buds against a dull sky; and the moon, finding a space between clouds, silvered the air for a moment, but there was nothing to see in its light.

The small tingling intensified, spread over her body; the air trembled as in a heat wave, then rippled and warped; the skin was writhing over her muscles.

:*Don't—*: Espinoza was whispering (something); but she was not afraid, did not feel under personal attack or in the presence of an enemy, only intensely interested, able to turn back at any time, and went deliberately toward that strengthening source, out of all contact with Khreng and Espinoza, padding down the silent road at midnight in a deafening silence.

She stopped, not knowing or wondering why, very still in the center of her being, though every hair of her body was on end, the knife burned against her side, her skin writhed and swirled over her body like an oil film on water.

A small whiteness spread behind her eyes, grew till it blinded her, went down every nerve, into every tooth, set her brain on fire. She sprang up on her hind legs, savaged the air with her claws briefly, and fell into blackness.

Khreng was pawing, pushing, growling at her.

"Where is this?" she whispered.

"One kilometer from the village, where do you think?" he grumbled. "You are a great traveler."

She lay panting. Whatever she had run into was gone, but she ached from the crown of her head right down her spine to the tip of her tail.

:Are you all right?: The image of Espinoza, quick swarthy man, touched her in the head, lightly. *:Are you all right?:*

"I am stupid."

"There you are not mistaken." Khreng pulled at her this way and that, heaved her on his back, her head lolled as if her neck were broken, her legs hung. "You are damn heavy." She was as limp as a trophy skin.

He headed back toward the shuttle at a slow trøt, the piston-bones of his shoulders moved beneath her jaw. In a great effort she stretched her neck, touched the tip of her tongue to the hairs of his ear. "Don't forget the meat," she whispered, then fainted.

She came to again in her couch in the shuttle. Khreng was rubbing down her sides and back with his pads, lightly oiled. "Now who is playing at great heroics, ha? I come looking and find you with your hair all on end as if you are struck by lightning."

"I am struck by lightning," she said sleepily.

:You sure you feel better?:

"I don't ache so much now. Do I find the Qumedni?" Khreng brought her a cup of warm herb tea, one of the few vegetable products Ungrukh enjoyed, and she lapped at it.

:Not exactly. You ran into his shuttle's energy field. He was starting up the engines.:

"Why don't I turn back?"

:There was nothing you could do against it. It paralyzes the nervous system, like a GalFed stunner, only this can be deadly.:

"Is he gone then?"

:I don't think so. From what I could see through Khreng, there was no blast off, and there wasn't a cutoff as if he'd been sucked into his time-warp. It increased gradually and died down the same way. I suppose he was testing.:

"Does he esp me?"

:I don't know. He's not too far away.:

Prandra sniffed. "He's no Kostopoler."

:He may become one yet—and you certainly will. Tomorrow

you'll both practice two-legged walking; if you want any chance of leaving this place, you'll have to hypnoform, get out there and find him.:

And suppose they found him, what then? Espinoza was grateful that Khreng and Prandra didn't ask silly questions like that.

Prandra didn't dream often, but perhaps she was stimulated by all the minds she had been esping. She found herself running shoulder to shoulder with Khreng across the red plains, as they had done often enough on Ungruwarkh. Tugrik and Emerald on their backs, each one a small warm weight with little claws prickling into the skin. And Espinoza, a young brown-skinned man with black hair and white teeth, quick-tempered and sharp-witted, was running lightly between them—how, when they were touching?—seemed to be blended half into each, with a hand resting on each of their necks, laughing. Was it her dream alone or one she was sharing with Khreng? Or Espinoza?

Friday morning they were up early; Espinoza had not slept. *:Everybody tells me I don't need sleep. Liars.:* His consciousness had been lowered by drugs for the Jump, but at his age they were too dangerous to use regularly. *:Anyway, this is my last trip.:*

"What do you do afterward, then?" Khreng was stalking stiffly about on two legs, preparing to hypnoform into a Solthree. He and Prandra were going to be a pair of travelers stopping over in Kostopol for the Sabbath. For some vague reason, possibly tribal conditioning in conformity, he felt all this business was unnatural and immoral.

:Not more so than coming across the Galaxy in the first place.:

"In the first place, I am better to stay home and die fighting."

"What do you say you do after you go back, Espinoza?" Prandra asked.

:Get put into some library think-tank as part of historical reference. Students come round, ask, "How long did the Thirty Years' War last?" That kind of thing. I'm too old to travel any more . . . you've got to get that tail curled up or you'll look like a pretty damn funny Solthree.:

"It's a meter and a half long, Espinoza. Do I chop it off?"
:*No, but you, Prandra, will have to chop off your whiskers. No use swearing. Solthree women just don't have long red bristles sprouting out of their faces.*:

Friday morning everybody gets up early. Chava and Braina and Freyda and Reisel and nearly a hundred other women jump out of bed while their husbands are still groaning and snorting with the misery of waking; wash hands, pull on old dresses, tie aprons, kerchiefs, flick the cloth off the risen dough, punch it down and turn it over to rise again. It smells like life, like a baby's flesh. . . .

Reb' Elya gnaws a crust, gulps tea, grabs shawl and phylacteries, and runs to shul. There is a film of dream around him yet, like a bubble ready to burst.

It never quite bursts, only rises and floats above him like a balloon on a string. Reb' Elya does not live in a bubble; he runs so that the damp from the early rain will not soak his old shoes, mud splashes his tattered caftan; supported by an impoverished congregation, he is a "poor man in seven edges," as they say in the shtetl, and he clasps to his breast the tallith and tefillin in their velvet drawstring bags so they will not be spattered.

:*Stop and eat now,*: Espinoza said. :*But don't gorge or you'll be sleepy.*: He enjoyed watching Reb' Elya, resting along his consciousness.

Espinoza was interested in psychodynamics, not physical or emotional privacies; he was not a voyeur, only an enforced observer of sentient life. He had a great fondness for Khreng and Prandra: they were fierce, quick, direct, integrated; their conjoined mind was a crystal globe without bubble or ripple; Reb' Elya's was faceted, asymmetrical, flawed and striated with pressures. Many parts of it were painful, some silly, some fine qualities blocked and thwarted by circumstance, and all of it fascinating. Sometimes Espinoza wished he had been a first grade ESP, could have had a ready insight into the psychological structures he had to build with so much time and effort. Sometimes, but not often. Class-one ESPs dealt with medical and psychiatric problems in many kinds of life-forms; a class-one ESP who could think like a psychotic decapod from Arcturus IV was as uncomfortable to be around as a Qumedni.

Reb' Elya pulled the string with the synagogue key from round his neck and unlocked the door. He knocked to warn demons and opened it. A bat flew out. Reb' Elya smiled and called out half seriously, "Good day, Ashmedai!" But the demon-king did not hear, or did not choose to answer. Elya slipped inside, whispering as always, "Lord, I love Your house, the place where Your glory lives...."

Khreng and Prandra ate cubed meat out of bowls, licking their jaws and grunting with pleasure.

Espinoza said, :*We have tapes for English, French, Russian, Chinese, Japanese, and Spanish. Unfortunately the languages you need are Polish, Yiddish, and Hebrew. What I don't know I'll pick up and feed you.*:

"Eat now, think later," said Khreng.

:*Think now, because you don't know what the Qumedni will do, or when. Remember: the rabbi doesn't like to speak Polish, the women don't know Hebrew, the scholars don't read or write Yiddish.*:

"You remember," Khreng growled. "I become a deaf-and-dumb Solthree."

Reb' Elya shook out the folds of his tallith and wrapped it round him. Having blessed this act, he sat down to wait for his quorum. Some of his congregation would be saying prayers at Tsippe's for the last day of Kaddish and enjoying a bagel and a little schnapps too; a couple of schnorrers, who went where the food was, Shloimeh-ha-Melech likewise, Reb' Nachman and Reb' Zalman who were important.... He could count on the company of Mordcha Pipick, whose huge belly was caused by a tumor, not by appetite.... He had an inspiration: he would use his small authority to appoint Mordcha temporary shammis.... "How can we do without a shammis over Pesach and with the Lubliner coming? Who'd complain? Who'd worry he'd hang on too long? Except for that pipick of his the man's thin as a pipestem, and, God be merciful, I think he'll soon be—oh."

Oh. The soul drained out of his body leaving Reb' Elya white as his tallith. Words said themselves:

HE'LL SOON BE DEAD HE'LL SOON BE DEAD HE'LL SOON BE DEAD DEAD DEAD DEAD DEAD DEAD DEAD

:Oh...oh...:

Khreng belched and scratched his belly with the tip of his tail, but Prandra cried, "Espinoza! What is it?"

There was a whimpering in Espinoza's mind. *:Dead, Dead. Oh, I don't know. Oh God. Tell me if there's something happening in the village. Quick!:*

Prandra scanned. "Twenty-three people are vomiting; eleven babies have begun to scream; seven men, thirteen women, and eighteen prepubic children have burst into tears; two old men and one woman have pain in the chest and trouble breathing; fifteen assorted people have headaches."

:And Reb' Elya?:

"The rabbi is unconscious."

Reb' Elya opened his eyes, pulled himself up to his knees, and began to weep. He gathered the fringes at the four corners of his shawl and kissed them, with trembling hands picked up the phylacteries, which he had pulled down in his fall, and kissed them as well.

"Blessed Lord our God King of the Universe, what have I done? Why have You struck me down? Lord of the Universe, did I sin when I said that Reb' Mordcha would die? Perhaps the Evil Urge made me call him to the attention of the Angel of Death? Spare the life of Your servant Mordcha, O Lord our God and forgive me, forgive me!"

Still weeping, still trembling in every limb, he pulled himself to his feet and began to wind tefillin, straining with all of his will not to drop or tangle them, crying out the prayers through chattering teeth:

"On the arm in memory of His outstretched arm, opposite the heart to subject our hearts to His service, opposite the brain to subject all faculties to His service, blessed be He . . . bring me long life and holy thoughts, and free me from the Evil Urge. . . ."

"Solthrees live half again as long as Ungrukh, and they are still afraid of death," said Prandra.

:*I am not afraid of death,*: said Espinoza with asperity. :*I have already died once. Something has constricted the cerebral vessels of everyone around here. Didn't you feel anything?*:

"A bit dull and sleepy. . . ."

:*You have a high metabolic rate, and you've just eaten heavily; that may be why you missed it. Turn up my oxygen a bit.*:

"Can you do anything for them?"

:*Plant a suggestion that they'd feel better with some fresh air. It's passing off already. The men will be praying, and that will get the air in their lungs. That was a very unpleasant feeling.*:

"What causes it?" Khreng asked.

:*Who would you suggest? Who do you know in the district with power to do that?*:

"*We* don't do that," said Khreng, with what for him was a great deal of forbearance. "There is no need to be sarcastic."

:*Sorry. I guess it's the effect.*:

The people of Kostopol did not quite know what had happened to them or realize it had happened to all of them. It was variously a sudden unease, nausea, depression, fear, headache, shortness of breath . . . a something. And it went away. Not quite. A thing, perhaps as small as a sand grain, perhaps as large as a flake of stone, remained. Lodged beneath the skin, or behind the eye, or back of the throat, or under the breastbone. . . .

The quorum who had been saying Kaddish for Zevi-Hirsch came out of Tsippe's house in a peculiar frame of mind. They had eaten bagels and hardboiled eggs, and had drunk schnapps, and the food knotted in their bellies and the liquor burned. . . . They did not speak much, and for them this was as if the world had turned upside down and day become night. They came raggedly across the marketplace, blinking, though there was no sun, scratching their necks, though there were no flies;

bearing toward the smithy where Shloimeh would leave them.

On the farther side, Janchik had just turned off the road and was shambling toward his day's work; sleepy-eyed, grinning foolishly, big shoulders swinging and coarse red hands hanging loosely.

They watched him.

That fist of his had gone crack! so, and the little man had fallen, scraggy beard jutting at the sky....

"Big loshek, what he did...."

"I don't know what got into him—"

"But you keep him around!"

"Give him meals, yet...."

"When he ought to be—"

"Yes, he ought to be...."

"—No justice—"

"Why don't we?"

"He's big, but—"

"—Ten of us—"

"And—"

"Do something about it for once, instead of—"

"Why not?"

It was strange that they did not look at each other and ask if God would wither their tongues.

:I think they've gone mad,: said Espinoza. *:They're planning to kill him.:*

From the other road approaching the village, a horsedrawn cart and driver were bringing Count Rosnicki, the landowner, to collect the black mare he had left at the smithy to be shod the day before. Riding behind him were a group of cousins from Warsaw who were staying with him over Easter, and he was going to show them his stables and his lands and his budding orchards and everything else that made for good country living. He was in a relaxed good humor, a state he could sometimes maintain for more than ten minutes.

The two parties were converging on that hapless Janchik, and Espinoza's mind hummed like a bee swarm with useless alternatives. :*God help them . . . :*

"Let us out, Espinoza."

:*Half an hour apiece to hypnoform and ten minutes for the lock-doors.:*

"We go without hypnoforming."

:*And make a big red target . . . Lord, I wish I'd never been born.:*

Khreng and Prandra looked at the blue globe, then at each other.

Reb' Elya came out of shul, like the minyan, in a very uncomfortable frame of mind. He did not know why it should have seemed so sinful, just at that moment, to think of Mordcha as a dying man, since he and everyone else knew he was . . . Elya pulled at the strings of his fringed undergarment, the minor tallith, as if the knots would undo themselves and solve his perplexity. He went across the market without seeing the minyan moving forward with death in its heart, or the count rounding the corner in a magisterial cloud of dust, driver beating the whipstock against his thigh.

Elya looked up and saw only Janchik, and his brow cleared. Surely the best way to be forgiven was to forgive. Blind to everything else, he hurried over to the shambling boy and plucked at his sleeve. "Janchik!" he cried. "Come have a glass of tea with me!"

Janchik blinked down at him, smiling. "I'd like that, Rebbeh, but I have to go to work now."

"Take a few minutes. . . ."

The minyan stopped short; Elya noticed them from the corner of his eye and turned his head. He saw two merchants, a blacksmith, a schoolmaster, a cantor/slaughterer, a cobbler, a carpenter, and three schnorrers. "Nachman," he called, "I have an idea, I want to talk to you . . . what's the matter?"

The ten looked at each other and saw much in each others' eyes. Their faces burned. "Nothing . . . nothing is wrong," the cantor said, choking. . . .

The galloping cart pulled up to them in a shower of dust.

* * *

:Very close, very close,: said Espinoza.

"Gut Shabbas, Rebbeh," the count said. It was a little early in the day for this greeting, but it was the only Yiddish he knew.

"Good day, Count," Reb' Elya said civilly. The count was no aristocrat in bearing, but a stocky, ruddy countryman, strong and glossy as his horses. His shrewd slit eyes glittered with ironic and capricious humor; he was not a wicked man, only nerve-rackingly unpredictable. The previous summer he had sent a couple of men to knock the cobbler around over the quality of the leather used in repairing his boots; a few days later he had sent the same men beating the bushes to find Elya's Moisheleh, who had gotten lost picking berries.

Elya did not even dislike the count, but he was so far from Elya's model of what a man ought to be; i.e., pale, with side curls and beard, black hat and caftan—that he found him totally alien.

The count said, "Feliks tells me his favorite sow didn't come home last night, the beautiful Sasha." He laughed. "I told him you wouldn't know where she is, but she likes to be around you so much I thought I'd ask."

Sasha? The stupid animal that rooted in Kostopol's vegetable plots? Tsk. Elya kept the glint out of his eye and said quietly, "No, Count, I haven't seen her." He added, "The children tease the pigs but they never harm them."

The count laughed again and jumped down to collect his horse. Reb' Elya looked around for Nachman, but the minyan had scattered. He sighed and turned homeward. Maybe it hadn't been such a good idea? He stopped in midstride and clapped his hands: of course! that's why I was so upset. I was turning Mordcha's illness to my own advantage, choosing a dying man so no one would complain . . . yes, I see it quite clearly—but God forgive me! we still need a shammis. . . .

:Now you know what you ate,: said Espinoza. *:The beautiful Sasha.:*

Khreng licked his jaws with his long rasp tongue. "I agree about her beauty."

"It's a pity Rosnicki is not the Qumedni," Prandra said, "nor his people."

:He's not far away now ... I've heard of a quorum of ten exorcising a dybbuk but never of any that was possessed by one.:

The fish are cut and simmering, spiced, in their pots; the women have dismembered and soaked and salted the chickens and put them on to boil; they punch down the dough, slap it on floured boards, divide and divide it, roll it in strips, braid and set it to rise for the last time.

The boys come home from yeshiva for the Sabbath and the Passover week, bringing friends whose homes are far away; they carry packs filled with threadbare clothes and books with raveled leaves; they march, unregimented, side curls bouncing, singing songs to ancient Biblical verses; they are seized upon, their cheeks are pinched to cries of "What are they feeding you, you got so thin?" None of their translucent spirits harbors a Qumedni.

Khreng and Prandra buckled on their harnesses, tucked away dozens of impliments, clipped remote switches for the hypnoformer on their forearms, put on tinted contact lenses to counteract the harsher rays of Sol.

:Your names are Jacob (my Hebrew name) and Sara, let's see, Katz—why not?—on your way from ... Krasniewic—I just made it up—to Warsaw, because, oh, because your mother's dying, your brother's been kidnaped into the army, and you have to buy him off, and—and your father's in jail for not paying taxes.:

"What a life," said Khreng. "How do I earn my keep?"

:Buy a little, sell a little, mend a little. The usual.:

"You must admit I have a very strange accent."

:That's the way they talk in Krasniewic,: said Espinoza. *:The first person you see, you'll ask where you can stay over the Sabbath. Somebody will find you a place.:*

The Sabbath loaves, risen at last into the shapes of cumulus clouds, are glazed with egg and put into the ovens. . . .

*   *   *

Hypnoforming an object is one thing. Hypnoforming a person into the shape of an alien being is something else: if he doesn't feel like an alien, he will never convince anyone else that he is. It's a good device for explorers as long as the two life-forms involved are roughly the same size and shape: a four-meter Arcturan serpent will never persuade anyone that he's a ten-centimeter Crystalloid from Vega, particularly since the two forms have never been able to communicate and you need to be assisted by an ESP of the race you're turning into in order to know what it feels like to be one.

For Ungrukh the process was relatively simple, but it was intimidating enough for Khreng to attach the electrodes to his skull and to Espinoza's connections.

He pulled the switch, closed his eyes...and over an endless half hour Espinoza gave him a life. Even if he never hypnoformed again, his mind would always be threaded with wisps of alien memory....

Strange shape, strange land, cruel time, a boy three years old dragged screaming into manhood and whipped in school over the shape of every black-flame letter, trailing at dusk in a shivering crocodile of children scared of demons, that thin child who crouched beside you snottering all day dead of typhoid, *mazel tov*, Bar Mitzvah, thirteen years and you're old enough to pray in a quorum with your cracking voice, your old man's wizened face, *mazel tov*, meet your bride, *l'chaim!* you're a father—sorry, it only lived an hour, anyway the Cossacks are coming....

:Not bad,: said Espinoza. *:No beautiful Jew, you're more a blacksmith than a scholar, but you'll do.:*

Khreng opened his eyes, upright, looked down and saw the long black caftan, through Prandra's eyes saw his face. Red hair and beard, fair enough; he looked in fact a lot like Shloimeh. Espinoza had picked the blacksmith as a good model for body type, big chest and shoulder muscles to mask the powerful torso and forefeet, heavy thighs to accommodate the tail. *:Keep your movements slow and close; any gross distortion and the field will crumble and break.:*

"I am choking, I think," said Khreng, pulling at his illusory neckband.

:It gets better later on. Now you, Prandra. You'll be a big girl, no beauty either, but we don't need the men chasing you.:

"Hah!" said Khreng. Prandra hissed, her equivalent of a giggle.

Who should be first to meet the strangers but Reb' Elya? He was everywhere, comforting the sick, pestering the healthy, blessing the newborn, collecting from the poor for the poorest. "Come home, stay with me," he said. "I have only the one room, but there's a little shed in back, where I keep the pickles—they only smell in summer—and I'll put in a stove, with blankets and a featherbed. . . ." He paused, looked at them, felt (they could tell) a little shiver, and added, to cover, "Come, come, you'll have a glass of tea? Then I have to meet the Lubliner, a big man, guests are coming, a busy time. . . ."

:He knows something,: Prandra told Espinoza. *:I can't tell what.:*

:Intuition . . . he's not an ESP: some kind of sensitive. . . . :

Chava, the Rebbetsin, was resigned to unexpected guests; they meant light eating on the following night. But lemon tea was a cheap drink and not a bad one. The Katzes refused cookies (more dog food).

"Where did you say you're from?" Reb' Elya asked.

"Krasniewic," said Khreng/Katz. He was relieved to be sitting down. Walking upright was hell; he thought his spine would crack and his tendons rip. Prandra was even worse off because she felt some of his pain as well as her own. How would they find the Qumedni if they were half crippled?

:No other way,: said Espinoza.

"Krasniewic?" Elya clasped his glass in both hands and blinked at them over the rim. "I never heard of it."

"Oh, you know," said Chava. "That place where they all talk like Litvaks."

The loaves come out of the oven, burnished, hollow when they're knocked on the bottom. The smell is superb.

"The Lubliner rebbeh," said Elya, "same first name as you, Yaakov Yitzhak, he's called the Seer . . . they say he can look at a

man's forehead and see into his soul. . . ." His own look seemed
to wonder what that seer might find within them. He was still
conscious of that something, that grain of sand or seed of doubt
which had been planted in him during the agonizing moment in
the synagogue.

The youngest of the little boys, not much more than a baby,
crawled about them on the floor. Prandra gave him a piece of
cookie and stroked his head. It might be possible to love such a
creature.

Elya picked up the child quickly and put him on the bed in the
corner. Then he blushed. He was a hospitible man; he did not
know why he felt uneasy.

Prandra, cramped spine and all, smiled to herself because she
had not thought of the child as a morsel.

Reb' Elya got up and Khreng followed; the women were not
expected to meet the Lubliner. "I can make up the bed in the
storeroom," Prandra said. Elya tapped the table with his
fingertips, hesitating, and to calm his uneasiness she took her
feelings about Tugrik and Emerald (separated by such distance
and danger) and placed them as well as she could among the
complicated folds of his emotions. "That's right," he whispered,
nodding. "That's good."

The children played and quarreled loudly. Chava grabbed
and scrubbed them for the Sabbath, rattled pots, tasted, jabbed
the chicken with a fork, all the while yelling personal questions
at the top of her voice and giving her life away in return:

"—terrible time with the little one, they thought I'd never—"

Prandra swept the hard earth floor, shifted the pickle crock,
laid down mattresses and featherbeds, her mind with Khreng
crossing the marketplace toward the road from Lublin.

"—certainly are strong, I've never been able to lift that thing,
Gitte-Frima next door got a hernia—"

Scholars and schoolboys in Sabbath clothes, the rich, the
poor, the important, the insignificant, all paraded to meet the
rabbi of Lublin. Everyone with a question, an ache, an Evil
Urge, a little money to help loosen the holy tongue. A few were
women, two barren ones who wanted to conceive, and one
pregnant with the twelfth who wanted to stop; the rest of them

stayed home putting their houses in order and shaking their heads over the foolishness of men.

"—married to a rabbi God bless him you're better off not every schlemiel in the street he thinks can give him a holy word I tell him if he got one word just one word from every schlepper he ran after he'd be wiser than Solomon if I didn't bring him the samovar when he got married he likes his tea so much I wouldn't see him Monday to Friday—"

:Just like my aunt Lena....: said Espinoza.

Even the count was there, with his cousins, to see what was so fine about the Seer of Lublin.

Prandra was scanning them all, using the quick network of relationship she had drawn up the night before. For Kostopol they were a crowd, actually only a few dozen; every one of them, count and all, held that odd hard thing only Reb' Elya was conscious of; for the others it was masked by anticipation of the Sabbath, the holidays, the honored guest—or perhaps it had simply settled down among the usual griefs and terrors of their lives....

"He's coming! There he is the rebbeh! There!"

Down the road, in a dust cloud, the rabbi came. Riding a horse, dapple-grey, a sleek trim animal, its hooves touched the earth as lightly as if it were dancing. It was like a piece of the sunless sky; behind it, six disciples marched, brisk of step and singing a song of the Joyous Festival:

> *He has divided the sea*
> *for His children, bim bam!*
> *but their enemies drown*
> *in its waters....*

As it came closer the procession slowed—

And Khreng's skin prickled, not from what he saw but from what Prandra was seeing through his eyes.

The pale horse picked its way through the dust cloud; the oiled reins rippled lightly on its neck, almost like snakes, wound themselves around a thin white hand....

Reb' Elya yearned, his eyes filled. He had no wisdom, no

learned tongue to speak with the holy and the pious. He would have been content with one deep look into the eyes of the Lubliner. But his own eyes were blurred with tears; he could see the billowing silk caftan, the shining black Cossack boots, the fur hat, the white hair and beard, could hear the pattering steps of the followers singing their songs of holiday and Sabbath—but the eyes were withheld from him: tears came between.

Prandra and Espinoza saw very clearly from their distance; they fixed their minds on the cloudy rider and the cluster of figures on foot behind him; they saw that there was no heart in that body, no human heart, no brains or bowels, none penetrable to an ESP. It was dense as stone, cold as ice, cruel as death.

:*There he is,:* said Espinoza. :*Now what do we do with him?:*
:*He knows we are here?:* Prandra asked.
:*I'm sure he does. Why should it bother him? He realizes we're helpless.:*

Prandra gave more attention to the horse: it was not a real animal, but a simulacrum created of dust and wind.

:*And those who march and sing ... they're not persons, only things made of dry leaves, branches and mud.:*
:*Yes. Golems,:* said Espinoza.

The people of Kostopol raised their voices and sang with the shadows: *He has divided the sea for His children. ...*

On a quick malevolent impulse, Elya's first son, Yehoshua, a boy gentle as his father, picked up a stone and threw it at the horseman. No one saw: it vanished before it struck and rebounded in three fragments. One struck Rosnicki in the neck; he clasped his hand to the spot and swore. Prandra, on the alert, picked up a message from Espinoza before he had time to implement it and covered the count's reaction swiftly: a Jew picked up/a stone/kicked up by the horse. The count only blinked and shook his head. Another fragment fell at the feet of Reb' Elya, who was standing with bowed head; in a dream he stooped to pick it up: it burned and he dropped it and stared at the small red spots on his fingers. The third struck Khreng in the forehead; he bit his tongue to repress a snarl. The Qumedni had acknowledged the presence of unbelievers.

:*When do we talk to this person, Espinoza?*:

:*Not while he's throwing stones. I don't know if he'll ever give us a chance.*:

:*Is this the only one?*:

:*I think so . . . his operation is modest, so far. I hope so.*:

Reb' Elya managed to confer the title of shammis on Mordcha Pipick, and at dusk he proudly summoned men to the bathhouse; it was never too late to become significant, and he was probably the most cheerful man in Kostopol; perhaps the others were overwhelmed by the presence of the Lubliner; the morning minyan who had prayed at Tsippe's had sweepings of guilt in the corners of their spirits, they could never know whether they would actually have killed Janchik.

Khreng sat in shul with the men of Kostopol and the Qumedni/rabbi, cursing his aching back; he prayed to the God of Solthrees with his voice and to Firemaster with his heart: *Unburden me of this Shape and this World, make me a man among men on Ungruwarkh and I never lift a foot off the planet again!* Perhaps the Qumedni had put flint in his heart as well.

Come in peace, crown of God, come with joy. . . .

Elya turned the pages of his siddur with trembling fingers while Reb' Nachman chanted, and tried and tried to see the face of the Lubliner; always at that point on his visual field a flickering came before his eyes like the disturbances of certain headaches. *We hope, Lord our God, soon to see Thy majestic glory, when the abominations shall be removed from the earth. . . .* What have I done, that I am blinded? Whom have I sinned against, O Lord? And what is the use of searching my soul? I have not done enough in the world, good or bad, to make it worth while for God to notice me.

He turned his eyes back to the letters of his prayers; these at least he could see clearly. *Angels of peace, may your coming be in peace; bless me with peace, and bless my table. . . .*

Prandra had withdrawn quietly into a corner while Chava changed clothes and blessed her Sabbath candles. She was satisfied that the Qumedni had been found and what was postulated had been proven, shaken because a Qumedni was an unsettling creature. What did it want with these people?

:*To inflame them into bloodshed.*: Espinoza had been quiet for a while, and she was glad to have word from him; it was becoming very lonely in Kostopol.

:*That's silly. There's so much conflict in the universe he has only to sit and wait.*:

:*He wants to cause it, not sit and wait for it.*:

Khreng, who had been receiving in silence, asked, :*Is that why Qumedni set up the time-vortices?*:

:*I think most often they use them to observe alien peoples the way GalFed Central does in controlled experiments. I don't believe they generally make mischief. I said before, this one is criminal or insane.*:

:*It is very hard to ask a mad Qumedni to help us get back to our ship,*: Prandra said. :*One thing strikes me as very odd. Is he responsible for the death of Zevi-Hirsch?*:

:*Likely. You wonder why he waited thirty-six hours after that to make another move? I can't tell you. Our Qumedni is a riddle.*:

:*Does he have any weaknesses?*:

:*None that I know . . . .*:

"Good Shabbas!" cried Chava, and Reb' Elya came into the house with his sons and Khreng.

Reb' Elya did not eat with Reb' Zalman and the Lubliner. He would have been welcomed, only a bit grudgingly, but he was frightened to be in the presence of those strange disciples and this saint whom he could not see clearly and whose words did not seem to have any meaning. No one else appeared to be bothered by the man; he wondered if he were suffering the onset of some terrible disease of the brain—madness, degeneration . . . even his guests made him fearful, and he did not know why. His mind unfolded a panoply of horrifying images: soul struggling in the meshes of slow decay while his wife and children watched in helpless anguish, were left to charity when he died. . . .

:*Stop this, Espinoza! I can't bear it.*:

:*The Qumedni's doing it. It won't stop till we get out of here with him.*:

Reb' Elya smiled with all his strength and broke the Sabbath bread.

Khreng closed the door of the storeroom as firmly as it would fasten. It was dark and they had no lamp because of the Sabbath; he had a tiny pen-light tucked somewhere in his harness but it was too risky to use it. "Do we wait till they're asleep?"

"No use. I doubt the rabbi can sleep."

Both fumbled at their wrists for the remotes and pressed them, dropping to all fours with a shudder of relief. Khreng snorted and muttered, "Trying to eat with a spoon is as bad as walking on two legs." It was chancy, dropping the hypnoform field, but they could resume it at any time using the remote switches until the machine in the shuttle had been cleared and reset, and Espinoza would warn them of danger. As uncomfortable Solthrees, they would get no sleep and be drained of their febrile energy.

They removed the contact lenses, which dimmed their night vision, and stared at each other. "I like you much better as Khreng," Prandra said.

"As a Solthree you find me tasty, I suppose."

She flicked his nose with the tip of her tongue. "Not bad."

:Take a scan with me,: said Espinoza. *:If nothing's doing, you can sleep.:*

Exhausted as she was, Prandra forced herself to scan the village and as far beyond as she could reach. The old dozed, the sick turned restlessly, the young made love in celebration of the Sabbath, babies snorted and snuffed like little animals, a child or two cried out in nightmare....

:Stay with me,: she said, *:I don't understand all this about Rosnicki.:*

In the big country house the count and his cousins were finishing their meal with brandy in the company of Father Chryzostom, who was there to discuss the matter of repairs to the church roof.

Rosnicki was shaking his head. "Money doesn't grow on trees."

One of the cousins grinned. "It grows on Jews."

Rosnicki, who knew that Reb' Zalman the Rich Man was no more affluent than any rag merchant in the Warsaw Ghetto, nodded. He didn't want to be shown up as a country cousin. "We don't do badly here."

"The way they go around in rags . . . you'd never know what they have buried underground in old pots and kettles."

"Those scrolls of theirs with silver crowns. . . ."

". . . always money to lend. . . ."

". . . give them a good shake. . . ."

Among those laughing men with their heavily blued jaws and glittering eyes, Rosnicki, began to feel that the conversation was running out of control. "They're my Jews—"

"No reason why you shouldn't get the most out of them, Oscar."

"I've done very well," he said with dangerous mildness. "I don't believe there's much left in them."

"Nonsense! If you were to get them together, for instance, when they are in synagogue tomorrow, and—"

Rosnicki got very red in the face with rage and brandy. "I don't—" *care to deal with my people that way,* he had been going to say, and hang city sophistication—and a small spot on his neck stung and burned where it had been struck. "I don't think that's a bad idea at all," he said.

:Espinoza, do we warn them?:
:How? Tell Reb' Elya you had a dream? He'll think you're crazy, or else he is, and he's near enough that now. Wait till tomorrow.:
Tomorrow.
And in one teardrop of his eye
the Rabbi sails across the sky. . . .
Rabbi Qumedni, we must find how to sail you off this planet.

At the inn, a ghostly horse was tethered, and six mock-men of clay and twigs lay upon benches. In Reb' Zalman's best bedroom the Qumedni, a pulsing vortex of energy, spun like a star. Prandra pulled away from that quickly and, with the recoil, fell asleep.

* * *

Reb' Elya did not sleep. How could he? He stared at the Sabbath candles until they guttered out in a fume of hot wax, and then at the lamp, which still had oil to use up and would be left until it went out by itself. The light meant nothing to him; his spirit was in darkness. The wife and children he loved were breathing softly around him, vulnerable and ephemeral. The people of the village, whom he had known all his life, had something wrong with them, that showed in a dulling of their eyes....

No, it is I who have something wrong, my eyes....

Was it that which had turned the Lubliner away from his sight? Had the holy man seen something in his eyes that repelled him and so avoided them? Even the count, with whom he had gotten along tolerably well for so many years, seemed to suggest some vicious threat with every look and gesture, as he thought back on them.

It is I! I! He screamed inside. O Lord our God, King of the universe, how can I pray to You?

He pulled himself out of bed in a sudden movement of terror and despair, afraid to look at Chava and the children in case he might see something ugly and filthy in them. He grabbed his head, pulled at his hair, in a twist of anguish found himself facing the door to the storeroom.

That ordinary, coarse-looking pair, from that Krasniewic he had never heard of—who were they and what, that they should have made him so uncomfortable the first time he had set eyes on them? In their eyes he had seen clearly enough a still, watching strangeness. No mistake, they had not blinded him. And yet their outlines, their very shapes, had never quite set or solidified. They had a shimmer to them that was—

Full of horror, unable to stop, he found himself picking up the lamp, which was never moved on the Sabbath, and walking toward the door.

Espinoza, who also needed some rest, had been drifting on the whispering memory of an old melody. Centuries of practiced instinct alerted him.

:Oh my God! Khreng, Prandra, wake up! WAKE UP!:

Prandra, chin resting on Khreng's shoulder, sniffed and went on dreaming. Padding down a vast hall till she came to the niche where Espinoza waited in his blue globe. "Hullo, Espinoza, you don't look a day older."

:Wake up, you damn fool, change back!:

"Ha, Espinoza, you always are a joker!"

In desperation Espinoza plunged into Elya's mind, but there was nothing for him to grasp at in its foaming turmoil.

Elya did not even have the choice of screaming or weeping now. His hand was rigid around the base of the lamp, his body propelled him against his will. The thought that the couple might be making love jetted into his mind, and a shameful desire to see them made him burn cold with sweat. He did not know how skillful the Qumedni were at turning a person's feelings against himself.

Espinoza knew very well, but he had no mouth to shout with, no eyes to close in despair. Khreng and Prandra were impervious.

Elya opened the door, his body vibrating like a tuning fork with internal tremors, lifted his lamp and saw the demons. Their deep-red bodies, heavy muzzles, slit eyes, and fearful claws. His trembling intensified, but he could neither move nor wake, and there was nothing for him to wake to.

One, which had been resting against the other, stirred and lifted its head. Elya's teeth unclenched at last. "Shaddai!" he cried in a strangled whisper.

"*Mazzikim!*"

Prandra opened her flame-colored eyes and stared at him.

:Oh God, Prandra, why in hell didn't you wake when I called!:

Prandra yawned, and Elya's body jerked in terror. Khreng growled softly; his nose twitched.

Elya, in the light of the trembling flame, hair awry and nightgown bunched in his other hand, was whispering, "*For he shall give his angels charge over thee, to keep thee in all thy ways, they shall bear thee up in their hands, lest thou dash they foot against a stone, thou shalt tread upon the lion and the adder, the young lion and the adder shalt thou trample under foot. . . .*"

:He really does believe we are demons,: Prandra said in some wonder.

:Don't try to change his mind or you'll drive him right over the edge.:

Reb' Elya, in spite of everything, managed to conquer himself enough to close the door and touch the talisman on the doorpost.

"Spare Chava and the children," he whispered. "Please...." Under his fear there was a terrible gulf of sadness that his hospitality had been betrayed and all of his love of God had come to nothing. "You are the ones who were called Jacob and Sarah, aren't you?"

"Yes, but—"

"Then take me if I have sinned, God help me, but don't—"

"Rabbi, Reb' Elya, we have not come for you. Not for you!"

"I think you have already taken the Lubliner and left some strange empty thing in his place...."

Prandra sighed. "No, rabbi, it's not so simple...." She got up on her hind legs so that her head was level with his. "How are we to talk to you?"

Elya shrank back against the door. Her solidity, the sleekness of her belly, and the faint rank smell about her suggested that she had borne and suckled demon whelps. "You are playing with me," he said sadly. "Demons are liars ... I knew there was no such place as Krasniewic."

Prandra watched him a moment while he stood immobile, eyes far away, drifting toward some depthless precipice.

:Prandra,: said Espinoza, *:if you don't catch him—:*

Prandra shrugged away Espinoza's mind, dropped to her forelegs, tilted her head so that the lantern could reflect its light in her eyes but avoid the eyeshine that would terrify him further. "Look at me, Rabbi. You are blind, I make you see."

He did not want to, he tried to keep his eyes turned away, but there was nothing else to see in that room. And her eyes were not hidden from him, nor were they anything but eyes. Light reflected from the inner surfaces of the corneas onto the translucent rims centered with black vortices; still they were calm sensitive animals'—no, person's eyes within any accepted range of creation.

"I don't mean to harm you or even touch you, only tell you what is happening, why you are so sick and unhappy. Your arm is stiff and aching, Rabbi, put down the lamp and let the oil burn out...." She took a small penlight from her harness—he noticed for the first time what a complicated piece of equipment she was wearing—turned it on and hung it from a nail; the other red shape behind her watched and blinked: "...You're free to speak and move... if you are too frightened, if you feel sick, you can go to bed and forget everything... do you want to do that?"

"No!" Elya cried, astonished at himself. "I want to know!"

Prandra showed her teeth, not too many, and gave Reb' Elya the short course.

She was quick. Almost instantaneously she drew from Espinoza everything she could understand of all he had learned of the psyche for three hundred years, collated it with her own experience, and turned the walls of Reb' Elya's mind to clear glass.

It was a violent act. Elya bent over, clutched his stomach and retched, but Prandra didn't hesitate. When he straightened, gasping, before he could think or speak, she gave him pictures: ... two demon shapes burning red in the evening light, going to and fro over the earth, lost on a journey from the unimaginable to the inconceivable/sucked into the trap laid by a sickly pale batwing creature, Ashmedai, King of Demons, who crouches over Kostopol and its people, and with a touch here, a twist there, turns them sick and drives them to rage/Janchik kills Zevi-Hirsch—Elya feels devoured by sin and faints in the synagogue—stammers his agony, his trembling hands wind tefillin/and the minya plans to kill—

"Oh, no!" Reb' Elya cried. "Never! They'd never dream of doing such a thing! You're ly—"

(...picks up the Sabbath lamp and opens the door to the storeroom to see if the man and woman are making—)

"Stop!" Elya's face was flaming.

Prandra grinned with all her teeth. "That is the way you usually behave?"

"No, no, but—"

"It is the demon Ashmedai that does this," she said. "That's what I'm trying to tell you...."

... as the minyan direct their rage at Janchik, Rosnicki is approaching...

"It is you who saves Janchik from being killed ... and your friends. . . ."

Janchik, come have a glass of tea with me!

"I didn't know—"

"Perhaps not, but you do what is necessary."

... when the minds of all Kostopol hold suspicion and unease like fragments of flint waiting to be sparked/the rabbi comes on his horse of dust and wind, with his disciples of twigs and clay ...

"I knew when I couldn't see his eyes. . . ." Tears streamed from his own. "Will he hurt Reb' Zalman?"

"Not now."

"Is there no true Lubliner?"

"He exists, but I don't know what is become of him."

... last flicker of imagery, a fragment of stone burns Elya's fingers/stings the neck of Rosnicki, who agrees to a plan. . . .

"It always comes to such a plan," Elya whispered.

"Now we ask: we want to warn your people but we don't know how."

"Do you really know what will happen tomorrow?"

"No, but this devil wants to drive men to fight and kill."

"Then what can I tell you?" Elya shrugged. He was leaning against the door, calm enough but feeling slightly nauseated, his heart bumping. "Men like Rosnicki makes these plans ... sometimes they wake up in the morning with headaches from drinking too much brandy and give them up. . . . If they decide to carry them out, we go and talk to them and sometimes manage to scrape up enough money to satisfy them. Sometimes even then they kill us."

"And you don't fight," Prandra muttered. Before he could answer, she went on, "We do what we can and make no plans. Still . . ." she kept looking at him and he turned deeply shy. "You are a good sensible man, not cowardly. Remember you are doing nothing wrong and are not thinking evil thoughts of your own will. You have nothing to be guilty about. Shall I make you forget what I tell you?"

"No, I want to remember." He had plenty to worry about, for himself and his people, but he was free of the sick fears of madness. These demons, and their adversary Ashmedai, were very far from the local ones of his belief, which had no Satanic majesty, no smoky splendor, but were shadowy stunted things that lurked and whispered, like fear and rage, in dark places. He wondered if he had fallen into some sin by listening and believing, but—dear God, Little Father, I am free to pray....

He said hesitantly, "You don't seem much like demons to me."

Prandra opened her mouth and closed it again. Khreng rose and stood beside her. "It is not necessary for demons to be what men expect," he said.

"I believe you," said Elya. "Good night."

"I almost tell him everything," Prandra said. "I want to."

:Just as well you didn't. That's a nice piece of hypnodrama you put on. I didn't know you could handle that kind of therapy.:

"Is that what it's called?" she asked indifferently. She was sulky with overexertion, crouched down and rubbed her chin on her forefeet. "It's risky, only for emergencies... I do that for my sister when she thinks it is her fault her baby dies."

:Be careful or you'll end up a class-five ESP.:

"Can we arrange to give the count a headache?" Khreng asked.

:That won't stop the Qumedni.:

What stops the Qumedni? Prandra pulled a shield around her mind, not to hide from Khreng or Espinoza, but to give herself a few quiet minutes to think.

... Not everything he does is successful... what weaknesses do powerful creatures have? On Ungruwarkh no one is stronger than Khreng and I, though there are many equal... the great power over us is starvation, and a Qumedni... needs energy most likely... and... Reb' Elya has stopped the Qumedni once—by being foolhardy and generous!

She snorted.

... But there are things we learn here that are useful, I'm sure... only Espinoza is too old and tired and Khreng and I are too inexperienced to use them....

Khreng said suddenly, "The rabbi does fight, you know.

Otherwise the Qumedni does not give him so much attention."

She laughed. "Are you sure you're not an ESP?"

"If I am no one puts me in any bottle."

It was not quite morning on Earth, in Kostopol. Khreng stood by the open door of the shed, watching the fading stars; no one he knew lived around them in this quarter of the sky.

:I wish I could be out there with you,: said Espinoza (a young man in his strength . . .).

"The sky is clear, it means bright sun," Khreng said. "I hate these scratchy lenses on my eyes."

"So do I . . . the sky is strange here with these clouds that move and change."

:Move and change yourselves, friends, or Chava and the children will take fits.:

Prandra laughed. "Maybe the children like the big pussy cats."

:I'm glad you can be so cheerful when we have no plans and don't know what to do.:

Khreng said, "On Ungruwarkh we act quickly and don't make secret plans because everybody knows what they are as soon as you think of them." Prandra laughed again, and he grunted. "This makes the men faithful—and the women happy. I think I die here soon if we can't get back."

Prandra asked, "Khreng, when you are a child, what do you do when you meet a bully or a bigger challenger?"

"I give him a good thump on the snout before either of us has time to think, and even if he beats me up, he thinks twice before he bothers me again."

"Ha, today nobody gets a chance to think twice."

Though it had slept beneath a clear sky, Kostopol woke a little tense and irritable as if there had been wind and thunder during the night. Babies disdained the breast and cried, children woke red-eyed and whined to sleep longer, banked fires ebbed, letting the Sabbath hotpots cool, and Janchik and a couple of other Polish boys dashed about, summoned by frantic wives, to shake and relight them.

Chava wrung her hands, but Elya for once did not complain

about the coldness of the tea. He barely saw around him, hardly noticed the guests at his table, and Chava, noting the strange expression on his face, did not question him.

He prepared for shul: put on a fur-rimmed shtreihel over his yarmulkeh, shook out his tallith from its bag and swept it over his shoulders. As he left the house with the three older boys, Chava following with the baby, he spread his arms as if to draw the children under his shawl, and as suddenly dropped them.

"Moisheleh, you look as if you have a cold, maybe you should stay home."

"No, Tateh, I'm all right."

The dread he did not feel for himself had driven its claws through them to pierce him. He had no desire to run, he had no world beyond Kostopol, and he did not know how to tell others to run, or where. The curious effect of meeting the demons, or whatever creatures of the night they were, had been to lessen his belief in them, and though he now only half believed, he thought, hoped, prayed that God, creator of angels and demons, would give him a sign.

The great rabbi of Lublin came to shul with his disciples, their faces pale as porcelain-clay, their shadows crisp and dancing on the rutted ground.

Reb' Elya pulled the shawl over his head and plunged his spirit into prayer. A few shafts of light pierced the dim synagogue windows and dust motes whirled in them briefly and drifted into shadow. *Master of all worlds! What are we? What is our life? What is our goodness? What our righteousness? What our helpfulness? What our strength?* The white-covered heads, striped blue or black, nodded and whispered on the drifts of the words, raised voices and sang, the sound was swallowed in a dead air. In his house among the orchards, the count and his cousins were perhaps holding their heads and groaning, swearing to leave off brandy and vodka, turning in their sweated linen sheets to sleep again. Perhaps not. *My offering, consumed by fire, a sweet savor to Me, you shall be careful to offer to Me at its proper time.* Jews shut into a synagogue set afire, burning and screaming, a sweet savor... the demon rabbi Ashmedai, standing on the beemah only a few feet away, turned the pages of a siddur quietly, raising his voice occasionally, keeping his eyes down. Elya wondered that the words of the prayers did not leap off the pages and burn in outrage, and then: What have I to say? I am here silent in his presence, and I have taken the word of the *mazzikim*—the word of the demons themselves!—that they will try to save us. How can I live under such conditions? *To thee, O Lord, I called, I appealed to my God: What profit would my blood be, if I went down to the grave? Will the dust praise thee? Will it declare thy faithfulness?*

Prandra, far back in the women's section, was far away. :*They are getting up...preparing to saddle the horses...they seem terribly cheerful...*:

:*I hope you know what we're doing,*: Khreng said.

:*The rabbi himself tells us when to move,*: Prandra said calmly.

:*You have more faith in him than he has in us.*:

:*There is no other choice.*:

Men rose to pray, swaying with fervor, and sat down again, rose and sat down again, raised their voices in curiously muffled song, picked up again the threads of the prayers. *Thou, O God, openest daily the gates of the east, and cleavest the windows of the sky; thou bringest forth the sun from its place, and the moon from its dwelling, and givest light to the world*... the dust motes swam and trembled; children whimpered and women hushed them, but did not let them out to play in the aisles as usual, or go out to the anteroom to gossip; nor did the men leave to conduct their weekly debates on Talmudic exegesis; they glanced at each other furtively and did not ask whether they were leaving and why not.

But Prandra rose quietly and went down the staircase to the lobby. To move at all was like pushing through shoulder-high sand, the air had become so thick and clotted; she expected obstruction. In Reb' Elya's terrified mind she had glimpsed a shadow of what was to come.

Reb' Zalman opened the curtains of the Ark and its carved doors, took out the Torah Scroll, and brought it to the lectern: its silver crown glittered, the bells on the crown's rim tinkled, the readers gathered round, it was unrolled... Prandra, breathing hard, reached the lobby and waited at the door to the sanctuary.

The outside door was ajar; a cat wandered in, a common short-haired animal, brindled. She looked at it; it gave her a quiet yellow stare for three seconds and leaped for her eyes. She picked it from the air and threw it out the door, quite gently, for her. "Qumedni likes to play," she said and smiled grimly.

The rabbi of Lublin came forward to read the first part of the week's portion.

Reb' Elya knew that his words did not have their proper shapes, that the sounds did not reverberate from the beams and timbers, and yet they reached some depth of the brain where images grew....

AND THE LORD SPOKE UNTO MOSES SAYING:
COMMAND AARON AND HIS SONS, SAYING:
THIS IS THE LAW OF THE BURNT OFFERING...

in the breast of every man and woman a small spark was struck from the stone fragment which had been lodged there, leaped to the dried-out tinder stored during thousands of years of insult and repression

THE FIRE OF THE ALTAR SHALL BE KEPT BURNING

a little flame kissed the altar of every heart for Zevi-Hirsch was dead, the signatory of a thousand, a hundred thousand, hundreds of thousands beyond

THE FIRE UPON THE ALTAR SHALL BE KEPT
BURNING THE FIRE SHALL BE KEPT BURNING UPON
THE ALTAR CONTINUALLY

Reb' Elya began to tremble

MY OFFERINGS MADE BY FIRE

fires leaped and licked among the spirits of the Kostopolers, and the pale disciples, smiling, nodded and swayed

FROM THE OFFERINGS OF THE LORD MADE BY FIRE, WHATSOEVER TOUCHETH THEM SHALL BE HOLY

the demon rabbi swept into the second part of the week's portion, Reb' Zalman's privilege, and the men of Kostopol did not move or blink, but sat like stone ovens harboring fire

A SWEET SAVOR UNTO THE LORD

they were given a vision: Count Rosnicki lusting for the silver of the Torah crowns, their gold-threaded coverings

WHERE THE BURNT-OFFERING IS KILLED SHALL THE SIN-OFFERING BE KILLED

saddling horses, gathering peasants with scythes

WHEN THERE IS SPRINKLED OF THE BLOOD THEREOF

Elya's heart fought like a bird in its ribcage

WHERE THEY KILL THE BURNT-OFFERING SHALL THEY KILL THE SIN-OFFERING

the readers on the beemah took one step back from the Scroll

THE BLOOD THEREOF SHALL BE DASHED AGAINST THE ALTAR

as if it had been spattered with blood, as if it were being consumed by fire

AN OFFERING MADE BY FIRE UNTO THE LORD

the unearthly voice rose howling like a chimney of fire

IT SHALL BE THE PRIEST THAT DASHEST THE BLOOD AND THE FLESH OF THE SACRIFICE

THE FLESH OF THE SACRIFICE, SHALL BE BURNT
WITH FIRE
IT SHALL BE BURNT WITH FIRE

Reb' Elya's lips quivered and moved without a sound, fire
moved from man to man and the heat of their passion scorched
him, the count came riding, smiling, calling out laughingly to his
cousins and his men....

Stupid, stupid, said voices in the ears of Khreng and Prandra.
Make no plan, have nothing to do, and you do nothing, stupid!

You, Reb' Elya, know no Names
you, Reb' Elya, are an ignoramus
an ignoramus!

He knew a thousand names for God, but none of the most
powerful commanded by great saints and towering scholars to
bring down the right arm of the Lord, His pillar of fire, His
burning bush

MOSES POURED OUT THE BLOOD

it rose pounding into the heads of the men

DASHED THE BLOOD AGAINST THE ALTAR

the riders were in the marketplace and Prandra, slipping into the
sanctuary, dared not admit a thought for fear of the demon

"Yes, the demon," whispered Khreng
Watch. Ungrukh, said the demon

MOSES TOOK OF THE BLOOD

the Qumedni delivered his strength to the men of Kostopol

MOSES PUT OF THE BLOOD

the Qumedni gave them his malice

MOSES DASHED THE BLOOD

and Elya, gathered his horror, his passion, his intelligence in one skein, one half second of mountainous despair, for in all those thousands of years those hundreds of thousands lay dead, saw with complete clarity that the men of Kostopol would wind their tallithim about the necks of their tormentors, in spite of scythes and pitchforks, break up the pews and lecterns for weapons, trample the Books—and then the King of Demons would withdraw his strength and the fire would grow veins outward, and the blood flow along them to Lublin, to Warsaw and beyond

threw back his head and howled "NO! NO! NO!" his whole being a bursting artery of fear and love, "Dear Lord God, King of the Universe, remove this abomination!"

Without a thought Khreng and Prandra pressed the switches of their remotes.

The count and his followers swarmed stamping across the lobby and into the sanctuary.

Khreng and Prandra crouched free in their bodies, fire-red in the flaked yellow light, and roared in pure pleasure, like forges, like dragons, like earthquakes, and leaped in unison three bounds over the lecterns scattering pages, straight on the Qumedni. Converging with Elya, who had sprung out in the first violent act of his life. All four vanished in a gulping implosion.

"Demons!" roared the count and his men, in one instant turning queasy with fright. "*Mazzikim!*" whispered the congregation, and trembled. Chava and the children screamed with horror.

As the Master of Demons disappeared, his works undid themselves. His disciples and his horse reverted to their elements. But they had this much life in them: the six disciples jumped up on tiptoe with heads thrown back and whirled crowing like cocks, for a quarter of a minute before they crumbled in heaps of earth-clotted twigs; and the horse, tethered in the inn yard, reared on its hind legs and brayed once, powerfully, in idiot discord and then turned transparent, dust sifted into the whirlwind. A great echo pulsed outward from it, rebounded, and died.

The count, with cousins and farmers, backed away from the

sanctuary; the congregation hurried out, pulling one another by sleeves and fringes, gathering Elya's family shivering among them.

Under the blazing noon sun, the metallic bell of the sky, they turned, twisted, peered everywhere. "What happened! Where are they? How?" They looked to the sky and the sun, to earth, trees and houses, and found no sign.

Over the southern horizon an odd cockle, a buckling of the sky's surface, was obscured by the sun.

Khreng and Prandra, tossed in a heap with Elya, stood up and found themselves in a bubble. Its surface, luminous semitransparent silver, shifted and mottled like soap-film; under their feet its stuff was not quite solid, of a firmness created by a force-field; it had a slithery feel. Beneath their pads, through it they could see Earth, a distorted ball as in a fisheye lens, the moon, a pale concave disc; above and around them a stunning collection of nebulae magnified by the warp of the field: spiral, barred, globular. It was a fearful panorama; it was meant to be so. The heavens between these lights were as blue as Espinoza's globe. But there was no contact with Espinoza.

Elya was only half conscious, and they lifted him between them, made a seat for him with their bent knees and a back with their entwined arms so that he was supported by a magnificent red throne of living plush; but it did not mean much to him, for he opened his eyes, took one wild look around, screamed and wrapped his tallith round his head. "I am in Gehinnom," he whispered through its folds.

They could not deny it. They too were intimidated. Their hair rose, their hearts beat faster; the earth under their feet, through the translucent film, was far away but not too far away to pull them down crashing. The nebulae above and around looked near enough to drag them as hideously burst and frozen bodies into their great orbits.

They breathed good air, their hearts beat time, but the space they were enclosed in seemed timeless.

Elya was well-rooted in time. He pulled the cloth half away from his face, enough to free his mouth though he kept his eyes shut, and said, "Kostopol? Chava and the children?"

Prandra could not keep her eyes from circling the surface of this sphere which had no door and was a mind-splitting window to the universe. "The demon has left them," she said. She hoped it was so. It was hard to reassure him: she was unwilling to frighten him with more esp, and without Espinoza she would have to pull the language from Elya's mind and feed it to Khreng as well.

Qumedni appeared, suspended before them. A spinning unradiant star, three meters across, nothing-colored, a few points of fire swimming within it like fish in a bowl, in its center a luminous globe small enough to hold between the hands.

Firepoints struck their minds:

YES YOU ARE QUICK AND CLEVER UNGRUKH AND YOU ARE INTERRUPTING MY GAME.

The bright globe darkened a little, and the huge bubble began to swing slowly, like a pendulum. Earth and moon went here and there beneath them.

Khreng and Prandra bent their heads and closed their eyes. "Stop, please," Prandra said. The bubble slowed and settled.

"Where are we?" Khreng got back his breath and his stomach. "What is this place?"

YOU ARE IN THE CENTER OF THE VORTEX. THE GLOBE I AM CARRYING IS ITS CONTROL THIS PLACE IS TIMELESS.

"Is there only one of you in this sector?"

THERE IS.

"You are a creature of such power," Prandra clenched her teeth trying to keep fear and contempt out of her mind, "why do you choose a small village and a few lost strangers to play games with?"

DO YOUR CHILDREN NOT PLAY WITH SMALL ANIMALS?

"My children don't play with people."

The Qumedni shrank quietly in one supple transformation and became a naked man. Without skin. Sitting cross-legged in the air holding the bright globe in his hands; beautiful in complexity, terrible in implication, he was a triumph of Qumedon mastery, no stupid animal of dust and wind. A red glisten of muscle laced in purple veins and pulsing scarlet arteries, shimmering blue-white in the fibrous sheaths between muscles and over the tendons of his intricate hands and feet; within his breast a heart beat *lubdubb,* his eyes were firepoints.

A smell of meat filled the place. Beyond control, Khreng and Prandra found saliva jetting into their mouths.

NICE FAT PEOPLE ON THIS PLANET.

Elya, between the two of them, shrank with terror.

Khreng spat his mouthful at the feet of the living model and snarled, "We do not yet kill or eat one, Qumedni!"

Qumedni moved the network of muscles in mouth and neck into laughter, tossed the ball into the air and caught it. The bubble trembled.

WHERE DID YOU GET A TASTE FOR MEAT, UNGRUKH? DID FIREMASTER GIVE IT TO YOU WHEN HE CREATED YOU FROM RED LAVA?

"Say what you mean!"

Laughter. OR WAS IT I WHO PICKED A PRIDE OF LEOPARDS OFF SOLTHREE AND CHANGED THEM ONLY A LITTLE, DROPPED THEM ON A PLANET TO SEE WHAT WOULD HAPPEN?

They swallowed that information in an unhappy lump without asking themselves if it were true. It was clearly within his power. "Firemaster has more effect on our lives than you," Khreng said.

YOU ARE NOT ON UNGRUWARKH AND HERE I CREATE THE EFFECTS.

Was he more forceful as a creature of unimaginable power who reflected the shape and texture of the cosmos—or as a flayed saint with the humanly evil mind of the persecutor?

I LIKE THIS PLACE, UNGRUKH. THAT IS WHY I PLAY MY GAMES HERE.

"Far away from Qumedni," Prandra said, risking jets of fire from those eyes.

YES. I'M A PERSON WHO BRINGS NEW IDEAS TO MY PEOPLE AND FOR THAT THEY WILL TOLERATE A LOT.

Everything? Without limit? Prandra became aware that the questions she wanted answers for, swelling nodes in her brain, were being contained by all this talk. But the Qumedni was turning his intensity toward the shivering Elya.

RABBI, YOUR SHOCHET, REB' NACHMAN, SLAUGHTERS AND SKINS MANY ANIMALS. DO I LOOK WORSE THAN THEY?

Elya whispered, "Ashmedai, a demon and a dead cow are not to be compared."

More laughter emerged between the white teeth among the naked muscles, and the Qumedni began to weave a skin, a tissue of capillaries, fibers, laminated cells, its surface horn-colored, puckered like an old man's and dotted with moles; sprouted white crinkled hair on his head, with side curls, mixed-grey brows and beard, body hair, provided himself with black breeches, black-and-white *tallith katan*, yarmulkeh, Cossack boots, tallith; cradled the globe in one arm against his heart as if its light were the white fires of space between the black-flame letters of the Torah Scroll. His eyes were nothing-colored. The Rabbi of Qumedni.

Elya turned pale.

YOU STOPPED A POGROM? MAZEL TOV, I'LL FIND ANOTHER GAME. I DON'T HAVE TO LIVE ON THIS PLANET, YOU DO... YOU THINK IT'S SAFER HERE WITHOUT ME? The telepathic voice, an astonishing homely Polish-Yiddish, was good-humored, almost gentle.

"When was it safe?" Elya said hoarsely. "My father died in a pogrom."

STAY ALIVE A HUNDRED YEARS, ELYA, MAYBE A FEW MORE... SEE THE SLAUGHTER THERE'LL BE.

"A hundred years ago and more," Elya whispered, "Bogdan Chmielnicki killed my people by the hundreds of thousands during the Cossack Rebellion."

THIS WILL BE TWENTY-FIVE TIMES GREATER THAN THAT ONE... the fleshy lips curved in the white beard... YOU COULDN'T IMAGINE....

Prandra said quietly, "When you say such things, I think even your own people must not care much for you."

The Qumedni's laughter was dark. EVEN THE KINDEST OF US LIKES A GOOD GAME. The laughter rebounded and circled the walls of the bubble. IRONY IS ALWAYS GOOD; YOU LIKE IT YOURSELF, RABBI—AND AT THIS LEVEL IT IS SUPERB. YOU HAVE SAVED KOSTOPOL!

Prandra began to tease out a thought beneath the whirling helix of laughter.

Elya raised his eyes. "And that killing, will that be your work?"

YOU THINK MEN AREN'T CAPABLE?

Elya closed his eyes and tears slid between his lids. His spirit shrank into a hard tight ball of anguish.

"Rabbi!" Prandra thought he was drifting into the abyss once more.

Elya opened his eyes and regarded the Qumedni. "Ashmedai, if you know so much, tell me if my people will die forever in that slaughter."

Prandra wound a thought firmly around the deep center of her being like fine wire on a spindle. "Your people are alive seven hundred and fifty years from now," she said. "After that I can't promise." Her voice sank to its deepest velvet. "Qumedni, is it Thursday when your shuttle breaks down? That day when you make no move?"

Firepoints grew in the eyes.

"You burn me out too like the ESP of the *Ruxcimi?*" she spoke very quietly. "That is an impulse, I think. Too bad to bring such attention to yourself."

IF I KILL—

Very quietly. "You manipulate fear and hatred very well, but do you know everything about reasoning? Perhaps you are only a novice joker."

—YOU ANIMALS—

"Must think for ourselves, because Firemaster, you know, gives no answer.

"I see the power of this Qumedni, and I ask myself: why does he let us live, when he can kill us with a thought? Because he needs us. Needs *animals?* We have a shuttle, and even Qumedni, with all their powers, need ships to cross the universe and shuttles to land . . . but if he can use our shuttle, he does not need us. Can you use our shuttle?"

Silence.

"Your energy field disrupts GalFed instruments? Some such thing? I know very little about those matters. Still, the vortex draws energy from the mother ship and Qumedni carries his personal energy source in his shuttle. Espinoza says this. The source feeds both him and his engines. Probably if it does not operate fully, he can still draw enough for himself for a while, but not enough to get him back to his ship. He realizes this on Thursday and perhaps is not sure what to do. And he takes notice of our landing. He cannot come to us and say: Ungrukh, I am in trouble, I send you up the vortex, leave a message with my people the Qumedni to rescue me. Why not? Because he burns out a valuable ESP—an act which likely upsets coexistence with GalFed—and maybe this game he's planning is a little too bloody even for Qumedni who are their own law...."

YOU HAVE A LOT TO SAY TO THE MAD RENEGADE QUMEDNI.

"All he can do is say: Look, I am a creature of a thousand powers, if you want to live you must do as I say—and he plays his game to please himself, to show off, to frighten us...."

"We believe in your great power, Qumedni, but still you are not offering to let us live—I hate to say so, but even if you are rescued, your people don't look on you too kindly. There's no way to avoid that."

THEN WHY SHOULD I BOTHER KEEPING YOU ALIVE WHEN YOU WILL ONLY BETRAY ME?

"Tsk, he's in a bind," Khreng said. "He can't decide whether to save himself and go home in shame or stay here and die with his pride."

Elya, who did not understand a word but knew a bargaining session when he saw one, sat quietly in a crouch with his shawl wrapped around him.

SOMETIMES IT IS BETTER—

Prandra moved her head in a gesture she had learned from Reb' Elya himself. "It's always better to be alive today."

Khreng said, "I think—"

And the bubble turned upside down. And warped, pinched, squeezed, they tumbled, screaming; Qumedni rolled with them, clenched around his glowing ball.

Outside a blundering roaring vibration gripped and clawed, emitted sounds, colors all over the spectrum, blue, violet, aquamarine, screaming ultra whines and bass rumbles out of the very pit of matter

what?

THE VORTEX HAS PULLED IN.

what?

alien creature?

hand, octopod, or

?flower with fire-petals bluing down the center into a black pit of suction

clasping the bubble like a hand and

turn off the vortex! Khreng/Prandra mindscreamed

NO MY ONLY CONTACT WITH THE—

then change time, change time!

Qumedni was no longer a rabbi, but the cloud of primary energy enveloping the globe. Khreng, Prandra, Elya slipped and slid with it in hills and valleys over those petal-fingers of terrifying intensity burning through the field, the globe in the Qumedni darkened all light what? disapeared where? and

brightened as the filmy sphere blew out to its former shape with an odd quavering warble. Silence.

"What in the Blue Pit is that?" Khreng picked himself up off Prandra, whom he had knocked flat. She was too weak to think, only lay panting.

The Qumedni seemed to be trying to pull itself together. Its fires were deep crimson, feebly wavering.

Khreng turned to Elya, who had somehow managed to sit up on the bubble floor and was coughing. Or laughing.

He threw back his head and choked with laughter. "Oh, Ashmedai, if that's not the work of God there must be far greater demons than you!"

"Rabbi, are you hurt?"

"How could I be hurt when I'm consorting in hell with the demons?"

"Don't depend on it," Khreng said. "Qumedni, tell us what that thing is."

...I DON'T KNOW.... The Qumedni's voice was as vague

as its body. THE VORTEX PULLED IT IN I'VE NEVER SEEN ANYTHING LIKE THAT...SOMETHING FROM ANOTHER UNIVERSE....

Prandra was a little lightheaded. "Perhaps it is Firemaster's apprentice!"

"Don't be fatuous," Khreng said. "Listen, Qumedni, if your vortex pulls in one more thing like that, I think you soon have no place to stay...and, Prandra, if you let me speak, I believe I can make a sensible suggestion. If the rabbi is set free and we are guided up the vortex, it is very simple to send a message to the Qumedni that one of their people lands on Solthree to explore and is trapped when his engines fail. It is not necessary to say anything else—regarding ESPS or games—and it is a way out of this impasse."

WOULD THEY BELIEVE YOU?

"You can believe us because you esp us. You know we cannot be liars and a radio message cannot be esped. When you are among your people, you make your own arrangements. You are very skilled at deception." In spite of himself Khreng's voice tailed off into a rasp of sarcasm.

Silence. The firepoints rippled and glittered in their aquarium of energy. The bubble trembled.

Prandra whispered, "I think if you stay on this planet your energy drains away till you are some shriveled black little thing like a burnt-out star...."

The firepoints intensified, their mouths went dry.

SAY WHEN YOU ARE READY.

Before they could react or speak: LISTEN, UNGRUKH, I HAVEN'T ASKED YOU MANY QUESTIONS SO PERHAPS YOU WILL ANSWER JUST ONE?

It sank and rested gently on the floor of the bubble.

WHAT ARE YOU GOING TO DO ABOUT ESPINOZA?

"What do you mean?"

HE WANTS YOU TO KILL HIM.

Prandra said sharply, "I don't esp that."

YOU ARE NOT YET A CLASS ONE ESP. WHAT DO YOU THINK ALL THOSE LOVELY DREAMS

MEANT...THAT PATHOS THAT POOR BODILESS BRAIN-IN-A-BOTTLE ROTTING IN A RUNDOWN MUSEUM?

"He—"

HE BELIEVES HE HAS ONLY TO ASK THEN YOU WILL BREAK THE BOTTLE AND LET THE BRAINS RUN OUT AND NO ONE WILL BLAME YOU BECAUSE YOU ARE SAVAGE CATS FROM A PRIMITIVE PLANET AND DON'T KNOW ANY BETTER, the patterns of fire swirled like arrows representing ocean currents on a map, I KNOW YOU WOULDN'T DO SUCH A THING BUT SINCE YOU ARE DOING ME A FAVOR I AM WILLING TO REPAY...UNGRUKH...IT WAS ON NO IMPULSE OF MINE THAT THE ESP OF THE *RUXCIMI* DIED....

Prandra kept her mind carefully clear and still. Khreng said stiffly, "Thank you, Qumedni, we manage our own affairs."

The Qumedni blinked out and was gone.

"Irony is always good," Khreng said. "Maybe we give up Firemaster and start worshiping the devil.... Come, Rabbi, you are going home." He helped Elya to his feet.

"Really?"

"Yes."

Elya stood on the shifting surface, wondered what thoughts to think and what to make of them. He reached under his tallith to scratch his head. Was he to thank these beings? How? And whom? He looked from one to the other of the red *mazzikim,* their savage teeth and claws, lashing tails and char-black chevrons. *Keteb miriri?* Khreng gave him one calm blink. *Machlat?* Prandra's eyes were warm and clear as a summer sunset. He nodded. "Thank you, creatures of God."

"Where? Where?" the people of Kostopol looked and found no sign.

"I am here," said Elya. Among them in the marketplace. The count and his men withdrew to one side of him, his congregation to another. Chava and the children threw themselves upon him with hysterical weeping.

"Elya! Elya!"

"Where have you been?"

"I have been among the demons and I seem to be well." He sighed. "I think."

"You're not—you're not—"

"I am not a demon rabbi, children—only the same Elya," he said though it was not true. "It was the false Lubliner that was the demon, Ashmedai himself."

"We know that, Elya—and you were with him, among the demons—in Gehinnom?"

"It seemed so."

"And was it terrible?"

"I have no words to tell you."

"Then how did you defeat them? What Names, what spells?"

"I defeated no one. God spared me." He sighed again. "I hope He did the same for the Lubliner, the true one."

"Somebody says his carriage broke down when he was setting out here yesterday . . . he'll have to go straight home now, he can't stop over with Passover coming. . . ."

They turned silent. Kostopol had been cut off from its promised glory and seized by demons instead.

"You seem strange, Elya," Chava whispered.

"What can I be, Chava? I've been frightened and I'm tired and sad." He gathered the children under his shawl. What could he say or tell? Mystics in wise books might claim a demon is this or that, but his own were indescribable. And as for what he had learned—Let it be a lie, Little Father, King of the Universe! Let it be a lie, what Ashmedai said. . . .

"Rebbeh—" the count came to him, reddened, rubbed his neck. "I don't know what has been happening."

"I'm not sure myself, Count, believe me." He turned to his congregation in their shawls and their beards, feasted his eyes on those worn and humble faces. "Rabbosai, we have to finish the service . . . I think we should begin reading Torah again—with a little less fire and blood. . . ."

There was nothing much to say to Espinoza. Prandra opened her mind and let him replay the scene for himself. Strapping herself down for lift-off, she said, "Is everything that Qumedni says true?"

:Yes. Everything.:

"And nothing can stop that slaughter? Nothing?"

:No.:

"Then we save our own lives, but I think we do nothing much for Kostopol."

:Prandra, you said it yourself,: Espinoza sealed his own fate. *:It's always better to be alive today.:*

They warped outward.

—ACCEPT COURSE CHANGE OR WAIT ONE ORBIT? the radio asked.

"We don't lose much time," Khreng said. WAIT AS MANY ORBITS AS YOU LIKE, FIJI. THAT COURSE CHANGE LEADS DOWN A QUMEDNI TIME VORTEX. . . .

When that was settled, he rubbed his head under Prandra's chin. "My old women, I'm sick of hypnoformers and contact lenses and civilization. I want sleep." He flung himself back on the couch belly-up.

Espinoza, the man without skin, flesh, bones, nerves, heart, lungs, limbs, genitals, said, *:Times I called you eisenkop I never meant you had an iron head. Maybe one day you'll wish you did. You too, ES Prandra . . . :*

"Espinoza!" Prandra rumbled sleepily.

:Yes?:

"You stay with us, be with us as long as we need you?"

:Yes.:

"That's good. . . ." She folded her limbs over her body, curled her tail about herself neatly; rising on waves of sleep, she considered, slowly and hazily, the shapes of minds, the organic structures that began them, the ideas and emotions that fulfilled them, wondered how a Qumedni functioned and what with, whether a mind-model could ever be built, how . . . she had time for five minutes of her life's work before she drifted off.

Seven hundred and fifty years spiraling downward the men of Kostopol sang:

> *This is the Torah*
> *that Moses set before the*

Children of Israel
the Children of Israel...

Reb' Nachman carried it in its tinkling crowns and glittering threads down from the beemah, around the synagogue, men reached out to touch it with their fringes and kissed them;

Long life is in its right hand
and in its left hand honor
it is a Tree of Life
it is a Tree of Life
its way are pleasant ways
and all its paths are peace...

Let it be a lie. Elya, his spirit a teardrop, his mouth a blessing, took the words of the most loving and gentle of all rabbis, Israel Baal-Shem, Master of the Greatest Name, in silence took the words, made them into a song and sang it:

Much, much have I learned bim bam!
much have I been able to do bam bim!
but there is no one to whom
I may reveal it bim bam bim!

2
THE KING'S DOGS

GALACTIC FEDERATION CITY ON SOLTHREE stands on tundra under a dome; a solar-electrified, water-recycling, self-supporting civil-service city in a civil-service world. Aliens from hundreds of worlds hop, skim, or lurch in tanks along its huge white-flagstone avenues. On its eastern rim the MedPsych Annex is enclosed in force-fields and white-noise walls. The ESPs within love privacy, and so, even more, do the non-ESPs outside.

For half an hour every dawn and dusk, two big red cats pace the hexagonal flags around MedPsych. Inevitably they fall into step, consciously break it, fall in and break. Prandra knows that when Khreng has matched her pace their minds are joined, and neither wishes to share one mind all the time. Distant outworld cousins of the leopard, they are leopard-sized, but their color is incongruously harsh against the white stones, among the green box-trees in cement tubs. Khreng is bright crimson, Prandra is much darker as if his shadow had rested on her.

Around his neck Khreng wears a medal, a diplomat's gold star. As the senior representative of Ungruwarkh on Solthree, he has been made its ambassador. He knows he has been given the honor because Prandra is the ESP, but he does not care; he is the stronger and the tracker; Prandra does not care for any reason. They do not know completely what ambassadors do: they are aware that neither one of themselves is very diplomatic. Prandra wears the ESP's insigne on Solthree, a steel medallion engraved with a lightning-bolt wound by a snake. It is sometimes called the Cracked Caduceus and other names; from her point of view it is a dogtag.

Khreng has caught through Prandra a thought in the mind of some passing lover of literature. "What is that about dogs and kings?"

"It is a piece of what Solthrees call poetry, like the words of singing, written on a tag by a man named Alexander Pope, who gives a dog to a king:

> *I am his Highness's dog at Kew;*
> *Pray tell me, sir, whose dog are you?*

"Is that directed at us?"

"Evidently."

Her mind is savage and morose; he pushes on: "Why does he think of us as dogs? We are not dogs of a king, nor serve any dog of a king."

"It is how their minds work. They put a tag on a creature they consider animal and call it a dog."

:*For God's sake, stop being so damn sensitive. Some idiot was making an absentminded allusion.*: Espinoza, their own ESP guide and counsellor, the centuries-old brain-in-a-bottle, is wheeling down the hall to have his nutrient pump adjusted. His mind fades past the walls of a white-room.

Prandra snarls, "Cats *are* sensitive and dogs are hypocrites." She hooks a claw in the chain and stops. Responsibility. If she does not work for GalFed, there will be no cattle or feed-grains for starving Ungrukhs.

"That's the price of being Earth-compatible cats," says Khreng.

"It is the price of being a bloody damned ESP."

Khreng leaves the walk and wanders about the lawn, sniffing some fascinating scent.

Whose dog are you, Khreng? Prandra continues alone. . . . I am alone here. Espinoza has his own affairs. Khreng is bored. She glances at the evening sky through the dome's roof. She and Khreng prefer dusk because they do not have to wear tinted contacts to dim a sun brighter than their own. She begins to trot, chain jingling. Here Rover! Here Rex! Here Fido! Good boy! She sneers. The sweat of fear is around her. *The jaws that bite, the claws that catch.* The literary mind, an idling engine, intrudes. Shut up, stupid! A leap, jaws closing on nape, *crunch!* Not here.

The angles of the buildings shift, the sky turns pink, then red as the plains of Ungruwarkh. Their children, Tugrik and Emerald, are growing across the dark emptiness, forgetting Khreng and Prandra. Half-grown now, Emerald mated, pregnant when we reach home? ESP Emerald chained, brains to be bottled in the dark globe. Not Emerald! Prandra gallops; no prey in the scant flesh dangling from bickering alien heads. Prandra skims the wall: too late to pass the gates, hurl herself at the dark city. Uncivil servants go to bed early in the short tundra nights.

Red, red sky, buildings elongated like spears, their few windows vanished; the sun is down. The spears are tipped with dying light like blood.... An opening among the spears: she smells blood. A shadow crouches, nipping at greens. Not Khreng. Big fleshy thing, no mind, only meat. From where? Saliva pools in her jaw, she is ready to rip meat from bone with her rasp tongue.

"Khreng?" Gone, white-roomed; she will save his portion. Drop it at his feet. Here, Khreng the tracker! Dog. Hyena.

Flesh hot in her nostrils; she goes to ground, thickens her haunches, tail lashing, up and out her powered thighs propel, red claws flash, teeth bare—

The shadow-figure turns, rises, is a man, Solthree, eyes wide, hands raised, pale star palms turned out—*Espinoza!*

Screaming

"Don't—"

"—pull me into your damned bloody dreams, woman! Hell's blazes!" Khreng's swipe sent her tumbling off the bed. "Hyena! Since when am I a hyena after hunting with you all the years?"

Prandra lay on the floor, tongue hanging out, feet slippery with sweat. She shook her head, stood and shook her whole body. She felt drugged.

"Are you sick?" Khreng touched her nose and forehead with his padded hand. "You don't seem feverish."

"I don't know... am I here?"

"What are you saying? You are in our room."

She lifted her head and looked at the pale walls, the great round velvet bed, the rough flagstone slab. She lay on that, scraped her back and flanks on it. "You thrash about so much I can't sleep half the time," Khreng grumbled, "and when I do you call me names."

Prandra crouched on the stone. "I never have such dreams until we come here. It's not in my mind to call you names. That's filthy."

"Whose mind is it in then?" he snorted.

"There are other ESPs here."

"Their thoughts don't come through these walls. What does Espinoza think if he knows you want to eat him?"

"Lummox!" she roared.

He grinned. "Names?"

"Who wants to eat some old brain?" She sniffed. "In my dreams he is not bottled; he is a man as he sees himself. I do not want to eat people. I am satisfied with the meat we get. Something is giving me terrible dreams!"

"We share the same food."

"The kitchens are not whitewalled. I know if drugs are put in the food. Something is wrong." She jumped from the stone and began to pace. "Maybe in my mind . . . from being in a strange place . . . with all those strange thoughts. Wearing a tag and being called a dog."

"That is from your dream."

"Not only. Who is not afraid of a creature that is thought of as savage here?" She sprawled on the floor, tail snapping like a whip. "It makes my head hurt . . . maybe we ask for separate rooms . . . if my head is sick you should not be joined to it."

He stared her in the eye, so close their whiskers melded. "That is not sickness, it is foolishness. If you can handle a Qumedni in a strange place hundreds of years back, you can get along here. On Ungruwarkh you know when a mind is sick, and you never say maybe."

"How do I know my own mind?"

"Your sister knows hers when it is unbalanced; she asks for help too—and you give it. Do you forget everything? Ungrukh know. Maybe not other ESPs. Whatever is bad here comes from somewhere else: we find out." He licked her neck. "If it is a

someone, likely it is happier if we separate and become more
vulnerable."

"That seems sensible."

"I am glad you think I am capable of sense."

She bit his ear and hopped to the bed. He followed, and they
writhed together in their fierce way.

After, they smoothed each other's fur, and Khreng said,
"Now maybe you sleep without dreams."

She hissed, "Now I am really awake. I want to go out."

"Better not disturb Espinoza now."

"Later. I want to think first." Before she reached the door he
had fallen asleep into a dream of Ungruwarkh and the children.
She paused to savor it. . . .

Down the hall padding in silence past guards in green
gold-braided uniforms; she had learned to move so that the
hateful chain did not ring; her red eyeshine reflected the dimmed
ceiling lights. The men on guard thought of jungles. "Here, kitty,
kitty," she muttered. Passed Espinoza's door. Not yet.

Don't—

Why Espinoza, whom she loved? Why leaping on fleshy
animal? Far back in the time-warp she had killed a pig, stunned
and butchered it, like any so-called civilized person. Certainly
she had lusted after it, but she had eaten its meat out of a bowl,
with Khreng. On Ungruwarkh there were no large food animals;
she had caught and roasted the diseased fish, like her
compatriots. And why were those low-ESP guards fearful? Big
red cats are fearsome, but if they mind their business. . . .

Their business is meat—

Stop.

Something was contaminating their minds.

She trotted, galloped, into the darkness. More guards. ESPs
are valuable and cause jealousy. No one else was out. Most went
to bed early in the short tundra nights . . . stop. That was in the
dream.

She looked up. The buildings stood in their right shapes and
proportions, unblooded. The flags had cooled. She smelt the
earth the plants were potted in and the worms that coursed it.
The sky was paling slightly in the east. She jumped the

ornamental fence of the children's playground and rolled in the sand, climbed the bars, slid the chutes, snaked the winding tubes. The patterned coolness of the metal soothed her. She stretched on the sand and watched the fading eastern stars.

Smelt flesh. Her head rose: she growled softly like an engine idling. The Solthree woman, Nema, was watching her, fingers clamped on an arabesque of the fence.

That odd one they considered so beautiful, whose mind was impervious even to the most powerful ESPs. The only Solthree of the kind ever discovered, perhaps the most valuable of her kind. Black eyes, smooth light brown skin, flowing dark hair, deep red velvet robe. Hands tight on bars, eyes fixed. Seeing what? Glowing coals in the head of red demon? Some transparent mind saw them.

The man Metaxa, tall, heavy, dark-bearded, put a hand on her shoulder. *Get away! Retro me, Satanas!* The literary mind.

Fool! Prandra stared him down, saw her red eyes in his. His arms circled the woman to lead her away. Her hands clamped tighter. He pried them off finger by finger.

Fear.

Not only of savage cats, but of/for—

:*Get out! Get out!*:

It was he who insisted on broadcasting to the universe. "Calm yourself, man. You are creating your own fears."

The woman let herself be drawn back. She moved oddly, bent legs placing one foot before the other with flattened soles.

Prandra leaped, cleared the fence in a red arc that blended with the shadows.

Metaxa, the man of immeasurable wealth, explored alien cultures and collected artifacts. The woman, Nema, like the Qumedni, was a mystery to Prandra who was not—and might never be—powerful enough to esp her. Metaxa was incomprehensible culturally: he collected facts and objects for their own sake.

Espinoza at end of patience: :*Because they're pleasing to look at! You've just been too busy surviving to make or look at things for pleasure. You've done extremely well at tool-making for a people without opposable thumbs, and if you had the kind of*

*climate that snowed you into a hut or holed you into a cave half
the year, you'd have been inventing games and artifacts as well.:*

"We have games—"

:Good—:

"But things *are* things."

:—God!:

"We are only savage and ignorant to you."

*:No! Get it straight! You're not savage because you don't kill
from ignorance. Your esp has prevented that. Otherwise you
might have become like many primitive tribes. That, and your
intelligence, have turned you off the branch that sacrifices to
gods. Add the survival crisis that makes you value lives, and
you've got an advanced ethical system. Plus complicated
tool-making abilities: that gives you a culture. You've still got
sore spots because your tribes compete instead of cooperating.
You and Khreng have got to change that. All you need now is to
understand and enjoy what's pleasing.:*

"Why should we gather things we don't need?"

:You don't have to! Just understand those who do!:

"Why?"

:Never mind. Just turn up my oxygen before you go.:

But who could understand Metaxa? The collector of things,
of snatches of poems (about dogs and claws) from books, had
found a child in the kitchen corner of a slum (community of poor
people with few implements, like the village of Kostopol in the
time-warp)—and what was he doing there? (*:Going slumming,:*
says Espinoza tartly, losing Prandra.) Filthy neglected child
who could not move or talk because of behavioral blockage
originating in the brain (called autism). Feeding and excreting in
silence broken sometimes by an hour's screaming, and beaten
for it.

Metaxa had taken her away and given his life to her, leaving
wife, children, mistress (subsidiary mate). Had fed, clothed,
tended her, found specialists to teach her to walk, use her hands,
signal her needs, though she never spoke. Metaxa had polished
her like a jewel. An ESP doctor had discovered her powerful
faculty.

And why?

*   *   *

"Hullo, Espinoza."

:Go to the window and watch the dawn for me.: Through the dome's struts the sun was rising out of a delicate lavender veil. *:That is beautiful.:*

She grinned. "If you say so."

:One more and one less.: The sun reflected a star from the dark bowl of his own dome. After a moment he said, *:Post-hypnotic suggestion.:*

"Ah . . . you *are* first class, Espinoza."

:If I was class-one maybe I'd know who did it, and why. But there is something going on—you'd have figured it out for yourself in a while.:

"The dreams make me afraid. Fear cramps reason."

:I can't move . . . and I'm tired. That cramps it too. . . . :

The room was tiny; the window took one wall. Nothing was there but Espinoza's globe on its stand, the pump humming. Prandra contorted herself to lie down around him. "I am ignorant. Please help."

:You need a class-one.:

Though Espinoza was class-two, she had on his testimony been granted pro-tem second-class ESP status as soon as she arrived. But she and Khreng had come not to be classified but to learn food-farming; in Terraform sector the embryos were developing, to be frozen for shipping. She was waiting in MedPsych because she was an ESP, and she expected to be ratified at GalFed Central on the way back to Ungruwarkh. "The number ones are odd here."

:Everyone is odd here. It's a backwater.:

"You want very much to be here when we are away."

:I always do when I'm away, and vice versa.:

"Espinoza . . . is this ugly thing reaching you?"

:I don't know. . . . :

"Wyaerl and the Lyhhrt are odd to me because they're from other worlds. Sheedy is a wasted old man, and the woman doesn't behave like a Solthree."

:Metaxa's the funny one. I'd say he was some kind of fake if I didn't know his mind.:

"But who will help, Espinoza?"

:*Nudnik, I'll think about it! Go get some sleep. You've probably had your share of dreams for the night. Leave the door open. All I get to hear is stupid thoughts, but they're better than nothing.*:

"I stay with you."

:*And break your bones trying to sleep like that? Go on, get out already!*:

But there was powerful affection beneath the thought, and in her mind she touched her nose to the cheek of the man-image, long gone, who had lived and walked beneath the sun.

Khreng sighed, "Now that I am ready for breakfast I suppose you want to sleep."

"Yes. Go eat. Now I know how I get the dreams, but not who does it or why."

"So I am right after all."

"Right. Fill your belly and don't say I don't listen to you." She flung herself on the wide bed and dropped into velvet sleep.

Espinoza is dead.

More dreams! She writhed, her claws flashed, her tail whipped.

"Pull in your claws, woman. It is no dream."

Grief . . . Khreng was licking her face, shuddering. A drop of sweat from his nose-tip, his only tear, fell on her eyelid.

She leaped up, electrified. "Espinoza!" she howled. Through the open doorway shivers ran down the halls. *Cracked shell spilling brains and liquids!*

ESPINOZA!

"Be quiet! They take him away." Khreng flung himself on her, pinned her down before she reached the door.

Espinoza . . . ?

"You were the last to see him alive."

MedPsych's director, Madame Yamashita, sat on a plain chair in the Committee Room: a small woman in a simple dark blue coverall with the insigne on its breast; her hair was gathered at the back of her neck by a gold and enamel clasp. The rest of the committee were faceless to Prandra; she recognized a few vaguely as Earache, Slipped-disc and Six-toes.

She said quietly, "You read me, Madame. I am not shielding." The pillars of her legs quivered, but she would not lie down to stop them.

Yamashita, a stolid and competent class-two, flushed slightly. "This is an inquiry, not a trial, Prandra. I know you are full of grief and anger."

"I regret expressing them so violently."

The director chose to miss the edge. "You discussed with Espinoza your troubled dreams and the possibility that they were induced by some outside agency."

"You know this."

"Please repeat it for our reports."

"Espinoza and I discuss the weather while he esps my problem, he says my dreams are perhaps engineered by post-hypnotic suggestion, I reply: if so, can you help? he promises to think about it and tells me to go sleep, I tell him I stay with him, he says no, I leave—and he is killed." Her voice tailed into a rasp.

"There were no witness to this conversation."

"What for? It is private business. He asks me to leave the door open when I go."

"When he was found, the door was closed."

"I presume murderers do not leave doors open."

"Why didn't you ask help from someone in authority?"

"I am fearful after having a terrible dream, and I have no friends in authority."

Yamashita clasped and unclasped her hands. "Don't you consider anyone else here your friend?"

Prandra said patiently, "Madame, I am a stranger and ignorant. I know Khreng is my friend, and Espinoza. I esp no one uninvited because it is not courteous, and perhaps I miss gestures that are offered in friendship."

They faced each other in perfect awareness: Khreng and Prandra had been treated correctly, even generously, but not with friendship. The faint frown line between the director's brows indicated that she was wondering why; it seemed the wrongness of the atmosphere had spread like a malign growth.

The pale brown hands steepled their fingertips. "Last night you were seen behaving strangely in the children's park."

"That is not strange for Ungrukh. We exercise the way children do here, but not for long, because we tire quickly." Get to the point, woman!

She did. "Espinoza was killed between four and six in the morning. There is no way of identifying the hour more exactly . . . he could have been killed either before or after you went to the park."

Prandra's fur rose. "The guards—"

"Those at the outer doors report you left at four-thirty and returned at five-fifteen. Metaxa clocked you at five. The guards in quarters don't recall seeing you at all . . . they have probably been tampered with. In some way."

Prandra felt caught in the hideous dream. "I am glad you are not accusing me of anything," she hissed.

"Be assured we are not. We are trying to lay down the basis for a full-scale inquiry. It is on record that while you were in the Qumed time-warp you used hypnosis to—"

Prandra, claw hooked in her chain, was on the point of ripping it from her neck and flinging it across the room. Then she stopped and thought. . . . What *can* I do, Espinoza?

Eisenkop, use your head for a change!

She inhaled deeply. Unhooked the claw from the chain and crouched down. Slapped the floor with the whole length of the tail.

Committee jumped.

She slapped the floor again. "Madame, I am ignorant of many things on this world, particularly the numbers of various articles of diplomatic relations among the worlds of Galactic Federation which state that since Khreng and I constitute an embassy we do not need to answer the kind of questions you ask unless put by an authorized GalFed committee." She stopped for breath. The sentence was sweet in her mouth. "Your inquiry in this area is extra-legal, your Committee unconstitutional, and I have the right to ask for advice from the legal department of GalFed. You strike from the record all exchanges following my account of what happens, and—and you leave me alone to be sad for the death of a friend I love." She rose and loped toward the door. Someone jumped to press the button and let her through. Committee was afraid she might claw down the wall.

Khreng was pacing the halls. "What now? Are we in the firepot?"

"Yes. While I am in there I have the feeling that something/somebody is counting on me to jump up and attack them. Is that crazy?"

"Why ask me? If it is true it is damned strange, and if it is not it is still damned strange."

"And that is pretty damned helpful."

"What else do you want? If the feeling comes from some particular person you tell me, and if you don't say so you feel it in everyone. It cannot exist by itself in the air." They were passing Espinoza's room with its bored guard, and Prandra shuddered. Khreng stopped. "Air," he said.

"There cannot be any scent left after all this time."

"Everybody and his mother is going in and out all morning so I can't get near, but ventilators are not as bad as wind for carrying scent away and maybe something is left."

"No one's allowed in here," the guard said.

"I don't want in," said Khreng. "Only to smell around, if you allow the expression. If you move down the hall in order not to overload my nose you may keep your gun aimed at me in case I break any rule or law."

The guard wrinkled his forehead, shrugged, and moved back, gun in the crook of his arm. Khreng inhaled deeply at the base of the door, raised his head, then his body, bracing himself by the forelimbs. "Don't expect much. Khreng the fearless tracker does better on Ungruwarkh."

"Any fool knows that," said Prandra sadly.

"We still must do all we can, woman." Sniff. "Here you are, and Yamashita—I see her this morning—some Lyyrt, they hardly smell, and—"

"Hurry up!" the guard snapped. "If anybody finds you here I'll be in trouble."

Khreng calmly lowered his head until his nose was buried in the carpeting. "A scale from Wyaerl, all those guards, very confusing... that one Sheedy is always pinching—"

The guard snorted. "He tries it with all of them. If he wasn't a blind old fool he'd get a few punches."

"—that woman, Nema, and . . . myself, of course—" he sneezed, "carpet fluff, and . . ."

Prandra finished for him. "And what is left of Espinoza."

"Tracked on somebody's shoes—"

"Which are now in some waste disposal."

"For God's sake, are you training to be a hunting dog or something?"

The guard found four savage red cats' eyes fixed on him. He swallowed. "I'm sorry! I didn't mean to insult you!" His fair skin was now hotly flushed. "It just popped into my mind."

"Maybe you ask yourself where it comes from," Khreng said quietly.

"Half the people in this place are visitors of Espinoza," said Prandra.

"All likely with good excuses." Ahead, an apartment door opened and a wisp of vapor escaped from it, followed by Wyaerl. Water and air tanks strapped to his back, he took his walk at high noon.

Wyaerl was not a telepath; he could only have been described as an inside man. He had a sense for the insides of things, and his people were used for surgery, metallurgy, mining, life and physical sciences. Sky-blue in color, he was shaped like an elongated pancake, two meters long; though his translucence made him look like jelly, he was tough as saddle leather. His rear half was a huge muscular foot that propelled him in the manner of a snail. His front end projected forty or fifty tendrils with specialized uses: light and sound sensors because he had no eyes or ears; prehensile digits; tools that split into almost invisible ends to explore earth or porous stone.

When he sensed the Ungrukh, he extended his foot to brace himself and raised his front end. His tendrils quivered. Across his half-meter expanse of belly was a slit opening into a pouch that held his generative organs, both male and female, and his feeding and excreting processes. Normally shy, like his species, he rarely invited esping and breathed through slits in his back; the only way he could speak was to extend his feeding tube, suck air, and expel it in an excruciating squeak.

Khreng and Prandra stopped. The breathing tube came out, sucked air like wind in a chimney. "What is, troubling you," said Wyaerl, "is something, inside something."

"Do you know what that is?" Prandra asked.

"No." Wyaerl withdrew the tube, flopped down with a thud, and pushed off in a cloud of his planet's ammoniac atmosphere.

"That is a very deep thought," Khreng said. "Everything is inside something."

"He goes to a lot of trouble to tell us," said Prandra. "Maybe he helps."

"Maybe something else helps...."

They glared at each other. "Say it, big man. You think I am too hard on Yamashita."

"I know she is an arrogant woman who deserves it, but—"

They choroused, "She is also somewhat afraid and unsure—"

Khreng huffed, "It is your thought in your head. You make her look bad and among her people; that is a great dishonor. She is only trying to do her work properly."

"I'm aware of it. To get us out of the stewpot I must apologize." She growled, "And you know how good I am at doing that."

"Then have your meal and think it over."

"No. I do it first; otherwise I throw up."

"Damnation, your stomach is iron like your head! Your dinner spoils."

"Ha. It is cold from their food boxes. You breathe on it and bring it to body heat." She grinned. "Meat tasts much better that way."

But she did not go at once to Yamashita's door; there were words to prepare. She trotted the white hexagons, eyes slitted against the glare of noon because she had not bothered about her contacts. It was hard to concentrate on apologizing (humbling oneself) with her mind still full of grief and fury.

Espinoza had wanted to die. But, as she had once done, he said: *It is always better to be alive today....* He had given her a gesture, his mental shrug, and she had given him the words. *Espinoza!*

Think of Yamashita.... She crouched on a patch of warm earth by the playground fence watching the children on the see-saws and slides. A little carousel tinkled faintly. Some of the children belonged to employees, a few were proto-ESPs. One good second-class, possibly higher, a couple of lower unknown quantities. Two or three of them looked delicious. She nestled chin on paws and thought of Yamashita.

"Hey, there's that cat!"

"I can see it, dummy."

Children at the fence, staring.

Madame Yamashita, I come to tell you it is not my intention—

A handful of sand fell on her back.

She opened one eye and met the stares of the children. Mischief. Pull Kitty's tail. The skin of her back rippled and shook it off. She was too warm and lazy to move.

—to hurt or embarrass you; I am deeply sorry to offend you. I only try to make clear—

Another fistful of sand.

At her eyes! She dug her head beneath her forearms, stunned by the mind-kaleidoscope of their fury.

"Aah, that's not enough! Get some gravel out of the pots, there!" Children outside the playground encircling her. Stones rained, one at her closed eye with stabbing pain.

On Ungruwarkh, she had survived ambushes. She sent feelers to their heads: puppets, bewildered. Some of them enjoyed stoning an animal, some did not care, some hated it: none knew why they had chosen that moment to do it. And there was a kind of shield between them and the adults; no one had noticed.

Prandra had several choices, some disastrous. First, she used most of her strength to break the shield; then, well-battered, she took the line of least resistance. As the stones rained down she rolled over on her back, exposing her belly with paws in the air, tail limp, eyes closed, neck crooked at an impossible angle with jaws gaping and tongue hanging slack. She looked like a horridly dead cat.

Guards began shouting, parents screaming, the hail diminished and stopped.

"Prandra!" Arms pulled at her. "Are you all right? Prandra!"

She opened her eyes slowly and straightened her head. Guards, clerks, one or two Lyhhrt in their curious little gold boxes on wheels. She moistened her mouth with her tongue and rolled over. Parents shaking and yelling at the children, slapping some of them. Good. "I am all right."

"My God, your eye's bleeding, we've got to—"

"Leave it. I attend to it myself." She pulled free and shook herself vigorously, not caring where the dust landed, then headed back toward the residence.

Damned good piece of acting, if I say so.

Her eye hurt badly, she was both exhilarated and furious. She would apologize and go home to Ungruwarkh. Fight and starve. Damned Solthrees, pretending to be civilized. Food and wisdom you get here, says Espinoza. Where are they, you dead fool?

At the residence doorway she sensed a significant presence and looked up. A tall man was leaning there, arms folded, ankles crossed. One of Committee. Six-toes. His name was Kinnear. "I am on my way to apologize to Madame Yamashita," she said. "That must please you."

He said, "That eye's swelling shut. I'll send you a medtech."

"Thank you."

As she passed he said out of the corner of his mouth, "Quite a good act you put on."

"I say so myself," she purred.

Prandra's rage almost negated the sense of obligation, but she wanted Yamashita to see her in this condition. She knew that was a shameful idea, but she could not control it.

She buzzed Yamashita's door and waited. No answer. The at-home light was on; she buzzed again, paced up and down, tried once more. Nothing.

She esped; a guard came trotting. "What happened to your eye?"

"Never mind. Madame Yamashita does not answer."

"Maybe she's sick. She gets headaches; I'll send somebody call in."

At the end they had to bring techs to remove the door.

Yamashita was sprawled across the bed wrapped in a brocaded kimono. Her hair was loose, the little gold and enamel clasp on the floor. Her face was almost beautiful in repose and her hair fine and silky; a thick tress lay across her throat but did not hide the deep claw slashes that sliced her arteries, nor the river of blood that flowed over the bed.

Prandra's belly convulsed; she gasped and choked. She let two guards lead her back to the room where Khreng waited; presently a medtech rolled in to inject her swollen eyelids and bathe her eye with drops to shrink the distended vessels.

She raged. "If I go earlier, I save her!"

"Now you are irrational," Khreng snorted. "How does an apology save her life?"

"Don't you see? It is like with Espinoza. How can I prove I do not kill her first and then go out to put on an act with the children? Even Kinnear knows it is an act."

"According to your memory, and it does not fail as long as I know you, Kinnear also knows it is an act of self-defense. You are too hurt and angry to think straight."

"That is true."

"And you tell him you intend to apologize."

"That can seem a misdirection . . . and those claw slashes. . . ." She shivered.

"That is not your style," he said dryly. "Any fool knows no serious cat kills like that."

"There is no shortage of fools here."

"Wait and see. One way or another we get out of this . . . take out our ship. . . ." He grinned. "At the worst a good bleach and a job in the circus. Here is fresh food. Now eat."

Day and night passed, and morning to the zenith. Prandra slept most of the time. Khreng watched over her, saw the swelling of her eye go down, called the medtech for a shot to calm her tossing; when she quieted and began to murmur the names of their children he lay beside her and slept.

"We go home." She was pacing. Round and round, tail slapping the walls. Her eye was better except for the odd dart of pain.

Khreng sprawled on the bed. "You are making me dizzy. We see what they have to say. There is no choice."

"They likely tell us to get legal advice in a hurry. I use my hurry some other way."

"And that makes the enemy very happy."

"What enemy? There is no substance, scent, thought-track. Nothing to hunt." The door chimed.

"Come in!" Prandra roared. Khreng tsked and pushed the button. Kinnear came in and leaned against the wall in his characteristic pose: arms folded, ankles crossed. He was very tall, with a bland oval face, thinning blond hair; broad shoulders tapered down to a wedge-shaped body. He had the small-pupilled blue eyes that are as good as an esp shield for hiding thought.

Khreng said, "Excuse me, I don't know your name."

"I'm the one Prandra calls Six-toes."

"His name is Kinnear." Prandra dropped to the floor, sulking.

"I am polydactylic," Kinnear said. "I had the extras removed from my hands; they weren't pretty. Most Solthree ESPs have some kind of abnormality."

Khreng shifted from the bed to the stone. "Sit."

"In a moment. I haven't apologized for letting Prandra be hurt."

"What's the difference? Espinoza and Yamashita are dead." Prandra blinked. "In Committee you are open-minded; so I know you have six toes. I am not, except for evidence; so how do you know I call you that?"

Kinnear coughed. "I have a habit of esping uninvited. I'm head of Security."

"Ah," said Prandra. "And still they are dead. Now I suppose you come to read us our rights."

"In a sense. The autopsy's been done." He smiled grimly. "And here comes Wyaerl now."

Wyaerl appeared with his inchworm step, air tank hissing furiously, food-pipe extruded. "I, hurried." Kinnear extended his hand. Wyaerl bent his top half, and with one tenacle dropped something into the open palm. Kinnear nodded. "Iron," said Wyaerl. "Not steel, it broke, with force."

"Look." In Kinnear's hand was a metal fragment shaped into the perfect replica of an Ungrukh claw. "From the wound."

Khreng grunted. "Who makes it?"

"We don't know yet."

"Then you are no further ahead," said Prandra. "It appears someone wishes to place suspicion on us again, or else make it seem as if the Lyhhrt are trying it because they do so much metal work."

Kinnear said, "*Suspicion* on the Lyhhrt? How do you know they aren't guilty?"

"Aah! Lyhhrt? Those little lumps of that stuff—"

"Protoplasm."

"—who make their workshells so fancy in precious metals so others do not look down on them? Do they make a claw in plain iron without all their stars and flowers?"

"But in this case—"

"Find me one. No Lyhhrt here would do that!"

On the surface of his sorrow for Yamashita, he was amused and a little condescending. "Can you esp a Lyhhrt?"

"Of course, but who needs to? You have only to look at them and it is clear as your day."

"You can esp Lyhhrt, ha? Then if it's not you or the Lyhhrt, where would you begin, Prandra?"

"Kinnear, I don't know or care. Khreng and I are leaving. If you believe we are in the clear, we rather starve on Ungruwarkh than stay here another day."

Kinnear flushed with embarrassment. "Um...one of your ship's engines has been blown up."

Khreng said, "Blown up...."

"A charge, of explosive," Wyaerl piped. Prandra was staring at Kinnear.

"We've put extra guards around your supplies and equipment," he said. "Two weeks of repairs."

"That helps." *Are you sure you don't do that yourself to keep us here, Head Security Man?*

His flush darkened; he said quietly, "I'm glad you didn't say that aloud."

Unrepentant, Prandra said, "No apologies yet. But you make sure *you* stay alive, Kinnear."

He laughed. "Did you know that only a class-one can esp a Lyhhrt?"

"Yes, but who cares?"

"I do. While you're waiting, why don't you take your class-one exam and you can have it ratified at GalFed Central?"

"From what examiners? Old raveled Sheedy or the Weird Lady?"

He said coolly, "We also have the Lyhhrt, and I'm a good enough class-two to sit on the Board . . ." he paused. "And . . . if you don't mind another brain-in-the-bottle Madame Chatterjee is really first class."

"Are all those on your staff?"

"Some of the Lyhhrt are here on their own business, like Wyaerl . . . what about it?"

Prandra considered. "Khreng, if I agree to this, do you tell me I have a swollen head?"

"Do you need to be told?"

Kinnear said, "You don't shield well enough yet, Prandra, and you'll need training. Chatterjee does that, and she can stick a pin in you."

"I worry about stones, not pins." She kept her eyes on Kinnear but was careful not to esp him. "You seem to trust us, Kinnear. Are you immune to psychological poison?"

"No . . . I've had dreams too. But what reason could you have had for killing Espinoza? He was the person you loved most on this world."

"He is tired and longing for death."

"You always knew that about him. You had a thousand chances to kill him and make it look like an accident—"

"After which we are esped and found out—"

"—or even in genuine kindness if you had a simpler morality."

"Savage morality," Khreng growled.

"Yes, our—let us say, enemies, try to make us seem savage and untrustworthy. We are expected to be accused of killing Espinoza and Yamashita—like wild beasts. I am to get insulted and jump on Committee, and rip up little children at play. Somebody thinks we have not much control."

"But if they want to get rid of you—" Kinnear scratched his

head, "—and then blow up your ship...?"

"Nobody tries to kill us yet, Kinnear," said Prandra. "It seems somebody wants us to leave—*but not on our own ship!*"

"Somebody wants you for something...."

"Yes. Isn't that interesting. And no one knows what." She cocked her head. "Yesterday I think you are esping me from the time I leave Committee until I meet those playful children...."

"I certainly never expected—"

"I don't mean that. During that time Yamashita is murdered."

"I know." He licked his lips. "I was fifty meters away from her and somebody shielded so well I never caught a hint of it. Same with the ship. And I'm stuck. I'm short of staff and I have to sit in as head of Committee too.... God, I wish we had Chatterjee on this, but she's so damn shy about that bottle she'll hardly ever come out of her room."

"How long?"

"Nearly two hundred years."

"Very nice for her." Prandra's sigh, like Espinoza's, was in the shape of a tear.

"If I don't get this cleared up in a hurry I'll be kicked out; we may not get our MedPsych division funded...everything happening...nobody will come into this kind of danger, especially with children." He stared at the metal fragment. "I'm going to trust you. I must, I need help. With my kind of funds I just don't have that many class-ones to—"

"Play around with," Khreng said, basso profundo.

Prandra having declared she would turn truly savage if she did not get out, the Ungrukh took their walk at noon. The sun sparkled through the dome, the flagstones were hot. After ten silent minutes, Prandra turned off the path, and Khreng hissed, "Oh no! Not the playground! What do you think you are doing, woman?"

"Something is not good there."

"And you make it better and get beat up again?" He hooked a claw in her chain.

"Don't stop me, Khreng." Knowing better, he let go.

There was an oppressive air about the playground, and the

children went through their games in a lackluster way; in the spirits of some, Prandra sensed a dusting of guilt. "Nine are sorry they hurt me, and four think it is too bad they do not hurt me more. Ha." She grinned. "There is no shortage of bent ones on Solthree." Since staff was rarely outworld, all the children were Solthrees.

"See those guards?" Khreng said. "The guns in their hands are not stunners."

"Is it forbidden for a big cat to play with a small child, since yesterday it is the other way around?" She pushed open the gate. Khreng, willy-nilly, followed; the guards shifted their weapons. Prandra paid no attention; she trotted to the silent carousel, pulled the switch, and jumped to the back of a yellow maned lion. "Come on, Khreng, take a ride with me."

"You are crazy." He found a zebra.

Kinnear's mind broke through her calm. :*For God's sake, Prandra, watch it!*:

:*Keep trusting, Kinnear.*:

Round and round they went, bodies undulating to the rhythm of the music. Khreng grumbled, "What *do* you think you are doing?"

"Enjoying myself."

The nervous parents at the gate were joined by doctors, clerks on lunch hour with sandwiches and coffee-bulbs; a couple of Lyhhrt in wheeled runabouts, two or three more gleaming in engraved workshells with multiple joints and stilt legs. Blind Sheedy with coffee dripping down his zipsuit as usual, one hand on the shoulder of his exasperated eye-guard. And even blank Nema with Metaxa. "What a marvel," said Prandra. "Maybe we are born for the circus."

"Shut up," Khreng said.

"Tcha! It is you who talk of a circus." She jumped off; Khreng stopped the machine. She rolled in the sand, stood and shook herself; if the air had been less humid the atmosphere might have matched that of the more habitable places of Ungruwarkh on one of its better days.

But she did not like the guilt on these spirits.

She began trotting in a circle, shoulder to shoulder with Khreng; the children backed away in a larger circle around them. She stopped short before one sullen boy about twelve. "You like dogs better than cats, hah?"

"Yes." An ESP-in-training who liked, or thought he liked, to stone animals.

:I don't bite children, baby.: His mouth turned down at the corners and she laughed. "Dogs lick your face and fetch sticks." She snorted. "Dogs play dead." With a twist she flung herself into her dead-cat position, then sprang up on hind legs. "Cats can play tricks too, and yesterday I play one on you!"

She dropped to fours and circled slowly, abreast with Khreng. The children were small statues of perplexity and suspicion. "I am not badly hurt, so you don't have to feel guilty," a breath of her mind blew dust from them and the air lightened, "but my eye is sore, and next time you think first when you feel like throwing stones—at anyone!" She found a girl of seven or eight, an ESP small for her age, but brash, and young enough to play the games of little children. "You like a catback ride?"

The child twisted her fingers and stuck her tongue in her cheek. "Uh huh."

Prandra's voice deepened. "Do you mean yes?"

"Yes, ma'am."

"Ask your mother."

The child drew a line in the dust with her toe. "She says all right."

Prandra crouched and the child bestrode her. "Not the chain. Hold the hair at the sides of my neck where it starts getting longer. Khreng gives rides too." Khreng said nothing, but the stretch of his nostrils expressed a lot. He accepted a squirming body.

Round and round in tandem spiral. . . . Now love, you know how it is on our world Ungruwarkh, with our children.

Red lava plains, pale sun, a nip in the air; one tongue of flame from a volcano in the north: Firemaster speaking from one of his many mouths; out of caves and fissures cats join, running until there is a tribe, an odd good-humored one, for each cat is ridden by a cub, thrilled/joyful/half-scared, little claws deep in the fur prickling the backs they ride on, patches of feverish heat between little body and big one, minds always open for the marauders over the hills. . . .

"What the hell do they think they're doing? What are you letting them do?"

The Ungrukh stopped.

"Go on! Go on!" the cubs/children cried.

"In a moment, children."

Metaxa, red-faced, shoving against watchers toward the gate. Nema still as a mannequin, hands on the bars.

"Playing with those animals!" Metaxa's mouth was a screaming cave. "Why don't you let them roll in the snakepit at the zoo?" His face burned with sweat.

Prandra watched, satisfied. She read confusion and anger in Metaxa and did not know what to make of them, but if nothing at all had happened she would have been deeply disappointed. Metaxa still yelling, "Don't you underst—"

Guards to either side grabbed him in mid-word, and Kinnear stepped up to him deliberately. "Are those your children, Metaxa?"

Metaxa's mouth clamped shut. He shook loose of the guards, barrelled his way back through the bewildered onlookers, and dragged Nema from the fence more roughly than he had done on that evening. She did not even blink.

The little girl yanked at Prandra's fur. "More!" Prandra wrapped her prehensile tail around the thin waist and set her on the ground firmly. "Everyone has a turn."

Finally they lay on their backs with the smallest children crawling over them like ants, rubbing their faces in the soft belly-fur and shrieking with laughter. Prandra plucked them off gently, one by one. "Enough now. Big pussycats get tired fast."

"Can we do it again tomorrow?"

"Yes, tomorrow." The children went back to naps and lessons; and the adults, somewhat bemused, followed. Sheedy was laughing and shaking his head; it had been a circus to him. The Lyhhrt skimmed or stilted away.

"All right, you've defused a lot of fear and hostility, and that exhibition was very pleasing—except for Metaxa," Kinnear said. "Now, Honorables, what were you trying to prove?"

"We are fishing, and there is a pull on the line," said Prandra.

"Also," Khreng said, "now we make ourselves nice kitty-cats; we are pushing. Killer is less apt to try blaming us and more likely to attack us instead of someone else."

"That's a fine improvement," Kinnear said. "Where does it leave me?"

"Blameless. We take care of ourselves."

"But how can Metaxa's blowup be a pull on your line?"

Khreng and his nose knew what to make of that: "Of all who go to Espinoza's door around the time he is killed—Prandra, Wyaerl, Yamashita, Nema, guards and all, there is no trace of Metaxa. Although he keeps himself very clean, there is no one I know who smells stronger—and there is no skin-flake, oil droplet, atom of sweat . . . he is never seen apart from Nema, and she is hardly capable of blowing her own nose without him. Today he is a very frightened and angry man. Isn't that strange?"

:Why do you always speak in the present tense?: Madame Chatterjee asked.

"Yesterday is before my birth and tomorrow is after my death," said Prandra. "That is what Ungrukh feel and how they speak." The blue glasstex globe on its stand, the tiny room, were exactly like Espinoza's. "May we keep the door open? I am tired of whitewalls."

:I understand what you feel—about the present. But I concentrate better with a closed door.:

Prandra sighed, a low rumble. And hallucinate better.

:That too,: said Chatterjee.

The bottled brains—they were called converted, and called themselves bottled—spent much time alone, of necessity; hallucinated much, because of lack of sensory afferents, and learned to control it rigidly, to keep their minds in order. Chatterjee was sufficiently down-to-earth. She had died of mutantt cholera at thirty-six, and maintained her self-image at that age: a small wiry woman with beautiful black eyes and graceful brows, hair beginning to grey.

"I don't mean to offend you," Prandra said.

:You don't, except to make me jealous of your freedom, as every embodied person does.: Image of a wry smile. *:It is not that good a motive for murder. I am not a superb shielder, nor a strong hypnotizer.:*

Prandra, shocked, said, "You are far ahead of me, Madame."

:I intend to stay that way.: She asked abruptly, *:Where is there a white, yellow, and blue ball?:*

"In the seal pool at the zoo."

:You did not break my shield then.:

Prandra grinned. "No, I remember seeing it when I am there." She added, "Calcutta has many green trees, though there is still much poverty."

:Good. Now you try . . . green . . . ah . . . why do you call your daughter Emerald, which is a green jewel in the English language, when your people are red?:

"Ha. Khreng hears it when he visits GalFed Central, and he likes the sound. Perhaps it is the beginning of an appreciation of Art in us Ungrukh."

Chatterjee permitted herself a smile-thought, and Prandra couched in the narrow space. "Madame, I think we can like each other, if you permit. And I learn as well as I can. But people are being killed, and I must find out why, and what the killer wants of Khreng and me. Can you help?"

Slowly: *:Oh, I am very willing to like you . . . :* and shrinking.

"I understand, Madame. Espinoza also spends over two hundred years in a bottle and does not care at the end. One day I too howl for death in my bottle, and there is nobody to hear. Nobody so kind to smash it, as even I cannot bring myself to do. From the bottle it is dangerous to think of flesh and bone; food, sleep, sex, running in the open air. Even drinking cold water when you are thirsty. Espinoza is lucky. Yamashita is lucky; it is too late to save her brain. So you stay in this room and teach ignorant people like me to do useful work—but you must also have to answer a lot of stupid questions, and you do not come out where the people are alive with their love and hate and anger—and I think that is narrowing and wasteful." She rose beside the door, but could not bring herself to open it, and stood there, head and tail hanging.

:I know.: The mind-touch was light as a peacock's feather. *:You spoke harshly to Yamashita and did not apologize. I have not been aware for so many years without understanding. What you don't understand is that even as an embodied person I was almost as retiring as I am today, and I regret it, but it is too late for me to change very much. I do want to help, not only by*

teaching you. I will gladly do whatever is necessary, but you can help me to work at my best by bringing me your thoughts and feelings as you brought them to Espinoza . . . I don't believe—I don't believe you will come to love me as much as you did Espinoza, but I am your friend, yours and Khreng's. Agreed?:

"Yes, Madame," Prandra whispered. "Agreed."

"Wyaerl, Kinnear asks me to help him in his investigations. May I question you?"

"Yes," Wyaerl piped. "You, may, esp." He withdrew his tube and flopped to the carpet like a relieved flapjack.

"Why do you come here?"

:On our world we have colonies of squatters from many places trading in illegal drugs and also farming and processing them from plant matter disturbing our economy ecology and moral which GalFed can't do much about because they don't extradite and because a good number are Solthrees especially some rare impervious types who cannot be esped I came here for help of which little is forthcoming there is no one suitable and we have spent too much credit already so I am going home soon with my disappointment is that enough?:

"It's certainly comprehensive. Can I ask you one more question without insult?"

:Go ahead I know you don't intend to insult my humble self.:

"You go to visit Espinoza some time before or after he is killed—"

:No no without insult I assure you that is not so though there were many times I consulted Espinoza he was most agreeable that was one time I did not you may esp as much as you please.:

"Thank you, I know you are not lying," said Prandra.

"I am sorry for Kinnear," Khreng said.

"Are you sure there is a trace of . . ."

"Old woman, I *know* I find a fresh undried scale with Wyaerl's personal scent and his planet's atmosphere on it. In Espinoza's doorway. If it is a plant it carried the planter's scent. That is it."

Prandra patted his forehead. "You are the authority. I accept."

* * *

"Who is there?" asked the speaking-tube.

"Prandra."

The door opened; Metaxa was drawn about the eyes, but the beard hid the rest of his broad high-colored face. He held a glass with a bent tube in it. "What do you want?" His control was brittle.

"I am allowed to ask questions, and you are permitted not to answer."

"Otherwise," he said coolly, "you will esp." He had pushed his sleeves up the arms and unzipped his suit halfway down the chest; grey hair burst from the opening and on his forearms. The hair of his beard was thick and lively brown; she wondered briefly if he colored it, and answered no. It was not himself he decorated with jewels or perfumes; his personal smell was strong, even to her unauthoritative nose.

"No, Metaxa. Sometimes you push your thoughts at me. I don't care for that because I don't esp without permission, except to defend myself. That is Kinnear's business."

"And you're working for him. . . ." He shrugged. "Come in, read all you like. I'm not hiding anything."

Metaxa and Nema had an apartment of several rooms; the walls were covered with hangings, reliefs, pictures, the floors crammed with furniture and figurines and things Prandra did not recognize, but she did not want to risk knocking them over. She tucked in her tail and crouched near the door.

Nema was sitting in a chair by the window dressed in one of her beautiful gowns, a blue shimmer. She was twenty-two years old, mature in body and with the face of a sleeping infant. Metaxa sat down beside her and offered the tube to her mouth. She sipped once, blinked, raised a fist, and swung with great power. Glass and tube bounced against the wall, splashing, and fell to the carpet.

Metaxa's face was expressionless as hers. He rubbed his arm, picked up the glass and tube and put them on a table. Prandra's skin prickled.

Nema's hands folded themselves in her lap and Metaxa turned to Prandra. "What do you want?" he asked again.

"Does the lady Nema go anywhere without you, or you without her?"

"No. We're always together, all the time." His forehead was wet; he did not wipe it. "Why?"

"It is the kind of question Kinnear asks. We try to help."

His eyes were shrewd. "I think it's the kind of question an Ungrukh asks. Kinnear would want to know where we were at the time of the murders."

"If Kinnear wishes to know that, he asks."

"He already has... Madame." His voice lingered on irony. "I'll tell you and save you trouble. When Espinoza was killed we were asleep here together, and when Yamashita was killed we were having lunch here together. Are you satisfied?"

No, Metaxa. Can you prove you are not drugged or hypnotized either time? That is the kind of question an Ungrukh asks. "I am grateful for your cooperation."

"You surprise me. Anything else?"

Before she could answer Nema stood up and headed for the door as if she were blind to the body in her way. Prandra scrambled to avoid tripping her, and Metaxa jumped to open the door before she crashed into it. Then he took her by the elbow and let her lead him where she would.

Prandra slipped out and watched them down the hall. Nema went blindly in her curious stilted walk. Metaxa glanced back once, but said nothing.

Pray tell me, sir: whose dog are you? Prandra scratched at her neck where the chain rubbed it. All at once her fur stood on end and her legs trembled.

A pinhole had opened involuntarily in Metaxa's mind, exploding volcanic fury: a firestorm of fear, dispair, disgust— and hatred for the woman, Nema.

Khreng came round a corner, sniffing, and stopped beside her. "Tune down, or they receive you in Ungruwarkh."

She was shaking. "I can't help it."

"What do you expect from a man with a ring in his nose?"

"I never try to put one in yours," she snarled. "What do you smell here?"

"Metaxa, Prandra, Nema, guards, Lyhhrt."

"Why Lyhhrt? They are not around all day."

"Ask them."

"They don't talk to class-twos."

"Then ask Kinnear."

"They don't talk to me, either," said Kinnear. "I'm a class-two, remember? They think in a way it's impossible to grasp unless you're a very powerful ESP. *You* must have picked up thoughts from them. What were they?"

"Yes, no, and maybe," Prandra said. "And some garble about Cosmic Thought."

"There you are. I had Sheedy question them and they say they weren't anywhere near Espinoza—or Yamashita."

Khreng growled, "Everybody is at Espinoza's door, and nobody is. Maybe my nose is playing tricks."

"No, but somebody is, and I don't pretend to understand." He pleated his hands. "Right now it's Metaxa I'm worried about. He's a walking hornet's nest."

"He's unconscious of it," Prandra said, "or he doesn't stay with her."

"I've never figured why he does. He's very proud; he's what used to be called a self-made man. Worked in a dockyard, at the beginning, earned everything he has, and learned everything he knows by himself."

"Yes," said Prandra. "The literary mind. And now we work for GalFed we *are* dogs of the King, hah?"

"Don't put on any stupid act for me. Now that's opened up he's going to blow—at you or Nema. You saw all the stuff crammed in his place. That's the Art. He's also got weapons collections. I don't have authority to confiscate them and if I did he'd find more—and bring in his lawyers too."

"I doubt Nema lets him hurt her."

"Then we'll give *you* some guns."

Khreng guffawed. "Without thumbs, Kinnear? First you spend a month learning to build up the grips so we can hold them, and days teaching us to use them, then we fall all over our feet and shoot our tails off carrying them? Knives are better."

"Carry knives."

"Kinnear, we are good with knives," Prandra said, "but we also play with little children. Even if I am attacked once, we still look pretty odd if we seem to need knives to defend ourselves from them. The kind we use best are in our heads and hands, and we leave it that way."

:Still your old self, Prandra,: said Chatterjee. *:You may need weapons.:*

"I am not shy about using a knife if I need one. We still don't know whom to fight. Our ship is ready in ten days and we are not staying longer."

:When do you want to set the exam, then?:

"In eight days if you believe I am ready. Otherwise I take it at Central. I still have a lot to learn."

:You can begin today by picking a lost memory out of my unconscious—within the bounds of good taste.:

"That is not what I have in mind."

:What I have in mind is my stock-in-trade, and you have agreed to learn.:

Prandra sighed and shut her eyes so tightly the bristles above them stood straight up. "The brass table from Benares . . . the one passed down through generations in your family, you plan to give it. . . ." Her voice tailed off and she twitched in embarrassment.

:I said unconscious, not suppressed!: Chatterjee's thoughts could sting like arrows.

"I admit I have no tact," Prandra muttered. "Begin again."

:No. I promised it to my daughter but she refused to see me after I was bottled. Not for many years. She came when she was nearly as old as I. I gave it to her.: Her mind went blank. She asked vaguely, *:What was I saying? . . . Prandra, you are blocking me! Tell me at once!:*

It seemed to Prandra that the pump had speeded up and the glass might burst. "Do you really wish to keep a painful memory?"

:If I avoided painful thoughts I could not be much of a teacher.:

"The brass table."

:Good. If you hadn't told me there would have been no exam.:

"Why? Because I block better than you?"

Grim smile-thought. :*Because a pupil shows courtesy—even to a humbled instructor.*:

"I am learning."

:*Have you always been able to block?*:

"On Ungruwarkh we call it netting because it is like catching the best fish out of a school of diseased ones—and our fish are terrible. That is why I am here." Prandra grinned. "Madame, there are many things I can do that I don't know the right names for or can't control properly. I am grateful to learn how to use them."

:*Before we are through you will teach me to block as well as you do. Now tell me the problem.*:

"Khreng's sense of smell is not evidence to the law, but it is to me. It tells us everyone is everywhere, and nobody admits to being anywhere. Even Wyaerl, who is as innocent as the morning dew, says he is nowhere near Espinoza on the night of death, and we know he is. Now—"

:*Prandra, you tell me.*:

"Ah, that is a block . . . but what matter in Wyaerl's head is so dangerous that it must be fished out?"

:*Perhaps . . . Wyaerl wondered if he could bring up to Espinoza the possibility you would agree to stop at his world on the way to Ungruwarkh, to help with his trouble. He didn't feel he knew you well enough then to ask you personally, and he was even shy of asking Espinoza—but you seem to have impressed him.*:

"I can tell you he is not all that shy when you get to know him, but I find nothing of that in Espinoza. I begin to see past that block: it is not desired for us to become too friendly with anyone here or leave too early—and our engine is blown up. Ha."

:*What else?*:

"The Lyhhrt are also among those who are not at Espinoza's door—they say."

:*Two of them, Administration and Liason, I've known well for several years; they work hard and deal honestly. The other three are visitors, and they have never seemed hostile. I don't intrude on their privacy, and they leave me with mine.*:

"They seem close to Nema."

:*No, they scarcely go near her. She's not really a staff*

member. More of a showpiece because her mind is so much like theirs. She cannot communicate very well with anyone.:

"Kinnear considers you much more valuable."

:I am not jealous.:

Prandra laughed. "There's no need to be jealous of that one."

Chatterjee said, *:I am beginning to look forward to that exam. What kind of illusion-form are you planning?:*

Prandra shrugged. "I'm not sure. I'm not a person with many illusions." She raised her hand to the door-button.

:Prandra. . . .:

She waited.

:I don't know much—not even where the danger lies—but it is enough to make me afraid. It was probably meant that you be captured and used for some purpose, on the premise that you were savage and ignorant, even though intelligent. Now you are stronger and have learned much more. Perhaps too much. . . . :

"I know. Now we are on the edge of finding out, I think . . . and we are meant to be killed."

:I feel responsible.:

"For what? Our feelings for Espinoza? and our curiosity? No. For helping me out of my ignorance? Kinnear suggests this training and I accept. I am responsible. For Khreng as well."

Two big red cats trotted the grounds in the evening light, followed by two armed guards ordered by Kinnear and mounted on foot-controlled mopeds. "There is nothing like a good run in fresh recycled air and escorted by guards to make one feel alive and carefree," said Prandra.

"As long as they keep behind. I am tired of smelling them."

They passed the zoo's reptile house. "There's a scent for you," Prandra said.

"Better than our fish." Khreng paused by the tiger's cage where the great beast lay snoring. "Over three hundred kilos, my guess. Khreng times three. I wonder what it is like to be that one." The tiger opened one eye and closed it again. "I think I keep on being Khreng."

Prandra laughed. "A nice toy for children." She stopped at the playground fence.

"No more bloody damned carousel rides!"

"Don't get excited...look: over there is where I see Nema and Metaxa the night Espinoza dies. My nose is not yours, but...if we close our eyes...smell: Nema, Metaxa, fear of/for—what? Her/him/them/it...."

Khreng opened his eyes. "It?"

"Yes. Let's go back." She seemed depressed.

Khreng rubbed his back on the stone slab and sat up. "What in Firemaster's name *is* the matter?"

She bit off a loose claw scale. "I believe...if we do not come here, Espinoza and Yamashita are still living."

"Maybe. And Ungruwarkh is dead as a stone."

"The tribes fight over what we have to bring them, and many die."

"Not necessarily. If so, they are better to die for hope than from starvation. What else?"

"Why ask?"

"I am with you all these years and I don't know you? When you twist your head twenty degrees clockwise, there is something you are afraid to tell me."

She sniffed.

"Are you afraid I am frightened or angry?"

She whispered at last, "I am afraid we die."

"That's how you save me?" He stood in a swift angry movement. "Woman, you better tell me pretty damn fast. I am a fine figure of a man on my world if I step down alone from the ship and tell everyone Prandra is dead because I am ignorant!"

"I always know you are vain," she hissed.

"I am vain enough to believe we are equals and can take risk together as we always do."

"I am afraid others may be killed. That is part of why my head is twenty degrees clockwise...everyone knows everything and nobody admits knowing anything."

"That is a contradiction. You are afraid they may be killed, and then they are all liars and conspirators."

"I don't mean that. *They* have information they are unconscious of, and *we* are ignorant. If they become conscious they are dead."

"Killer cannot murder all of MedPsych."

"There is no need. (One) when we are not here nothing is upset, (two) we arrive and Killer finds some use for us, (three) Killer finds us too hard to handle and becomes enraged and frustrated so he (four) kills us and returns to (one), leaving what is not conscious, unconscious."

"(One-a)," said Khreng sarcastically, "only having to explain two big dead red cats."

"Not if they die by accident or foolish mistake."

"And you have in mind?"

"We lack that carefully hidden information...but—I want to get back to our people on our ship. Forget the exam. If we stay under guard until we leave, we are safe."

He hacked with laughter. "Do we sit safe in that village long ago and let the Qumedni kill the Rabbi and his people? Whether the test means anything or not, you spend the rest of our days hurting your spirit because you let Espinoza's murderer go free."

"If we move, we risk other lives."

"Whose are you counting?"

"The helpless ones who suspect, like Chatterjee, perhaps Sheedy."

"Why don't we ask them about risks?" He opened the locker, tossed a knife-harness to Prandra and buckled on his own. "This is not the first time I play the fool for you."

She sighed. "The trouble is, we are not playing *with* fools."

"What is the use of the game, otherwise?"

Prandra slid Chatterjee's door open a crack.

:Yes, Prandra?:

"Madame, Khreng wants to sleep in front of your door tonight. Do you object?"

:Of course not. In India I was always very fond of cats.: She added with deeper irony, *:Good hunting.:*

"She takes the chance," said Prandra. Khreng crouched at the door, a heraldic beast. He did not intend to sleep.

"I've never seen anything like that before," said the guard.

"Make sure you don't miss anything else." Prandra ambled down the hall. The chain jangled, the scabbard bobbed against her side. She wrenched at the chain until it broke and let it drop. Not only because she hated the Cracked Caduceus: in a fight it might choke her. She stared at the medallion lying on the carpet and remembered the little gold and enamel clasp near Yamashita's bed. She went on, pushing her mind against the tangle of occurrence and evidence.

Metaxa goes everywhere with Nema; Nema always carries trace of Lyhhrt. There is something about that shield I break in the playground that smells like Lyhhrt. But—

No Lyhhrt here would do that! says Prandra.

:They scarcely go near her.: says Chatterjee.

Then what have they created: Nema, Metaxa, Lyhhrt? *Something inside,* says Wyaerl. A structure forms; and while it is building, pieces are taken away. Stupid Nema; Metaxa's love/hate/anger; courteous Lyhhrt....

One room open and empty: Sheedy, the one she had not questioned—she quickened around a corner and ... blink, the guards were gone.

Behind another door, silent screaming: *Leave me alone! Help! Please don't!*

She stopped cold. Ambush?

She whacked that flimsy door off its mooring with one shoulder and flattened it with a terrific crack on the tiled floor of a laundry room. Sheedy, gagged with a pillowcase, was being pummeled by four of the guards.

Her breath went out in a burst of mingled relief and disgust. She roared. The attackers had left their guns behind. They jumped, gaped and fled whimpering, clawing at each other to get out. She ripped off the gag. Sheedy coughed and flailed his arms. "What? What?... Prandra?"

"Yes," she drawled. "None other."

He fell to his knees and began to sob. "Prandra.... I can't see."

She took one of his hands and guided it to her neck. He clutched her round the throat with both arms. "You saved my life!"

"That shoulder is a bit sore, Sheedy. Get up. You are not hurt, only your pride."

He dragged his sleeve across his nose. "I have no pride."

"Find some." She stood on hind legs and hauled him up. "Hold my arm, look through my eyes; I take you to your room."

He whimpered, "You despise me."

"I don't despise you. I need you." Sheedy *was* first-class when he wasn't drunk or chasing the boys who hated him. It was his self-hatred she couldn't stand.

"Oh, now I see! I see! Cat's eyes, beautiful strength and graceful ... everything bright, so strange ... marvelous, Prandra, oh—"

"And very hard walking hind-legged. Come on, Sheedy, I lend you my eyes another time."

Khreng waited. He did not know what he was waiting for. On Ungruwarkh he knew what was to be hunted, Prandra knew approximately where it was, and he found the way to it. Simplicity itself. Why am I sitting here like a stupid lump of a dog? If I wait long enough I get fleas. He blinked, and the hall began to spin. He blinked again, the hall spun faster. He thrashed against the engulfing dizziness, but his head was being dragged down and down until it thudded to the floor. In the center of a black vortex a tiger's eye flared briefly and died.

Sheedy's room was unlit, but bright enough for Prandra's eyes. Sheedy gulped whiskey, still marvelling at seeing through the eyes of a cat. His hand trembled on the bottle's neck, his lip quivered at the glass's edge. "Tremendous, gorgeous, cat's eyes. I should get a cat."

"There is a nice big one in a cage out there. Sheedy, put down the whiskey for a minute, and I don't mean inside your gut. I want to talk."

"Talk away, talk away, long dark nights, hah? meant for talk, all day I talk, Khagodi, Xirifri, Yefni, every lizard, serpent, thing with gills, talk-talk, nights I get nothing but cats, whiskey talks, says good things to the old gut—"

"Now it's time for Nema, Metaxa, Lyhhrt, Sheedy—"

He belched.

:Sheedy!: Ah, what a wretch! How she could have grabbed him by the neck and shaken him, broken him, scooped his brain by the roots, picked it for nits, and smeared it on the wall!

"That's right," he giggled. "Brains on the wall. Living sculpture. Freeze it and give it to Metaxa." He choked and coughed.

She slumped. He was doing everything possible to shy away

from the knowledge that might kill. And she had no right to push further. But.

I have no pride.

:Do you not, Sheedy? You let me look?:

:Look away, Big Mama, you look. You find it, I'll buy you a drink. You and this flabby old bastard.:

She startled. Like the bottled ESPs, Sheedy also had a vivid self-image; but this one stood back and observed. He was a strong supple young man with ugly contempt for the sagging flesh that imprisoned him; he took unceasing and demonic revenge on it. This was not quite a separated personality of the multiple type—Prandra had met just one in her life—but it was the self that hated Sheedy.

Sheedy babbled on, gruesome nonsense of cats' eyes and mashed brains. Prandra addressed Other: *:Young one, if you are so clever, give me information I need that does not get you into trouble.:*

:I don't care who gets into trouble. Least of all him. Anyone who's stupid enough to let glaucoma blind him without having it treated deserves trouble.:

:If foolishness is a sin we are all in hell before we start. He sees enough of himself. You are claiming superiority you do not yet show.:

Sullenly, *:What do you want?:*

:Data on Lyhhrt you gather and file for Kinnear. I have his permission.:

:That's a whole world you're talking about.:

:I don't need the whole world. You esp what I want, boil it down. You know how, it's your specialty.:

Faint noise made Khreng raise his head. He thought he might have had some kind of blackout, for he had no sensation of waking. He noticed vaguely that the ceiling lights were out in the hall, then caught the scents, both perfumed and personal, of Nema and the suggestion of Lyhhrt that always came with her. He padded down the hall, following. She seemed to be moving ahead. If she turned she might see him, but he was the tracker, and silent, so silent he could not have been heard among thorns. Even the guards did not see him because he was so silent, for they did not stir. There was an open door with a blue creature standing in it and waving tendrils furiously, piping, "Don't—" but that slow one could not catch him. He heard a thump behind, did not turn because what was ahead was so important. What was so important he barely saw, a flicker, a shimmer. And always the scent.

Guards turned to statues by enchantment.

His mind was a dark cone; at its small end a tiny Prandra roared and reached for him. Ridiculous. She knew he was the tracker.... Across the lobby through open doors into darkness, past the guard mounted on moped staring at nothing, no swerve toward the infants' park ... scent always steady and faint moonlight on the shimmer ...

pausing at iron gate and snicking of bolt ... vanishes—

Hot and rank hit him a blow. Green eyeshine lanced his brain.

HA HA HA says voice from the sky POOR KHRENG IDIOT KHRENG GOES CRAZY WITH VANITY HE WANTS TO PLAY WITH

Tiger!

He woke, shook darkness from his head, skittered back growling.

Tiger on four feet waved its tail gently, stepped softly across the cage and with one paw pushed open the creaking gate.

And roared. The air split.

Prandra relaxed, began to luxuriate in the flow of information.

:—not just formless masses of protoplasm, they have complicated nervous systems and muscles of thin fiber. They need food and water to reproduce, but if they're stranded without it, they grow skins, shells, scales, whatever they need to wait for good conditions. They reproduce by fission: not often, they're nearly immortal. Before reproducing a group will fuse to exchange genetic material, hardly any two have the same genes. On Lyhhrr they lie about by thousands with joined pseudopods, like the ends of nerve-cells, in marshes and lakes, on hills, under seas, thinking Cosmic Thoughts, don't ask what those are, would have been doing it for millenia more if GalFed hadn't

discovered them, shown them how to use the false limbs to build true bodies. They chose metal, I don't know why, probably body chemistry. Once they got separate bodies they became individuals, maybe not such a good idea. They work well enough for GalFed, but it's hard for them to communicate. Superb artistry in those workshells, maybe afraid people won't respect them because they don't look like much....

:More? The sticky part, private but not classified. Two of them were posted here eight years ago, Administration and Liason. Liason had been important at GalFed Central, but got to be a nuisance because he began insisting that workshells were too clumsy for minds with so much power, ought to be controlling animals, insensate life-forms, instead. GalFed hit the roof in whatever they call their Intergalactic S.P.C.A., as well as Human Rights Div. Who knows what'll turn out to be sentient? Sent him out of the way rather than squash him. The shuttle crashed here. Admin was unhurt. Liason disappeared except for his empty workshell. Theory was he'd crawled somewhere, wounded, then died and dissolved. After a while Admin asked to be allowed to fission to carry out the work of both. That took three years because it's a long way to Lyhhrr. Three years more, and Admin-L'ason asked for more staff and these three showed up. I suspect an investigating committee. That's all.:

:Investigating, after eight years?:

:I said it's a long way. Give the old fart my regards.: Young Sheedy's image collapsed on itself and folded away.

"I've been enjoying our conversation, Prandra," Sheedy said over a hiccup, "but it's time for some serious drinking, and—"

"I am enjoying a conversation with young Sheedy."

"Glad to hear it. He's quite an interesting fellow."

"He has a tough mind. Both of you together make one good man.... Sheedy, why not let up on the bottle a little?"

He snickered. "I'm hardly likely to get any *in* the bottle, am I?"

Tiger shrieked.

Sheedy knocked over bottle and glass. "What was that? My God, the power's off, no whitewalls!"

Prandra slammed the t-screen's buttons without raising a flicker.

"The door won't open! I'm locked in!"

Prandra pushed the manual release and dragged open the heavy door. "You can get out. Take my advice and lock yourself in." She bounded down the hall.

KhrengKhrengKhreng? Khreng and Tiger! She found the blue lump, Wyaerl, forced herself to stop. Flattened, great welt across his back. His bottles had been wrenched out; she replaced the tubes in their slits, clumsily, because she was not wearing finger-prostheses for fine-muscle work.

"Badly hurt?" She smelled Metaxa.

:*Temporary paralysis, nerves pinched by swelling, and—:* his mind was remarkably clear, :—*inside something—is at the zoo.....:*

Not only. She picked up Khreng's thought-track now. Nema and Lyhrt. Nema plus Lyhrt.

She broadcast to all quarters. *Chatterjee, give your head! Sheedy, put down your fear and help! Lyhhrt, are you hiding when you know the lost one is an insane killer?* Two of them now, and one in Tiger.

In the darkness and without whitewalls, Prandra felt as if she were out in space in a lattice of stars, each star a soul with its flickering intelligence: Kinnear, Committee, guards, Chatterjee, Sheedy, Lyhhrt—asleep, hypnotized, fearful, cold as stars seemed from their distances...and on the edge of the universe, Khreng facing Tiger.

One half-crazy mind cackling hysterically:

THEY RETURNED FROM THE RIDE
WITH THE LADY INSIDE
AND THE SMILE ON THE FACE OF THE TIGER

Khreng did not deceive himself. Compared to a tiger he was a runt. He backed up, roaring. Tiger advanced, silent now, jaws open, the stub teeth between the fangs a steel gate.

Khreng, crouching, dared not reach for his knife. Tiger's jaws wanted to grip on a limb, tail, or throat. He saved his breath, wrapped the long tail around his loins. Claws reached, Khreng snaked under, Tiger reached out again, and raked his side. Most terrible was that part of his self adored Tiger, gold under the moon and black flame stripes leaping up his flanks. Ungrukh in the volcanic zones had once worshipped a Great Cat until the Prophet of Firemaster had risen in their tribes. Blazing green eyes. O Great Cat!

His pads slipped in driblets of his own blood, his side stung. He was half-stunned, could not even smell the beast, an immortal engine, gold and flame rippling. It leaped.

Prandra howled.

Jolted, Khreng ducked beneath the belly. "Away! Get away!"

"There is a Lyhhrt alive in that beast!"

Tiger paused and turned toward her.

"Save yourself, I sacrifice to the Cat for you!"

"Idiot!"

Tiger was bent on killing its challenger, the cat. Lyhhrt Six on murdering Prandra. Nema, harboring his fission-brother, Lyhhrt Seven, lay in bed, smiling; Metaxa in forced sleep beside her, face twisted in a hideous grin.

The eyes, turned away from the moon, had darkened. Prandra regarded them: she did not worship the spirit of Cat. She had conceived, brought forth in blood, given the teat, cleaned the excretions, and disembowelled the prey; she had burrowed too deep in living matter to respect any ghost. She drew out the knife, wound her tail round its handle and held it against her side. Tiger-Lyhhrt moved forward, gathering speed.

:Wyaerl! Wyaerl!:

Whisper of thought: *Beneath the ribs. . . .*

Khreng roared and leaped. Tiger clawed his forehead before he landed, then rose over Prandra, claws out.

:Chatterjee! Sheedy!:

They were trying to rouse the others. There was nothing else they could do.

She slewed, twisting, her teeth caught the skin of the throat, jaws came down slamming the crown of her head as Khreng's knife dashed in and out among the stripes of the flank. The beast turned aside, roaring; Prandra rolled out of reach of the claws, fireworks bursting before her eyes from the pain in her head. Khreng's blade slithered under the loose skin, blunted itself along the steely ribs. A few red lines ran among the stripes. Tiger did not stop. A claw slashed Khreng between the eyes and he retreated.

Prandra backed away, snarling. Lyhhrt wanted her badly, if Tiger did not. She thought briefly of the shelter of the cage; Tiger wheeled and planted itself before the bars: Lyhhrt reasoning.

The three cats made points of a triangle. Khreng whetted his knife on the flags. Prandra's head was pounding; she shook it, flicking droplets of blood from her brow-hairs.

Ah, but Tiger was beautiful. She shook the beauty away with her blood. Lyhhrt hidden among the vitals. She was tiring; Tiger could eat bullets, and his jaws were as wide as the sky.

She pulled Khreng under her shield. Have I learned at all, Chatterjee? It was not safe there, but dark and lonely. She levelled an arrow of thought at Khreng. He tossed her his knife, she clamped her tail around it with the other. One more effort.

She and Khreng charged from two directions, screaming. Tiger-Lyhhrt, intent on Prandra, was not prepared for the fangs driving into the base of its tail and reared, howling. Prandra took a knife in each hand, an awkward maneuver achieved in desperation, and drove them upward hilt-deep under both sides of the ribcage.

Lyhhrt died in a silent convulsion.

Light flashed, sound burst: Tiger's eye exploded. The head, falling forever, hammered her to the ground.

She dragged herself from under, gasping.

Kinnear was on the steps, cradling his heavy gun with its lights, sights, triggers, tubes, grips. Any number of people had gathered behind him. She had not heard them coming. She did not care that they had come.

Khreng began to howl. He circled the fallen beast, dripping blood, howling prayers to Firemaster, to the Great Cat, to the gods of the equatorial zones of Ungruwarkh where tides ravaged the sands, begging forgiveness, absolution, vowing repentance.

"Khreng!"

He went round and round, raising hideous voice. She forced herself to stand, planted herself before him, cursing. He swiped her aside. She dropped and let him go.

In a few moments the zoo keeper, a little stick-limbed black man in pajamas and hastily-wound turban, came and shot him with a tranquilizer dart. He made one more round, still howling, and collapsed.

The zoo keeper stood scratching in his thick grey beard and looking at the tiger. "He is not badly hurt, your man." He added, almost sorrowfully, "In my native state in India, Tiger is called the dog of the gods, because he does always what they wish."

She raised herself on trembling forelimbs. Kinnear gave his gun to somebody else, crossed the bloodied stones. He bent to pull the knives from the tiger's belly, wiped their blades on his sleeves and held them out to Prandra.

With the last of her strength she grabbed and flung them away into the darkness. "Civilization." She spat. "Take that thing apart until you find the Lyhhrt."

Khreng woke up in a fearful temper. "Zoo keepers! Tranquilizer darts!" He screeched outrage. "Haven't they the decency to use a stunner?"

Prandra growled, "Stunner gives you ten days of headache, and we need to lift off."

Both had been crammed with antibiotics; a few hairs had been shaved off Khreng; the skintex sprayed on his wounds gave him a couple of sickly pink stripes. The temper was caused by sheer humiliation that he, the rational being, had found himself almost grovelling to a foreign god.

"For a groveller you do great fighting, so shut up," Prandra said.

The door buzzed and opened. Kinnear was standing in the doorway with his hands up. "If you feel like throwing things, I'll leave," he said.

"We're not quite that peevish," said Prandra. "What I feel like is a fool. I say Lyhhrt have nothing to do with the murders, and I am completely mistaken; I know I must not take risks, and I behave irresponsibly and risk lives; then I cause the death of an insane person and an innocent beast, and that is horrible."

"I suppose that's the truth from your point of view. But we did find the Lyhhrt; Wyaerl would be dead if you hadn't replaced his air and water: now he just has a big bruise. Most of us are grateful that many things we couldn't grasp before are becoming clear—and there is one Lyhhrt who is not guilty who would like to speak to you, if you're willing."

"We're willing," Khreng said. "Don't pay attention to the old woman's grumbling. Without that shot of yours we are still fighing Tiger, if not Lyhhrt."

"Listen who is talking," Prandra snorted. "The rational man!"

Kinnear laughed. "I'd better send him in right away."

The Lyhhrt who appeared in his most magnificent workshell was one of Admin-L'ason; in near Solthree form he was wearing all of Lyhhrr's art in precious metals and inset jewels. He was taller than Kinnear, and his shell's head was shaped something like one of the primitive masks on Metaxa's wall. Prandra remembered her conversation with Espinoza, and his pleasure in seeing the morning sun even through her alien eyes. And then the ashy bleakness of the planet where Ungrukh struggled and fought. Primitive.

Admin-L'ason's mind opened to welcome Khreng and herself, and she glimpsed a planet, swirling in marsh and fog, that was even more dispiriting than her own: its crawling lives had been taught by others not only to create their magnificent gleam and brilliance, but painfully to speak to the peoples of the Galaxy. Inside some part of the cold metal was a slug-like thing who deeply admired the grace and beauty of the Ungrukh.

: *So much so, unfortunately, that some of us wished to make workshells of you.*:

"We are honored to speak with you, don't blame yourself," Prandra said. "There are so many questions to ask I don't know where to begin."

: *At the beginning,*: said the Lyhhrt; he was very literal-minded. : *Our former Liason was so powerful even we could not esp him. He called our shells clumsy and did his best to convince us that others considered them pretentious and ridiculous.*:

"Then he is certainly mad," Prandra said, half-blinded by the reflected light of the creature whose people were called the Shining Ones by many weaker ESPs.

: *An unfortunate combination of genetic material—particularly since he is a killer. But he is a genius—and in that other respect he is quite right, when we must go about on wheels or walk in such a graceless manner.:*

"Like Nema," Prandra whispered.

The Lyhhrt hesitated. *:Yes...at first he tried to control animals—wild or domestic insensate beings on several worlds— by telepathy; he found this unsatisfactory; when he decided that he must work from within he was declared a menace to Lyhhrr and our organization in GalFed and sent with what we felt was a qualified guard to what we believed was a safe post—here. We were horribly mistaken. I-brother are culpable and will of course resign.:*

"I think Kinnear prefers not," said Prandra. "You better stay. I say once already if fools are sinners we're all in hell."

:There...were...other curious deaths here before you came.:

"I'm not surprised. It is why you ask help. So your rebel gets inside..."

:In Nema—we suspected that—and he sent a fission-twin to the tiger, because he admired strength and savagery—:

"And stupidity."

:No. He was aware those others were hardly more satisfactory than metals. He was waiting for someone like you.:

Khreng, reading through Prandra, shivered and cried to suppress the involuntary memory of a case of intestinal flukes for which he had been treated with hearty doses of emetic.

Lyhhrt had little sense of humor and could not smile, but they did their best. *:No, not exactly. We are not—what Solthrees call Protean—not shape-changers: one could not crawl into things, like a worm. Once inside, our man extended pseudo-axons and hooked them into the host spinal cord. To get inside—:* he sprung open a little drawer in his belly and held out a small steel object shaped like a flattened egg. It split, a dozen tiny knives were packed inside. *:We are superb surgeons and dissecters, and we leave no scars. This came from our brother in the tiger.:*

"And the false claw is made I presume by Nema-Lyhhrt," said Prandra. "It is interesting that the genius who despises metal work cannot do it very well. And what do you do about Nema?"

:Guard her, and report the case to GalFed Central. We are certain, but Khreng's sense of smell is not evidence against Nema, and you were forced to kill fission-brother to save your lives.... Before I-we go it must be said it is good to speak at ease and at length with an outworlder, as you know we rarely can.:

"Thank you—particularly since I'm still class-two."

:It is unfortunate that the situation remains essentially the same.:

"I hope not," said Prandra.

"Prandra, it's no use throwing yourself around," said Kinnear. "You and Khreng are going to stay under guard just like Nema and Metaxa until you lift off out of here—only, unlike them, you're staying together so you can scratch each other's eyes out."

"In my dreams I tell Espinoza I am too stupid to trap his killer!"

"And what does Espinoza say to you?"

"He tells me he is content and...I must remember Yamashita who is so much worse off, and—and—"

"Espinoza is a wise man even in your dreams," Kinnear said gently.

Prandra was not to be put off. "You tell Metaxa everything?"

"We told him what we suspected."

"And he is angry?"

"Angry enough that we decided to put Nema in a room of her own, with Lyhhrt guarding her—and a nurse to take care of her. If he did try to attack her ... well, he might find himself putting a gun to his own head."

"I think he is angry at us."

"No, he's angry at having been taken. At first he thought we were accusing him of murder, but we all believe she did the work. He knocked down Wyaerl, we fished that out of his mind, but he was obviously under hypnosis, and no one will charge him. It shocked him enough so that he began to put things together, realize how he'd been chosen to be her guardian from the start."

"So he goes free...."

"Eventually. We haven't discussed that with him yet. We want him under surveillance, but we don't want all his lawyers. If we can put up a case he'll be a witness—but he'll go free. It's strange that in spite of everything he knows and feels in one part of his mind, the part she controlled doesn't hate her: it still believes he chose her as a collector's piece. He'll go into a rage and end in tears."

"She goes free too," Prandra growled.

"The body with the useless brain will go some place where it'll be taken care of. The criminal—I'm sure the Lyhhrt will keep after that one if it takes thirty years. I gather that any evildoer who disrupts the Cosmic Thought keeps the world at one remove from God—and whatever that is, it's a deadly sin."

"In thirty years I may be a live brain, but I am a dead cat." She scratched her nose with the tip of her tongue. "You think Metaxa tries to free her?"

Surprised, Kinnear said, "How can he?"

"You think she can't find a way with opportunity? And all her power? Especially when *he* is going free? Nema is two: infant and Lyhhrt. We know about her. But Metaxa is three: love, hate, and doubt. We know about him too: he is malleable. Those three parts can be turned off and on; she does not have to be the only one who pulls switches."

Kinnear let out his breath in a long whish. "You've just beaten my head in with the unthinkable."

"It is not forbidden to think about it, surely."

"I will. Believe me, I will."

"Good. You find your cat friends helpful... but Kinnear, remember one thing. No harm. I am not just speaking of Khreng and myself. *No harm.* Ungrukh have ideas about sin too."

GalFed's ESP examinations are open to the public in order to dispel the ESP mystique; they are rarely well-attended: the exam to a non-ESP is as kriegspiel to a non-chessplayer.

Prandra, at one end of the Committee Room with Khreng dozing beside her, looked half-asleep. She was crouched on the rough flagstone brought in for her by an earth-mover; she did not want to grow too comfortable. She was sulky as always before some difficult task; she would be worse later. Her half-closed eyes skimmed her audience: armed guards, curious clerks, a couple of outworld ESPs she did not remember having met. Wyaerl, a blue rug with a purple welt; Chatterjee, reflecting the window on her dark globe; Sheedy, looking as if the light hurt his eyes. Metaxa was openly yawning; he had been allowed to come because he had not much else to do.

Kinnear, somber and a bit nervous, sat with the rest of Committee, a conglobation of faces. The Lyhhrt were the surprise, all five in a golden row: they had considered the occasion important enough to come in force, leaving Nema attended by three crack shots in a portable whitewall cage. Prandra was the day's star and could esp as she pleased, but she caught nothing from the Lyhhrt. Committee was backache, triplicate reports, and thank-God-it's-nearly-over, get-rid-of-these-damn-cats-and-back-to-normal.

Yes.

The door closed. The silence lengthened.

"Are you ready?" Kinnear asked.

:*Yes*,: said Chatterjee. Prandra grunted.

"This is an examination for ESP class-one status of the candidate Prandra daughter of Tengura of Ungruwarkh, Galactic Catalogue Feldfar five-five-three, Anax Two, Candidate was perviously attested class-two by this Committee on evidence of Sector-Liason Diego Espinoza. Examiner: Sita Chatterjee. Begin."

:*Forms obligatory*,: said Chatterjee. :*Search, collate, shield, lock, block and break*.:

An hour of silence punctuated by aborted snores from Khreng. Metaxa got up and left halfway through, and the guard who followed him seemed grateful.

Prandra was tempted to make slips, out of mischief and impatience. Damned savage trouble-making cats, hah? Respect and affection for Chatterjee stopped her. She picked thought-trains tossed from ESP to ESP, set them in order, flicked them back, sometimes with force just short of headache-making, until Sheedy winced. She took pity and subdued herself. She needed all her control. Set up shields and blocks and withstood battering against them, drove herself against the shields and blocks of others.

Played childish games with adults and wished she were back on Ungruwarkh, where life was simpler.

*   *   *

Metaxa had been allowed to keep his guns and the obsolete projectiles they used; his guards wore metal- and explosives-detectors. There was one half-forgotten weapon hidden and unnoticed behind the wine racks in his refrigerator, a more modern version of the zookeeper's tranquilizer gun, made of plastics and tiny enough to be palmed. He had carried it in earlier years through the dark places where he made his deals. It was not lethal, he was no murderer, but it was just as effective as the stunner and far less harmful. Its crystal darts had lain preserved in the cold place where they could not sublimate and were good for a day of body heat. He did not need a day.

The corridors were almost deserted. He paused at a door. "I want to use the washroom."

"Your own place is up one floor. Can't you wait?"

"No."

The guard shrugged and followed him in. As he was turning to shut the door, Metaxa touched him lightly beneath the ear with the little muzzle and pressed a stud.

"Hey...." The man staggered and within three seconds fell. Metaxa came out alone and slipped into the next doorway, an elevator.

The whitewall cage was a collection of wire mesh panels fastened to a platform with runners, and blocking Nema's door. The men inside were sleepy and hot from crowding. There was no one else in the corridor. Seeing Metaxa alone, one of them, through a yawn, said, "Where's your guard?"

"He had to use the washroom."

They did not react; they could not esp him, and as usual were a bit stupefied from boredom. He stopped before the cage. "Couldn't...couldn't you just let me look at her?"

"No, sir. We have orders."

"Just to look, please?" He flattened a hand against the mesh in appeal. "Please?"

"Mr. Metaxa, I'm warning you, get away from here!" The man grasped his weapon tighter, unwilling to raise it before wealth and power. "You know you're not supposed to be—hey, what are you do—"

Metaxa slid the panel aside, touched him under the jaw, and shoved. He fell against the others so hard they were too crowded to aim their guns, and Metaxa had them. He closed the cage and pushed it aside gently, careful not to trip up the wire that carried the current. Slid Nema's door open. The nurse by the doorway, holstered and armed, was weaving something useful with complicated bobbins and spindles. He put her to sleep before she had time to look up. Seven darts left. He did not think he would need more. The door closed.

"Darling?" Nema in a chair, blank as always, hands folded. Always when he saw her everything changed. "Didn't you think I'd come for you?" She looked at him.

"Nema!" He came forward, hands reaching for hers. "My skimmer's still on the roof. I've been watching with the telescope and the portway's hardly guarded—"

She sat up suddenly, incisively, pushed his hands away and signed with her own in the language he had taught her: *To the apartment.*

"But darling, why? I've put out the guards, we can get away now, from here." Once again he treid to take her hands and she pushed them aside.

To the apartment.

He shrugged, helplessly. "You know I always do what you want. But that's so danger—"

She stood, put a hand on his mouth, grasped him by the wrist, and pulled him across the room to the door.

He was forced to put out one more guard they ran into rounding a corner. A burly one who thrashed and kicked even with the dart in him, and Metaxa had to use another. He began to sweat.

Forms ended. There was a wearied pause. Prandra nestled her chin into her forelimbs, whisked the tip of her tail back and forth, tick-tock.

:*Forms-optional,*: said Chatterjee. :*Category: illusion.*:

If the other part of the examination had bored her, this one Prandra had been dreading. What was demanded was the creation of an original illusion—by mass hypnosis—of a person, place, time, situation, real or imaginary. She was aware that she was not imaginative or original enough to impress an audience of sophisticated ESPs. She came from a long line of realists: she was one of the few people on Ungruwarkh who had never seen the "plains-companion," the hallucinatory cat-companion which often accompanied lonely travellers over the vast barrens, and her own great-grandmother had made a career of convincing the tribes that the phenomonon was psychological rather than supernatural. She had not been helped by researching the examination records of earlier candidates who had produced marvels. She could extrapolate, reproduce, modify. What could she show here? A sunny day on Ungruwarkh? She had done that for the children, and it was worthy of children. Her experiences in the time-warp? She had given those, in exhaustive detail, to historians exobiologists. She could bring Sita Chatterjee embodied in her finest sari woven with peacocks on gold, a perfect eye blazing in each tail-feather... or Yamashita... too painful. Espinoza?

Oh, Espinoza....

:*Do you want a recess?*: Chatterjee asked.

"No...."

Khreng raised his tail and let it fall. Prandra swallowed and stood up on fours. "Madame Chatterjee, members of Invigilating Committee and audience...."

"What are you doing?" Metaxa, perplexed, stood watching in the kitchen doorway.

Although Nema could not take care of herself instinctively, like normal Solthree humans, she could use her hands to perform other actions—everything, perhaps, a Lyhhrt might do in a workshell. *I am preparing this for you.* She had run a half-liter of water into an ice bucket, found a small metal box, taken out several vials of crystals, shaken them into the water, swirled them to dissolve.

She took the bucket into the living room, in her even mechanical walk, and set it on a table beside the couch. He followed, a man in a dream. She faced him, slipped the gown from her shoulders till she was bared to the waist. Her mouth formed the shape a primitive sculptor might have created and called a smile.

Metaxa had never felt sexual desire for her, perhaps never had been allowed to. "What is it?" he whispered. Her breasts trembled with pulses. She pulled down his zip and peeled the cloth from one shoulder and arm till he showed a forequarter of grey hair and aging flesh that might have been the record of years in a foreign service. His arm moved as if it were submerged in water. "Don't...can't you see the danger? What—" His fingers groped, in slow motion, for the sleeve.

Leave it. She moved back, still with the terrible alien smile. The pale skin below her ribs quivered and rippled. She motioned toward the couch and he sat, slowly. She pushed down his shoulders until he was reclining. Then she took a small metal case from her pocket, opened it, removed a tiny blade, and set it lengthwise into his flesh below the seventh rib.

He was too numb now for shock or horror. He stared at it, watched a drop of blood gather and run down his skin.

She picked up the bucket and held it at her waist; in her own abdomen an opening appeared, a few centimeters long, a drop of blood gathered and ran, a tiny blade pushed out slowly, came clear, fell into the folds of her dress. A tentacle emerged, a pseudopod, like the tongue-tip from a mouth; inside the skin something writhed struggling among layers of muscle.

Metaxa did not know how long it took. In the time he knew, it was an eternity until the creature freed itself and slid into the basin: a Lyhhrt, half normal size. A newborn, newly divided Lyhhrt-brother enveloped in the crinkled transparent membrane of fission.

"Dearest, I know...I understand..." there seemed to be a thickness in his speech, "you're making sure...we'll be together...always...wherever I go...." He could not tell whether he was babbling wildly or muttering to himself. Inside his head a person struggled and screamed.

And the Lyhhrt was not ugly, better looking than an octopus or starfish. It was translucent pink, the size of a hand, and looked more like a flower; its five true limbs were rounded at the ends like petals, and on its back there was a star-pattern of deep red spots. Underneath was a tiny pulsing heart, and just below the surface veins, nerves and muscles extended. It was a brain with limbs, a fearful intelligence. It lay placidly in the water, absorbing nutrient into its birth-membrane, swelling and gathering strength. Nema's wound closed, a little blood crusted on its lower lip.

"Always together," Metaxa babbled. "A part of you in me...."

The Lyhhrt grew, absorbed half the liquid, reached three-quarters of the way toward adulthood.... Nema knelt beside the couch and offered the bowl, like a priestess. Offered Metaxa to the bowl. The Lyhhrt stirred; its envelope was smooth, the skin beneath would grow to match. It extended the tip of one limb into a thin tentacle and hooked it over the edge of the bucket on its way toward the blade embedded in Metaxa's flesh.

Metaxa shuddered, pulling on his strength. Sat up cautiously, not to disturb the knife, drew on saliva and swallowed before he got words out:

"Did you really think you could?"

"...although I believe I qualify as a class-one ESP," Prandra said, "I have no ability to produce the illusions you expect in these examinations. I create only what I see or know. I am also affected by what happens here. I cannot show you imaginary rainbows or fireworks when people are murdered and I want justice. Therefore I set myself the humbler task I consider most useful, of—can you show yourself, please, Kinnear?"

Heads turned. Kinnear stood up, hands knotted white. His image wavered, ripples, reformed... darkened. Blond hair and blue eyes turned brown; his face grew ruddy, beard lengthened and thickened. And he was Metaxa.

"Thank you for your help, Metaxa. Members of the audience, for my illusion I set myself the task of convincing you from the time you come into this room that Metaxa is Kinnear and Kinnear is Metaxa." She added dryly, "Convincing the murderer is, of course, the work of the Lyhhrt."

Still life: the man on the couch, Nema, the bowl with its reaching Lyhhrt.

The man's outline wavered, his face and hair paled, his beard dissolved... and he said much more sharply, "Administration-my-brother, do you witness?" He looked straight into Nema's eyes, wondering if Killer could see through those blank dark disks, and what he saw.

:Yes, Kinnear. I witness and will so testify.: Over Kinnear's shoulder spidery metal limbs unfolded themselves and hooked, pulling up the small steel workshell of Lyhhrr's official Administrator, who had accomplished two marvels of his own: speaking to Kinnear for the first time, after lying crowded and uncomfortable against hot flesh for two hours.

"Thank God," said Kinnear; his face and chest were running with cold sweat. But the gun was in his hand; while Admin scuttled to drop the lid of a cloisonné vase over the bucket, he shot three darts into Nema's neck.

Admin grabbed the bucket as Nema jumped up in a convulsive whirl, gave a single shriek, and crumpled.

Kinnear addressed the t-screen. "All right, CommUnit, cut the video and ring Committee. And Admin—will you get this goddam knife out of me before I split open?"

A Lyhhrt could not laugh. But it tried. *:Take it out yourself, Kinnear. It is barely cutting your skin.:*

In the Committee-Room the t-screen buzzer sounded, and everyone jumped.

The door slammed open. Metaxa rushed into his apartment and stopped short. "You said she wouldn't be hurt!"

"She wasn't hurt," said Kinnear and sighed. "No harm. She got three darts—a tranquilizer for her and two to paralyze the Lyhhrt; they won't have any effect on her. We made up four of them."

Metaxa fell to his knees beside Nema. She lay curled up, her breath came in whimpers. Her gown was tangled about her waist; he pulled the bodice up over her back and breast, the skirt over the plastic covering of her diaper. The look on his face was something to turn away from.

Kinnear, drained, raised his eyes to the red shape in the doorway. It was Khreng, planted square, the whack of his tail keeping all comers at bay.

"Where's Prandra? What's happened?"

"Nothing," Khreng said. "She is gone back to quarters to sleep, what do you think? She leaves a message: tell Kinnear he is a brave man."

"Brave? Anything and everything could have gone wrong. I was half crazy with fear."

That has nothing to do with bravery! I think," Khreng considered for two seconds, "you are maybe even as brave as I am."

Ambling back to quarters, Khreng paused at the open door of the deserted examination room, where a blaze of reflected light caught his eye. One chair was still taken by an empty workshell brought by the four Lyhhrt to sit in while its usual inhabitant was occupied elsewhere.

:Well, Prandra, are you satisfied with your status?: Chatterjee asked.

"It is good to be class-one," Prandra said quietly. "It remains to be seen whether I become first class."

:Yamashita would also have been your friend one day, if....:

"I know. Now I know we have friends here, and we can say goodbye to Espinoza through you."

A committee had formed in the lobby of Administration Quarters: Kinnêar, Sheedy, two Lyhhrt, and Chatterjee. Wyaerl, bubbling quietly, was there too because he was leaving for his world with Khreng and Prandra.

Khreng wrestled the chain of the gold star over his head, untangling it from ears and whiskers. "Kinnear, I thank you for the use of this beautiful artifact, but a gold star does not make me a big man on Ungruwarkh."

"I'll want to know how you're getting on," Kinnear said. He seemed to be trying to find something else to say, and failing.

:We will get on beautifully!: Wyaerl's mission had succeeded and he was filled with happiness. *:Although you may find it somewhat boring on my poor world—:*

"Good!"

:—where we hunt the eggs of the plaak or lie about at the edge of the waters and sleep—:

"That's exactly what we like to do," said Prandra.

:—and occasionally the drug-runners have a fight and kill each other but otherwise—:

"Your world is the marvel of creation!" Khreng rumbled. "It is on the way home to ours."

3

NEBUCHADNEZZAR

"DIRHOB TWO IS OFF LIMITS."

The faceless bureaucrat was the Third Assistant Junior Secretary of the Second Associate Representative to the Fourth Senior Deputy Vice-Minister of Transport for GalFed Central on Dirhob One, and was assigned to deal with bewildered outworlders knocking on the golden doors for help. He paused, as if the five words explained all to the two big red cats flanking what appeared to be a bright blue bathmat with a fringe at one end. The fringe trembled, but the bathmat did not speak. It had no mouth.

The round pink head of Faceless bore kilometers of regulations lighted by asterisks and buttressed by footnotes. It was as well that he was not an ESP. The slightly smaller, rather darker of the great red cats was considering how neatly and quickly he might be dismembered and stuffed in the disposal. But the 2nd Asst Jun Sec, an ESP, was on vacation, and Prandra was not good at finding her way among the lower bureaucrats or unravelling footnotes.

Khreng asked with controlled civility, "Why are we not supposed to go there?"

The man steepled his fingertips (*why* did Solthrees do that when they were assuming superiority?) and spoke with the loud distinctness reserved for morons and foreigners, "Yirl, as they call it, has not sent word from the GalFed Observer for nearly a year, trading ships have been warned off with threats and given up delivering supplies and collecting protein—"

The fringes quivered, Bathmat sat up suddenly, startling Faceless and rattling his own air and water bottles. He balanced

127

on his muscular snail-foot, the feeding-tube popped out of the slit across his belly, sucked air, and squeaked, "And still, the drugs, get delivered, to illegal, customers here!" The tube withdrew and the blue creature thumped flat, the fringes drummed sinister little tattoos on the bare parquet floor.

The secretary pursed his lips. "Their shuttles slip under our radar. I don't see what—"

"Our shuttle also slips under radar," Prandra snarled, "perhaps better, because it is from GalFed, with modern conveniences."

"We cannot allow a GalFed ship—"

The eyes of the female cat flared, and she lifted her tail as if to slam it on the floor. Khreng said quickly, still quietly, "Let me speak, please. Our ship and shuttle with equipment are made by and belong to GalFed, but they are registered to me, Khreng, and this woman, Prandra, of Ungruwarkh, under permanent loan, and we take good care of them. We do not land on Dirhob Two: we drop our passenger, a Yirl national, at his home from which he is picked up by GalFed some while ago and is promised return. If you dare not return him, it is you who are remiss, sir. Our only request is to store equipment under GalFed protection on this world so we need not tow it all the way to Yirl. *That* equipment has nothing to do with smugglers or other dangers. We orbit Yirl, land our passenger, and return for our supplies. It is a pity that world is not under GalFed protection for the sake of the poor and deprived, and the many parties whose livelihood depends on it—otherwise it is policed and you have less trouble with its criminals, hah? Now may we have permission to store supplies here under sealed and frozen conditions for whatever price you consider suitable, to be charged to GalFed Central Terraform-Agricultural Division in reference to Sector Feldfar Five-Five-Three?"

The Asst Jun Sec got his mouth closed, opened it to clear his throat, and croaked, "I will make arrangements."

"Good."

The deskman fumbled out a couple of pills, swallowed them with a squirt from a water-bulb, and stared at the retreating backs. He was relieved to see that the blue one did not leave a trail of slime on the shining wooden floor, kept bare for its

beauty: Dirhob One had marvellous trees and used them well.
All the creature had left behind were three translucent scales and
a faint but pervasive stink of methane and ammonia from the
atmosphere of that poor relation of a planet, Yirl.

"What an admirable speech," said Prandra. "For a non-ESP
you are picking up officialese very fast and learning to lie better
all the time."

"Yes," said Khreng. "If I stay much longer I get to be a
class-one diplomat. Let's get away from this place."

The interworld voyage lasted eight days. Wyaerl, the Yirli,
was accustomed to a watery life and did not travel well in space;
he had taken a stasis pill and was wound unconscious in a net
cocoon. Course was automatic, but there were many manual
controls for rearranging spaces and living equipment on the
ship: GalFed had refined it at every stop, and also enlarged most
of the buttons and pressure plates so that the Ungrukh did not
have to wear finger-stalls over their broad padded digits to use
them. Khreng was intensely interested in mastering all the
devices and once nearly ejected Wyaerl as radioactive waste. He
was driving Prandra wild.

"*Can* you stop your bloody damned poking about and leave
this one single cabin alone for one single hour?"

He flicked a screwdriver point at the remote on his wrist and
the cabin walls stopped shuddering. "I like to think we last long
enough down there to keep on using this ship a while."

"Play somewhere else." She was stabbing buttons to flash
pictures on a screen: charts relating to Ungulates-Solthree,
free-running and domestic, edible; care and feeding; butchering.

He grinned. "I always see those on the screen, but never the
ones for food-farming."

"I like to think of my food first."

"You don't yet look at the message."

The lucite cube was hanging in a net bag from a hook beside
the port. She did not glance at it. It had been delivered during
their stop at GalFed Central; a touch of the stud on one of its
corners would show fluorescent red images of their children,
Tugrik and Emerald, on their red planet, scuffling, racing,

growing.... "You see it already. You know nothing is wrong. They are well."

"You don't come into my mind to look; you block it off."

She hunched her shoulders. "They are well, they are growing, they are cared for by others. I don't know how time passes on these travels and I never learn."

"Agreement, agreement," he muttered.

"I become their tame ESP and they feed us. Agreed."

"But why do you not look at the children?"

"If we come out of this one alive I look. Are you satisfied?"

"No. That is the stupidest thing I can think of."

"Damnation! Leave me alone with it now!"

"Try not to feel so hurt." He licked her neck, but she shrugged him away, flicked another chart on the screen. He growled. "What in the Blue Pit of hell is that?"

"Some of our friends in GalFed think they have a sense of humor and that we have a peculiar taste in food." The chart was of *homo sapiens sapiens Galactensis Solthree*, male, marked out with butcher's cuts. She shivered. "We make jokes like that because we know we mean no harm. Theirs become stale and ugly. The savage ignorant cats."

He groaned. "That again. *Why* do you not go into stasis?"

"It is two hours to orbit... let me have the goggles."

The prismatic lenses allowed her wide-set eyes to focus close up. "Ha. Now I can't find the damn button with these on. Enlarge the skull for me... that is not a GalFed chart. Look where the lines wobble... it is a tracing... and no anatomist calls that part of the bone zygomotic."

"Not with your interest in bones! Who is the joker?"

"Somebody who tells the whole world we are coming. I presume every criminal on Yirl knows that now." She stared at the chart. "Maybe this is no joke. Maybe they think we enjoy a taste of Solthree meat."

"The species doesn't carry much, except around the hams, and I suspect most of that is fat." He switched off the projector and whacked her rump lightly with his tail. "I can think of something I enjoy much better right now, and I don't think we get much of *it* down there."

*   *   *

Wyærl had been wakened with an injection, and he was a bit drowsy, mainly because of the hypnotic in the needle. He was alert enough to be trembling with fear as Khreng and Prandra strapped him in the shuttle. He could not move because of the bindings, but his mind was never less than logical. :*Their radar is tracking us!*: His feeding, excreting, and hermaphroditic sexual processes were packed into his belly-slit; all his sense organs were in the fringe of quivering tentacles and they were fine enough to register molecular changes in the ship's hull and the edge of the atmosphere it was skimming.

"I know, man," Prandra said. "They also have a ship pacing us, but the grapples are not good enough to hold a GalFed Surveyor." That did not make him feel much better, and she added, "Look, Wyaerl, we all understand the risks. You are a man of great courage to come all the way to Solthree to ask help for your world, and we take the time...the time not only because we respect you, but because we also know what it is to have a world that is becoming a ruin. In your bottle there is a drug to keep you from feeling sick while we land, and a little sedative to make you calm."

:*I am calm now.*:

"Good. Now tell me."

:*Once I have dropped into my tidal basin I must tell every one, every Yirl I know all I have learned about you, and they must tell each other one they meet.*:

"Yes. If the spoilers come after you with ESPs to find out what they think are secrets, you have no secrets. Nobody must get hurt or killed on our account. Now...we have the masks, and the ointment so the air and water don't burn our skins, and the dreadful food concentrates, and the knives which I hope we don't use...."

Khreng glanced at Wyaerl, who was drowsing again, and hissed, "I'm sure this comes to mind very often, so excuse me for repeating. Down there they want a GalFed ship. Once we are in the open what is to stop two well-aimed bullets from perhaps a dozen guns—"

She pulled the lock switch. "I give them credit for a little curiosity."

*   *   *

The shuttle slid into fall, and the breath pushed out of him. "What being is one called Don Quixote?"

Remembering everything else, she had as usual forgotten to take her own dizzy-pill and said over a wave of nausea, :*I don't know. What are you saying?*:

His mind blurred, his speech thickened. "Nothing. It is something I hear from some techman at GalFed in relation to those damn fool Ungrukh...."

Wyaerl fell, free of his bottles and with his back slits puckered closed. He clove the whipping wind, thick foot pointed toward the sweep of the sea, barely caught the *plaak! plaak! plaak!* of the winged reptiles circling the tidal basin, slipped through the cloud and froth of ammoniac spume, down like a leaf-shaped spearhead into the waters; he added hardly a ripple to the breakers, headed with the tides toward the basin's wall where he would hang, separating his scales to exude the adhesive that would maintain him in wind and thunder and crashing surf on his tough back, while his tentacles reached busily into the wet straw-lined crevices for the fresh, beautiful delicious eggs of the plaak. He paused only briefly to touch feelers with his mates, siblings and cohorts in greeting and message, he was so homesick, so exhilarated, so hungry.

There were two big moons in the pale sky; Yirl did not know of them except by their effect on the tides and the light they gave at night. "The sky is more interesting here than Ungruwarkh's, but the ground is certainly duller," said Khreng. They had circled the seemingly deserted GalFed Observer Station, which was attended by a few aimless plaak only because it was near the basin and the sparse grasslands provided linings for their nests.

"I expect the ground becomes interesting soon enough," Prandra said. They headed inland toward the barrens of ashy dune and scree that seemed common in the area. "Gravity is one-point-one-five Solthree, bad; oxygen point nine-one, good, but air stinks, bad; nights rarely clear but moons prevent darkness, indifferent; thirty-four-hour-standard days, also cloudy and ditto—"

"And enemies some thousands of percent," said Khreng,

adding an involuntary "oof!" as the shuttle ploughed, on purpose, into one of the low dunes of loose ash. He slipped the restraining bands and permitted himself the last luxury of a good long yawn. "Hypnoforming compatible with surroundings." He turned a setscrew on the remote and the whine began in the bulkhead. The fact that the shuttle was blending with the ash-heap and becoming invisible did not strike him with wonder any longer. "Equipment stowed ... hypnoform complete. You want to open the lock and let in the fresh air now?" He gave Prandra a sharp look. "What is that lump in your pack?"

Prandra tried to push by him, but he stopped her with one heavy shoulder and slapped at the lump. "That is a half-kilo of weight, woman, but it feels like ten after fifteen kilometers over the scree at this gravity."

She muttered, "It's the picture cube."

"Ah. After eight days doing nothing aboard ship you intend to pass the leisure hours on Yirl with that?"

"It is something I do not intend to leave aboard the ship!" she snarled. "Do you need another reason?" She pulled the mask up over her face.

"Don't ask me to carry it, that's all." He masked his own head and opened the lock.

There was nothing to be seen of the ship except an uneven hump of ash. The material had blown so far from its original source that there were no volcanoes visible at all. These were all extinct now, but if the ash in the wind had not been so fine, it might have wrecked the shuttle. They did not turn back to look. Khreng had a good sense of direction, and a beeper in the remote if the former betrayed him. He raised a paw covered in crumbled powder and stared at the instrument. "This is a fine piece of work but a stupid one to find hiding places for."

Prandra with a rise of one shoulder indicated it was his problem.

"What do you esp?"

"A few plaak are complaining of having their nests disturbed by alien farmers growing herbs in their grounds." The powder was pushing into the spaces between her digits and beneath the loose skin over her claws; she dared not complain even with so little overweight as half a kilo. But she was growing surlier by the minute. She knew cold, but none so damp and penetrating. It was unjust that when two living worlds circled a sun one should have all of life's richness.

"Nothing else?"

"The plaak see moving figures but they may be Yirl, they are too far away."

"Maybe it is better to hypnoform ourselves. I am tired of always being the target."

"Last time we go walking on two legs I get all of your backache as well as my own. Solthrees here still have eyes and ears if many are ESP-impervious."

"That's right," a loud, slightly blurred voice said, in *lingua,* and two masked men in ash-colored suits moved out in front of the Ungrukh from hillocks to either side. Both were armed, one with what appeared to be a small cannon.

Khreng and Prandra stopped.

There were no features to be seen below the hoods, behind the masks. On one forehead, a lock of hair blew free with flecks of ash caught in it. An eddy of pale flakes whipped round them, and a dozen plaak, stupid but curious, circled above. The men were impervious non-ESPs: the featureless suits told nothing except that they were what Solthrees called humanoid.

And it was what Solthrees called unearthly to be standing on a desert planet in a dust devil facing statues bearing death.

"You are early," Prandra said. "We expect to meet you at the Station."

"We thought we'd make sure we got the remote before anyone else did. Just lift that paw so we can get a look."

Khreng stared into the gun barrel and raised the forelimb bearing the remote. He made no move to take it off.

The man with the big gun gestured, "You other one, take it off and give it here."

Prandra did not move, and the men hesitated. A shot could destroy the instrument, and these robbers might be afraid, even with their guns, of getting too close to Ungrukh teeth.

"Get on with it!"

The circling plaak tightened formation and with one black swoop dove into the whirlwind, squawking.

The man with the big gun was knocked over; in reflex he fired a burst of flame that sent the plaak screaming in all directions, half of them singed. Khreng and Prandra had neither moved nor been touched, but there was no remote on Khreng's wrist.

The fallen man scrambled to his knees; his mask had been knocked askew. "Devil, you did that!" he yelled. "Kill them, Jens!" Rifle aimed, Jens hesitated for one second; Khreng whipped his tail out and around the barrel and jerked it from his hands. The long prehensile tail coiled it like a snake, he backed away and aimed it at both while Prandra kicked the flame-gun aside. It was hot and she yelped a little.

The kneeling man straightened his mask and rose in a crouch. "There are many more of us," he said in a voice trembling with fury, "and many more guns."

"We don't come with guns," Prandra said. She raised a padded hand, shot out its claws, and withdrew them. "We have these, but we don't come for killing or eating people, and we don't use your drugs or trade in them. The remote is safe. Some plaak, slightly singed, thinks it is an egg, and puts it in a nest. You can look for it. I am sure you are interested in knowing that it works only with Khreng's body chemistry and his alone— before I mention that Khreng cannot possibly fire that rifle he is holding because we don't have the fingers and thumbs necessary to use it."

Khreng let fall the rifle, and they passed between the two grey figures and ambled ahead. No flame seared them. No bullet hit.

:That is a neat trick,: said Khreng. *:I hope you have some others planned.:*

:Planned! Who is planning? Hell's blazes, man, I am happy to be alive!:

"Get on!" The muzzles of flame-gun and rifle jabbed their flanks.

:I don't see much to be so damned happy about,: said Khreng.

The Observer's Station, little more than a large hut, stood half a kilometer from the basin. It had begun as a metal framework supporting plastic panels and had gradually been built up outside with compacted blocks of scree and ash; their bonding withstood the weather. At the back were the ceramic tanks of hydrochloric acid, added in small amounts to turn Yirl's sea into water drinkable by Solthrees except for ammonium chloride; a converter removed the salt. Each world's visitors added their own necessary chemicals and drank. The hut was much like the shelters on Ungruwarkh and many other worlds, except that there was a radar installation on its roof. Around it, and occupying much of the basin's perimeter, were the plants growing in cold-frames with their glasstex panels tilted slightly open to let in water and protect them from windblown dust.

Life on Yirl depended on wind and water; the Yirln glued themselves to the basin walls where the winds drove air into their breathing slits and the tides pushed the great amounts of ammonium hydroxide they needed into the openings beneath. When they lay in masses, their backs looked like faces, blank except for silently speaking mouths.

They fed on one thing only, the eggs of the plaak who made their nests on the basin's edge and even in its wall's crevices. For the plaak were foolish: they did not seem to mind having their eggs stolen: they laid them daily. Yet they were not so badly endowed. Slightly more than half the eggs were empty shells: the live ones bedded among them and were kept warm and wet; the shells were many-layered nettings of living protein formed in beautiful patterns. While a Yirli at a plaak's nest was probing with his fine tentacles for the vibration of life, a plaak might seize a live egg in its claw and fly to another nest. Then the Yirli was left with a mass of rapidly decomposing protein packed in moldy straw. More often then not he found one edible egg, extruded his food-pipe with its edge of tiny saw teeth, bore through, and sucked.

GalFed did not find enough that was valuable on Yirl to make it a Protectorate; they established an Observer to collect data. Soon after, salvage operators landed rusty scows and gathered discarded eggshells by the metric ton to sell for processing into fertilizer, food additives, and glue. The Yirln did not mind having their planet cleaned up a little; they got a percentage of the profits.

Two other things happened: GalFed discovered that the most intelligent Yirln could use their tentacles not only to find eggs but to palpate almost any substance and tell something of its internal structure. These Yirln, like Wyaerl, were persuaded into part-time scientific careers and learned to talk by using their food-pipes. Last, a few of the seeds from the straw the plaak ate and nested in somehow blew into the food of one of the Observers, and a new psychotropic drug was discovered. This discovery was kept confidential, but it leaked as usual. The new merchants landed. The next Observer who went down found himself a captive until he died.

Thousands of plaak were scared away by poison and weaponry from the scrubby dunes along the basin. Most of those that survived retreated to inland marshes, flats of hummock and muddy water where Yirln could not follow, ships could not land, nor men work. They were content. The protein traders, terrified of converging gangs, were not. Neither were the Yirln. All they had were the few hundreds of nests in each basin of the coastland cliffs, and they were becoming hungry.

The Station had an airlock; it did not work very well, but the air inside was breathable. The place was bare and shabby, a working space leading to small bunkrooms.

A trapdoor opened in the floor, and a woman's head popped out. Red frizzy hair stood out over her head; her thick lips turned back like the ends of a scroll. "Hey Grever, you got it?"

"Not quite." He explained in a few profane words while she helped the men out of their suits. She was in her thirties, rather thickset, wearing a shapeless coverall stuck with graindust. "Who *are* they?"

"GalFed agents."

"Huh. Now I've seen everything. Don't expect me to feed *them*." She flounced downstairs, yelling orders to somebody below. Echoing curses answered.

Prandra stared at the trap: a storeroom dug out beneath, probably with more space than the Station. Grever, guessing her thoughts, said, "No doors out of there." He was a wiry hawkfaced man with a thick shock of white hair. "Get those packs off." He hung the gun on the wall. Jens aimed the rifle. This one was round-faced and stocky, with black hair and brows. From his movements, muscular but without grace, he seemed lubberly.

As many peoples in the Galaxy had done, Grever was regarding the two red cats crouching beside their belongings. "Ungrukh," he said. "We know about you."

"We're not agents," Prandra said.

"Why were you heading for the Station?"

"To see the Observer."

Grever laughed. "You're late." He sat in the Observer's chair and put his feet up on the desk now cleared of paperwork forever. He said to Jens, "What about that bonding business?"

"I've heard of a remote like that. You activate it, a little sensor pushes under the skin and identifies blood or serum."

"Maybe there's a spare. Hand me the gun and go through everything."

Jens sighed, dropped to his knees on the floor, and went through everything: dismantled the masks, unscrewed the knife mountings, opened every food package, and crumbled its contents. There was no spare. He brushed crumbs from his hands slowly and stood up.

"Now that picture cube."

Prandra growled, "Leave it alone!" She drove forward, and Khreng pushed her back sharply with one forelimb.

"Stop that," he said. "Those are only shadows."

"They are mine!"

"Ah," said Grever. "Quite a reaction."

Jens said dryly, "I doubt it's a bomb."

"No, I don't think these are crazy people. It's a message. You—she-devil—come here and push the button."

Prandra's eyes burned, she crouched, her claws shot out—

Jens said quickly, "Please don't. We don't want to have to kill you."

Khreng pushed down on Prandra's shoulders with both padded hands. :*Woman, these men are tricked and humiliated. We back off.*: Aloud, he said, almost pleadingly, "Allow me to play the cube for you."

"All right. Play it."

Prandra's eyes flared again, briefly, she dropped to the floor and curled into a sulk. Screwed her eyes tight, shut out the evil men, the ruined supplies, the—

Khreng pressed the button, the cube crackled for an instant, and then two luminescent red cubs sprang to life in it, wrestled, raced, stood and spoke, leaped and ran again, growing as they ran in perfect feline grace, stopped and spoke with increasing dignity in deepening voices. . . .

"That's your language they're talking in?"

"Our tribe's dialect. By now they probably know some *lingua*."

"What are they saying?"

"Grever, it is only the little things all children say."

"What are they saying—and quickly!"

Khreng closed his own eyes to shut out Prandra. "'Mother, Father . . . we are well and everyone is good to us, but we miss you. Come back soon . . . our second teeth are all in now. . . . Mother, the ESP lady says I am going to be a class-one ESP because my range is one whole kilometer now. . . . Father, Mother, when are you coming home? Father, there are poachers in our fishing waters and I am going hunting for them with the men tomorrow. . . . Mother, oh Mother, I am becoming a woman . . . there are men asking for me, Raanung is the strongest and almost as good a tracker as our father. . . .'" The cube crackled and darkened. Khreng sighed. "Maybe you find the secret plans in that." He touched Prandra's vibrating shoulder.

Jens found a plastic bag in the desk, kneeled on the floor again, and began to pack in the broken bits of food.

Grever said coldly, "What are you doing that for?"

"They've got to eat, haven't they, until we find the remote?"

Khreng pointed to the pills scattered from a broken vial. "Those are tranquilizers. You permit me to give one to my woman?"

"Yeah," said Grever. "Give her two. She's got enough fire for a brace of lionesses."

"Leopard family," Khreng said absently. "Twice removed. . . ." He stroked her head. "Unfortunately this is a violent woman who loves peace."

A probing Yirli was surprised to find a strange object in a plaak nest during one of his crevice searches. He did not know what it was, but he knew, because of its internal structure and because he had been told all the news, that it had something to do with the GalFed ship. He exuded solvent to unstick himself, dropped into the sea, and swam with tail-kicks until he found Yirl, the Yirli of Yirln. The person who bore this honorific did not hold any office; he was the only present descendent of the first Yirli who had been taught to extrude his food-pipe, draw in air, and expel it in the sound, approximating "yirl," which gave the planet its name.

The pair tapped sensors like xylophone players. ((In a plaak's nest I found this instrument which I think belongs to the one-and-one who came with Wyaerl and I am not sure what to do with it.))

((The message from others is those ones have been taken by the Station ones,)) said Yirl. ((We should ask Wyaerl.))

It took time to find Wyaerl. At great risk he had strapped on a tank of sea-water, crawled a half-kilometer after sundown, and plastered himself against the Station window for half an hour. Luckily none of the Grever crew were ESPs. Neither was he, but he learned enough by vibration about the talk within. Exhausted, he was sliding down the cliffside when Yirl found him.

((Have they been taken?)) Yirl asked.

((Yes.))

((Are they lost then?))

((Not as long as they are alive what is the trouble?))

((We found this instrument which we believe belongs to them in the nest of a plaak now what are we to do?))

((It is part of the ship's control and if it was in a plaak's nest they probably wanted it to be hidden.))

((Then we must replace it.))

((No I believe they want it hidden for a time longer and all of us ones know about it and some ESP might find it too quickly so give it to one and tell him to give it to another whom he will tell to give to another and put it in any nest he may come by then let him stay away from that place and the person who gave it to him.)) He said to the other Yirli, ((Gather as many eggs as you can and when you have fed yourself give the rest to the other ones and say: stay in the sea as long and as far apart as possible because it is dangerous for more than one to work a nest at the same time and the cliffside should be nearly bare now tell this to one who will tell one and one.))

((Those ones will complain a lot.))

((Let them try the open sea and fight for eggs with the Out-Cliffers if they choose better hungry than dead.))

Khreng and Prandra ate their crumb rations out of an old plastic bowl with dirt in its cracks. The woman, Megan, served Grever, Jens, and two other men scrambled eggs made from powder. They did not seem to be enjoying their supper more than the Ungrukh. Prandra thought non-ESPs might be more talkative, but these were a surly lot, and obviously would have affairs they would not discuss in the presence of spies. She got a nasty jolt when she sensed Wyaerl hooking himself over the basin's rim and heading for the Station.

Khreng picked her up on it. *:Keep eating.:*

:My mouth is dry. They kill him!:

:Not if you don't give him away.:

And the idiot plastered himself against the window! She curled up in a corner and shut down her mind. She dared not even esp him. But the window was dirty and reflected light from within; she slipped suggestions into his brain so subtly that he believed he had thought of them himself. Presently he went away, and her appetite came back.

"Every goddam thing tastes rotten," said Grever.

Megan said wearily, "It's a cheap hotel." Her curled lips made every word come out a sneer. Grever too had a fixed expression, of wanting to hit someone. Her or anyone else. But he held in because he dared not upset a balance. She touched his shoulder, its pebbled black jersey, in grudging conciliation. She loved him.

They all smelt lightly of fear-sweat.

Khreng had not been quite fair in blaming GalFed for not protecting Dirhob Two, "called Yirl." Since there were no other planets in the system, Number One considered the other under her jurisdiction, as if it were a moon, and with some justification. GalFed did not sit itself down anywhere without delicate negotiations, especially about financing, and traders in protein and even smaller amounts of minerals and methane gas did not bring in much money. The drugs did, but they were illegal anywhere, unless that particular psychotropic (so new it was simply called "seed") turned out to be some kind of miracle drug, and so far it had not. Dirhob One would hardly admit to knowing of it.

GalFed would and did; Khreng and Prandra knew what they knew: there were six or seven gangs in operation; Grever's was one of the smallest, but it controlled the Station, and had a ship of its own. Three other small gangs shared a ship: they were the only ones not at war with each other, a loose business partnership. The one that wracked Grever's nerves the most was Quantz's Company, a highly efficient group encamped only about twenty kilometers west. They had a ship, heavy arms, and a powerful ESP. The ESP who had come down with the Observer years ago, as GalFed's Liason. A traitor.

Not a prisoner, says GalFed. *No ESP as powerful as a Khagodi would let himself be taken prisoner.*

Ho ho, says captive ESPrandra, tapping her tail in the corner.

She turned her mind to the anatomy chart with butcher's cuts. Grever was cold and cruel; he had probably killed the Observer and would almost certainly get rid of the Ungrukh once he took control of their ship. She did not believe he amused himself with grisly jokes. She said to Khreng, *:I don't think our choice cuts of Solthree come from Grever.:*

:If it's supposed to be a joke I doubt he is capable of making one.:

:But I am sure everyone here has some unpleasant plans for us.:

:Please! The food is bad enough. I don't care to choke on it.:

:That has so much preservative you turn to stone first. Think! Some other gang comes after us, and there is a fight, and then a third, who may join this side or that—:

:Leaving us dead before the remote is found. "There is not much to do on our world but lie by the water and sleep!" says Wyaerl. It is absolutely crazy to come here.:

:On Solthree you fight a tiger three times your size—:

:Grever's men together weigh much more than that, and they

*are not stupid either. You are thinking about that Khagodi. If
you are so keen on thinking remember that Grever has the
Station—but Quantz gets the ESP! So there must be plenty of
fighting going on here already.:*

A pattern of buzzes sounded at the lock-door. Megan,
Grever, and the others jumped for guns and masks. They circled
the lock; Grever pushed and released.

The pump hummed, drawing air. In a few minutes another
pattern rang, the door opened. A black-suited man stumbled in,
leaned against the wall, ripped off his mask. He was red-faced
and gasping.

Grever dropped the gun and clawed his shoulder. "Where's
Ed? Where's the skimmer?"

"I—I—skimmer's under the overhang on hill fifty-seven in
the shadow—"

Grever grabbed the cloth of the suit with both hands. "Ed!
God damn it, where's Ed!"

The man swallowed. "He's there—they got—"

Grever screamed, "My brother!" Slapped his face, palm and
backhand; his impatient hand had found the target.

Prandra winced. The man was not impervious. Though his
face, his only visible flesh, turned darker under the blows, his
mind's jumble of exhaustion, fear, and fire-images settled itself.
He took off his gloves and said coldly, "I was sent to disable
Quantz's tank and I did that." His temper broke and he dropped
his gloves and jabbed Grever in the chest with the fingers of both
hands. "Not to mind your goddam baby brother!" He turned;
the back of his suit was slashed to the lining with a scorch streak
and caked with wet ash. "We had to run away from that, and if
I'd turned back I'd have got it in the face. The ESP's hidden
somewhere, locked up." He unzipped and shucked down the
suit. "I don't know if this can be patched."

"Is he dead?" Grever's voice cracked on the word.

The man's shoulders sagged. He sat on the floor and yanked
at his boots. "I don't know. They were punching him up...." He
looked up. "I'm not going back, Sam. No sir. I'm..." his head
fell forward and he yawned, "a demolitions man."

"I'm not sending you back," Grever said, as if his lips were
stiff with cold. "Megan, get Harry something to eat." He turned,

as stiffly as he had spoken, in a semicircle, looking nowhere.

Harry lifted his head and peered at Khreng and Prandra. "Are these them? Looks like we're starting a zoo."

Jens said, "If we'd gotten the Khagodi we could have." He shambled across to Grever. "Sam, we have to get ready for a siege. We've got no ESP to prove these two or look for the remote tonight, all we've done is put a burr under Quantz's tail and he'll be after us. We've got nothing to bargain with."

Grever shook his head like a wet dog and pulled himself together. "No. Their tank's out, their skimmer can't hold more than three hundred kilos and is too easy to shoot down. They won't come out in the landcar tonight when we can have an Imper in the shadow of every dune waiting for them. We've got five wetsuits and ten hours of darkness. We'll put Jack on the roof and you watch this pair, and we'll start digging out those dirty nests ourselves. Right now."

Jens said slowly, "I don't know. . . ."

"I don't care what you don't know. That's what we're doing."

Jens sat at the desk with his feet up and the rifle in his arms, looking bored and irritable. Khreng and Prandra crouched in their corner. :*I think Grever makes a bad mistake,*: Prandra said. :*His demolitions man is not impervious, so the Khagodi must know all that goes on here.*:

:*Impers are as hard to find as ESPs, so maybe one in hundreds of thousands is a demolitions man. If he wants one he has to take his chances. You yourself think that Khagodi may be a prisoner, so he probably doesn't tell all he knows.*:

:*Even I can be wrong. I am a good ESP with a five km range, and anything further gives me one hell of a headache—but a Khagodi is the most powerful in GalFed and can fry a brain a quarter-world away, so why is he a prisoner?*:

He looked at her in disgust. :*That is a grandfather story. Do you know of a Khagodi ever frying a brain? Their little heads are so stuffed with Ethical Ideas it's a wonder there is room for the esp. And to be practical, how does he get his three-hundred-kilo lump of a rear end off the world? With wings? Who controls his food and water, hah?*:

:*You are right . . . and I am sure they have lower-grade ESPs to monitor him . . . but he can shield and still send. I wonder if that great ESP out there likes to talk to this humble one?:*

Khreng, startled, said "Humble?" aloud, and Jens jumped up. "Nothing. I am clearing my throat. You can go back to sleep."

"You better watch your big mouth, Ungrukh."

Prandra catches one blink, one flash

"Why? Do we live longer then, Mister Jens? You already kill the Observer."

of a windowless room with two basins for eating and drinking and a hole for excreting

"We didn't murder the Observer. He was caught in the crossfire during the fight over the Station with Quantz."

and the huddled lizard, old, very old, heavy leather collar around the neck and—hurts!—chain leading from it to the wall. . . .

"Ah," said Khreng, very gently. "That puts things in a different light." He was unwilling to give up the point, but not anxious to inflame the man who had shown the Ungrukh a minimum of kindness. Jens settled back, grudgingly, in a silence broken by the snores of the demolitions man asleep in his bunk and the dull beat of wind and waters. There was no one else in the Station; Megan was out on the cliff in a wetsuit with the others.

Prandra's thought was icy: *:That traitor of a Khagodi is an old sick creature chained in a cell with his own dung! He is not let into water for nearly two years, and his skin is diseased and his gills inflamed from the filters.:* Khagodi were amphibian, but preferred water out of necessity: they could scarcely haul their great weight about on the ground with such short legs, and the volcanoes of their mountainous world were very much alive and rained fire-storms daily.

:That is the prize? How does Grever expect to bring him here even if he can free him, when skimmers don't hold more than three hundred kilos?:

:Remember Quantz has a landcar. That's also a prize. Most of the battles here seem to be fought over equipment.:

They looked at each other. *:Unfortunately,:* Khreng said, *:Neither of us can handle a landcar or a skimmer.:*

:No. We must find someone to do it for us.:

Both stared at Jens. He stared back. He tapped the rifle barrel on the desk's edge. "If you two are up to something, remember there's more than one way to skin a cat."

"Who, us?" Khreng asked. *:That one is already treading on Grever's toes. Using him delivers a death sentence.:*

:The Khagodi is too weak to drag around also, and I don't want to give him to Grever for a present. Quantz is already in a fury over his tank.:

:And Grever enraged over his brother. So what is the difference? Tomorrow they are both marching out with blood in their eyes, and we are in the cross fire, maybe unmurdered, but still pretty dead.:

:The ESP says Grever's brother is still alive, until they beat the rest of the information out of him. . . .:

:So?:

:There's more than one way to skin a Quantz. More than one way to move the Khagodi. We arrange a cease-fire between the two parties so they co-operate until we let them find the remote.:

:You are becoming a dreamer. How do we make Grever swallow that?:

:He has no choice. Neither do we if we want this to turn out according to plan.:

:Well then, which of us gets to bundle up Jens? You want to play a game of tooth-tail-toe?:

:Why not just co-operate?:

They both stood and stretched, yawning, then crouched and in one leap cleared the desk and landed to either side of the startled Jens, an open-clawed hand heavy on each of his shoulders. Khreng purred in his ear, "While you are shooting one of us the other is killing you. It is better to give up the gun."

Jens broke into a sweat and shrank from the brush of the stiff red whiskers. "You can't get away—" Rough whiskers, hot breaths, sharp claws closed in from both sides, and he pushed the gun across the table.

"Good," said Prandra. "We are not escaping. I am trying to bring back Grever's brother for him, in return for which he allows us to stay alive. Khreng is waiting here. We also try to stop Quantz from wiping you out. You can tell this to Grever, though I doubt he believes you. No, don't cry out, I make sure your dreaming demolitions sleeps very deeply. I care even less for killing than you do, so you needn't fear for your life, but if you seem to give in without struggle I think your bad-tempered friends knock you about quite a lot. Do you prefer we give you a thump on the head and stun you a little, or do we tie you up?"

Jens wet his lips. "There's some baling wire in that locker." He even helped them bind and gag him. Prandra gave him a few light scratches on the face and hands, enough to show, not enough to become infected.

Khreng took Jens's chronometer. Khreng had all the fine senses Ungrukh non-ESP males developed in a society where most of the females were ESPs: smell, hearing, direction, and the ability to read subtle facial expressions. But time was something only his stomach told him.

Outside was wind, tide, and distant thunder. Cold and damp. Much of the cloud cover had blown away, leaving fine mist, and the two big moons were out, their visible limbs touching like lovers. Around them, atmospheric ice crystals had formed a linked bow with softly flaming moondogs at their vertical and horizontal axes. The Yirln could not see them; Khreng and Prandra had no time to marvel at them.

The steps to the roof were in shadow at the back of the building. Khreng kept watch while Prandra climbed. The man called Jack was still patrolling around the radar dish. Prandra crouched at the top of the stairway, waiting for him to come round. There was no need for silence; outside the soundproofing blocks, the noise of the weather burst from every direction. It was a terrifying moment for Jack when a hundred and ten kilos with claws landed on his shoulders. He buckled and went down on his knees.

Prandra shrugged aside her mask and growled, "Throw away the gun, Jack, or you get a nasty bite." She clawed off his hood and planted a hot kiss on the back of his neck. He shuddered and threw the gun aside.

The rank atmosphere was seizing her by the throat. She replaced the mask in time to stop a coughing fit. "Good. Now you take me to hill fifty-seven where the skimmer is hidden." She dipped into the head of Demolitions and fed the data to Khreng. "Do not try to go somewhere else. I know where it is."

"You can't get away—"

"That is what people are always telling me." She directed him down the stair, a heavy hand on his shoulder and claws piercing the flesh. "We are not escaping, man. Khreng is staying here for hostage. You need him because of the remote."

"What about me?" His voice cracked inside the mask.

"You are every bit as safe as Khreng."

"For God's sake, what do you want?"

"I want to bring back Grever's brother. You drop me three kilometers from Quantz, so I save a little strength. Then you take the skimmer and hide it nearby, or come back here as you choose. You are the one who is spending the fuel. After that, if you don't hear from me in three hours, by radio or esp through Demolitions, you assume we are both dead. You better hope otherwise."

"Why are you doing this, goddam it?"

"To give plaak eggs to the Yirln," Prandra said. She added quietly, her voice pulled away by the wind, "And I swear when I come here there is to be no blood spilled." She came round in front of him and pulled down her mask so that the moonlight gave back her eyeshine in burning red disks. He could not avoid looking at them or doubt that she told the truth.

Under the glare of Jens, Khreng waited in his corner. The chronometer hummed in his ear: the risk of a dead Prandra kept him alert. He measured off an hour and fifteen minutes to reach the skimmer over that terrible landscape, and three quarters for Jack, with margin, to drop Prandra and return; he would not radio when Quantz could pick up the message. There was no hubbub, no Grever storming in in a fury. The man and his skimmer had decided to wait. Good. In a little while Khreng would create his own hubbub.

Three kilometers from Quantz, Prandra stood with ash and pebbles crunching between her toes, thunder rising in the west, and cloud beginning to dim the moons. She did not listen to the buzz of the receding skimmer.

She was no better humored than any cat, but as a member of

the only sentient cat species she knew she rarely failed to take
pleasure in her own body movements: fine balance of head and
tail, easy swing of limbs and belly and oiled-piston of shoulder
blades under the loose ripple of skin. Like all big cats she also
tired easily. Within the last ten hours she had travelled over 10
km on foot, lost her temper several times, been frightened, made
melodramatic threat and counter-threat, and was surrounded
with enemies. Now, sore-footed, covered with ash stuck even to
the hairs in her ears, half-suffocated by the filter-mask, and
about to start the whole damned cycle over again—she was very
nearly dangerously sore-headed.

:*I understand....*: The faint whisper of thought came from
Lokh, the Khagodi, painfully cramped and diseased from
huddling for years in a dark and filthy cell.

She was ashamed. :*Just stay where you are, man. The old
woman is coming.*: She flopped to rest for a moment in the
shadow of a dune and with her tail scraped away the irritating
muck from under her knife harness. The knife was a new one.
During stopover at GalFed Central someone on a whim had
asked her what she wanted most. Never shy, she had asked for
and gotten it: a knife of the finest steel in the Galaxy made at the
Great Forges of Chlis, the moon of Barrazan IV. It was not a
weapon, but a tool for gutting and scaling the contemptible fish
the Ungrukh would keep on eating until they mastered the
techniques of raising cattle and farming the grain to feed them;
she had brought the knife not to threaten or kill but to cut Lokh
free of his damned collar and chain.

She shook her head to clear her brains of body irritants. Her
shield was set as firmly as her GalFed teachers could have
wished; only a Khagodi, or perhaps a Lyhhrt, could penetrate it;
Quantz owned no other class-one ESPs.

But that was all he lacked. She picked details from the
buzzing minds at Quantz's headquarters. The man ran an
efficient paramilitary organization with none of Grever's
sloppiness. His hangars, processing plants, and quarters were
grouped in an L-shape that partly sheltered the seed-fields
growing out from their angle. His buildings had slanted roofs
that did not buckle under wind, rain, or soil; solar cells that
trapped whatever energy could be collected from the stingy sun;

protected walkways for patrollers and their guns. Thirty men, nineteen Solthree, the rest various; ten women, seven Solthree. Quantz kept the men happy and the women busy. All wore uniforms with insignia.

Prandra snorted. Once on Solthree she had worn an insigne on a chain—for a little while. She laughed, in her peculiar hiss, rose, and followed the shadows. They had paled slightly because of the diffuse cloud, but her fur was dull at night, blended in shadow.

She scanned for Quantz, the controlling mind. No faceless bureaucrat, he was on patrol with his men, gun on shoulder, radio receiver in ear. Suited up against the weather. She searched for him as his men saw him, if they saw straight, or as a woman would see him, whomever he chose. Tall, muscular in limb, and heavy-bellied. He did not stint himself. Cropped round head, hair of no particular color, thick brows, deep eyes, red slab cheeks, stippled chin that never shaved clean. . . .

She paused before the mind. He had no esp, but he had ESP guards always to front and back with guns. He had even learned to shield fairly well. He was a determined man, a fighter and hunter. An enraged man. The butcher.

She blocked the guard ESPs, slipped through the shield; it was a lattice, no barrier to her. He knew about red cats and admired them greatly—for their skins: fine carpeting for cold floors. She laughed again. He was some piece of meat, himself, *homo sapiens sapiens Galactensis Solthree,* in butcher's cuts.

Woolgathering. Dangerous to admit how tired she was.

Lokh was kept in a room off the cellar warehouse that stored the dried seed; Grever's brother, battered but still alive, was nearby. Adjacent were the arms depot and garages for landcar, tank, and big-wheeled trucks. Quantz's crops were loaded and conveniently driven down a ramp from outside, but its entrance had heavy doors and guards. The main entrance lock in the other wing led to the cellar steps through a long and well-lit hallway, and supposing a big red cat traversed that, leaving a muddy trail. . . .

Oof. Her head was beginning to ache, she thought her shield must be ravelling around the edges. . . .

    :Door beside ramp with steps leading to cellar. . . .:

:Ah. Thank you, Lokh.: Sensible. She should have picked it up herself. But her head was dull, tiredness always hit so suddenly. She yawned, wanted to lie down and stretch and make a nice rug for Quantz's floor, with Khreng a beautiful matched pair—

She speeded her pace, forgot stones and ash. Bounded.

The building was a heavy black bar resting on the horizon. The arms of the L pointed north and east, ramp doors inside the longitudinal one, now in shadow because the moons were past zenith. She skirted the field, did not want even a smell of the seed with the wind blowing at her. Men patrolled, Quantz watched, chewing on his rage and planning attack, workers repaired the tank. Half the personnel were resting for tomorrow's efforts, but too many remained awake and alert.

Prandra knew what she wanted to do, but not how to do it. Ungrukh were limited by continuous awareness of ESP and a primitive time sense; they were not long-range planners but created strategies on impulse and tactics on the run.

She cast about. When she had taken her examination for class-one ESP status she had hypnotized many people at once. It was part of an exercise: they had been waiting, even wanting to be hypnotized. Here were enemies. One or two . . . but there were forty, and separated. . . . She snarled and twitched with nerves.

Plaak! plaak! Two or three of the reptiles circled the seed field, frustrated by the heavy glasstex louvres protecting the crop. On the cliffsides they dove at the nest-robbing Yirln with sharp beaks and talons, and a Yirli, tough and clever as it was, might be defeated. But the panels covering the fields did not give way at all and could not be pried apart beyond the few milimeters allowing ventilation. She stared at them: they reflected odd-angled squares of cloudy sky. Here plaak might destroy themselves, break claws and beaks, batter brains. A few had done so: several black splotched shapes lay rotting among the transparent squares. *Plaak!*

"Plaak yourself," she hissed. For those she had enough power. To the south the sea gleamed between bars of spume. Plaak were hovering there. She could not see them, turned northward among dunes for what she wanted, a hillock where dark lava showed through ash at its peak. She flung herself at it, panting, clawed thick soft ash. Swore. On the western side, scoured by wind, she found the hard surface of the lava, stubbed her toes on it and swore again, exposed a hollow where rock had collapsed and dug like any scratching dog, kicking out fragments as if they were old bones. Too small . . . ah, at last one chunk, twenty-odd kilos. She clawed it free, shoved and rolled it with head and shoulder out and down toward the field.

Her breath rasped and bubbled in the mask. She squatted by the frames of the louvers on the base of thickened haunches and spraddled tail, grasped the rock in forelimbs, raised and hurled it, it did not have far to crash into the cloud-field. Glass shattered, hinges sprung, forty panes around it snapped open. She called plaak.

They came in a black coil shrieking above her head.

Plaaplaak! plaak! paaplaak!

:Plaak, eat! Plaak! Eat, eat, plaak!: She laughed, hissing, shuddering with tiredness; the plaak shrieked and cackled, dove into the frames in furor and turmoil by the tens and scores. She pulled in breath till her diaphragm swelled, dragged off her mask, and raised voice in a howl that ripped harmonics from all the scales of sound. In the thin air the noise was alien and terrifying, even to her ears. But satisfying.

When the armed men came swarming down the walkways of the plaak-infested seed-field, she was loping among shadows roundabout toward the dark bar of the L and its door to the cellar.

Quantz was still on the rooftop scanning with infrared glasses. Her shield was tight around her. She had an alley of darkness to run in beneath the roof's overhang; one man had been left to guard the entrance. She did not want the plaak either slaughtered or scared off too easily. With part of her mind, she drove them to gorge on seed and duck the weapons the men used as flails; they would not waste ammunition on plaak now.

The guard at the doorstep was craning his neck to see what was going on; she was too busy to waste hypnosis on him. She knocked him over sideways, rolled him prone, careful not to disturb the mask, and sat on him while she opened the lock-door. He did not know what had hit him; grunting sounds of terror came from his squeezed chest. When she rose and vanished through the door, it took him three minutes to gather the breath and brains to get up. Quantz was shouting from the roof, the noise in the field ebbed. Most of the men were straggling back.

"What happened to you!" Hands grabbed the watchman's arms, he shook stars out of his eyes.

"Something sat on me!"

"Something!"

"I think it got, I think it got in the cellar—"

Quantz danced downstairs from the roof. "One of Grever's Impers?"

"Grever! Where'd he get some hot and heavy thing with fur?"

"Hot and heavy?" Quantz whispered. "Fur?"

"I got its filthy tail whacking me in the face. Christ!"

"Ah," said Quantz.

Khreng glanced at the chronometer and rose, yawning. Jens had given up glaring; he was tired and stiff, half-hypnotized by a primitive awe of the red disk eyes of the waiting cat. "You get free in a short while," Khreng said. "Mind your tongue when you do." He pulled the mask over his head and went out the lock without hurry.

The sky was light with cloud. The cliff's edge to the south was a black line curved like the edge of a cauldron from which the boiling spume arose. He headed for it.

Grever's men had begun their search at the watermark and climbed up, hooking their way into the rock wall with grapples or by limb's pushed into crevices. Khreng stood watching them for a moment. There were a few Yirln about, and those kept dropping in water to reappear farther away along the sea line. The searchers were sweeping upward to the east, and two of the black gleaming figures had nearly reached the cliff top. The highest, intent on nest-grubbing, was only half a meter from Khreng's head. Obviously none had found the remote. Khreng shoved his snout over the edge toward the bowed head. "Hullo," he growled.

The figure flung arms wide and let out a female shriek. It was Megan; her line barely kept her from falling on the head of the man below.

In a few moments five persons with three guns circled Khreng. He waited some seconds for a break in Grever's stream of vituperation. "Remember the remote," he said gently. "No one is hurt, yet. Prandra is gone for your brother—"

"Why? What for? What have you to gain?"

"Why man, our lives, eventually. Your brother is due back here in half an hour. Maybe you go back to the Station and be ready to care for him?"

"You're so goddamned sure of yourself, you bloody beast," Grever snarled.

Khreng cut off the beginning of a growl and with great forebearance damped his voice down half an octave. "Prandra is sure of herself. *I* think maybe thirty-five minutes."

With the outer lock hissing open again in back of her, Prandra was not so sure. As far as she could see ahead she had three minutes in which to do an hour's work. Half the vast chamber was lit, illuminating the crew repairing the tank. The rock walls were dry, the floor clean except for a few driblets of oil. She hid from the repair crew behind the landcar and tried to think past the clamoring of men outside.

She asked Lokh, *:How long can you keep forty people asleep?:*

Lokh struggled a second with the number of questions compacted in one. *:I am an old man, and Khagodi do not believe in—:*

:Three lives supersede here, Khagodi, and you are a damned tough old man. How long?:

Lokh struggled two more seconds with the implications of Khagodi ethics and philosophy. *:Ten minutes.:*

:Keep us and Grever awake.:

:Now?:

:Hell's blazes, man, now!:

Khagodi power could be subtle. The depth of sleep in fifteen bodies increased; twenty-five others slipped into unconsciousness so gently their combined fall was almost soundless.

:Unfortunately, I believe someone slid downstairs and broke a collarbone,: Lokh said mournfully.

:Khreng and I make restitution to Khagodis gods for you,:

Prandra said. *:We drop Quantz down one of your volcanoes.:*
:You do not seem to appreciate our ethical system.:

Prandra was already outside Ed Grever's cell door. The area here was less clean, the drops on the floor looked and smelled like dried blood. *:Now you wake somebody. That is Demolitions at the Observer Station, he is not impervious. Tell him this: the she-devil says, if you want your brother alive radio Jack in the skimmer to pick him up from the rooftop at the L's angle of Quantz's Headquarters building. You have six minutes and no more to pick up and clear out. Your choice.:*

As Grever and crew stepped into the Station, Harry the demolitions man sat up in bed with a yell.

Prandra blinked at the grating of Ed Grever's door, but there was no light inside. *:Is there a combination to this lock?:*
:Only a simple pressure-plate.:

The cell door slid open, grinding with rust. By the ceiling lights in the corridor she could see the dark outline of a figure on a mattress against the wall. A whimper came from it. The place stank, and she stepped back, not from the smell but to give the man a look, no matter how frightening, of herself in an unthreatening posture: feet on the ground, jaws closed, knife sheathed, mask hanging from her neck.

In reflex Ed Grever's arm rose before his beaten bruised face, and a chill of empathy ran down Prandra's haunches. She said very quietly, "I am not here to hurt you. You know who I am and that I am not your friend, but I want you alive and free. If you do not do as I say you are dead, because Quantz plans to kill you tomorrow."

"What—"

"I know you are in pain. Do you have broken bones?"

"My left arm, but—"

"If your legs are sound, you escape. Turn left out of this door and right along the corridor. Follow it for twenty meters until you reach the angle of this building and you find a stairwell. Climb the stair through the roof-lock. Jack picks you up from there in the skimmer. Take this mask. You have four minutes starting ten seconds from now. *Move!*"

Ed Grever dragged himself from the mattress and staggered to the door. Prandra hung the mask-strap over his wrist. "Don't stop to look at the bodies you see lying about," she said. "They come alive soon enough. Go!" She turned her back on him and headed for Lokh's cell.

:*For a person admittedly without time sense you are tossing the seconds about most expertly, Ungrukh.*:

"I am using *your* time sense, Khagodi. I cannot tell one hour from another." She grinned. "I am also aware that you are allowing me to borrow your intelligence and planning capacity." The second cell was open. She could see quite well in the dark by now but kept her eyes down; she knew Lokh would be shamed to be stared at in his stinking filth. Khagodi males were half as heavy and powerful as females, but many times more beautiful, in the bright, deeply marbled colors of tropical vegetation. Their beauty lasted to great age, but its loss by neglect or maltreatment was an extreme humiliation.

:*You may look at me,*: said Lokh. Like most lizards and all Khagodi, he had no voice. :*This is no time for propriety.*: He added, :*You have five minutes and some seconds. You cannot cut through my collar in that time and if you did Quantz would find something crueler to replace it with.*: He shook the heavy chain with his small pearl-clawed hands. :*What are your plans for me?*:

"You have six hundred and some days here. How many plans have you?"

:*Six hundred and thirteen. There is no escape. My plans are for mischief.*:

"Lokh, choose your favorite."

Lokh, no idler in his imprisonment, had by continual scraping worn down the link of his chain that attached it to the wall; it was thinned enough for Prandra to wrench free with the hilt of her knife. Lokh paused only to sweep his food and water dishes with one whack of his massive tail into the excretory pit, tucked the chain's end into his collar so that it would not trip him, and hobbled away stiffly in a three-pointed hippity-hop on his powerful legs and his tail's base.

Four minutes, fifteen seconds. Prandra was in the stores,

choosing explosives. Under Lokh's guidance she selected, for noise and limited damage, reels of fuses strung with little time bombs. She flung them about the two empty cells, set the timers and raced upstairs.

Two minutes, ten seconds. It was a nice coincidence that Quantz's suite was almost directly over the cells; the only useful coincidence she had met with since landing. It was a pleasant and comfortable place, floored with carpet-tiles. In the bathroom Lokh was already running warm fresh water into Quantz's luxurious tub. He could not drink the distilled water, but it was more than adequate for his first bath in nearly two years. Prandra shut the bathroom door from outside and shoved the blunt scaler's edge of her knife into the crack between door and frame. If the Forgemasters of Chlis had known they would have ripped out their tendrils, but the blade did not even bend.

:*It would have been simpler to lock the door.*:

"A locked door proves your complicity. A skewed door may result from bombing, which is my nefarious act. Also much harder to open. I doubt you get much shock in there. Enjoy yourself."

A smart little explosion rattled the brandy decanter on the table by the bed. Forty seconds. She ran.

Then stopped for a half-second's indecision. She could not pass by the cells where the bombs were popping, one per second now. She saw down the hall that the inner door of the front entrance-lock was open; she hopped over bodies into its chamber and shoved the door to. Pushed the button and held her breath as the air began to withdraw, and—

Sleepers woke, forty bodies came to life. Alarms added shrilly to the racket of explosions. Voices cried out. The air pump stopped.

She thumped buttons and scratched at doors fore and aft. They did not budge.

She sighed. She had expected to be taken; she did not like to be taken in an enclosed space. But though apprehensive and weary, she was not discontented. If Jack had picked up Ed Grever he had done it undetected. Not one of those forty in there was thinking of the skimmer: the explosions had covered its noise. Lokh, shield down tight, was rocking gently in the waves of his tub watching the luminous colors of his scales come alive. Quantz's magnificent purple face was something to deal with before she slept, but at present she had nothing to do but rest on the floor, lick out and spit away the ashy detritus from between her claws, and wait.

Megan had splinted Ed Grever's broken arm and was swabbing the bruised face. Jens was washing his own scratches and the score marks of baling wire on his wrists. The rest were stowing the gear. Khreng waited for the hard questions.

Grever's narrowed eyes settled on him, finally. They were odd eyes, brown, and beady because they were set in a face colored for pale grey ones. "I don't think you've been doing all this out of kindness of heart—particularly when you tied up Jens and hijacked the skimmer."

"Prandra and I don't expect you to agree with our plan," Khreng said. "As for kindness, Grever, we don't like you at all, but we don't want you to be hurt. Jack can tell you we swear no harm is to be done, and you may find that oath amusing but Ungrukh do not."

"Ungrukh, you're talking around it! That tiger-woman of yours is still out there with Quantz. What are they doing?"

"I doubt she is seducing him," Khreng said dryly. "Probably he is pointing a gun at her and she is persuading him not to shoot. In all the places we go, there are ever so many men with guns and so willing to use them."

"You're very sure of yourself to be making jokes."

"I am not joking. If Prandra is dead in that place I make sure to follow and you have no remote." He paused a moment to nerve himself for the difficult part. "I remind you that we come here *only* because of a promise to the Yirln that we help them get food. Your affairs complicate the matter and have nothing to do with us. For the sake of gaining something we are willing to give something up and so must you. If nothing is done Quantz comes here tomorrow with superior forces and weaponry and wipes all of us out. So Prandra is making a bargain, Grever. You hunt for the remote together with Quantz and his ESPs, and—and you and he share the GalFed ship."

Grever's face flamed. The butt of his rifle swung back.

Khreng had been expecting the blow, and, half-turning, hunched his shoulders.

But the arm controlling the gun was hooked and dragged down by Ed Grever's good one. Streaming with the sweat of exhaustion he held on, and spat in his brother's face. "Shit on you and your filthy temper, you sonofabitch! I like staying alive!"

Prandra knew that beyond the door there were enraged men waiting with ropes and guns. As the door whirred open she was allowed a moment's reflection on the endless fear, anger, and suspicion among those who were banded together to do no good. And she must bargain with such.

A noose flicked over her head. The line jerked, and she rolled head over tail into the midst of the group whose hard laughter echoed in the halls. She stood up, coughing, and faced Quantz. She no longer found his uniform ridiculous; she had never found guns laughable. Quantz smiled and his face's color ebbed to its normal red.

The rope pulled once more. She gagged. The men, and the few women among them, snickered. A few in that company were scaled, and one or two had tentacles, but all were what a Solthree would have called "humanoid." She and Lokh were not, and she knew what the difference meant to Quantz. A pair of skins....

She choked. "You want to speak to me, or you kill me here?"

"Both," said Quantz. "I have had enough of Grever, and very soon I will have had enough of you." He bent to loosen and pull the rope from around her neck. His touch on her head lingered, brushing the fur wrongways, and her neck stiffened. "I like to be frank right from the beginning," he said. "I know all about you. The Junior Assistant Sec you dealt with on Dirhob One was our man, you see."

Prandra cocked her head and nodded. She was bone-weary. Every time her eyes closed in a blink, she seemed to be falling in a bottomless pit. But she still admired a good ploy. "He is a fine actor."

"And an even better ESP. Perhaps better than you."

"Most likely," said Prandra. "I am only a novice."

"You are too modest," Quantz said in polite irony, and then barked with laughter. "He particularly enjoyed your desire to stuff him down the disposal."

Prandra purred, "It is a pity I restrain myself."

Quantz barked with laughter again. "So do we here, for the time being."

She had expected to be interrogated in the usual foul cell, but found herself in a lounge, also carpeted, where electronic screens with game boards were set into the wall—and four or five men with the usual guns surrounded her. The air smelt much better than at Grever's place. She had even been given a dish of water. Quantz was amused by the sight of a big animal lapping water like a dog. Many things amused him.

"I do not, however, care to be tricked," he said. "I know what happened with Grever's brother. The diversion was very clever. What have you done with Lokh? You are blocking very strongly on that."

Between the game boards, the wall was hung with guns. Not collectors' items, but heavy weapons that could pierce metal or slice flesh into smoked meat. She did not think Quantz would use them if he wanted skins. She licked drops of water from her whiskers. "You claim to know everything. Then you know I come to bargain. I am left without a mask, so I cannot get far outside, but I do not like to be taken easily. I give Grever back his brother hoping he is willing to bargain with you because I don't want people to be slaughtered tomorrow, including Khreng and me. Lokh is unharmed. I hide him only so I can have something to give back to you, as I give back Grever's brother."

Quantz sat back and said with contempt, "And that's your bargain? Lokh has never been any use to us because we've never trusted him."

"I know. You keep him as a counter in one of your games. Grever has the Station, you have the ESP. The ramshackle Station with out-of-date equipment—and the ESP you make ramshackle too."

"Then how do you expect—"

"To use Lokh for bargaining? In two ways. You want to keep him because even you are nervous about killing a Khagodi, except by constant maltreatment. Your men are searching for him now, and if they find him you say I have nothing to bargain with. That is not true. Lokh is willing to work for me."

"The GalFed ship . . ."

"How much does your little secretary know about that? He is a minor official on an insignificant world. How many do you place in GalFed Central—or on Solthree where the ones like myself are taught to block?" It was dangerous to allow herself so much as a smile. "Your man on Dirhob is competent, your ESP monitors are watchful. . . ." She pointed to one of the game boards. "That has black and white squares. So does an ESP. You know a few of my white ones."

"Why should Lokh work for you?"

"He respects me."

"Ha. And me?"

"Lokh can kill himself with a wish. If you put him back in a cell. . . ."

"We have a cell for *you*."

"Quantz, your men are coming back to tell you they cannot find Lokh."

Without turning his head, Quantz yelled at the man who had appeared glowering in the doorway, "I know! I know!" Neither he nor Prandra moved. "Why do I need Lokh to get the GalFed ship?"

"Tcha! You have Grever's brother here with the answer, and you do not think to ask!"

Quantz said evenly, though his eyes were picking out angry glints of light. "I thought it was one of the usual raids."

"And blowing up the tank is Grever's diversion."

"So? Where is Lokh and how do we use him?" One of the ESPs was turning the noosed rope this way and that in his hands, and Quantz watched it. "Shall we dance?"

"Recall, I only do small damage to the plots and your rooms and do not touch your equipment." She added rather hastily, "The remote which controls both ship and shuttle is bonded to Khreng. Originally it is hidden, but now it is lost so that even I cannot find it. I am almost certain that Lokh can. Of course you can find the ship and shuttle, but without locking codes the controls self-destruct. Often including the ship."

Quantz said thoughtfully, "A GalFed ship is a marvelous

vehicle in which a man can cross the Galaxy almost unchallenged. Possibly the finest thing I might ever own . . . and you are promising to give me this in return for your life?"

"No, man, no! I am not giving it to you. That is not the way to bargain. And I want much more than my life."

"Go on." Quantz hooked up the loop of the rope with one of his fingers, then let it drop. Perhaps he was counting on Prandra's being so tired and fearful that she couldn't think straight; he was not rested himself.

She stood up slowly, very slowly, not to make those guns jerk up. "I know you are impatient, but I am very tired—so I take a rest by giving you back Lokh. The price for him—" she dared a grin now, "—is treating him with care and decency. He is too old and tired to escape or to harm you, but he cannot work at all if he is stupefied by filth and darkness."

"I agree to that," he said easily.

"Then let me show you." She did not think it would endanger herself or Lokh to give Quantz the small jolt of seeing a non-"humanoid" in his bathtub. She had allowed Lokh to choose the place because it would seem so incongruous to such a man as Quantz that it would hardly occur to him. She and Lokh had also worked on him a little to reinforce the feeling.

The man with the rope stood up to accompany them, looping it round his shoulder, hefting his gun. As light fell on his face close to the ceiling panels she noticed something odd about it, a strange puckering. Two faint mauve scars a couple of centimeters long extended from the corners of the man's mouth, buckling like badly fitted zippers. Quantz had done that himself, to punish, neither hid it. Prandra folded the information and her feelings down into one of the hypothetical black squares of her gameboard. :*Your part is over*,: she told Lokh, in the depth to which the ESP monitors could not reach. :*He makes certain promises*.:

:*Yes. He is a great liar*.:

:*I know*,: said Prandra. :*But so am I*.:

The explosions had heaved the bedroom floor and driven a pile of furniture against the bathroom door. "You find Lokh behind that door. In the tub. I think you don't mind that he takes a bath. You like to deal with those who are clean and elegant. I need a bath myself, but I don't include it in my terms."

Ten minutes of heaving and wrenching disclosed Lokh, refreshed if not rejuvenated. One flash from him gave Prandra the scene, through the eyes of Demolitions, of Ed Grever's return and Khreng's narrow escape from attack. Grever would have to concede. It was her turn to make the same deal and she would rather have risked Grever's hasty temper.

Back in the lounge, Quantz said, "That was very clever. But now we get back to the matter of the ship. The ship, remember? You seem very willing to give up so precious a thing in exchange for your life and Lokh's bath."

"I tell you I want much more." Prandra swallowed. "Grever has Khreng. You and he must bargain."

Quantz's face darkened. "I was under the impression that bargaining with Grever meant that I wouldn't attack him."

"Not attacking him results in his agreeing to share the use of the remote. Listen, Quantz! Grever is a thorn in your flesh, but his band is small and not very resourceful. And he is a very hot-tempered man who is fiercely determined to keep that Station where he has access to GalFed communications channels and the seed-growing location is very good. And you *know* if you try to get rid of him he is savage enough to take many of your company with him. You are much cleverer: on your poorer location you grow ten times as much with greater efficiency and buy the best equipment. You have all the advantage you need.

"A GalFed Survey ship is not a freighter! It can tow a fair amount rather awkwardly, but it carries no more than a metric ton. You can use it only to establish contacts, make deals, and display samples. For that you can make arrangements that more than satisfy both you and Grever...."

A feeling she could not define frightened her horribly in that moment. Was it that she had shown she knew too much, too well, for a being inferior in his eyes? She dared not probe his mind because of the monitors or even intensify her shield. She believed that he was on the verge of agreement, and yet his eyes (she could see through them) were fixed above her head on the wall where there were three—not guns but objects with straight stems and curved crossbars. A glance only, and without detail. Solthree religious articles? Quantz—religious? Then, weapons?

The hand holding the noose jittered. She wished for a moment that she were male and "humanoid."

"Go on," Quantz folded competent elegant hands. "The rest of the terms."

"The rest! After asking you and Grever to make peace, how much more can I demand, Quantz? After that hurdle do you think I am letting the ship go too easily? That there is some catch? I want Khreng and me to stay alive, and that is the most important to us! I doubt GalFed thinks much of the deal, but Ungruwarkh is a world where more than half of the people are ESPs, probably over five hundred thousand; if we can persuade one in a hundred to work for GalFed they more than make up for the worth of the ship. We find a way to collect our equipment and carry it home, we don't need a ship for anything else now.

"The last of the terms—Quantz, it is so simple I am beginning to sound like a teacher of small children. You are scaring away the plaak so my friend Wyaerl and his people cannot find enough eggs. If you and Grever are willing to broadcast one tenth of one percent of your seed near the basin's edge so the plaak can feed and nest on it . . . we don't care what else you do with your seed. That is not our business. We want only to bring food to hungry worlds."

"A noble thought. The ship is very easily identifiable by registry."

"I am sure you have skilled forgers and camouflagers. I respect your abilities. And you are safe on this world as long as your man in Dirhob can keep it off limits."

"And how do you expect to get off the planet?"

"Both you and Grever have shipments ready to be delivered. If one of you takes us aboard your ship you refuel some place where GalFed has no warrants for you and you have no business, and we are out of your life."

Quantz crossed his knees and folded his hands around them as well as his belly would let him. "It would be simpler to kill you once your usefulness was over."

Prandra had been waiting for this. It was the sign that the bargaining was over. It was a piece of hyperbole for the moment; having agreed to so many terms with an enemy he wanted to see her wriggle.

There were few things for which Prandra truly admired Quantz, and one was that he was a worthy opponent. "Who would look for you?" He went on. "Your starving Ungrukh? There is no record of your even landing on this world."

She shook her head. She was not taking bait, and for once was so tired that she was willing to give up the last word. "You see I come alone. I already put my life in your hands. I must trust you."

"Good. I'll find you a room."

"One moment, Quantz. You do not say in so many words that you find the terms acceptable. I know Grever must agree to them."

Quantz folded his arms and said, as if after great thought, "I agree to discuss them."

She was so near to keeling over her breath came ragged. "Then, to seal that degree of concord, allow me one request. Let me go back to my man. Otherwise he waits up for me all night and gets very cross. And stubborn . . . and you need him. Lokh is happy to monitor us for you."

"And keep an eye on Grever too." Quantz smiled. "Good enough."

And he had damned near made her beg.

An hour before dawn Quantz's CommUnit transmitted the first plaintext message ever sent on Yirl:

Quantz to Grever:
1. On receipt of your agreement all controversies between our two parties dissolved without retribution either side.
2. Propose discussion-bargain of valuables for salvage you name time-place.
3. Skimmer returning cat where drop?

Grever to Quantz:
1. Agreed.
2. Will call you sixteen hours confirm details.
3. Any place.

* * *

Prandra woke as she was being dumped on the ground. The skimmer rose with a whine and disappeared. She half-expected to find herself in a desert place where she would choke in the noxious air until her swollen windpipe suffocated her. But a shadow came between her and the paling sky and a hand slipped a mask strap around her head. She breathed. A foot nudged her flank, not gently, and she pulled herself to fours and followed the dark figure to the Station. She recognized the mind of Harry the demo man, who had not appreciated being wakened either.

Outer and inner lock-doors opened, hissed, closed, and she was within walls again. Quantz? Grever? The latter was slightly less intelligent, devious, sadistic. Otherwise not much to choose.

Harry took his place with the gun. She settled in the accustomed corner and rested her head on Khreng's shoulder. His eyes were closed but he was not asleep. "You are all right?"

"I am dirty, tired, sore, frightened, dizzy—"

"Good night." His tail curled round her waist and she slept.

She woke, choking in a noose, clawing the wall where the strange crosses hung.

"Wake up," Khreng said. "You are having dreams."

"I am choking!"

"I think you are overtired." He dropped pills on her mouth, dunked her head in the water dish with a splayed paw. She drank. "Get to sleep and stay asleep."

When she woke her limbs jerked and trembled for minutes before she could stand. Jens, on guard now, nudged the food bowl under her nose.

"What time is it?"

"Past noon. Grever's out there parleying."

"Where?"

"I dunno. They picked some place and called it neutral."

"Who are *they*?"

"Grever with Ed and Jack. Quantz and two of his boys."

"Who takes over in case of an ambush?"

"Hah, you think of everything. Each party has a skimmer circling. No ambushes."

"I am sorry to be rough with you."

"You haven't had it so smooth yourself." He gave off no

feeling of resentment. Khreng paced quietly. Megan's voice echoed hoarsely in the cellar and the dull beat of the waters pushed at the walls. The light was dim as always through the dirty panes and occasionally the shadow of a plaak flicked across them. Jens kept squatting by her as she ate. "You certainly pulled it off last night."

"Very expensively." She coughed on a crumb. Bad enough when it was fresh, the food had dried from exposure and picked up dirt from the floor. She did not understand this man. She had the odd feeling that he would have liked to touch her head, not as Quantz had done, but as the first alien visitor on Ungruwarkh had touched Khreng so long ago, in a gesture of greeting. She wondered how Jens came to be with Grever, and why he stayed; it was a question that might have been asked of many.

"You have a funny mark on your neck," he said suddenly. He reached his hand out and paused. She lifted her head and allowed him to examine the fine parting in the fur. "Looks like a rope burn. It may need antiseptic."

"Cat skin heals fast. It is from a rope."

"A loop, a noose...man with a scarred mouth, wild yellowish hair?"

"Perhaps...yes."

"He likes to play with ropes, that one. Kind of funny in the head."

"All Quantz's men are funny in the head."

He laughed. "Us too?"

"You expect an answer?"

"I often wondered how he got the decoration."

"Sleeping with a woman Quantz considers his personal possession—and he does not shield well enough."

"I won't ask what he did to the girl."

"Neither do I," said Prandra. "Jens, tell me what is in the shape of a cross, the longitudinal piece thicker than this digit and measuring two-thirds of a meter, and the crosspiece curved down at the ends, about half a meter?"

He sat back on the floor and looked away a moment, scratching his stubbled chin. "I've heard Quantz sometimes likes to do target shooting with crossbows. You know what bows are?"

"Yes."

"This is a very sophisticated kind . . . it uses an arrow that can go through a steel plate."

"Is it used by Solthree military people?"

"Not for centuries. Just for fun now."

Talks did not go smoothly. Four or five times during the next two days Grever's team came back and took their meals silently with lowering faces. Megan did not try to speak to them. Harry, Jens, and a gorilla named Higgins, all morose, took turns guarding the Ungrukh, stacking bales of harvested crops, and sleeping. None of them appeared to use the drug at all. Prandra, appreciating their wisdom, wondered if a taste might have made them better-natured.

The Ungrukh did not rest much during that time. They spent more than half of it patrolling the cliff top under guard with Lokh, who was attended by one of Quantz's ESPs. Prandra was grateful it was not Puckermouth.

Once Wyaerl and Yirl climbed up to speak to them: Quantz immediately took it into his head to take them captive as well. A mind-touch from Lokh sent them dropping back into the sea. Quantz did not know it, but he did not need them. Although by that time Prandra had really lost track of the remote and would have needed seven or eight days to follow it, Lokh had traced the complicated transfer-route within ten minutes of his first look into Yirl's mind.

Lokh would have liked, but did not dare, to ask when they intended to give up the remote. Prandra would have liked to dare give Khreng's answer: "There is a rare time in tribal parleys when everyone is tired and angry and sick to death of talking. Then somehow a solution comes up and leaves everyone weak with relief. Unfortunately it *is* rare."

Rare or not, it would come. It would be the time of greatest danger for the Ungrukh, when their enemies were free to dispose of them, but it would give them control over the time.

:*Forgive me for saying so,*: said Lokh, :*but I am very tired.*:
Prandra sighed. She and Khreng had no way to save their own strength for the future, but Lokh's life span, five times their own, was behind him; he was near its end. He had had his

adventure and was free of his terrible chain: now he was being paraded back and forth on a cliff's edge lashed by vicious alien waters, and becoming as ravaged as he had been in his cell. And doing it for the Ungrukh.

Khreng glared at Prandra. Prandra dared. :*Lokh, it is time for you to faint.*: A good faint it was—safe, convincing, and an extremely awkward two-hundred-and-fifty kilo burden for cursing men to drag to peace and comfort.

The first thing Quantz and Grever agreed on was to take the ship out of orbit as soon as they got possession of it and put it to work. Then they argued over the sizes of their respective crews and loads, over routes, navigators, communications, and codes.

"Niggles," said Megan caustically. The rest of the men were busy elsewhere, and the Ungrukh had been left in her charge, that is, in the locked cellar among the stacked bales of seed while she loaded them on sledges that would be dragged upstairs on pulleys because there was no other way out.

"Quantz's arrangement is more convenient," Prandra said.

"Yeah, but it's slow to open and close." Megan did the work of three men and looked strong as an ox. Although she was a homely woman she was not repellent, and there were occasional signs of good humor in her face. But there was a gun butt hooked into the waistband of her jeans sticking out beneath the edge of her shapeless oiled-wool sweater. Prandra thought Grever did not likely tangle with her much except in bed, and wondered idly whether some of the other men found their way once in a while to a few of the women Quantz did not choose.

It was almost pleasant in the cellar, considering the alternatives. There was no noise; the seed gave off a light fragrance that was not hypnotic in the dry state.

All at once the negotiating crew tramped in again, thumping and cursing overhead. "Ah hell," said Megan. "I hope they got it settled this time." She kept on stacking; she was content to run the business and was contemptuous of intrigues. The yelling and table-thumping in the normal style of conversation among Grever's crew went on, sound but not meaning filtered through the ceiling.

Prandra began to pace. :*Something is being decided. They have a lot to say.*:

:*Not much good for us.*:

There was a moment of quiet. Then one clear word: *"You!"*

The door opened and Grever called harshly, "Megan, get up here right away!"

"Bite your goddam tongue," Megan muttered. On the stair she passed Jens coming down. "Hey, you got no gun."

"I—don't need one."

"It's your skin."

Grever yelled, "Everything, Jens! Tell them *everything!*"

Jens said nothing. His face was shocking. Even under the ugly light it was a strange putty-color. His mouth opened and closed like a fish's and his usual rounded shoulders were slumped even further. :*You know what I think?*: Khreng said.

"Where I can hear you!" Grever yelled.

Prandra spoke to Jens. "You are not here to guard us."

He sat on a bale, hands hanging between his knees. "No."

She whispered, "What about standard issue?"

He touched his armpit. "You think they'd let me keep that?" Then looked up and said dully, "When did you find out?"

"That you are from GalFed?" Khreng asked. "Just this moment."

"Perhaps earlier," Prandra said. "It may be a thing we know and are not conscious of. You are not a very good actor, Jens."

"I kept it up a year and a half," he said tartly. "Not much of an agent. Stolen ship, terrific cover, crashed in the sea and lost everything."

"How do *they* find out?"

"I was the only dissenter in an important vote."

"Oh? What is that everything you are to tell us?"

"Quantz has the remote."

"Hah." If Quantz had waited half an hour they could have handed it to him on a platter. "Does Lokh give it to them?"

"No...he was so tired—maybe they exhausted him on purpose—one of Quantz's ESPs picked it out of him when he was half asleep."

Lokh would be ashamed of that. Prandra reached out to console him...and found nothing. No thought, dream ...nothing. She snarled, claws up and out, "You tell me fast, Jens, or I don't care what you are! Is Lokh dead?"

"Don't for God's sake!" He crossed his arms before his face in a futile shielding gesture and cried out in a low impassioned voice, "You have nothing against me! He's making me tell you because he's ashamed to do it himself. You saved his brother's life."

"Jens!" Grever yelled. "I never said—"

"Oh shut up you dumb bastard, I'm trying to give you *some* credit!"

Grever yanked the door shut savagely. "God," Jens muttered. "What does it matter what we say now?"

"It matters to us whether Lokh—"

"Nobody murders a Khagodi. It's an ethical concept they've managed to spread across the Galaxy and I wish they'd extend it to some other species. He was drugged—so he couldn't let you know—"

"That Quantz doesn't intend to keep to his bargains? Quantz makes only two real promises: to discuss my proposals with Grever and to treat Lokh decently—and he sticks to both, after a fashion."

"He added one term... without it the others were to be nullified." He was a big man, fairly young and strong, and he kept kneading his hands.

"That important vote—has it to do with you?" Khreng asked quietly.

"Me? I'm nothing to him, I'm garbage, I'll end up in the sea I came out of. It's—"

"Ah, hah," Prandra half-sang. "Two beautiful cat skins, three crossbows—"

"What? How did you—"

"Quantz is not exactly impervious, Jens. When is he coming with the remote, or are we carried to the King?"

"He'll be here in an hour or two, and—"

"After they use the remote—"

"—while they're getting the shuttle and loading it down here—'

"You Solthrees have an English song called 'Three Jolly Huntsmen'?"

He turned his face away. "Don't, for God's sake! The man's mad!" He rubbed sweat off his forehead. "He wouldn't let anybody share the kill. Him with the crossbow, a couple of ESP outriders—all on mopeds." He stood up suddenly, yelling, "You're sitting there making jokes!"

Khreng said in his quiet voice with the deadly overtones, "I think Prandra is a bit lightheaded with weariness—and disgust. I expect Grever already makes an agreement with Quantz over this. That is the vote."

"He had to, once Quantz got the remote, or give up his part in the ship."

:*Clumsy of us,*: Khreng said to Prandra. :*Grever is to have the remote.*:

:*Quantz is smarter.*: "Why does Quantz not simply discard Grever now that he has what he wants?"

"He'd be back where he started, with a fight on his hands, and sometimes I wish they'd had the damn thing."

"Where are we to be hunted?" Prandra asked.

"They agreed to three hours," Jens said. "Any place you can get to on this filthy planet in that time."

"I see." Prandra roared, "Grever! Open the door and let us up!"

The door kicked open. Grever waited with the flame-gun. "Put away the gun, man, or you spoil our beautiful skins and get a nasty slap on the wrist from Quantz."

"Don't try to start us fighting."

"I spend all my time here trying to stop you."

The crew were sitting around the table, except for Harry, absent probably because he was a non-Imper. Ed was pale, Megan red around the eys; the rest looked merely bored.

She ignored them. "Do we Ungrukh get a choice of weapons?"

Grever laughed. "You prefer guns or knives?"

"We cannot use guns. Our knives are made for gutting fish. We want these." She bared her fangs to the guns. "You give us what every hunted animal is allowed?"

"What do you mean?"

"In our equipment, unless you have broken them, there are contact lenses and nose-filters. We want to run without masks."

"Give them that," Ed Grever said in a flat voice.

"It makes breathing harder," Khreng said.

"I believe we must risk that."

Grever muttered, "Quantz may guess something's—"

Prandra's ears stood up. "What of Quantz?"

"You're not supposed to know about the hunt," Ed Grever said.

"Simply get shot? That's not very sportsmanlike."

"I imagine Quantz will let you know when he feels like it," said Jens.

"What is the excuse for our being sent out?"

"You're to be heading out with packs for another establishment fifty kilometers north-east along the cliffs."

"Then we wear masks too. How much head start?"

Ed Grever looked at his interlocked hands. "About twenty minutes."

"Generous." She hissed with laughter, trotted to her old corner, and dropped to sleep at once.

They stared. "She's crazy," Ed Grever said.

"No," Khreng said. "She tires fast, and lately she does the work for both of us. She leaves me to finish what must be said. Grever, you are trying to be fair to us in your somewhat crooked way, and that is a mark in your favor."

"Thanks," said Grever.

"We are fed and sheltered, and so far you do not harm us. True, you do not thank us for saving your brother's life, but Ungrukh are not schooled in fine courtesies, and we accept your warning as thanks. Now Jens is sent to spy on you, but without success, and he works with you for some time, and does not betray you, as you know because he is always under your eyes. What do you do with him?"

"Leave him to Quantz."

"That seems sensible because Quantz's hands are already very bloody—but Grever, it's a dangerous precedent. Quantz has the remote, the forces, the arms, and likely in a while he has more and more of the ship, your stores, your powers. I think quite soon you are licking his backside—"

"Shut up, you damned animal!" Grever roared. "What are you trying to do?"

"I am trying to warn you that you have very little now, and in very little time, nothing. I am not subtle or diplomatic so my words sound ugly, but if I think there is nothing worth saving in you I leave you in the mess. Let Quantz have the prize ship! Keep what you have and defend it! If you give in to Quantz now by letting him have us and Jens—"

"If you think you can save your skins now it's too late—so shut up or I'll shut you up, Quantz or no!"

Khreng knew he could not help Jens, and there was little worth saving in this pack of jackals now. He gave up.

The hum of Quantz's shuttle rose in the west. Grever breathed deeply. "Wake the little lady up, and give these two what they want."

Ungrukh did not have hands, but their slightly elongated feline digits gave them almost plantigrade hind feet and forepaws with "fingers" that could bend enough to grasp a coarse object like a bar or branch. They were adept at using finger-stalls tipped with simple tools like screwdrivers and socket wrenches. As he slid the remote over his wrist and the stalls on his fingers under the careful eyes of Quantz's and Grever's communications men, Khreng wished he were not quite so adept.

Whatever he thought was not available to them; in their concentration they did not seem to notice: Prandra had built her gameboard before she saw any of Quantz's, and had placed Khreng in a black square. He did not feel the hair-thin sensor penetrating his skin, but the remote buzzed faintly. The watchers let out their breath.

The instrument did not have external buttons. No larger than a chronometer, it opened up in leaves like an ancient watch or locket. He touched a blade to a setscrew.

"Wait, it could be explosive," said Grever's man.

"Only enough to blow off his arm. I told Lokh if that happened we'd kill them all."

Khreng turned the screw and the lid sprang.

"Blue stud, hypnoformer." The remote beeped faintly.

"Good. That's the direction finder. Now, careful...."

"Black bar marked with theta, lock in controls."

Quantz stood arms folded, eyes hooded. "Why all the drama? Those things are standard."

"These cats aren't standard—and GalFed is tricky."

Jens squatted in the corner beside Prandra, who was sprawled carelessly, tail slowly whacking the floor. Her contacts and nose filters were not visible externally, but he had worn them often enough to know they were agonizing. The heavy-duty filters, no matter how carefully fitted, were hard enough on Solthrees: in the narrow convoluted nostrils of the Ungrukh they would be many times as painful—and the contacts were worse. They were not simple disks made to float on the cornea, but hemispheres impregnated with gel to protect the whole eyeball and useful for only a few hours in poisonous atmospheres where mask goggles cut down half the sight needed in certain search-and-rescue operations. Her lids had been painted with insoluble gel, but seemed already inflamed. He dug his face against his knees and wrapped his arms around his head.

Leaf after leaf opened on the remote, thin as membranes. On ship and shuttle the controls locked into place, computers tested and directed them. The leaves were translucent; their microcircuits were wired with filaments finer than spider silk. The ship, invisible, blinked and chattered to itself, and the last leaf turned.

"Bay emergency latch controls." Communications ticked with his tongue.

Grever asked, "That's all?"

"The lot."

Quantz smiled, grabbed the remote from Khreng's wrist, slammed it on the desk and smashed it with his gun-butt.

And turned to the Ungrukh with his arms spread, embracing the universe. "Now you are free, my friends! The whole planet is yours!"

Prandra said, "Quantz, it is not the freedom of Yirl we request but a passage on your ship to the first refueling station."

The man with the puckered mouth thumbed the rope tucked in his belt and Quantz's voice hardened. "We need the weight for our crops on all the ships. You've been told you'll find an encampment fifty kilometers northeast. You must realize terms get modified in discussion. Do you realize?" He placed a foot on Khreng's tail and jabbed his haunch with the toe of the other boot. "You are lucky to have what we're willing to give you. You understand?"

Khreng did not move by so much as a tremor.

Though there was nothing to be done, Jens could not help himself and jumped up. Guns rose on him, and Prandra tapped the backs of his legs with her tail: *down*.

"You do understand?" Quantz asked again.

"We understand. Of course," said Prandra.

Khreng added, "And of course we wish to thank you for sparing us, and remind you that we do not harm *you* in any way." Blunt-mouthed Khreng was the chosen among Ungrukh for the expression of irony. He was a master of ambiguity. He and Prandra put on packs and masks, taking the time they needed to do it with care; the lock was opened for them. They did not look at anyone, not Jens, or Megan, or the Grevers, not Quantz or Puckerface. They passed through the locks and vanished from the minds of men.

Prandra's shield was down around them both.

"Twenty minutes: one kilometer on this terrain. You still have that damned cube?"

"I know what is in it. I leave it." They headed northeast, racing. No use letting Quantz know that Grever had given him away.

"Get rid of the packs," Khreng said. He pulled his mask off. "We need to lose the weight. Five minutes are gone."

"How do you know?"

"Jens gives me his chronometer."

"It takes too much time to bury them."

"Drop them in the sea. Open them first, so they sink. We don't need the food." The dark awkward shapes fell into the vicious bite of the waters. Even under her thick ointment coating Prandra felt the sting of spray. Two or three plaak squawked from crevices, a few Yirln hung in the water line.

"Still east? I'm sure Quantz stakes the terrain."

"Separate," said Khreng. "You north. Quantz is counting on the matched pair."

"And you are trying to save me!" Prandra growled.

"You stupid woman, we have only eleven minutes!"

Prandra, who had outwitted a Qumedni, killed a tiger harboring an insane Lyhhrt, gone into Quantz's own lions' den, was shot with a jolt of pure panic deadly as the bolt of a crossbow. The filters and lenses were driving her wild, the sea water stung with a thousand arrows, the loneliness—for she thought of Khreng and herself as one, always—the foul land and the unremitting cruelty and stupidity of its inhabitants—she began to turn and turn madly, like a dog chasing its tail—

"Stop it! Stop!" Khreng roared. Her nostrils flared, she was slavering.

circle   circircle   circle

"What's that?" Khreng whispered.

She had stopped. She was a statue. An unearthly whisper answered:

cir   circle   cir   cle

"Lokh is awake."

"No, that's not Lokh," said Prandra.

Khreng glanced at the chronometer and said nothing. He was grateful to have Prandra at least halfway back to her own senses. "I know," said Prandra. "We give this one minute. You measure."

Plaak! Plaak!   Plaplaak!

They looked out over the cliff where three or four plaak were circling...

and dropping eggs on the backs of the Yirln!

"Trap?" Khreng asked.

"I hope not." :*Where circle?*:

Northern sky. Setting sun.

"Yirln minds, I don't know where, saying circle north and around to west...."

"The men come back with the ship that way and see us."

"If we hurry, we miss them. *Now* separate."

They heard the distant growl of the mopeds. "Five minutes to go. Even here he cheats."

Prandra ran northeast, Khreng northwest; they changed and crossed tracks, changed and crossed again. Their track made a chain bracelet arcing northwest.

Once Prandra stopped for five seconds behind a hillock; she could not breathe by mouth and her nose was running. The roar of a moped burst out of nowhere and a *thang!* sounded in an ash heap on the other side of the hill. The machine circled furiously once around her: Quantz was on it, hooded and masked, jowls darkly flushed and glistening, crossbow in hands, aiming.

Prandra stood. The breath bubbled in her nose. Quantz's gauntleted hands raised the bow, she could see the silver arabesques set into its black stock, but his thumb did not press the button that turned the windlass, nor did his other hand pluck a fresh bolt from the quiver in his belt. He laughed and skimmed away. Playing.

The noise rose again, and Prandra came forward, ready to crash head-on and spoil the game once and for all. But this was only one of the ESP outriders come to retrieve the expensive bolt. Mediaeval weaponry was in short supply on Yirl, and he was armed with a flame-gun. The machine was foot-controlled, and the weapon was aimed, but he would not spoil Quantz's game.

As he slowed, Prandra waited until he was within ten seconds of her, then grabbed one end of the brass shaft as a dog would a bone, and yanked it to the ground; she leaped forward and reared with claws out, roaring through her teeth.

Prandra had never had the opportunity of jumping on a water buffalo twice her size and crunching its neck precisely, but she had the ability. As the outrider tried frantically to brake, she slipped aside and sent the fledged end of the bolt cracking across his mask filter. The moped skidded and went over with its rider, the gun flew out of his hands and arced through the air. Another leap brought Prandra between gun and rider. She stood and waited, still gnawing the bolt.

The man pulled himself out from under the machine, discovered that he could still stand, but not breathe very well. He stared at her for a moment, gasping, righted the moped and raced away; his shoulders jerked with coughing.

Prandra scanned for Quantz: he was nearly half a kilometer away on Khreng's track; now he turned. She jammed the bolt's steel point into the bared lava near the top of the hillock, grabbed the gun and hammered it in with three blows flat to the surface as if it were a nail, and smashed the fuel tank on the lava peak. Then she ran.

Something like a mental snort from Khreng. : *You are not supposed to be good at judging time*.:

:*I am learning.*: With her forelimb she swabbed the runny nose she had forgotten. :*On a world like Yirl the man who carries spare fuel, power cells, and extra bolts for ancient crossbows is a fool for not bringing another mask.*:

:*The course the Yirln plot for us brings us right back to the Station. We are perhaps fools.*:

:*We never intend to leave it. Why complain?*:

'*It's that ugly face of Quantz I must see on the way.*:

Their paths crossed again and separated. :*Outrider One back to Station in disgrace, replaced by—damnation!—Puckermouth coming up with rifle and handgun.*:

:*Good.*: said Khreng. :*Now we get roped like farm animals before shooting.*:

:*Look out, Khreng! Quantz is on your tail!*:

:*He already treads on my—*: He turned, expecting to see Quantz coming up behind at a distance. But Prandra was exactly correct. A wind had risen, and under its noise Quantz had cut down his motor; his grinning face and primed bow were coming up at leisure just twenty meters from Khreng's tail. Puckermouth was a very competent shielder.

Khreng stopped for an instant in which Prandra flashed the answer to the unasked question. :*Outrider Two stopped one quarter km southeast with grit in foot-control.*:

There was no shelter. The land was flat, the sky flat, the wind blew tiny eddies of ash-dust.

Even with the racing wind Quantz could have killed from the distance of a quarter-kilometer. If he were a normal hunter, for food, pride, thrill. If he had been worried about spoiling the skin he could have hit an eye from half that length. But, as in work he delegated authority only when he must, in play he needed contact with the victim's fear and desperation. So, playing, he laughed.

Khreng—of a hunter's tribe whose food animals were nearly extinct and who hunted only the packs of marauders raiding for catches of sickly fish and valuable females—had learned to understand this kind. He bounded to one side, did two reverse summersaults, and leaped on Quantz's back. His jaw shoved down the head, his arms went round the bull neck, his legs and tail round the waist and thighs, he clasped his hunter like a lover.

Quantz gurgled and swerved wildly on a serpentine course. Khreng hugged fiercely. The gauntleted hands could not budge one claw. Finally the moped, overburdened, lurched violently on one of its swerves and went over, as the outrider's had done. Khreng jumped off before it hit. Quantz, like a beetle on its back, struggled wildly under the machine.

:*Outrider coming up*,: said Prandra. :*Get out, I am shielding*.:

He drove himself and met her northeast in five minutes.

The ground rose in ripples of hillocks. They crouched among them. "The Station is south," he said. "You can see it round the hill."

"I know. Wyaerl says, head for the cliff."

"Our friends are driving us to suicide. The shuttle comes over in a few minutes."

"Not with that thunderhead in the west. It makes a bad storm, the pilot is waiting for it to pass. Wyaerl asks trust, and on Solthree he does much for us."

Khreng grunted. "What other choice is there?"

They ran south for the station. In the east, Quantz and his riders were circling furiously; in the north, the shuttle's crew were waiting for the storm to pass. West, men were loading Quantz's crops on his shuttle to meet the GalFed ship and transfer them by EVA because they could not dock with it. The storm cloud was diving over their heads to unload itself. At the Station Grever was at work in his own shuttle. There was one clear lane due south: no one was about on the eastern side of the Station. For the moment.

Sore and exhausted, the Ungrukh ran. When they were within a few meters of the Station the storm broke; the cloud settled toward the ground and dropped its waters in stinging sheets. Khreng and Prandra floundered in mud, shivering and coughing, and flattened themselves by the wall, invisible under the cloud.

Crews stopped work and groped their way to the building.

Khreng and Prandra dashed upstairs to the roof and huddled on the lee side of the radar's base. Their eyes and noses burned; their throats were raw. Raindrops bounced back at them, stinging.

The rain beat and beat. The cloud blackened, the ashy ground turned lighter under it, pocking into waves and ripples, foaming. On the roof a flock of plaak landed in puddles and flapped their leathery wings, the only creatures enjoying that pitiless attack.

To Prandra, it seemed spiteful, the utter withdrawal of the god Firemaster. The feeling was not unfamiliar, she knew it was irrational; it beat on her with the water and there was no shelter from it. *Give up.* Faintest shred of thought. The plaak danced in the puddles, their little eyes glittered, picking light from nowhere.

Voices sang: *to the to cliff iff cliff*

"I am wrong," she whispered. "it *is* a trick."

"Maybe," Khreng said. "Get on." He nudged her. She did not move. "Back there you are a match for ten of Quantz and telling me to trust Wyaerl. Now you are a lump."

They crouched on the steaming slathering roof of the world, wrapped in cloud, convulsed in burning alien air and water. "I am finished. I am a fool to let us come here. Give up."

"Next time we give up, I promise you," said Khreng. He gave her one almighty heave that sent her skittering and tumbling across the roof and over the edge.

She landed on four feet in the mud and raised her head and howled with all of the rage of the storm—so that the very wind snarled in her teeth—that he was a faithless, betraying, treacherous dog-son of a foul mother and improbable father to be spitted roasting and spinning in the Blue Pit until—

He dropped beside her, the fires of the Pit in his eyes.

"To the cliff, woman!" he roared.

The storm whipped away as swiftly as it had come with the snap of a last whirlwind, like the sting in a scorpion's tail. The sky lightened, the Station's air lock hummed.

They ran toward the cliff, not knowing why. It was the end of the world, and the storm still raged in its basin. A shot skimmed Khreng's ear. The waters were a vision of hell with their slamming breakers; they flattened in terror at the edge under the fusillade.

And the voices rang again:

> *fallfallfaFALL fall*
> *FALL fa fall   fall fallall*
> *fall fall FALL FALL! FALL! FALL!*

They looked downward, for the one instant they dared pause, and saw a vision far more strange than the waters or the storm.

The sheer face of the cliff just below was lined with a solid carpet of Yirln fifteen meters broad. It had not occurred to Prandra that most Yirln might not be colored in variations of Yirl's sky-blue, but here there were not only much lighter and darker blues, but Jade-green, ivory, coral, pearl, grey, mauve, pale yellow, aquamarine. They gleamed like semi-precious jewels in the whitened sky.

FALL!

Men shouted, guns cracked behind them; the Ungrukh let themselves fall.

As they slid down the ripple of bodies, the carpet detached itself from the cliffside and curved over them like a dome, so that they hit the waters in a bubble of air, for the Yirln had joined themselves together with their own adhesive for the purpose. Free-swimmers kicked forward to pull and press at the structure, hauling it downward, and further downward while Khreng and Prandra bobbed like corks in their pool, with both water and air nearly smothering them, but still alive.

Both fought off the panic created by water forcing itself into nose and mouth; when they were convinced of drowning from the inevitable leakage of air in their dome of bodies, they found themselves thrust into a rock fissure where an uprush of tidal waters washed them into a maze of angled stone and solidified lava. Here they floundered, sputtering until the tide withdrew and left them in a V-shaped gutter under a vault only slightly larger than their living dome had been. Immediately water came at them from ahead. This was of an entirely different chemical compositon than the sea, hot and sulfurous. In comparison it was fresh, to them, and they stood in it neck deep and snorted the sea from nose and throat. The place steamed from the meeting of waters.

Yellow and orange lights from the waterway beyond lit up the place like dim fires. The lights approached, upheld on

standards by a dark shape below the surface of the pool. "Oof!"
said Prandra. "That is an animal." It was a harmless eater of
water-weeds, but it would crush any object in its way.

: *Here.*:

She realized that there was a shelf to her left: Wyaerl and a
dark jade companion were lying on it. She and Khreng climbed
up beside them; they had small lanterns in their tentacles and air
and water tanks on their backs because the differing water and
atmosphere here were inimical to them.

"Thank you for your help," Prandra said. "We do not know
how to thank you enough."

: *You might thank your friend Jens,*: said Wyaerl. : *This place
was discovered by the exploration of GalFed before he was sent
to find what happened to the Observer. We did not trust him
when he came down with his equipment and showed us how it
might be used in case of an emergency until Lokh told us just a
little while ago that he was from GalFed.*:

"It is a pity he cannot use it himself," Khreng said. "I think it
is the chimney of an extinct volcano. We have many such on
Ungruwarkh and they are also good hiding places, but
dangerous if the volcano is not extinct. . . ." He ended on a yawn.
The vault was dark and damp; the steam eddied in the clashes of
hot and cold air, but for Khreng and Prandra then it was the
most comfortable place on Yirl, and they found their eyes
closing and their bodies slumping. . . .

It was two hours later by the chronometer when they woke;
the sun would be on the horizon. The Yirln had been waiting
patiently in the same positions.

Prandra pulled herself up stiffly. "How does all this come
about? It is surely a mysterious and complicated plan."

: *I am Aarl,*: said the jade Yirli. : *I caught the message from
Lokh it is a wonder he was able to make it clear to me and I hope
I can explain it as logically—*:

Khreng said, "Except for Lokh, you people are the most
logical—and rational—" a dart of sarcasm in Prandra's
direction "persons on this world."

: *—but before we lost all trace of him I hope he is safe he told
us he suspected a connection and an intention in the mind of the
hunting one between a certain dangerous weapon and the red*

strange one-and-one who are you we cannot tell color nor what is red but he said the plaak would know and he put it in the heads of one plaak and all the other ones that if they saw the red ones running in the open away from the Station followed by Solthrees~or machines the plaak would drop their eggs on us ones and if we found eggs raining from the sky we were to direct you to this hiding place and he told us all this in an instant because of the danger in trying to reach you and we were also afraid so perhaps you did not understand us ones very well.:

"That is only because you don't use the word *jump*," said Prandra.

:*We don't need such a word.*:

"You do very well without it," Khreng said. "Lokh is safe for the while. I wonder if *that* is a plan he patches together in his cell?" He looked about. "Is there another exit here? I don't think we have the strength to go by sea again."

:*Both parent crater and siblings of this volcano are extinct for as long as we have known the world but there is an opening to this cone where storms washed out part of the plug it would have been easier for you to come down that way but also easier for others to follow. Yirl is up there now on guard for you.*:

Khreng jumped up. "Damnation, man, get him down! When he can't see anything up there he's in terrible danger."

Wyaerl said, a bit stiffly, :*You high-temperature beings much more than we humble ones give off waves of heat and chemical components to which we ones are extremely sensitive. If anyone comes Yirl will tap a signal and we will sense it.*:

Prandra laughed shortly, "You ones are brave to the point of being foolhardy, like us high-tempered ones. Those who want us dead can kill from great distances." :*Yirl, come down at once. It is too risky up there.*:

:*Only because you have ordered it, Prandra-she.*:

"And you claim there is no one in this place but enemies!" Khreng said.

"I am getting old for my years, whatever they are."

Wyaerl said, :*If it is dangerous for Yirl up there it is much more so for you and you must stay here we will find a way to bring you food.*:

"No more risks, Wyaerl! If necessary we eat the monster of

the deeps, that one with lights—but we have work still to do, and Jens of GalFed is without a friend."

"I think we must share the water with that monster upstream to get out of here," said Khreng.

:*No the stream comes from below,*: said Wyaerl. :*It forced the opening undersea during the eruption and the cone opens up here just beyond this shelf and leads up to a cleft in a lava hill in a location I understand but cannot express.*:

"Just beyond the northwest corner of the Station." Prandra snorted. "Not so very—Yirl is gone!"

"What do you mean?"

"I'm not sure...." She cast about wildly for a moment, then leaped off the end of the shelf and landed in the darkness of the opening above the steaming water. Khreng followed. The cone was nearly as spacious as the cave; storms had washed down bits of ash and gravel to line the bottom, but the cylindrical wall reamed straight upward fifty meters to a dim crescent of light.

The walls were seamed and rugged; they could be climbed. But before the Ungrukh could lift a limb on them, there was a great clattering from above as of objects falling. Khreng and Prandra shrank back toward the cavern opening as the noise grew in unholy echoes and the fearful orange lamps of the pit creatures rose in inquiry behind them casting their shadows hugely on the crater wall.

Before the objects landed Prandra felt the jet of terror and surmise that told her how others might have learned of the hiding place. The clattering things drove into the soil heap at last: they might have killed both her and Khreng if they hit; what horrified her was to find Yirl's air and water bottles, their black and silver scarified by the fall.

The Ungrukh climbed, scrabbling, panting. Prandra expected a shot: it came. One fireball dropped, almost lazily, scattering sparks as it ricocheted off the wall in its jagged path; it was a teaser, they ducked it easily. It burned itself out beside the bottles.

:*Come down!*: There was something painful and forlorn in the shadings of Wyaerl's thought-call. :*We will help you!*:

She snarled. :*Get out of there! That place is not safe for you any more and we cannot live in the sea!*:

"Death is upstairs," said Khreng, but he did not stop climbing.

There was no one in the crevice under the hill, no one in sight through the opening, no sign of Yirl. Nothing but a few meters of scree and a sliver of sky dully glowing with sunset.

A moment's silence.

"Come on out, Ungrukh," Quantz roared. "You have nowhere to go!"

Prandra said in a voice of pure red plush, "Why don't you come in, Quantz?"

Quantz laughed. "We have something for you." A pale heavy thing dropped three or four meters away from the entrance, and Prandra winced with its pain.

Yirl had been shot in the side and, out in the air, was losing his pale blood rapidly; his water-receptor was puckered closed. Yirln lived long healthy lives and knew nothing of medicine. They had no defence against such predation. No one in the Galaxy could have saved this one, and if Prandra could have taken him down the cone for his water supply, he would be dead before he reached bottom.

Prandra thought all of these thoughts and went outside into the light without looking at Quantz or his men or their guns. "Come, Yirl, we take you down." She touched him with the harsh tip of her tongue. He quivered once and was still; there was nothing in his mind but pain. His skin had been opaline blue, and was darkening in the evening rising from the east.

"We cannot do that," Khreng said quietly.

"She *is* crazy." Prandra looked up and saw Puckermouth, aiming his rifle, the ends of his scars pointing lividly from either side of his mask. Perhaps he was right, but it was the same madness that had made Khreng kick her off the roof and drive her toward the blasting sea.

Quantz had men with him, perhaps ten. There was no hate or anger in them; they were mildly amused. Between their bodies, in the dulling cloudlight of the west she could glimpse the GalFed shuttle, white with the gold ringed-planet symbol and registration numbers. It stood on a flat expanse north of the Station, meant for light craft to land on; there was no pavement, for the ground was too shifting to take it, but it was tramped down now and darkened from use. Crew were loading the boat; one moved away and stood staring at them: Grever. There was a bruise down one side of his face. The battling would have started already.

Prandra looked down at Yirl again, and up at Quantz with his flame-gun. She growled wordlessly.

The men stepped back. Quantz grinned. He had given up on skins and wanted suffering. The gun rose. The game was over.

Khreng and Prandra separated abruptly and skittered around like red lightning between him and his men. Any of them could have shot, but they knew better than to interfere with Quantz and his lust.

Quantz swivelled, yelling, "Get away from them, you sonsofbitches!" They divided gratefully; Khreng and Prandra came together, then, scuffling, nearly clawing in their efforts to shield each other.

Quantz began to sweat with rage; there was no way to satisfy himself killing creatures so intent on their protective fury with each other they had become a writhing, muddy mass without another thought between their heads. He gave up trying; the gun steadied.

"Quantz!" Grever ran forward. "Save one of them at least, take it with us! You don't know how that ship—"

"I know about the ship. All I need."

Grever did not get within three meters of Quantz. One of the men shoved him away with a gun butt to the belly and he fell. The Ungrukh had stopped, huddled, still.

And Yirl leaped. He was insensible, but a spasm of death or some unconscious urge to defend made him rise and spring a few centimeters off the ground. Quantz caught the movement from the corner of his eye, swung, and shot a bolt of flame. It shrieked, blazing down Yirl's flesh and he died as he fell.

Prandra took the pain in the center of her skull, a blast of cold fire. She pulled away from Khreng, snorted to clear her nose, and drew breath. Several of the ESPs bent over in nausea for a moment.

:*What a lot of pain they must know with that man.*:
:*Why not?*: said Khreng. :*He is the mad one.*:

They drew back slowly. Quantz, laughing, raised the gun for

the last time. "Still trying to escape?"

Prandra said softly, "I think we give up on you, Quantz."
Before the trigger finger began tightening, she had taken Yirl's
pain and the torture of Puckermouth and all of those casual or
thoughtful brutalities, and she gave them to Quantz between the
eyes. Her anger had so sharpened and whitened that her own
spirit cooled and turned still. She felt Lokh stirring in her mind
and plucked at the knotted thread of his ethos to draw power.
Puckermouth fell to his knees; another ESP fainted. Quantz
stood rigid, his fist closed on the massive cocked trigger.

Prandra, with the scorch of Yirl's death in her tortured
nostrils, very nearly admired him again. Khreng growled, and
she recalled Tiger, rearing under the Solthree moon, whose
beauty had very nearly killed Khreng with admiration. She drew
from wherever power came and smashed the brittle walls of
Quantz's mind to free the red beasts of fear and rage among the
synapses. His knees bent slightly, he grunted, blood ran down
his chin under the mask from bitten tongue and lips; his fingers
did not loosen. Light dimmed, men turned away from tasks,
drew closer.

To be a Lyhhrt or a Khagodi, to be a Qumedni with princely
powers. Ah....

YOU ANIMALS, says Qumedon.

"—those animals!" howls Metaxa of Solthree.

"—you bloody beast," Grever snarls.

*Cool thought: on Solthree, brain in a dark globe sustained by
nutrient pump, body in gold-woven sari long whispered to ash,
two-hundred-and-twenty-five-year-old instructor ESP first-
class Sita Chatterjee: :Before we are through you will teach
me....:*

Men still. Quantz on knees. Hands down resting on gun. One
rises rips mask. Mouth open. Scream. Tusks thrust from jaw.
Scream into bellow. Nose thickening, snout. Hand frozen in
mid-air, nails grow twisting and join to hoof-cleats turning
against himself savage the cloth encasing him, he is naked,
springing with hair, horns burst from forehead coiling like a

ram's, head tangles shaggy hair and fur darkens, brindling. His very eyes, great and yellow, are screaming, the bellow goes on and on, he tries and tries to stop, biting again the thick papillated tongue, blood clots in the hair on his jaw. He lashes his burr-clumped tail, trips on it and rolls as he crawls back and back among the cold-frames, smashes panes with his hooves and shoves his snout into the seed. He gobbles, bellows, gobbles. His mind screams in horror, and Prandra suffers and cannot stop. Men and women are running, some toward the cliff's edge. Puckermouth, until now a statue on his knees, jumps up with a shriek, claws the rope from his waist and whips it about his head in a lariat, whirls it about the neck of the beast and yanks at it, whooping, shrieking, capering. Grever gapes and whimpers.

"Stop," said Khreng. *"Stop!"* he roared.

STOP. That was Lokh.

Prandra's legs collapsed. She slumped.

Quantz stared at her, mad-eyed, human as he had been, clothed as he had been, mask askew, blood crusted on his lips and on the hands gripping the glass-shattered frames. Puckerface still howled and jumped; someone tore the rope from his hands, freed Quantz's neck, pulled him up. Men and women blank-eyed, Grever's and Quantz's, guns dangling from slack hands. Quantz twitched and snivelled, others held him. Turned their eyes from Prandra, as if she did not exist, dared not let their minds rest on her.

But for Khreng's hand on her head she was alone. She, who had admitted not having enough imagination to impress an ESP examining committee, unable to hypnotize minds en masse against their will, had done it. To Quantz's men, to Grever's Impers, to Khreng. Beyond the turmoil of their minds, the frantic urges to repress, she found the emptiness. Lokh had not helped. Chatterjee was parsecs distant, perhaps by now dead.

She had done it alone. She had no one to thank and no one to blame.

Several of Quantz's men dragged him aboard the shuttle, determined to carry out the plan as if it had not been interrupted; they did not look at her or ask what would become of Quantz in his state. She did not know. Someone kicked Puckermouth away from the ladder and he fell in the scree, rolling and howling, ignored, until others pulled him into the unloaded landcar and headed west. Megan was clinging to Grever, pleading.

"Grever," Prandra said, "let the ship go."

Grever pushed Megan away. "Shut up, both of you! You, you stupid bitch, I'm tired of your blubbering! And you! I'm not waiting around until you turn me into one of *him!* I like *him* the way he is; all right, you've handed him to me on a platter and he's paying for everything he tried to do to me! I'm not letting him out of my sight for anything, and without him his bunch is going to fall apart the way he did. I have all I want, all I ever wanted, and that doesn't include this dog here. That bloody little mind of yours can't take me apart so easy and I don't play games. I don't care how you get off here, but if I find you when I come back you're dead."

Prandra said very quietly, almost sadly, "Grever, first tell me where Jens is, and then have your men drop Yirl's body into the sea. Or else you get a little piece of my mind—and you only need a little."

Grever pumped up his defiance. "He's in the Station. *I* didn't do anything to him."

Darkness had settled. Megan stood, head bowed, arms clenched about herself. Hood dropped back, hair blowing, the white nape of her neck so vulnerable she might never have laughed, cursed, fought, and labored in fierce loyalty to such a useless man. She, Khreng, Prandra were alone on the plain. Harry, the demo man, crouched against the radar dish's base, eyes away from them, turned toward the north where the shuttle had disappeared.

Prandra nudged Megan's elbow, very gently. "Come, woman, we need you to bring in that food of ours they dumped out of the shuttle. And I think Jens...."

Jens was on the floor, hands and feet trussed behind him, mouth gagged, teeth missing, face bruised black and red. His eyes, barely open, were full of shame.

Megan cut the gag, and then the wire. "They made me tell," he whispered.

"I know," said Prandra. "Forgive yourself. Are you badly hurt?"

"Think I'm all here." He spat. "Except for the teeth." He tried to smile. "Mostly implants anyway. Bad teeth run in the family. What happened?" Prandra dropped to the floor. He rubbed his wrists and ankles. "Same old baling wire." He looked at Prandra and did not ask again.

Khreng told him.

"Huh. He enjoyed doing all *this*. Wish I'd seen—no, no, I'm glad I didn't." He tried to rise on his cramped legs and fell. Khreng pulled him up. "Who else is here beside her?" Megan, sitting at the desk, had buried her head in her arms.

"Harry. He is harmless, I think."

"Yeah. Maybe we better warn him off. We've got the radio now. And a few guns, in case anybody else comes round." He sighed, rubbing his wrists, spat another gout of blood on the dirty floor, and staggered into the radio room. When he came out a few minutes later the grin looked weird in his gap teeth. "We'll have a fast cruiser here in three days, be back on Dirhob One in six. Too bad about your—"

Khreng was laughing. "Just in time to meet our ship."

"What—" His teeth gaped even wider.

Khreng passed him on the way to the radio room. "Pull the old woman's ear for me and tell her one death is a great tragedy but better than average for the places we go. Then come help me with this radio. It looks old and cranky."

"What for?"

"Jens, I am tired. Help me if you like, or let me work." He clawed the filters from his nostrils and flung them in the disposal without paying attention to the threads of blood running from his nose. "This goes on the ear, not so? and the call signals...."

KHRENG-PRANDRA TO GALFED SURVEYOR 668X327, CODE VOCABLE—he picked up the microphone, "Ungruwarkh," giving it all the resonance of native pronunciation ranging from cat's meow to tiger's roar,—MOD 885 CONFIRM IDENTIFICATION.

CONFIRMED. RELEASE.

GOOD.

STATE REQUEST KHRENG-PRANDRA.

CONFIRM COCKPIT SEALED.

CONFIRMED.

RESTATE LOCKING PROCEDURES AS PREREQUESTED AND CON
FIRMED BY REMOTE.

LOCKING PROCEDURES RECEIVED BY REMOTE: BAR-THETA,
BLUE, GIMMEL, INTEGRAL, SIGMA . . .

CONFIRM CHAMBER SUPPLIES.

AS REQUESTED LIST IS—

DON'T BOTHER. I'M SICK OF THIS STUPID CONVERSATION. MY
EYES ARE ON FIRE AND—WAIT. ONE MORE. CONFIRM DESTINATION.

DIRHOB ONE. YOU WISH TO CHANGE?

NO, YOU IDIOT MACHINE! RECORD THE FOLLOWING VOCAL
MESSAGE AND BROADCAST THROUGHOUT SHIP AFTER BAY DOORS
and ALL COMPARTMENTS ARE SECURE.

He picked up the mike once more. "Quantz, Grevers, and
assorted beings. You are bound for Dirhob One GalFed Center
landing field where you are arrested for stealing this ship and
carrying contraband. The controls are locked and the cockpit is
sealed as well as the compartments you find yourselves in. I
advise calm because any weapon fired causes release of
extinguisher foam which lets you breathe but is damned
uncomfortable. You get explanations on landing because I am
tired of talking. If you are locked in a compartment without
provision there are stasis pills suitable to blood hemoglobin in
wall compartments. Red, iron; blue, copper; white, vanadium;
black, manganese. According to information this covers all
necessary. If not, regrets. Otherwise, sweet dreams." He signed
off. "Jens, *can* you stop gaping and wash your hands so you get
these filthy lenses out of my eyes before I go blind?"

"There is no trick to the remote. It is only a new thing GalFed
tries on ignoramuses like us."

"Never mind the humility business." Jens dropped the lenses
he had taken from Prandra's eyes into the disposal with the
others and wiped his hands on his coverall. "Let me guess. They
left the controls standard but switched around the components."

"Correct. Now it becomes standard GalFed issue. Individual

combination for each remote. Memorize and burn instructions. Deep hypnosis, locked in when hypnoform in operation, released when code vocable confirmed by ship's computer. And unavailable without brain damage, even to ESPs like Lokh. They choose me because Prandra is harder to hypnotize—and my brain is less valuable." He said this without malice.

Prandra had picked herself up and was trying to persuade Megan to eat and rest, but she would only sit with her hands covering her face. Jens studied them a moment and said, "let me try." He turned back for one more question. "It was all planned, wasn't it? You wanted them to have the remote."

"The purpose is to bring some of the worst offenders together and shunt them off with the evidence. That gives GalFed a big fat foot on this world. Plaak get seed. Yirln get eggs. We are not very neat about it, but it works."

It seemed reasonable that Jens and Megan should find themselves comforting each other in bed, two not very beautiful people, one temporarily rather repulsive. She had washed and bandaged him; he had treated her with a gentleness she was not quite sure how to respond to.

"She goes back to Grever when he gets out of jail," Prandra said cynically. They were crouched in their old corner, eating food from the freshly opened packs.

"Maybe not," Khreng said. "You seem content to stay with a gentle soul like me."

"Hah. At least Grever is bound to lose some of that grit in his teeth."

In the following days they would bring Lokh to the Station, watch the bizarre burial ceremony of Yirl, endure the thanks of the Yirln, tempered as it was with grief. Now. . . .

"Next stop is home," Prandra whispered. She and Khreng looked at each other and for the first time she noticed that the white V centering the black chevron of his forehead had filled with pink-white hair to the depth of a centimeter. His fur's color was turning with age. *Mother, we are nearly grown now. . . .* "I wonder if I am still fertile?"

"Why not find out?"

"On the ship." She cocked her head. "In there, those two are doing all that is necessary for now."

Khreng snorted and dug into the food again.

The cube was under Prandra's hand. She touched the stud and the cubs galloped over the plains of red lava. *Mother, Father....*

4

A JUDGMENT OF DRAGONS

UNGRUWARKH, LISTED IN GALACTIC CATALOGUE
as Feldfar 553, Anax II, had no cities, industries, crops, tourist
attractions, or exotic flora. No great mountains or marvelous
views. It had slight incline and few seasonal changes. Separated
from Anax I by a wide asteroid belt, it was near enough to its sun
to sustain life, barely. The air was thin and dusty, and the
temperature dropped sharply beyond the equator. Many
watersheds decanted water from the broad icecaps, and shores
were almost tideless except in the tropic zone where three small
moons pulled the waters in and out of the sands. The seas were
mainly shallow; archipelagoes rose from them spiralling from
pole to pole.

Across the broadest archipelago, some twenty degrees north
of the equator, a fault line had pushed up a long range of
volcanoes; over millennia its effluents had covered thousands of
square kilometers with red lava plains relieved only by
occasional low clusters of hills or broken hummocks. Once huge
pits of fire, the volcanoes had through ages developed so many
daughter cones that, though they were in almost constant
activity, they did little more than spit and dribble. Yet, at times,
the god Firemaster magnificently inflamed a dull pink sky with
their fury.

Ungruwarkh had no archaeology, little paleontology, and no
recorded history. It did have a large and busy Galactic
Federation Observer Station built solidly into the lava plain
fifteen kilometers south of the mountain range and well out of
the way of volcanic bombs. A small part of the station was
occupied by offices, quarters and infirmary; the rest housed food
stores, skimmers, transports and dredgers.

*   *   *

The Sector Co-ordinator had spent what should have been his vacation by coming out with the two members of the new Observer team to wait for a ship soon due on this world. All were Solthrees, the Co-ordinator an ESP class-two like the woman; the other man an Impervious. They were awkward with each other. The Co-ordinator did not like to remind them that he had no jurisdiction in their sector and was not their superior; he tried to keep out of their way.

But, two days before the ship's arrival, twitching with restlessness begotten by inactivity, he wandered into the infirmary to watch Orbin at work. The Impervious was a competent man with clearly defined tasks: he dealt food supplies and gave medical attention when requested to all comers among the world's million and a quarter inhabitants: big red cats, leopard-sized and -shaped; nearly half, mostly female, were telepathic. Although the adults weighed a hundred kilos or more, and their teeth and fangs were very sharp, he was not at all afraid of them. They arrived in tribes, carefully scheduled to avoid conflict. With the help of a fleet of machines, he doled out rations of specially prepared catfood from an enormous stockpile of crates. Smaller robots helped the cats build and load rafts made from the crates, and they poled their way southward among the archipelagoes, towing nets full of live fish bred to resist the parasites which had been plaguing both fish and eaters for thousands of years. For overland travellers the fish were packed in polar ice, of which there was plenty on Ungruwarkh, and the rafts set on wheels and dragged by harnessed Ungrukh, who swore and snarled on the way but generally reached home safe and content. Even the savage Hills raiders had submitted to these peaceful measures and came on schedule for their shares. They did not care to starve either. No one thanked the suppliers. GalFed had plenty of use for half a million telepaths, and one day payment would fall due.

Medical attention was another matter. Not even GalFed could afford the care needed by such a population; hopeless diseases were accepted with resignation. Ungrukh, with the aid of their ESPs, were clever enough to learn why they hurt; they had discovered a few medicinal herbs in their sparse vegetation and came to the Station when cure was possible and they could not help themselves.

The Co-ordinator paused in the doorway of the infirmary, arms folded, ankles crossed. "Do you mind if I watch a bit? I always like to see a good pair of hands at work."

Orbin smiled fainlty. "If you can bear what you see."

"I've seen a fair amount."

"I should imagine so."

The Co-ordinator wondered why, though he respected Orbin, he did not like the man. They were strikingly similar in looks; the doctor was about fifteen years younger; both tall, tapering from broad shoulders, oval-faced with thinning pale hair and blue eyes. Perhaps because the woman, Malvina, preferred Orbin: he did not seem to be interested in her.

The first patient was a yowling cub brought in on the back of its mother and firmly held there by her long prehensile tail. She was a magnificent woman, deep crimson, strongly marked by the black V, centered with a white line, that began at her forehead and branched down along either flank. But she was diffident.

"Thorn," she said haltingly in *lingua*.

The Co-ordinator, perched on a stool in the corner, said, "Left rear paw, between second and third digit."

"Thank you," said Orbin. "I have learned some Ungru'akh."

The Co-ordinator flushed. "I didn't mean to interfere."

"Not at all," said Orbin coolly. He laid out forceps and antibiotic needles, plucked up the cub with no regard for its yowls, flattened it on the table with the length of a muscular forearm, swabbed, probed, withdrew the long wicked object, flicked it into the disposal, swabbed again. plunged a needle into the rump of the still screeching cub, and replaced it on its mother's back. She had been absolutely still. She left without a word.

Orbin turned to the keyboard and punched in a record of condition and treatment. "Next on schedule: drain abscess. You want to stay for this one?"

"A short while," said the Co-ordinator. He folded his arms and hooked his heels into the rungs of the stool.

Orbin shrugged, took an apron from the cupboard, put it on. He washed his hands, opened the autoclave, removed lancets.

The patient was old; he had the silver diamond on his head, a patch of pinkish-white hairs filling the peaked chevron and extending to the tip of his crown. Orbin spoke a few words, and he climbed to the table and stretched out on the unoffending side. There was a bulge at the base of his left ribcage. Orbin palpated with hands neither harsh nor gentle, and the old man accepted them without complaint.

Orbin stuffed padding under the belly, washed his hands again, swabbed, injected a local, picked up a lancet. Orbin cut. Pus jetted and ran down his apron, and he pressed either side of the wound to quicken the flow.

The Co-ordinator watched his face. The planes seemed rough-cut, immobile. He unhooked his heels and stood up.

Orbin raised his eyes. The lights of the room reflected from them in a dizzying glitter. "Feeling queasy?" There was the lightest touch of sarcasm in his voice.

The watcher smiled. "My line of work, I've been splashed with brains."

The Ungrukh's tail rose once and fell, and he began to groan.

Outside, the Co-ordinator stared across the dim red plains. He could still see those bright spots, felt slightly giddy and distinctly uneasy. He had the feeling that *he* had been probed—by an Impervious, and it was nonsense. But it was strange... he made an effort to pull his thoughts into order.

There was no love lost between Orbin and his patients. So what? There were plenty of frozen-faced doctors in the universe. Had he examined the cub earlier? Not likely, with so many. Then why not check and see if the child was harboring another thorn or two. *Because he knew?*

The line of reasoning broke when he saw that a transport rolling down from the north with its load of polar ice had skidded and stopped, lurching, a quarter km away. The cabin door opened, an Ungrukh slithered out and crouched near the wheel base, poking ineffectually at the treads. Ungrukh had taken a fancy to machines but did not yet know much about their functions.

To avoid disturbing the men working around the base, the Co-ordinator climbed the low gradient toward the stalled vehicle. He needed the exercise. But he had not brought extra oxygen and soon found himself winded. It was a weak rescuer who approached the transport. He called in Ungru'akh, "Do you need help, man?"

The heavy cat head swivelled, the Ungrukh skittered to face him in a crouch, snarling, tail swinging.

The Co-ordinator stood astonished and panting, empty hands turned out. :*It's only me, friend. What's the trouble?*:

The head rose and the Ungrukh said in a civil voice, "No trouble, man. The tread slipped on some smooth matter."

"Oof, let me get my breath, and see...." He squatted by the chassis. "Get back in now...go forward by half a meter...stop." He reached in beneath the huge machine and pulled out again. "There's a crack in the right front tread—you need that repaired—and it picks up," he pulled to his feet, "this." He offered the dark shiny ovoid in his palm. "It's called a tektite, a piece of glass Firemaster spit out long ago, and it makes the tread skid. Keep it for luck."

The Ungrukh had come out to examine the tread damage. "It is no luck when it stops my carrier." He climbed back in slowly. "You want to ride back with me, big man? I think you are a little weary." He said this shyly, as if to make up for the show of anger.

"Thank you, yes," adding very carefully, "but by the way you move your shoulder, Ungrukh, I think you are in pain."

The thick brow hairs drew down again, the whiskers stiffened. "It is only the cold. I am a Tidesman and I don't like the north."

"The doctor can help you with that."

"No. It is only the cold. I need no doctor."

The Co-ordinator knew, from a swift and unauthorized probe of his own, that the pain was great and likely caused by bursitis, but he said nothing more. He was also aware that the Ungrukh had reacted in a hostile way because he had mistaken the Co-ordinator for Orbin.

* * *

Intuition born of long experience told him to store conjecture. He headed for the Station's conference room, a pretentiously termed cubicle with doubled white-noise walls for privacy, where he felt a dose of Vivaldi flute concerto would clear his sinuses. The at-home light was on above the lintel. He buzzed anyway.

The door slid open. "Oh. It's you," said Malvina.

"Yes," he said pleasantly. *"Me."*

She was what his Scottish ancestors would have called sonsie: almost the female of his body type, tall and well-built in good proportion; she had short wavy brown hair and grey eyes, round ruddy cheeks, strong fleshed-out arms and hands only a little smaller than his own. Ideally a sexual spark should have flashed between them. Perhaps they were too much alike. But then, she was interested in Orbin. . . .

She made no move. He said, "I was getting a little starved for oxygen out there. This room's got the best supply, but if—"

She moved back. "There's enough for both of us. I was just looking at the tape again. I wanted to know. . . ."

She had the title of Planetary Engineer, though in practice the work was that of sanitary engineer, teaching Ungrukh to feed the fish and clean the enclosures, manage the dredgers that dug and spread layers of ooze in the right locations to wait for the coming of seed; maintaining recycling systems and sludge purifiers. She hated the work; she had been a sociologist in a crowded profession.

She wanted to know what Ungrukh were like. They were like leopards. The tape had only begun unreeling, and on the tri-v screen a leopard was running, muscles stretching and bunching, tail dipping behind in a casual curl.

The Co-ordinator sat behind her, folded his arms and watched the leopard transformed to a yellow outline circling a running skeleton; the background darkened. The yellow outline shifted to red, the tail lengthened. *Tail vertebrae increase by five to twenty-seven,* said the commentator. The display was computer output now. The figure slowed and stopped. *Prehensile.* The red tail spiralled about an abstract blue bar. *Rump muscles thicken marginally to permit squatting with assistance of tail in order to free hands.* Ungrukh skeleton squatting with forelimbs raised. *Note similarity to position of begging dog.* Just think that around some Ungrukh, Mister Teacher, and your head will get bit off. *Lengthening of digits by average one point five centimeters gives near-plantigrade stature to feet and increased gripping power to hands.* Figure holding green-striped ball. The Co-ordinator ground his teeth. Malvina did not hear. *Expansion of average leopard skull capacity by three hundred and fifty cc is not enough to account for sentient intelligence explained in theory by deepening of sulci and greater number and extent of convolutions.* Skull growing slightly, replaced by outline holding deeply pleated brain. The Co-ordinator sighed.

"You think this is childish?" Malvina asked.

"Just right for people like me, I expect," the Co-ordinator said.

She smiled slightly, "We'll skip the stuff about optimum development of speech centers and conjectures about ESP." She thumbed a button, *bleep* and blur, and a true Ungrukh was running, running, cub on her back and tail a lazy curl, something of disdain in its very shape.

A shiver ran down his back. "That's her."

"Prandra, you mean? That's an old picture. How do you know? But I suppose you've seen it—"

"Never. But I've seen the expression on her face a few hundred times. Doing her duty for the birdbrains. That's Emerald on her back."

"It could be Tugrik. They must have looked very much alike then."

"No. Men carry boys, women carry girls. Primitive tribalism."

"I'd have thought you'd be the last to say that about Ungrukh."

"They'd be the first to admit it. They *are* intelligent." He stood up. "I guess I've got my wind back. I'll leave you to your education."

She said, almost shyly, "You like them a lot, don't you?" Everyone was being shy today. Except.

"I . . ." he could not bring himself to use the word he wanted, "I like them very much."

She rested an arm on the back of her chair and cupped chin in fist. "That story of how they were brought here, leopards I mean, by a Qumedni, just on a whim and then...changed. Do you believe it?"

"I don't really know. I'm sure I wouldn't want to ask the Qumedni."

The door closed behind him. Nothing there for him, not even Vivaldi. And two goddam more days.

Run, Prandra, run!

Hardest was meeting the two strangers: Tugrik and Emerald.

Khreng and Prandra came down the shuttle's ladder, heads lowered in the guest-position, into the alien land: their own.

They waited, heads down, decontaminated of foreign substances; cheated of seven years. Khreng's chevron filling slowly with the silver diamond, Prandra mopish as always on landing because she never failed to forget the pill for motion sickness. They had come back not to lead a tribe, but to teach its teachers and live their own lives.

Araandru, the Tribesman, came forward and said softly, "Big man, look up."

A bounding in dust-puffs, a wind-eddy in familiar odors, the heads rubbed against their necks. "Mother, Father...."

Prandra bit her daughter's ear gently. "Mra'it...." Few Ungrukh could wring their mouths around the name Emerald, not even that young woman.

You worry? Yes. You think we forget you? No. Or that we no longer care? Perhaps.... Four minds, same questions.

Khreng and Tugrik reared simultaneously, father cuffed son's head with sheathed pads and roared, "Two beauties!"

And a tribe of over a hundred, many of whom had never known these two.

Prandra looked into the eyes of her son and grinned. Like most males Tugrik had missed the ESP, but he was a Stiller: in every successful tribe there was at least one who spoke quietly and calmed roaring tempers. "I don't ask if you are well. Many care for you here, my loves."

Heads up now, surrounded on the plain, the known and loved mixed with the unknown yet to be sorted. "And my mother in her cave as always."

"She is blind, Prandra," said Araandru.

"I know." :*A good day, Mother,*: she said with very little sarcasm.

:*And a good time for you to be home,*: said Tengura sharply.

:*And for you to pull your old bones out of that place, lady.*: Prandra laughed, hissing. "No contest of wills today. I go see her." She sniffed the dusty pink air, sneezed, and drew breath again, more deeply. "Soon I learn to love my home air again."

Khreng had caught sight of the tall figure waiting at the edge of the crowd. "Another we know!" he cried and bounded forward. "Kinnear!" The way cleared for them, the Co-ordinator unfolded his arms at last, braced himself for their combined four-hundred-plus kilos, two hot and heavy great crimson heads on his shoulders, twenty claws in his ribs.

"Easy! Easy, friends!" Kinnear laughed and panted. Two rasp tongues shaved his cheeks.

"What are you doing here, Head Security Man?"

"Sector Co-ordinator, please! I got kicked upstairs for what *we* did about the Lyhhrt on Solthree. I came to see you before I got too snobbish and too busy."

"You don't call us in the ship. Why so secret?"

"No secrets. You had more important people to see." He rapped their heads gently with his knuckles. "Go to them, Ungrukh. We'll talk later."

"I trust you are content to see your old mother still alive," said Tengura.

Prandra saw that her mother's blindness had completed itself and there was nothing to be done for it on this world; her stubbornness would not have let her accept treatment if it were possible. Yet the leucoma of the corneas, which had left them whiter than the veined eyeballs, was shocking. "I don't pretend we are great friends, Mother, but I love you very much and I'm happy to see you alive. Why do you stay in the dark when there are so many to see for you?"

"I don't care for what they see *of* me," Tengura said. "Now here is that man of yours who takes you away from us."

"And I bring her back too, my-Mother," Khreng said patiently.

"Leaving strangers to take care of your children," Tengura

was as wound-up as usual, "and your Mra'it what-you-call-her is becoming a wild one, that Raanung she chooses is a Hillsman—"

"A marauder?" Khreng asked sharply.

"He swears loyalty to Araandru, and he believes he means it, but he counts family by tens and twenties in the Hills, why do you think he is not out to meet you?"

"Perhaps he is afraid," Prandra said.

"Of what? This silverhead here?"

"Mother, that is enough," said Prandra over Khreng's growl. "Maybe *she* is afraid—"

"Afraid! That one—"

"But if Araandru accepts him so do we—Mother. Those people want food and fertile women, and if they get them peacefully so much the better."

Tengura sniffed. Silent, talking, asleep, her mind kept up a continual buzz like the faint crackle of white-noise. She had had a hard life ground between the millstones of a scientist mother and an adventurous daughter; she did not care for status by association, but early blindness had kept her from any other. She was a dreadful nuisance, and respect for her position and compassion for her handicap would not have prevented the tribe from driving her away except for two compensations: she was a stronger ESP and a better shielder than anyone else.

"What about the Solthrees?" Prandra had picked a nugget from the shifting scree of that mind.

"The one called Orbin is distrusted by everyone except the woman. She is not stupid, only a bit of a fool. The ones here before are much better. You notice *he* does not come out to meet you: he is too busy curing the natives." She spat. "They bring children to him, but otherwise they don't come unless they think they are going to die."

"Does he mistreat them?"

"No. He treats them like," she picked an image from Prandra's mind, "an animal doctor handling cattle."

"Who keeps your food bowls clean and puts up the windscreen so the cave mouth does not fill with dust?"

"The woman." Tengura grunted. "She is not a bad one."

"Why are you shielding so heavily, Mother?"

Tengura's shield was unique. Because of blindness and loneliness on an almost featureless world she was subject to hallucinations, like those ESPs on other worlds who for GalFed's sake allowed their brains to be preserved in tanks at the moment of death and used for hundreds of years. Unlike them she stored up every scrap of observation, memory, and hallucination to fortify her mind's walls, so that outsiders approaching it grew confused and disoriented. Prandra asked anxiously, "Is anything the matter?"

"Not with me. Your Co-ordinator has a thorn in his paw. You find out soon enough."

Khreng and Prandra spent the night in their old cave with Tugrik and Emerald, but not as in the past when the children had made a game of fighting over slivers of fish. Adults, they lay still now, minds open, sharing the seven years of experience that would form networks to bind them again. The young learned of the time-warp and its alien Qumedni, the perhaps even more alien Rabbi with his people; of the god Yahweh/Elohim and his analogy in Firemaster; the battle with the distant relative, Tiger; of elusive Lyhhrt and wise, ingratiating Yirln, and the marvels of GalFed Central. These were experiences given not as prizes, but as pieces of living that fit seven missing years.

And Khreng and Prandra learned of the coming of Solthrees with machines to help the world grow crops and feed cattle, tame and wild. The embryos were circling space, waiting to be brought down in blocks and frozen in polar ice until their land was ready.

The fire of branches and thorns flickered and sputtered at the cave mouth; the sky was a mauve bar on the horizon, rising into purple and then blue-black, showing its stars above two of the three moons. No one had mentioned Raanung; he was a fire-shadow in the back of Emerald's mind.

Prandra rubbed her back against the rough side of the cave wall. "Mra'it, you are Raanung's woman, and we do not yet meet him. It doesn't seem right that you are here without him."

"You meet him soon, Mother-Father. I live with him in the Hills now, but you are newly here so I stay with you a while."

Khreng rubbed noses with his daughter. "Emerald, Raanung

is welcome here, you come with or without him, it is for you to choose."

Emerald said nothing more, but composed her long graceful body and slept at once.

Tugrik, who like most Stillers had very little to say, spoke at last. "The men in the Hills don't trust us yet."

"They must learn," Khreng said.

The sun was high and GalFed Station was at work.

"Kinnear," Prandra said, "I want to talk. Can you scramble?"

"That's one I never learned," said Kinnear. "We have a room with double whitewalls."

"I don't like those little rooms. I have a scrambler for us."

"Then let's take a walk up the hill and get out of this garble." He had his oxygen with him this time and the climb was much shorter. He looked down from his vantage point. "Excusing your presence, Prandra, this is the damned dullest inhabited world I've ever been on."

"A home need not seem exciting, though it usually is."

"Your scrambler on?"

"It is on before I speak, Kinnear. Do you notice and enjoy the stillness in your head?"

Kinnear laughed. "Go on."

"My mother, whom you may call a busybody though she can scarcely move more than her tongue, says you have something on your mind."

"I'd hoped I was keeping it private."

"Not from my mother."

"I see...." He replayed the scene with Orbin for her. "It's only a feeling and doesn't have to mean anything."

"Maybe not." She paced to and fro a few steps. "Impervious often have a slight field of elasticity about them before you reach the impenetrable. In your mind Orbin seems very hard. This may not mean anything either—but I don't like the dizziness. I think I go feel for myself."

"Be careful!"

"I am always careful, Kinnear."

"Hah." Qumedni, Tiger, Lyhhrt, Quantz the drug-dealer. "By the way, who's doing your scrambling?"

"My mother the busybody—and one day I expect to

learn . . . Kinnear, I am afraid to ask. How is Madame Chatterjee in her bottle? I owe her much learning too."

"I—she's dead, Prandra. Peacefully, of natural causes, thank God."

"Good. I thank all the gods."

Prandra readied herself with shield, scrambler, locks and blocks.

"I am coming with you," Khreng said.

"Why? Whatever may be wrong about him he hardly starts anything right now."

"He is not treating you like any head of cattle either."

Prandra did not argue. She wanted Khreng's firsthand opinion of Orbin. She finished licking down her fur, and put on her most innocent face, if an Ungrukh could be said to have one.

Orbin, punching data on the recorder, looked up when the dark shapes filled his doorway. "Ah, Khreng and Prandra! I've seen the tapes of you many times, and I've been looking forward to meeting you."

So why not come and do so, Mister Orbin? "We too, and we come partly to say hello and welcome you to this world," said Prandra. "But those tapes are made when I am young and beautiful." She ran tongue over whiskers in a vainglorious gesture.

"You are still a beauty, Madame."

"Thank you." She grinned complacently. "I may be growing too old to conceive children, but we wish to have another, or a pair if we are so lucky. I miss the youth of my cubs, and that is painful. I hope I am pregnant. Can you test me?"

Khreng found the one free corner among pieces of equipment and curled into it, watching through slitted eyes.

"Very easily," said Orbin. "just lie on the table on your right side." He felt for and wiped down the great vein of her thigh, drove in the heavy needle—empty, plunger carefully depressed—and let it fill with blood. His face was expressionless. He decanted the blood into a tube and added three drops of some chemical. The dark liquid clarified to the color of a ruby. Orbin smiled. "The answer is yes."

"Ah . . . good." She scrambled off the table.

"But aren't you going to stay and talk for a while, Khreng-Prandra?"

"Thank you, Orbin, but you are busy and we have good news to tell. You please us both very much."

"I hate to say, Prandra...age does have its risks."

"We know that, man. Oh yes, we know that."

"Well the old man still has some strength left, hah?"

:*When you get over your attack of self-congratulation, tell me what is wrong about Orbin.*:

:*That's easy. He has no smell.*:

:*How can you say that? The room is full of smells.*:

:*Yes, doctors smell of cleansers and disinfectants, so some people feel they are impersonal or even inhuman. But doctors are persons, and every person I meet smells of skin, hair, scales, secretions. We know many of the cleanest people can smell strong enough to take your head off. Orbin smells of clenasers and disinfectants. Putting it extremely: not human.*:

:*Kinnear.*:

:*Here with you.*:

:*He is extra sociable, by all counts, but no tricks. That mind is really hard.*: She described the test. :*Is that usual?*:

:*It's an old standard. My wife had it and I'm a grandfather now.*:

:*Congratulations.*:

:*It's you who have them coming. Maybe my mind was working overtime, or I was suffering oxygen deprivation, and Orbin's just a plain and simple bastard.*:

:*I don't think so, Kinnear. Khreng says he smells of medical cleansers, synthetic chemical material, and has no personal scent.*:

:*Are you sure?*:

:*Of course he is sure! Is there some type of person on Solthree—or anywhere else—like that?*:

:*There's non-carbon life forms, that aren't quite persons— but any kind of organic life ... I'll have to think about that one.*:

"Now I wonder if I don't make a bad mistake."

"How?" Khreng asked.

"By bringing this matter out into the open. Kinnear leaves in a few days. He is the only one in the world with a chance to get off it—"

"So can we and the Solthrees, with our ship. That's a foolish idea."

"But if anything goes wrong—"

"A sector Co-ordinator is missed by many people. In the meantime Orbin is doing his job and not making trouble. I don't think we worry about him yet."

"Where are you going? I am ready to make supper."

"I have my own fish to roast. I come later."

"Aha? Make sure you don't get burnt."

Ungruwarkh's year is roughly equivalent to Solthree's, but the world revolves more slowly, and twilights are much longer. Khreng paused to watch the lengthening shadow of the shuttle, guarded by three strong young women, powerful ESPs with knives loose in their harnesses. Khreng had put aside knife and harness for his own venture.

Tugrik loped up to him. "Father, are you coming home to eat now?"

"I have work to do first, my love. Your mother knows where I am."

One of the young guards cried, "Tugrik, we're lonely here. Come and play with us." Firemaster had given Stillers the gift of greater size and strength than most males, and women liked them for this and for their mild tempers.

Tugrik called, "You come round when you are off duty and teach me how to play."

Khreng said with a straight face, "None of those is a bad choice."

Tugrik grinned. "I like all of them."

Khreng went on with contentment in his heart for his son and anxiety for his daughter. He kept an easy pace. The cluster of hills south of the volcano line was nearly ten kilometers west, and he wanted to save his strength and prepare the clarity of his mind so that whoever esped it would do so with accuracy and fairness.

By the time he reached Hills territory the twilight was very deep, and stars were out. As he had expected, a figure came from behind a bush and barred his way. This was a female of his own age, rather gaunt, but armed and sharp-eyed. He stopped.

"I know you are Khreng the Plainsman," she said. "I am Raanung's mother. My name is Nga."

"You allow me to call you my-sister?"

"That, or my name, as you choose."

"My-sister, you know I am unarmed. You permit me to speak to Raanung and Raanung's father as well as yourself?"

She thought for a moment. "Wait here. I find a replacement guard." She disappeared, and he stood watching glimmers of firelight reflected from the hill slopes.

Two shapes returned and he followed one up the stony path that grew steeper, winding among conical humps. Fires were built at their bases, for there were not many caves here. They passed several families preparing supper, but no one turned to look at the visitor.

Khreng had travelled halfway across the Galaxy, but never to the heart of this place ten kilometers from home. In the open spaces there were a few patches of thorny scrub, and chilling wind-eddies hissed among them. He smelled fish roasting, and bones and scraps rotting where they had been tossed aside. Hillsmen were not good housekeepers, but he had not come to study their habits. His mind was open, and his tribe was too far away to esp him. Like most Ungrukh men he accepted the absence of esp as part of his maleness, but now he wished for it if only to know whether any of his tribe had been foolish enough to follow him.

"No one is following you," said Nga. Privacy was another habit Hillsmen lacked.

"Good."

Families were smaller than usual here. In the system of springs whose water supplied the hills, GalFed had found a chemical dissolved from rock that slowly sterilized the females of both fish species and Ungrukh. This was one reason why Hillsmen raided other tribes for women. Now, courtesy of GalFed, they were drinking distilled water and eating imported fish. Whether increased fertility would change their customs remained to be seen.

Nga's family was a large extended one, and Khreng suspected

that Raanung's father was Tribesman. The group ate in the open round a big smoky fire, disdaining wind and cold. The ground about them was strewn with bones, emptied water bags, charred twigs.

Khreng stood at the edge of the circle. Nga went round it and crouched in a space reserved for her. She tilted her head to the left: "This is Raanung's father," and to the right: "This is Raanung." She hooked her claws round a twig in the fire, pulled it out, and began to eat the fish spitted on it.

Raanung's father, an old silverhead who still looked very powerful, said, "Why are you here, father of Mra'it?"

Khreng, who in other circumstances might have had his teeth in that throat within a second, was calm, almost amused. "That fish smells very good, my-brother."

The members of the circle twitched and shifted in surprise. "You have dinner at home," said Nga.

"And a long way back in the darkness. If I know I am to be offered nothing I bring my own provisions." He stood unmoving, tail curved around his flank, ears still. Faces around him glowed with eyeshine, an intimidating sight; he kept his own eyes slightly diverted from the fire; he was not taking this challenge.

After a few moments a space opened for him. He crouched in the debris and plucked a fish from the fire, neither the largest nor the smallest. He ate in the same speed and manner as he would at home, tossed the twig and bone comb into the flames; they sputtered for a second.

"I come to make sure you know how I feel," he said. He looked at Raanung, who was about Tugrik's age, and lean and rangy like the rest of his fierce tribe. "Raanung, I feel that Emerald need not hide from me in her own home." Then he kept attention on Raanung's father, though he did not miss the flicker of Nga's eyes to one side.

Emerald came out from behind a hillock but no further and stood adding her eyeshine to that of the others. It was a shrewd guess: he had not seen her during the day.

"I also feel sorrow and worry," he said. "But you who esp me know that I am sorry for leaving my children so long and worry that they hold it against me. As for Raanung and—and Mra'it, I am content. I think they make a good match for each other in both senses." He thought Raanung's fire might cool a little in the process of making Emerald's steel a bit more malleable.

"But there is one more thing I must not leave unsaid without being a coward or a liar." He spoke very quietly so that some pushed their heads forward to hear, and the pattern of eyeshine was broken. "There are times you come down to the Plains to raid us, and I believe I understand why, a little. You have trouble with fertility and food supplies. But times change: soon you are more fertile, and also we interbreed—starting with my daughter . . . and willingly. The world's life changes whether we like it or not. That is the real price of this food we enjoy, not just a few brains in bottles."

Raanung's father sprang to his feet, fangs bared. Khreng watched him without a flicker. Even among Ungrukh, Hillsmen were known to have a great taste for passion and drama as well as fighting. "Father of Mra'it," he growled, "are you warning us? threatening us?"

"Neither," Nga said dryly. "Be calm."

The old man shut his mouth, but remained standing with nostrils flared.

"My-sister knows what I mean," Khreng said. "We are fishing in reverse. First we choke on the hooks for a while, then we enjoy the bait. I know you are a hunter tribe, and if you do not hunt you become restless. So first we grow grain, and then we breed animals. Some are dull quiet ones for us mild-tempered plainsmen to slaughter," his voice rasped a little in irony, "and others are wild and free-running for those who like to hunt.

"But if we keep raiding and bickering, nobody works or eats. That is no threat. I am talking of trade and commerce. It is no bribe; I ask for cooperation. We must help each other because GalFed is not always going to stay here with their beautiful machines. When we can take care of our own affairs they leave, and you remain a strong and independent hunting tribe."

"And do I live to see that?"

"Perhaps not, nor I neither. Your son and his children do. How well can we control ourselves for their sakes?" He got to his feet slowly. "I have no more to say now, except—" he turned to Nga, "my-sister, I think you cook better than my woman. But if you are willing to eat what we offer you are welcome at my fire."

They were silent, with what emotions he could not tell. But as he was about to leave, Nga cocked an eye at Raanung's father, who said in a low rumble, "My name is Mundr," and his teeth bared again, at the name so long used to strike fear. "Soon I come down to your plains to share your food—if your people are willing to welcome me."

"I make sure they welcome you," said Khreng. He paused. "Mra'it, you are a Hillswoman. You come down with Raanung when you choose."

Emerald came forward a few steps. "Father, there is no need. You give me the name Emerald, not so?" She pronounced it with great effort. "You call me that name."

A cool one. He grinned. "Emerald, my love, we wait for you."

Nga guided him down the steep and winding path in silence. After she had resumed her sentry post and allowed her substitute to return, she said, in the dry tone much like Tengura's, "A cool pair, I think." She added with amusement and a light touch of malice, "Your Sector Co-ordinator is coming out after you, and he is in a terrible fury."

Khreng had never realized that his world was so quiet. He trotted under the stars, without hurry, and heard clearly the *whish* of Kinnear's landcar kilometers away, speeding toward him. He could not feel Kinnear's emotions and did not worry about them; he was thinking of Emerald, who would not willingly become an enemy of her parent tribe, and of Raanung, who must become his own man as well as his woman's. Of course he had not lied when he told those sharp-eyed people he was content with the match; if his spirit ached for the warm ball of fur Emerald had been, that was his own young past haunting him.

The hovercar almost skinned him, then reversed in a screech of cinders. "Get in, God damn it!" Kinnear snarled. His face was flushed. There was a stunner on the seat beside him.

Khreng cleared the window neatly, pushed down the back of the seat, and flicked the stunner into the carrier with his tail before he crouched down. "It is good to have a ride back," he said mildly.

The car shot up to the limit. "I used to think you were fairly intelligent," Kinnear said through his teeth. Khreng noticed traces of spittle at his mouth corners and smelled fear.

"I visit my family," Khreng said. "Why are you so fearful?" He had never seen the man in such a state.

Kinnear licked his lips and swallowed. His words pulled like a fish at line's end. "My wife is dead . . . Espinoza is dead. Chatterjee. Yamashita."

"How old are you, Kinnear?"

"Forty-eight," Kinnear muttered.

"That is not so old for you, is it? I am thirty-one years old. It is kind of the Qumedni to give us twice the life span of the leopard, but fifteen years from now, when you are a hearty sixty-three, I am dead or dying. Espinoza once tells me: *Your tribes compete instead of cooperating, and you must change all that.* Do you think fifteen years is enough? I must start at once and teach others before I die."

"You could have got killed tonight."

"And you lose a friend? I love you, Kinnear, but I am not here to be your friend—and Hills people are fighters, not murderers. Tcha! Prandra is waiting supper, and she is probably in a bad temper too!"

Prandra greeted him with a blow, which he deflected neatly. "So she is a better cook than I, hah?" she roared.

He gripped her round the neck and bit her ear. "That is what they call Diplomatic Relations. How do I know what kind of cook you are now? Last night you are too tired and Emerald feeds us very well, and this morning we eat the dogfood. You don't cook for seven years, and if Nga cooks well it is a marvel because her campsite stinks of garbage. Now let me eat in peace with those I love."

"From eating two meals you rumble like all the mouths of Firemaster at once."

"Then get your head off my belly so I can sleep," Khreng said.

Prandra pillowed herself on his shoulder, which was silent, if harder. After a moment she lifted her head again. "Araandru is coming. Which do you prefer, armed or unarmed combat?"

"We make no jokes about this," Khreng said.

"Diplomatic Relations!" she snorted. "I want sleep."

Khreng grunted. He flicked out his tail, twined it round a stick, and poked the fire's embers. Except when engaged in special tasks, Ungrukh kept "civilized" hours for evening meals and visits were not welcomed on a full belly. "What is the trouble, Araandru?" he asked civilly.

The Tribesman's dark shape reddened at the fire. "Khreng-Prandra, gossip says you invite Hills marauders to eat at our fires, and that does not sit very well on our stomachs."

Khreng and Prandra rose and faced him. "Gossip can keep its head shut," said Prandra.

Araandru sniffed. "I am afraid it is Tengura, Prandra."

"The same goes," Prandra said tartly.

"It is true I have no authority to give an invitation to a Tribesman," Khreng said. "But I invite Mundr to *my* fire because he is now my-brother, and I want Hills people down here in peace because it is no longer time to fight. It is *not* the old days."

"Mundr is a savage beast and his woman is no better."

Khreng said softly, "It seems to me they are much like us. In any case, he is the mouth and she is the head, and anyone who lies on top of her is bound to get a belly full of thorns. Mundr says, *I eat at your fire if your people are willing.* I promise that, and if I cannot keep it I leave my people because all my work becomes useless."

Araandru grunted.

"And Araandru, I promise *you* that no Hillsman comes down to the Plains with an unsheathed knife. I go back there and tell that to everyone if you wish."

"That is not necessary," said Araandru in no great humor. He disappeared in the darkness.

"Into the fire pot again," Khreng growled. "Life is simple when we have only Tiger and Qumedni to fight. Why bother to come back?"

Prandra laughed. "You stop before you begin, big man? Peace is never easy. We spend seven years learning for their sakes, and you convince them that without Khreng-Prandra on the Plains there is no future."

"When do I ever suggest such a thing?"

"It is stirring from every hair on your body."

"No one can say I am that arrogant!"

"Ha."

Kinnear woke startled and sweating out of an obscene dream centering on Orbin and Malvina. There were no images, words, colors to it, only a sense of filth and a deepening horror as he realized his own tumescence. His hand was shaking so badly he could not find the light switch. He rolled off his bunk onto hands and knees, dragged off his sleepsuit, and crawled on all fours to the shower stall, butting his head on a chair corner without feeling it. He touched the cubicle's door, it slid, the light came on, found *Why?* the button, water *Why?* beat on his back like *Why?* rain, crouched on knees and elbows, shook his head, spattering drops. It did not clear.

Why?

The place, no good, I'm not wanted, *I'm not here to be your friend,* says Khreng. Prandra? No, no. Flesh like peaches, and loves that *thing.* Oh. Thing. Sorry, sorry, sorry, Thing! No, no. I am a thing. Kinnear-thing? Nearly two meters and a hundred and seven kilos? Like Orbin. No. Orbin-thing is like Kinnear. Because. Look at this hand. It shakes. By itself. It has a little motor in it. It is aut-o-matic. Tic-tic-tic. Turn off water, hand. Bring towel. Out of this place. World. Drink. God, a drink. Nothing. Bring me a drink, God?

Towel on his shoulders, he crawled.

Dopestick. Bad habit. But she's dead, they're dead. Sitting at desk. He says: *You deserve a holiday, Kinnear.* For good work. *Because you're going crazy. We'll put you in a nice. Safe. Place. Upstairs.* Dopestick.

It was in his mouth, lit. Thank you.

Aagh, this tastes like shit. He dragged a hand from the floor, yanked the stick from his mouth, flung it behind him into the stall. It sizzled. He hung his head and began to cry. He shivered, wet and cold. Sobs wrenched him.

:*Unlock the door.*:

"You're not God," he whimpered.

:*You're damned right I'm not. I'm not Orbin either. Unlock the door, Kinnear.*:

He got to his knees, found the release in the dim light of the stall, and pulled back. Prandra slipped in. No dream. Heart-pounding heavy deep red furred body. Her eyes shone briefly as they turned to the stall and she sniffed the dope. Then back to him as she rose on hind legs to draw the towel around him. He saw the growing studs of her teats and shuddered. She dropped to fours, and he sat back, gripping his knees, and stared at his toes, six on each foot. He began to scratch furiously at each hand in turn, at the invisible scars where the extra fingers had been removed.

"Too many ESPs," he said dully. "Too many strange ones."

"Solthrees, maybe." She laughed, hissing. "Don't say that on Ungruwarkh."

"Why did you come?"

"You are about to send all of the Plains into fits before we block you. I and my mother."

"There's whitewalls."

"I think somebody turns off their current. The lights are working." She turned all of them on, to their brightest. "ESPs do have the worst nightmares. No need to spread them."

"I'm not good for anything."

"You remind me of someone."

"Which one? The one you called old ravelled Sheedy? You used to call me Six-toes."

"When I believe you are my enemies. But I am wrong. Even enemies deserve to be called by their right names. Now, Kinnear, if you keep on being angry, and not at yourself, I think you find the energy to dry yourself and put on clothing."

"I'm not cold any more."

"That is because I am such a hot body."

Kinnear finally woke to his situation; he flushed and grabbed the towel about himself. Prandra was laughing so hard her body was bent into an arch and her hiss filled the room. "A little joke is good for you, man! You are warm because I turn the heat up." She pointed to the dial. "You remind me of that little Rabbi in the time-warp, who thinks he is a sinner because he has terrible thoughts. He is a little man, younger than you, who is half your size and looks twice your age. He is brave too."

"Like me." He stared at the hands which had been shaking and twisting.

"I know how it is to have a poisoned mind when the poison

comes from outside. Your thoughts are irrational configurations. You are offended because Khreng says he is not here to be your friend. You forget that he tells you he loves you in the same breath—and on Solthree, when you do so much for us, he says you are as brave as he. *I* don't know if there are men braver than Khreng, and I don't want to know—but he gives you the best compliment he is capable of. Now listen, Kinnear! It is true you must leave this place, but with a straight head, and I don't use hypnodrama on an experienced person like yourself.

"You call yourself a thing. You are no kind of thing. If there is one it is called Orbin, for now. He is out of his quarters, away somewhere, and you must clear your mind before he comes back. Malvina never goes near him. She is afraid of men, does not know how to help herself, and I have no time for her. Look at your feet. They are not warped like your fingers, and nobody counts your toes but yourself. Tcha! Once we have an Ungrukh with two heads, but they are so bad-tempered they bite each other to death."

"Come on, Prandra, that's not true!"

"No," she said. "It is a fable. Not as good as your old Aesop or your great Shakespeare, but suitable for Ungrukh."

"Why? If Orbin's doing it, why?"

"I don't know. Don't ask. Leave here and go back to your work."

"I was thinking of quitting," he muttered.

"No! You do not do that!"

He looked up and into her eyes. "No...I'll go back and work."

"Yes. There are those on Ungruwarkh and over half the Galaxy who love and respect you. Sleep now and refresh yourself."

When he looked up again she was gone. He dragged himself back to his tumbled bed and slept.

Prandra loped in darkness toward home cave and fire.
:*Thank you, Mother.*:
:*You can thank Grenna and Orenda too. You have the best ESPs in the Plains working for you. Now maybe you explain this business.*:
:*When I learn to understand it, Mother.*:

* * *

She was not pleased with herself. From the time Kinnear had said, *I'll have to think about that* she had, in violation of her own ethic, remained inside his mind without permission—until he thought himself to near madness. She might have blocked his thought-train; that would have been a grosser violation. Instead, she had let him risk his sanity and had been forced to battle for it in the depths of his mind. She had gained a pause. Only a pause.

The peaceful fires glimmering in the hollows and crevices of the foothills reminded her of the village of Kostopol, its Rabbi, and the terrible power crouching over all. The skin of her back rippled and shuddered.

She had the chain of thought. Nothing would have stopped her from forging it herself, in time, but Kinnear had done it first. She was next in line to be strangled by it:

hardest Impervious I ever came across and no scent/think about/ Khreng damn fool what's he think/all right I was the fool but I/no I'm not your keeper/times like this could use a bottle/dopestick/no I want to think/putting it extremely not human/ Khreng said it don't blame me/wish I had the bloody drink/meant not a Solthree but what/robotics nobody's good enough yet, criminal with ideas of running illegal ESP racket only has to hire or be ordinary Impervious/Orbin's an ordinary Impervious/Orbin's Ordinary no he's not/damn eyelid twitching/he's not, not, not the way things've been going/ Lyhhrt in a workshell, been that route, they smell/same host-parasite/wound up try dopestick/first try chemical life-forms it is to laugh so damn chemical they think in formulas, try/a couple of those blue capsule things and maybe slee************************no no no no no no no no no no no no/no/Prandra/get away/I'm busy crying on the floor/don't come near me you have teats like a Solthree woman like her like them but eight is too many and I have twelve toes and that is too many/where do I find a list of nots you count them like toes?/not one not two/not allowed/yes I am?//I am?//not Impervious? not a Solthree? not a robot? not a parasite? not a Crystalloid?//that's five nots get away Prandra get away damn you!/not a/not allowed to say/don't make me. oh. oh./

not.a.shape.changer/no?/not.a.Praximfi?/why not? because
they're shy and stick to their own world and change into their
plants and animals part of their religious practice something like
getting high on dope and drugs are you satisfied now God damn
you to hell I'm sick

> *not? not a Qumedni?*
> *oh God*

why not, Kinnear? among shape-changers, energy-form is
the one you forget. after all, the world begins with Qumedni. no,
this one I think is not our old adversary. I defy the old evil one to
meet *me* again without recognition, and Orbin-Thing is nowhere
sophisticated enough. he even forgets to give himself a scent.
think. remember. a Doctor Ekkart is to be Malvina's workmate
and he sickens from that parasite, Schoebl's disease, coming out
from Yskeladar. GalFed looks for substitutes and Orbin turns
up studdenly aboard ship. poor Orbin. Ekkart is supposed to be
his model—before Orbin gets rid of him—instead of lying sick
light-years away covered with painful lumps. but never
mind—Kinnear is experienced, knows how to behave with the
peoples of a hundred worlds. three bound for one dim world are
expected to exchange civilities. waiting Qumedni with plans
awry—and what plans I don't know—learns and becomes
rough-cut Kinnear. Malvina, who wants what she is sure she
cannot have, is simple for him to deceive. don't get too close.
Kinnear? mind full of lost wife and friends, looks forward to
meeting his big old cats. too bad he drinks little for fear of
wanting too much. how about dopesticks to muddle depressed
mind? finds them in baggage, thinks he bought them in
spaceport, absent-minded. here Orbin-Thing gets a little stupid,
doesn't probe far enough. Kinnear smokes three dopesticks in
life, has five minutes euphoria plus one hour painful allergic
reaction. . . .

isn't it strange, Kinnear, when you are on hands and knees on
the floor and cannot rise, how dopestick turns up in your mouth,
lit, out of shelf in cupboard near ceiling? where they are
otherwise left forgotten?

. . . why send out an Impervious to a caretaking job when
there are only a few hundred Solthrees of that kind in GalFed?

do you wonder aboard ship why he is happy to have the least-preferred bunk nearest the engines, or whether his rem-counter and rad-strip are genuine—or why he stays away from the foredeck where a Qumedni's energy-field distrupts our instruments—or for what reason he is observed to make pilgrimages to our power plant here every two days?

sleep, Kinnear, and don't wonder too much

Stupid-clever Orbin, why are you here? and how do you attack next? you must attack now I know you. Why must I push so? *Run, Prandra, run!* says Kinnear. But no powers I have let me—us—run far enough.

The fires guttered; the moons and stars moved in familiar patterns; Khreng dreamed of old days. Tengura's mind crackled with barely suppressed questions; in the darkness of a lovers' niche Tugrik rubbed necks with Orenda and they growled in fulfilment.

But to her ears was silence—no, a peculiar *shluff-shluff* approached and her skin tightened. Round a hump trotted a strange Ungrukh, male by his smell, and Impervious.

Not another one! I cannot stand one more Impervious.

Then: this my attacker?

But no: he passed five meters away. Yet, coming abreast, they paused and looked at each other and between them flickered that miniscule spark of hostility that each Ungrukh carries for every other Ungrukh in the world.

The dim fires caught his eyeshine faintly, and she thought for the first time how strange a phenomenon it was, and how very strange it must appear to the alien. Then he grinned and passed with his odd shuffle.

:*No, Mother, don't tell me, don't ask, don't think. I don't want to know, I want rest, enough is enough.*:

She had no nightmares, but eyes rose on her dream-surface as out of dark water: disks of eyeshine, Orbin's blue-and-white porcelain knobs reflecting ceiling lights, Kinnear's membranes bloodshot, Tengura's white hemispheres staring out of the dark cave; and the Qumedni's windows into northingness.

She opened her own and saw Khreng's warm familiar ones regarding her. "What a night," he said and ripped a tab from a package he was grasping with his tail and spilled the contents into a bowl. Prandra was surprised to find herself with an appetite.

A weak autumn sun carpeted the floor, and she stood to shake off dust. Alive. Unharmed so far. Almost unreal. "I need a night's sleep."

"Today we do some work and maybe you get one."

The workaday world began for Ungrukh: they scraped algae and gathered dead weed from the fish pools, dumped them into compost pits; processed excrement; dredged ooze; hauled out the treacherous thornbushes by the shores and compacted them for fuel and compost, and substituted the seedlings of compatible shrubs, woody and thornless, with galloping root systems for retaining water. Khreng and Prandra, wanting to be useful, joined these activities until Malvina reminded them rather sharply that, especially in the light of Prandra's pregnancy, they had come to teach; she dispatched Khreng northward in a skimmer to survey the best locations for frozen embryos, and Prandra to a storehouse to sort out seed packets for experimental plots: there would be many of these, and many would fail.

While Prandra was on her way to unpack seed-grain, Kinnear woke. He had slept late and did not feel refreshed. :*Prandra, you've been blocking me! I can't get anything straight about last night.*:

:*It's not you I'm blocking, big man, it's everyone else! I don't want those ideas to spread too far yet. I don't dare try that on you after Chatterjee gives me hell and blazes for doing it to her. I think you are suppressing, and for good reason. When you need to remember you find your head clear enough.*:

:*But what are you running around in the open for when—*:

:*I come home to work, man. That's—*:

:*Prandra, you're in dan—*:

:*Dear friend, shut up!*:

Obscenity from Kinnear, flavored with desire for hot coffee. Prandra went about her business.

The sun shone, as strongly as it knew how; the sky was pink

with dust. Far to the north, a volcano spat, and the wind turned colder. Prandra paused to feel the first quiver of fetal movement. Eighty days, perhaps, to come, and she hoped for a double in the warmth of those inside sacs. There were no other signs from within; the first primitive synapses controlled autonomic systems, and even at term there were few communications from a dark furred underbelly world. She envied for a moment the Solthree women who bore their huge-headed babies out front with access to light and a sense of the red comfort of the womb. But she would be satisfied with term. If.

:—*if you think Tugrik is any wiser than his sister think again*—: Tengura as usual, :—*because he makes a choice in Orenda even if he does not admit it and Araandru can be happy for his daughter but even if she has a good head there is something missing at the other end when many men cannot make her pregnant no matter how often they tr*—:

:*Mother, save the bad news for later and tell me who is the strange Impervious skulking around.*:

:*Him? That one is called Kriku, or sometimes Feet. A nomad his tribe drives out because he has seven toes on each foot and his parents give an unpronounceable name so it cannot be used to call down curses and bad luck. Those Scrublanders are superstitious as the Blue Pit and they never have good luck anyway.*:

:*The tribes accept him?*:

:*Why not? He is a bit stupid but he works hard when he needs food and is otherwise harmless.*: That explained, then, the shluff-shluff of the walk.

He has a good coat and a clear eye... I wonder if he is so stupid. :*Better keep him out of sight of Kinnear. How much work can he do with those clumsy feet?*:

:*Nothing clumsy about them. Those seven toes grasp and turn almost as well as Solthree hands, and they climb and dig much faster.*:

Prandra heard a chuff, something between a snort and a laugh, and turned to see Kriku the Feet grinning at her, all the while skimming weed off the water surface with his paws as quickly as his fellow laborers were doing with their implements. She did not know what to think; she was afraid to think anything, and said a bit sharply, :*Maybe he is our next evolutionary step.*:

:—*but about Tugrik I think you must*—:

She shut off her head.

In the shed near the staked plots, packets were waiting in sealed crates with the Master of Stores and his flame cutter. In years to come, meat would feed on their crops: cow, pig, sheep, reindeer, antelope, caribou. Soybeans, oats, and barley in their hardiest mutations; weed-grasses, coarse lichens, and seaweed. Thirty crates of fifteen kilos, all that the shuttle had been able to bring on its first pass.

"We don't sort all this today," the Storesman said. "What do you want to do now?"

"Check-count random samples first."

Flame bit into the plastic and the ventilator blew the acrid smoke away. He hung up his burner and wheeled out the big standing abacus, a heavy nylon base and beads running on steel rods; it would outlast a thousand beautiful electronic calculators of much greater speed. The storesmen and their forebears of the male line had been headcounting and tallying food and instrument supplies on knotted twine for hundreds of generations: the abacus was their rational advance.

He squatted on haunches, flicked packets with his claws and beads with his tail. He laid out trays on the floor, clicked beads until the crate was emptied, and grunted. "Maybe I count again. My head is dull today."

"Your head is good. Count again." She knew what was coming. Ordinarily the seeds would have been packed sensibly, one or two types to a crate. Since she and Khreng had gone through so many dangerous situations, she had asked AgriBureau to pack mixtures so that in an emergency whatever could be saved at all would be valuable for its variety. As a result, of course, every crate had been two or three hundred grams off-weight and each had required a long packing list.

"There is a shortfall of one-twentieth tundra, one tenth north-south temperate, three-twentieths equatorial. Do I go through all of them?"

"No. But this is not a big enough sample. Take four more at random."

Flame bit through plastic again. Flick-click, flick-click. "This one counts out." He rubbed his sweaty pads in the dust. The sun climbed. Cutting agin, rank and smoky. "This too. Enough?"

"Count the other two," she said implacably.

He snorted. The flame bit and both of them sneezed. "Ah. One-tenth equatorial, one-twentieth temperate." He attacked the fifth crate with more enthusiasm, but it tallied out. He looked at her doubtfully. "I go through all of them if you say."

"No. We end up counting at midnight in the middle of a big mess. Sort the grains into regional categories, reseal the crates, and put them aside."

"GalFed is clumsy, or else we have a thief."

"GalFed is careful and nobody here eats grain. But somebody is clumsy."

She left the Master of Stores scratching his head with his tail, and scanned for Kinnear. :*Hell's blazes, Kinnear, what are you doing there?*: He was in the infirmary surrounded by hungry or ailing Ungrukh, punching the file console with one cub draped around his neck and another digging into his armpit.

:*What does it look like? I'm locum tenens for our friend Orbin, who has not been seen all day, God love him, nor has his bed been slept in, which I doubt he sleeps in—*:

:*Are you feeling well, Kinnear?*:

:*Not having a medical diploma or a dietician's certificate I'm off my head from feeding and healing. But my dope is being recycled in the manure pit—and I'd still like a drink.*:

So the packing list promised forty ten-gram packets *Festuca duriuscula* and delivered thirty-seven. GalFed was careless. :*Hold on. I am coming to help.*:

The river meandered northeast-southwest with plot lines and irrigation ditches staked off wherever vegetation might grow; the temporary Stores had been carpentered up on the northwest shore two kilometers east of the Station. Prandra took an arcing course up the northern slope; no one was working in the area and she was too tired and irritable to give anyone a good day. Khreng was somewhere around latitude sixty hovering over ice fields and would be lucky to be back my midnight. Tengura, mercifully, was asleep.

A flash from the north caught the corner of her eye, and she paused. Thunderstorms were very rare on her home plain and almost never rolled in from the dry volcanic north. She had seen thunderclouds and their lightning only twice on Ungruwarkh, at the western border of Hills territory when storms had quenched a battle with raiders. Lightning flickered again now, between two peaks where the sky, though dusty, was cloudless.

It rose like a star over the valley crest and like a falling star descended. And grew, not in size, but in brightness. And approached. It was a ball of white fire, rolling, spinning at great speed, jetting sparks, heading directly toward her.

She stood still to watch this curiosity and did not want to move. Could not. "It seems I am the sacrifice," she said and did not know what she meant. She knew she ought to be terrified and enraged, but was only mildly curious whether she would go up in a great burst of flame.

The ball of light was no more than a half-meter in diameter, but horridly hot and bright. When it was less than five meters away and she could not have dodged to save her life, seared and blinded, the spell left her, and she had time only to snarl in defiance.

A blow from nowhere struck by nothing visible, knocked her to one side; she landed on her flank, smothering a streak of fire in her fur. She sprang to fours, howling, eyelids clenched to douse the twin stars in her retinas.

When she opened them, Kriku was standing below her on hind feet, holding the flameball in his seven-digit hands, eyes on fire. He flicked the lightning orb with one claw, tossed and caught it. She scrambled away from its heat. Kriku the Feet opened his huge fanged jaws, tipped the white fury into them, closed his mouth over it; it glared for a moment through the ivory bars of his teeth. The sound of a bubble popping, the hiss of flesh on fire, and it was gone. He dropped to fours and, turning toward her, grinned for the third time.

The gates of his eyes opened into the nothingness of space beyond cosmos. She stood trembling with terror and fury.

"Qumedni," she said, "you are better looking as a Solthree. Without skin."

WOULD YOU PREFER ME TO TAKE THAT FORM?

Terrible, never-forgotten ringing in the mind.

"I think you frighten the natives."

YOU ARE STILL IRREPRESSIBLE AND THAT IS GOOD BUT YOU ARE ALSO HURT.

"My skin is tingling a little and my fur is scorched. What are you doing on my world?"

GOING UP AND DOWN AND BACK AND FORTH AS USUAL. YOU DO NOT SEEM TO BE GRATEFUL THAT I HAVE SAVED YOUR SKIN.

"From whom?"

ORBIN.

"Ah, we have two Qumedni instead of one. That is some kind of improvement, I suppose."

ONE IS PROTECTING YOU FROM THE OTHER. WHO DO YOU THINK IS REALLY DOING THE SHIELDING AND BLOCKING?

"I understand. But this time for once you are nearly a failure." Her shuddering legs gave way at last and she dropped.

I CANNOT BE EVERYWHERE AT ONCE. IT IS REGRETTABLE BUT SOMEONE WILL DIE....ORBIN WANTS SPECIMENS AND HE WILL GET THEM.

"Even to *Festuca duriuscula*," she said. "I understand what but not why."

ALLOW ME TO CURE THAT BURN.

"No I want to keep it for a while." Her voice dropped to a whisper; she felt feverish. "If you want to do a favor, bring me Khreng."

Khreng appeared, startled and blinking. "What is happening? Where are we?"

She realized for the first time that they were surrounded by a dim splotchy blur. "I don't know. Or care."

WE HAVE MOVED BESIDE TIME, said the Qumedni.

"This is our Qumedni of old acquaintance—in a new shape," Prandra said. "Our damned dull world is now a center of intercosmic traffic." She opened her mind to let him sort the information.

He shifted it aside. "You are not hurt."

"Not badly. Not for long."

"Oh. Are we expected to be killed again, as usual?"

"Only by Orbin, because we know too much, as usual."

I AM GLAD TO SEE THAT I CREATED YOU WITH A SENSE OF HUMOR.

"You give yourself to much credit," said Prandra. "You confuse us with dogs, perhaps. Cats *always* have a sense of humor—especially when they are staring death in the face. Is Kriku your true name?"

QUMEDNI HAVE NO NAMES. ONLY WAVE PATTERNS.

"That is a ridiculous name, but I don't know how to address you as a wave pattern—so, Kriku," she pulled herself painfully to her feet, "explain yourself."

YOU ARE SINGULARLY UNGRATEFUL.

"We save *you* once, Qumedni. Do wave patterns know gratitude?"

IT WOULD BE EASY TO LEAVE YOU TO ORBIN.

"For specimens? I doubt you are willing to give up that much. Do you stay here always with a hidden energy source? Are you the hallucination that walks with lonely travellers in the desert?"

I HAVE NO TIME TO BE A FRIEND AND COMPANION TO LONELY TRAVELLERS. I COME HERE ONCE IN SOME TENS OF YEARS TO FIND OUT WHAT HAS HAPPENED.

"May I guess then that Orbin is searching for your shuttle to put you out of order and takes the opportunity to throw his spitball in my direction?"

Kriku did not speak or move. Khreng said, "I don't like arguing with these ones. There is nothing to get one's teeth into."

THAT IS A VERY UNHAPPY EXPRESSION.

Prandra sighed. "Kriku, you save my life, and I do thank you. But Khreng is right. You are putting on the god: the savage beasts cannot possibly understand your exalted affairs. Free us; we piece together whatever we can and try to save ourselves without bothering you."

YOU CANNOT PIECE TOGETHER WHAT IS HAPPENING NOW.

"No? You say once that you are a bringer of new ideas and for that your people tolerate a lot. I think your people run out of tolerance and are getting back at you through us, the one you consider your creation. I don't understand why they need specimens; it is easy enough to kill us."

Kriku-Qumedni said, with some malicious glee in his cat-manifestation, THEY DON'T PLAN TO KILL YOU. THEY PLAN TO SELL YOU. Khreng and Prandra looked at each other and then at the companion, who was stretched out comfortably running his many-clawed hand through his whiskers. THIS IS REALLY AN AGREEABLE SHAPE.

Khreng said, "Those so-called buyers like cat meat, or red skins, or just hearth pets?"

THEY WANT TO LEARN HOW TO CHANGE A STUPID ANIMAL INTO A SENTIENT BEING BY AN ACT OF WILL. IT HAS BEEN DONE ONLY ONCE IN YOUR COSMOS—BY ME—AND NO ONE ELSE KNOWS HOW.

"And your...compatriots are trying to find your trade secrets before they sell?"

YES.

The Ungrukh fell silent.

YOU DON'T SEEM TO ACCEPT THIS EXPLANATION.

"It seems strange that people as powerful as yourselves want to sell a lower order of beings to a higher one."

YOU ARE HIGHER THAN MANY OTHERS BECAUSE OF ME. DOES NOT GALACTIC FEDERATION SHOW ITS POWER BY EXPORTING TECHNOLOGY? AND IS IT NOT ALWAYS REACHING FOR MORE POWER?

"And of course you are fond of power too, ha? You prefer to sell us yourself?"

Kriku disappeared and became Qumedni, the three-meter globe of being writhing with furious darts of fire. NO! I OWN SOMETHING NO ONE ELSE HAS AND I WILL NEVER GIVE IT UP!

Khreng and Prandra stood ground. They knew this one. They did not like him but they knew him. Khreng growled. "Qumedni, now you tell us when—"

Abruptly the Qumedni disappeared, and they were in their own space and time. Air ruffled their fur, distant motors sputtered, the descending sun threw long shadows on the ground. Khreng shook himself. "I am not sorry to see that one go, but I want to ask him when the transaction takes place."

"He doesn't know," said Prandra. "Why do you think he leaves in such a hurry?"

"So much for great powers...the burn hurts you. Why do you not let him cure it?"

"I want Orbin to see it. I think he is in the district."

"Into the other tiger's den? Come now, woman!"

"If he sees no effect at all he gets suspicious. He doesn't dare refuse to treat it."

"And you tell him—"

"Exactly one half of the truth." Pain and fear at last undermined her; she fainted as abruptly as the Qumedni had disappeared.

She woke gradually to the sound of the landcar and Kinnear's curses. "—traveling alone, and *then* she called you when she was with that—that—and you could both have been—"

Khreng was calm. "She knows I get *very* annoyed if she dies when I am not around...she faces lonely hundreds of years in that bottle, Kinnear. Anyway, why does Qumedni kill her after saving her life?"

"Oh, shut up!" Kinnear snarled.

Prandra yawned. "Nothing to get so excited about, big man. Is Orbin back?"

"Yes, and I was even glad to see that son of Belial. Stay still and we'll get you into the infirmary."

"I do my own walking," Said Prandra, and Kinnear dared not argue with her fangs.

"*How* did you say you got this burn?"

"I am coming from Stores to help because you are away, and a lightning ball comes over that sharp crest between the Twin Hills and runs down the slope toward me, and I am watching because it is so curious, it seems hypnotic. Then I suppose it hits me alongside and I roll over. Everything is very confusing, and Khreng is with me and then Kinnear."

There was no expression on his face. Frightening as it might have been, she would have taken grisly amusement in seeing him pop with fury into the fire-dotted globe of Qumedni. She was also glad that he did not.

He brushed off the broken hair ends lightly and rubbed ointment into the burn area. "It's not serious. I won't give you a painkiller on account of the pregnancy." Or because he knew she did not trust him enough to take it. "But one more scrape like that—"

"Lightning is *very* rare in this area," said Prandra.

"What happens to my skimmer?" Khreng asked. He was piling branches for the fire, skillfully quiet because Prandra was dozing.

"It'll come back the way it was supposed to, on auto," Kinnear said. Not being neat-handed, he squatted against the cave wall doing his best to eat some healthful concoction out of a plastic bag.

"Maybe one day we get fish good enough to eat raw," said Khreng, "but tonight I learn to cook. Today is a day for education." He dipped two sticks into a small cup of burning fuel and pushed their flaming ends into the heap.

Prandra said, "Yes. I learn that no one can esp a Qumedni." She got up and shook herself gingerly.

"Everybody knows that," said Kinnear.

"I don't think so...Espinoza says, *You cannot esp a Qumedni*, and of course I cannot, and neither can you or any ESP I know. We assume that because Qumedni can esp us they can esp each other—but not necessarily. Maybe they speak to each other in some way like radio."

"Kriku and Orbin each know the other is here."

"But Orbin cannot seem to find Kriku or his ship," Khreng said.

"Kriku told you he was shielding."

"Shielding us, yes. But Kriku says *they* are planning to sell us, and if *they* are a fleet of Qumedni, either orbiting or landed here already—it is strange if with all their powers they cannot find the single Qumedni who is in their way." Khreng stared at the pile of fish waiting to be cooked. "In the long run I guess it does not matter whether we get to eat raw fish or not."

Kinnear rolled up the plastic bag and pushed it into his

shoulder pack. He stood up, folded his arms, leaned against the wall that curved over and pushed his head down so that his chin rested on his chest. He seemed to be folding into himself. "I wonder who their buyer is, their great mysterious Being.... Qumedni are the most powerful we know in the Galaxy—"

"Why must this customer be so great?"

"Because he has something valuable to buy with—and the nerve to deal with Qumedni: Some say they have access to other universes through warps or black holes, and that may be nonsense ... our own universe is horribly big to us ... still, they seem to have some Great Big Man in the wings. They know Kriku's got a project here, and they're trying to sell it. They don't know exactly what it's good for, but GalFed's investing a lot in it, and Kriku's inordinately proud of it; they've gotten the impression that some great and unusual power is invovled, and they're trying to find out."

"If Kriku *is* the original founder," Khreng said.

"I don't see why he'd be skittering around trying to protect his project if he wasn't. I think they might have almost unlimited life spans as long as they have energy sources. And you're probably right when you say that if they haven't been able to find him by now they can't esp each other. But....

"You indirectly asked Kriku what was so valuable about you, and he gave you an indirect answer. In short, no answer at all. Now—"

Prandra said, "Kinnear, don't twist yourself out of shape with tact. We know we *are* only sentient beings in a form that Solthrees kindly refer to as the lower animals, and except for our ESPs we are no great marvel. If you clarify what you mean by the term 'gold brick' we can all speak more directly."

"Don't mistake me! An instant ago, as these things run, Kriku found or stole a group of short-lived and comparatively small-brained creatures from an obscure planet and changed them into sentient beings without all the clumsy and lumpish developments every other people has gone through. You're on a level with the most intelligent Solthrees; that's a marvel. The tremendous esp faculty is a marvel too. But in that instant you have made yourselves a people who may be primitive by many standards, and savage by some, and ignorant by others—those things are of no account—but you don't kill people except in self-defense, have never made live sacrifices, don't live by superstition, value respect and don't shame others ... and even demand justice for others as well as yourselves—and that's a miracle!

"But it's no news to you, and maybe not to Kriku. You don't need more marvels. But when the other Qumedni realize that, and their buyer finds out there are no miracles for sale—then there's going to be hell to pay." He hoisted his shoulder pack and went out without another word.

"The fire is hot." Khreng sighed. "Now the Marvel tries the great experiment."

"You don't need to learn cooking tonight," said Prandra. "Here are the children—and Raanung!" From somewhere she found genuine warmth for her words: "Long life and blessings, my-son! It is good to meet you at last."

:*And if they find time to visit their grandmother that does not hurt either,*: said Tengura.

Araandru appeared again at the cave mouth after the meal. He was oddly constrained. "Can you come to talk to me and my family, all of you? I ask to speak here, because it is a private matter, only there is not enough room."

Khreng threw dust on the fire and the group followed him. Raanung whispered, "I go home in case I cause trouble."

"My-son, *you* are no trouble," Prandra said.

Araandru, like Mundr of the Hills, had a big family and had always lived in the tribe's biggest cave. Khreng, when he was Tribesman, had never demanded it; his parents and brother had died long ago in an epidemic and he had travelled too far and too long to beget more children.

Araandru, though surrounded by siblings, mate, children and cousins, was uncomfortable. He settled himself head on arms, legs and tail tucked in, and took time before he spoke.

"What I want to say is usually a cause for happiness, but this time it is not ... Tugrik declares he wants my daughter Orenda for his woman...."

Prandra realized that the timely presence of Emerald and

Raanung was meant to back up their brother.

"Orenda is a beautiful woman and a powerful ESP," Orenda lay at the back of the cave, crouched, eyes slitted in withdrawal, "a fine daughter we love dearly—but by all evidence it seems she is sterile, and—and because Tugrik's experience is very limited we presume he is not. Tugrik is not only your son but a member of my tribe, and with all the work there is to be done in these new days he cannot be allowed to throw seed away. He is a valuable man. I want him very much for my-son—and with their permission and I hope with your approval, I offer him my other daughters and my nieces. He refuses, in all courtesy, and I do not know how to solve this problem. I ask your advice."

Tugrik stood up in an easy movement, looked round for objection, and finding nothing but embarrassed silence, said, "I don't care to make speeches, but this one time I must. Father of Orenda, my mother has a sister Ypra living in the Upper Plains by the river. Ypra's daughter Embri is badly scarred in the eye and jaw from an accident as a child, but I know of nothing else wrong with her except that she is unhappy. Men don't ask for her, but I think that is because of her unhappiness since she is not unbearably ugly. Because Orenda already agrees, I am willing to ask for Embri and have my children with her if nobody else objects." Because the faces around him seemed to be full of consternation, he added, "I know that multiple mating is not common in this generation, but it is not forbidden."

Prandra, staring at her son over the dim embers, finally found voice. "Tugrik, my love, that is not what we are worried about. Do you give us permission to esp?"

"Yes, Mother." He waited patiently in the same position.

Prandra knew that Espinoza had considered Ungrukh, though intelligent by any standard, to be psychodynamically simple. At the time she picked up this thought she had not quite realized what it meant, only that no offence was intended. Later she came to disagree and felt that Espinoza himself had modified his view. Now she understood that early judgement. Tugrik's mind was as clear as a dewdrop, without ripple or warp. There was no twist in his willingness to take an ugly woman for the mother of his children so that he could also be happy with one he loved. An innocent.

"Tugrik," she said gently, "you don't understand the feelings you stir in Embri by such a situation. She is already unhappy. Make her a vessel for your children and give your love to Orenda, and you see just how unhappy *your* life can be."

"Mother, any of these women in Araandru's family is enough to make a man happy, and they all have many choices. Embri does not. Do you think I don't expect to love my children and their mother too? Unless both you and she believe this, I don't ask for her. Every healthy child she has makes her more valuable to the tribes, and it is possible that someday another man wants her to bear his children, and she makes her own choices again."

Khreng said, barely audibly, "And takes your sons and your daughters away from you?"

"Or leaves them with me and Orenda as she wishes. In any case I give the Tribe the children it requires."

Araandru said sadly, "This seems to be too simple to be good."

"There is no law forbidding it," Emerald said in a voice as clear and cool as the jewel she was named for. "Orenda, what do you feel?"

"I love Tugrik." Her voice turned bitter. "No matter how fine an ESP I am, if I cannot have children I am as wounded as Embri."

Prandra said to Khreng, :*We are in too much danger to spend more time over this.*:

:*I agree.*: "Araandru, Tugrik's plan may not work, but it is reasonable enough. Let him try it. When we see what comes of the arrangements, we discuss it again. Does that seem fair?"

"Yes," said Araandru with relief, and the meeting broke up immediately. Tugrik and Orenda remained in the cave to talk, and Emerald came back home with her parents.

"Mother, I hope that you are not offended because I speak up for Tugrik."

"No . . . I am sad for her and her family."

Raanung said, a bit crisply, "Do you feel now that because you accept a different one like me you must accept her?"

"My-son, do you still doubt our welcome? We long to give it to Orenda . . . but her intelligence and beauty may be wasted and that is sad."

* * *

The last bar of cloud on the horizon blackened. Twilight winds on Ungruwarkh were very mild; a lazy dust-whirl sent one or two small rodents scuttling.

Kinnear was leaning against the Station wall with his eyes closed, observing not intrusively. Prandra's memory had reminded him of Espinoza's pleasure in this activity. There was often much poignancy in it, and he tried, with less success than Espinoza, to distance himself from it.

Orbin's voice said, "They're very much like primitive Solthrees." There was some perplexity in its tone.

Kinnear opened his eyes. Orbin was leaning beside him; his arms were folded behind his back and the slight stiffness of his attitude suggested that he would never master the easy gracelessness of the body he had chosen for himself.

"Well... they are primitive Solthrees, you know. That's almost exactly what they are," said Kinnear. He pulled himself away from the wall and went inside, leaving Orbin with this thought.

There was an idea buried in the depth of his mind that very badly wanted to rise and could not. But he was walking hot coals and dared not disturb them. He let it lie.

Kinnear dreamed again: no horror. He got up out of bed and went into the hallway. Malvina was standing at her open door, leaning against the lintel in her sleepsuit, normal dream costume. There was a narrow edging of eyelet lace at her neckband and sleeves; it gave a soft, almost childlike touch to her strong capable body. *Come in and have coffee, Orbin.* He was not surprised, only a little disconcerted that when he tried to say *No, I'm Kinnear,* the words would not come. They were in bed: *I like you, Orbin, I think I love you/No, no, I'm* her fingers closed his lips. She smelt of peaches, as he expected, but he felt very little. His senses damped down, his feelings diluted; she saw him as one of Blake's angels, winged and sexless, all she could accept in a man. Oh, in the pit of her mind was a horrible something, hidden and fearful, out of her childhood and bound with teak staves, steel hoops. *Trouble with Psych. Kicked out of sociology.* This thought that did not belong began to loosen the dream's bonds, and soon he dreamed himself back in his own bed ... not satisfied ... not horrified ... falling into calm sleep....

... until the hour before dawn, when the unearthly wailing jerked him out of bed, dream forgotten, and sent him fumbling with the door latch. The open door gave him a blast of cold air and the grief and fury of a tribe of Ungrukh minds.

Orenda was dead.

Hair tossing, still in sleepsuit, he ran into the twilit shadow world.

"Taking the last watch—"

"—blank out of a few moments, like that disease in the head—"

"Petit mal epilepsy."

"—hits everyone, and when we come aware again—"

Orenda's body, dark flattened shape, lay flung like trash beneath the wing of the shuttle. Kinnear pushed his way through the circle of Ungrukh and squatted beside it. It was crisscrossed with lines of beaded blood: dissection cuts.

Araandru and his family, howling, ran about unceasingly. Kinnear wanted to put his fingers in his ears, feared to give offence, ground his teeth. :*Prandra, you must have been out some hours. Not even a Qumedni could do all this in a couple of minutes.*:

:*She is the sacrifice,*: Prandra said and knew what she meant this time. Tugrik the Stiller was standing beside her, head bowed. The two young women who had been standing guard with Orenda were screaming loudest in self-reproach.

"Shut up and stop blaming yourselves!" Khreng roared. "This is not your fault!"

Araandru snarled, "It is my daughter, and someone is to blame!"

Khreng said much more quietly, "She is someone I love whom I cannot now make my-daughter." Araandru's throat rattled in fury and grief.

Kinnear stood and regarded the shuttle. No Qumedni would steal either that or the mother-ship: Qumedni energy-fields would wreck the controls. No Ungrukh would be allowed to escape in it either. He went back to the Station and found Orbin's infirmary and room as empty as he had expected. He dressed and knocked on Malvina's door.

"Who'sit?" she answered sleepily.

"Kinnear. I have to talk to you, quickly!"

"Oh, Kinnear, not so early...." Her door opened a handbreadth. He went rigid. In the streak of blue-white light he saw that her sleepsuit was edged at sleeves and neck with eyelet lace and the dream/reality hit him with knives of ice at the back of the throat and the base of the spine. "You're letting the cold in, Kinnear. What do you want?" Her voice was cold too.

"Orenda's been killed!"

"I know. You're letting the cold in."

"Oh God! Malvina...." Last night he had not been able to tell her either.

"Don't shout at me. I can hear well enough."

"You know what the danger is. My mind's open."

"What do you want?"

Her voice was almost toneless. She was being controlled. He pushed anyway. "I want us to take the shuttle and ship and get out of here. Or if you can't stand me," he added bitterly, "take the ship yourself and I'll direct you. You're the only one I have a good chance of saving."

"I don't care."

"But Orbin is gone!"

"He'll be back," she said calmly. And he would, too.

"Even if he comes, he's not a man, Malvina!"

"He's as much of a man as I want."

She was tying him in knots. The conversation was irrational. He said carefully, "I don't know whether he wants you."

"How do you know. He came to me last night." Helplessly, he felt his face going red. But he had been like a robot, and she was no longer Malvina, the warm-hearted sensible woman cruelly cut off from love. Orbin had bound her to this world, his quarter of it.

Kinnear no longer tried to argue or cajole, and dared not force; greater effort would bring down the power of Orbin. "Goodbye, Malvina."

"Don't come again, Kinnear. I am going back to sleep."

*   *   *

The storm of emotion was still raging; he could not calm it.
:*Prandra*.:

:*With you, Kinnear*.:

:*I want to use the radio. The message will not affect the
Qumedni in any way. Try to make sure Kriku understands that*.:

:*I do my best*.:

:*Okay. Pick out the call signals to Anax One from your
radioman*.:

The first planet was Ungruwarkh's only neighbor in its solar
system apart from the asteroids. It was too hot for colonizing,
but bearable enough to support a spacelight relay.

Kinnear sat with fingers resting on the toggles, trying to find
the right way to express himself. There was no right way.

TO GALFED RELAY ANAX I FELDFAR 553 FROM
CO-ORDINATOR KINNEAR OF SECTOR 492 AT
GALFED OBSERVER STATION ANAX II:

TO CRUISER *BERRINGER* DUE PICK ME UP STAN-
DARD DAY 2482 MESSAGE: DO NOT ORBIT OR LAND
ON ANAX II REPEAT DO NOT ORBIT OR LAND
BYPASS ANAX SYSTEM. END MESSAGE TO *BER-
RINGER*. TO RELAY ANAX I: QUMEDNI OCCUPYING
ANAX II. NUMBER UNSURE. KNOWN SUBJECTS 2.
SUSPECT QUMEDNI FLEET ORBITING. CHECK. TAKE
NO FURTHER ACTION REPEAT NO FURTHER AC-
TION.

He did not know when to expect an answer or if he should,
but rather than go out and face the emotions of the Ungrukh he
sat where he was and struggled with his own.

After twenty minutes the call signals beeped and he stared at
the screen. ANAX I RELAY TO KINNEAR. NO QUMEDNI
FLEET MOVEMENT RECORDED PREVIOUS EIGHT
THIRTYDAYS. DATE 2476 OBSERVERS RECORDED
SINGLE SHIP. THIS INFORMATION NOT VALIDATED.
ANY FURTHER DIRECTIVE? CAN WE HELP?

The suspicion in Kinnear's mind surfaced with an explosive
headache. He shivered. FROM KINNEAR THANKS. RE-

LIEVED NO FLEET. POLICE, MILITARY OR GALFED
FORCE USELESS HERE, POSSIBLY DANGEROUS.
KEEP THE *BERRINGER* OUT OF IT. END.

Now he had bound himself to this world.

The half-sun was orange and the lava plains brown-purple.
He had not previously noticed how the magnificent color of the
Ungrukh was dulled and washed out against a background color
so like their own. Through their big-pupiled eyes they saw their
world brighter than he did but paid no attention to such
gradations. Standing among them, however, he felt very much
an animal of a different color, pale pink in skin and bright blue
in cloth. He had an impulse to crouch down and be less
conspicuous, but it was not in character. "Get Kriku."

"I don't know if he comes," Prandra said.

Araandru growled, "Now you tell us what this is about,
Solthree!" His tail whipped. He was not a show-off with fang
and claw like Mundr, but no less respected.

"I am trying to do that, Tribesman."

Prandra snarled through her teeth. *"Kriku!"*

"I think he hides and leaves us to Orbin," Khreng rumbled.

"I don't think so," said Kinnear.

Kriku appeared—it seemed from nowhere—and shuffled
forward. Not quite so easy now in his cat shape, feet splayed over
the crumbled ridges of ground. The Tribe made space, as if they
felt the waves emanating from him. He stopped in front of
Kinnear and raised nothing-colored eyes. Kinnear swallowed.

"It is not the time for tricks, Qumedni," said Prandra. "Show
yourself and explain."

I GIVE FRIGHT TO YOUR PEOPLE. The mind-voice, in
Ungru'akh, was incongruous.

"We know great fright. We have more coming. Be kind
enough not to do it too suddenly."

Tiger-by-the-tail flicked into Kinnear's mind, but which-the-
tiger did not answer itself.

Kriku lost his color, and his features, and his outline, and
slowly expanded into the fire-writhing sphere of Qumedni.

There was no fainting, no gasping, very little stirring.
Perhaps the Ungrukh were too enraged, or some ancestral

memory had prepared them for the sight, or they had learned enough of him from Khreng and Prandra. But the sense of power he gave off was greater than they had ever known, and they pulled back further.

And Qumedni explained. He could have done this in one-tenth of a second; in deference to organic brains he took ten minutes. He added, deserting Ungru'akh for greater directness, DO NOT BLAME KHRENG-PRANDRA FOR NOT TELLING YOU EARLIER THEY WERE REASONING BY CONJECTURE AND I WOULD NOT HAVE ALLOWED THEM TO TELL IF THEY HAD KNOWN FOR CERTAIN

Araandru was trembling. "What of Orenda?"

TRIBESMAN I DID MY BEST TO PREVENT THIS BUT I CANNOT BE ALL PLACES AT ONCE EVEN WITH ALL MY POWER

Araandru reared now. "Why? Why?" he howled.

QUMEDNI ARE NOT LIKE YIRLI WHO ALWAYS KNOW IN DETAIL WHAT IS INSIDE . . . I AM THE ONLY ONE I KNOW AMONG MY PEOPLE WHO HAS THE ABILITY AND IN THIS SITUATION ORBIN WAS FORCED TO DISSECT AT LEAST ONE HEALTHY SPECIMEN

Kinnear said, "Yes, he thought it was quite all right to waste Orenda because she was sterile." He pushed down the thought that Araandru himself may have directed Orbin's attention to Orenda's sterility. "Now you can explain why there's no fleet and you and Orbin are the only Qumedni here."

I TOLD YOU WHAT I BELIEVED TRUE ORBIN SAID MY PEOPLE PLANNED TO SELL THE UNGRUKH AND ALL I KNEW WAS WHAT I LEARNED FROM HIM

"Because you couldn't esp him." Kinnear sighed. "Kriku, the Qumedni always knew of your experiment on this planet, didn't they?"

YES

"And they didn't object because there was no threat to them . . . but they never did—I'm just suggesting this, it's a feeling I have—they never did find out what happened in the time-warp—and it was Orbin who came to pull you out?"

Silence. The Qumedni spun.

"GalFed and Kwemedn don't like each other very much, but they do have a few agreements for the sake of coexistence. Qumedni land and observe where they choose, but they don't interfere and rarely make mischief out of caprice. They allowed your experiment here, but they didn't consider it especially valuable or GalFed wouldn't have been allowed to come near it, least of all make a treaty with the Ungrukh. It's not all of Kwemedn that wants to sell this world—only Orbin. Otherwise he'd have been heading a fleet instead of coming in disguise—and even that's not the way they behave. We may not agree with their standards, but they have them and maintain them. Except for one or two rebels."

Prandra said, "This one . . . he is a great sinner . . . and yet I believe he cares for his creatures, as well as any Qumedni can."

The Qumedni bloomed fire. YOU WOULD DESTROY ME IF YOU COULD

"No, Kriku. It is only the way you people think. Always the worst. But that is not so at all." She bowed her head. "Thank you for coming to speak to us."

The Qumedni disappeared.

The Tribe rounded on Prandra, snarling. "Why do you send him away? We understand nothing yet!"

Khreng whacked them back with his tail. "Fools! If we batter at his pride any more in his presence he does not protect us at all!"

"What protection? That other one is also a killer, and he plans to sell us! We have two of those damned fireballs here—and how do we tell them apart?"

"I doubt Orbin stops to talk," said Prandra.

Kinnear rubbed cold sweat off his forehead. "Why didn't we think of this before? Because Orbin wouldn't let us get our thoughts together until Kriku had been shielding us for a while. And why did Kriku believe everything Orbin told him?"

Prandra said, "In the time-warp we try to arrange matters so that our Qumedni," she said it almost possessively, "does not have to confess his mischief to his people. It is our bargain that each helps the other out of a trap. What I think is that when Orbin comes to rescue him from the time-warp he puts together what the trouble is. Then perhaps he makes Kriku beg him not to tell his superiors. That is only what I think. But if it is so I don't want to ask Kriku to admit it to us. It is *not* the time for Kriku to shame himself before his creatures."

"Creatures!" Araandru roared.

Khreng said, "It is hard to swallow, but it is better to know how the Evil thinks when we sit down to eat with him."

"With a long spoon," said Kinnear. "So Orbin had something on him. They kept a close watch on each other. When Orbin made the deal and Kriku found out and came running, he was told a story—and of course he believed the worst—that Orbin had betrayed him and had the rest of Kwemedn behind him."

"He is frightened," Prandra said. "Otherwise he is not such a fool as to think his people want to sell a bunch of cats to a Big Thing in the sky."

"Orbin does," said Khreng, "much good it may do him. But I don't like to think what it does to us."

How much do you want, Orbin? Kinnear asked the sky. A tribe, a hemisphere, a world? No answer. And that Being...must be very powerful...and very stupid. He packed up his feelings and headed for the infirmary. Ungrukh still needed food.

He could not help the sick who crowded jostling about him, but he recorded their complaints. It was depressing to think that he was likely the oldest organic life-form on Ungruwarkh and in the normal course of events would still have survived nearly three-quarters of the inhabitants. He urged all visitors to take what they were allotted, return quickly, and try to keep from congregating in large groups. He found explaining difficult and did it clumsily until Raanung and Emerald came to help; they worked with him throughout the day.

Araandru and his family, like most of the Tribe, kept to their caves; Khreng and Prandra watched over Tugrik. He appeared to be in a stupor: it was an advanced state of rage, and they did not try to relieve it. Malvina stayed in her room.

The Caretakers of the Dead, chosen by lot, washed Orenda's body and bound it in dried herbs and twigs; toward evening they poled it on a raft across the river to the southeast and set fire to it on the further bank; it burned for hours and the reflected flames gleamed and rippled downward in the slowly, moving water.

While Prandra was watching the pyre and thinking of

Orenda and her brief pleasure with Tugrik, Emerald said, :*Mother, my-father Mundr and his family are coming here. I am sending Raanung to tell them to go back.*:

:*No!*: said Prandra. :*Let them come and be welcome.*:

:*The Solthree says it is too dangerous for many to be together because of that one who is planning to gather us up.*:

:*Raanung's family is not all that large, and I want to meet them . . . at least once. Bring more food from the Stores.*:

Khreng and Raanung built a great fire in the open, and from neighboring caves snouts pointed and eyes shone. "Come out and eat if you want!" Khreng roared. "Tonight we have peace!" And added under his breath, "Whether anyone likes it or not."

The Tribe, except for Araandru's family, crept out in twos and threes. Presently one gaunt old shape came forward on shaking legs. Prandra ran to guide her mother forward.

"Stop your damned pity," said Tengura.

"Mother, my love, it is better than anger."

Mundr and eleven of his family loped in silence along the stony plain toward the hummocks where his son's family lived. They kept their heads up, but each had slipped an arm from the knife-harness; the scabbards slapped loosely on their flanks. They paused before the fire. The Tribe moved away to give them exactly one half of the warmth. The Hillsmen glanced at the pyre and its reflection for a moment, then crouched without greeting in their established order, Mundr and Nga to the forefront. Emerald took a place beside them, Raanung with the Plainsmen. They said nothing; they seemed to understand what was happening.

:*Don't think they don't send spies, peace or no peace,*: said Tengura.

They stared at her white eyes and did not ask why the disabled one had not been driven from the tribe. She stared back at them blindly until Mundr grunted and looked elsewhere.

Khreng presented him with the biggest fish; Mundr ate quickly, paused, and tossed stick and bone into the fire. A group from the Plains rose to serve the rest.

As the last bone was tossed, Tengura said in her dry ratchety voice, "Now who is to speak first?"

"I speak first," said Mundr and stood. He made no display this time, but only swivelled his head to look at all of his observers. "My woman says you Plainsmen ridicule me as some kind of joker. Hah?" With sheathed pads he aimed a blow at Nga which, if meant in earnest, would have broken her neck. She dodged easily. He looked down at her, grinning. "I tell you it takes both brains and courage to choose this one for my woman."

"No one is calling you a joker," Prandra said. "When you are our enemy we call you all the names we can think of. When you come in peace you have our respect, especially when you have the courage to say what you think."

"I come to offer my tribe in battle along with you against whatever danger must be fought. But in all my battles I never fight an enemy like the one facing us now, and I ask you how I am to direct my force. No Hillsman is afraid to fight and die."

Khreng said, "My-brother, it is not a matter of fighting and dying. Any brave man or woman can do that with claws or teeth or knives. Those are no use against the enemy. Neither are the weapons of Galactic Federation, and we have none of those. This enemy can kill with a thought. What he wishes to do is not kill but gather together as many Ungrukh as possible and drive them to another world. All Ungrukh, from all tribes."

Nga snorted. "Let him try gathering the Scrublanders with the Spotted Pinks, and they kill each other before he has time to think."

"They are dead before they have time to think of fighting," Khreng said dryly. "Self-destructive specimens are no use to him and a great loss to us, even if you do not care for them."

Mundr roared. "Then how do we fight?"

Khreng turned his head; Kinnear, who had been leaning against the hillside of Khreng and Prandra's cave, approached and stood at the edge of the crowd, arms crossed. "Tribesman," he said, "we have one of the enemy's kind who is our ally for the moment; he is shielding our thoughts and fighting the enemy as well as he can, but we cannot expect him to defend our great number of Ungrukh. We have only one other way. If the enemy considers it to his greatest advantage having Ungrukh together, Ungrukh must separate. You must take food supplies and go in small numbers all over the world, with never more than two or three of you together at once, and you must never stop to camp for more than one meal or one sleep—"

"That is cowardice! I make my tribe kill themselves on their own knives first!"

Kinnear sneered, "*That* is cowardice if you are willing to die rather than fight in a new way!" He came forward and pulled a burning stick from the fire and planted it in a crack so that his angry face flamed in its light. "The enemy is *not* invincible!"

They must join and corroborate before I die, says Khreng. But.

"When the enemy is flesh like you and me, Ungrukh can defeat him no matter how powerful he is. If his mind-weapons are only esp and hypnosis, no matter how great and subtle, Ungrukh can hold him off. But when he is not flesh and has mind-weapons beyond what we can imagine and tremendous physical powers as well—Ungrukh who stay together deliver themselves to be imprisoned or slaughtered." A buried hysteria made him feel like the parody of an ancient Roman hero addressing his legions. "If you want to see the enemy and learn how to fight him, you must run, not huddle together and grumble."

Mundr checked his temper. "Solthree, I am surely not here to fight against my people. Don't think I am Tribesman because I fight without experience, or that I gain experience without learning. And don't believe that even at my age I cannot learn more."

"I understand and honor you, Tribesman."

"When do we move?"

"Not now, not all at once. That gives warning. The enemy does not seem to be moving, so perhaps we have a little time. A few days. I know that Ungrukh are not accustomed to making plans, and that is in their favor. I myself do not much consider plans until tonight, and I speak because you are here. If you leave your homes, beginning tomorrow, in small groups, three or four times each day, without making special preparations, it is the usual pattern for Ungrukh who often go scouting or hunting. You may have to eat a few bad fish for a while. When you cross the territories of other tribes you must try to warn them...but...it is hardest for me to tell you: if they pick quarrels with you, you must run away. You say yourself you do not wish to fight your people, and no one who risks dying that way can fight this enemy."

Tugrik had been prodded gently out of the cave by Khreng and crouched quietly at the edge of the group. He would fight when necessary, but like all Stillers considered even a battle preferable to great uproar and argument. Now, when his emotions prevented him from exercising his normal calming function, he found the atmosphere unbearable and slipped away to be alone. He thought there might be peaceful darkness away from familiar places in the shadow of the Station.

There was a dim square of light from one of the small windows and this disturbed him; he wanted silence and loneliness, but it seemed that Malvina was up and about, and he did not trust her now. Then he thought he heard voices. His hearing was very sharp, but these sounds were blurred by the noise of the tribal gathering, so he moved closer: there was no one else who ought to be in the Station now. He listened, crouching beneath the window.

There were two speakers. One was Malvina and the other Orbin. His hair rose; his skin tingled. Qumedni-Orbin did not appear to notice his presence. He was being shielded or considered not worthy of attention.

"—stay and send reports as usual," Orbin was saying.

"Yes, Orbin," Malvina whispered. "For how long?"

"Five or six days. Then you can call for help. Tell what happened, but that you didn't realize what was going on until it was too late." He added, "That's not exactly a lie. I'll make sure you're believed."

"But you won't hurt them?" Her voice was childlike. Tugrik's pulses were hammering; he trembled.

"Of course not."

"And you'll come back, after."

A pause. "Yes, I'll be back."

"I . . . don't think . . . I believe you . . . will."

"You believe I will."

"Yes . . . I believe it."

Orbin came out the door; Malvina stood in it, a silhouette. They were three meters from Tugrik. A bound could reach them; he had never attacked. Nothing could hide him; he had never run away.

The fury crackled in his throat.

Orbin turned. His expression did not change; he became outlined in flame. Malvina threw herself at him screaming, "Orbin! Oh, Orbin!"

Lightning flashed. Her scream cut short.

Prandra's scream lasted forever.

Malvina was crumpled before the doorway, face purple, eyes and tongue bulging. Tugrik lay twisted, bleeding from mouth and ears. The beautiful, gentle son was dead.

"You damned Orbin!" Khreng howled. "You damned Kriku, where is your help?"

I SENT MY SHUTTLE TO DOCK, said the voice. I AM ALSO BOUND TO YOUR WORLD NOW.

"You fool, what is that to us!"

The tribes wailed and swarmed; Prandra heard nothing but the rushing in her ears.

A stranger sound rose in the south. The Ungrukh quieted to listen and esp.

"It's the ones who were visiting the Station today," Kinnear said. "They're coming back!"

Hundreds of Ungrukh from twenty tribes were running north, splashing in panic through wetlands and rivers, driven by a mindforce that sent them wild with panic.

Panic inflamed the Ungrukh of Hills and Plains alike, and they swirled, eddied, stampeded northward, roaring. Kinnear cried out to stop them and was pushed aside like a straw in a frothing river.

In the north all the volcanoes opened at once, shooting to the sky in pillars of fire and thickets of smoke; burning sprays cascaded their sides.

Mundr's roar, awesome as the voice of the Qumedni cut across the noise: "Plainsmen, are you throwing away your heads *now*?"

Kriku-Qumedni pulled himself out of whatever terror his kind might feel and laid down his shield over them. The rush stopped. Hundreds of red eyes burned in the light. Prandra was given back her senses. She joined minds with Nga, Emerald, Tengura, Grenna, pulled the rest of the women into the network: :*Emerald, east and warn the other Plains—Nga, drive your Hillsmen away—Grenna, Merra, stop those fools from the south!*:

It was too late. Ashes, lava, fire bombs were bursting down the hills, and still Ungrukh drove toward them from the south as if they had been carried on air.

Abruptly as they had begun the volcanoes subsided, rumbling and spitting over their burning flanks, still blocking passage. The smoke hung, a black roof showering ashes and cinders; it blotted the stars. The moons, tiny dim things, gave no light.

The Plains were covered with Ungrukh farther than anyone could see or sense, bodies dusted with ash or crowded half-submerged in the shallow waters. Orbin-Qumedni appeared. Qumedni now, twice the size of Kriku, twice as bright with darts of fire, and skimmed over them. They roared in one massed voice and were silent.

The southern sky began to shake. It rippled; its darkness seemed pale around the point of blackness that broke in the center of its ringed waves. The eddies of movement among the Ungrukh slowed and stopped; their growls died in broken sounds.

Khreng and Prandra, Araandru and his woman Merra, were quiet as stones. Their sky had already broken like a dish, and they had seen the nothingness in its cracks.

The point of blackness grew into a mass that shrugged the sky away with the little moons and faint stars. It claimed a quadrant of the heavens and emerged with its own lights, stunning points of brightness. The Qumedni paused between earth and heaven and became pale before it.

A rush of air whipped dust and brushed the smoke away; the black shape was beyond the universe, and yet almost near enough to touch. Its blackness was absolute; its lights were fierce. It spread downward in a fan of petals or limbs; there were not many but they writhed and twined and blended so that they were uncountable. They were armored with suns.

On the plain nothing moved but the tiny points of light on Orbin-Qumedni.

"Illusion," Kinnear whispered. "Illusion?" He was kneeling in a cave mouth where he had been shoved by the press of bodies, hands clasped between his knees, trying to clench his chattering teeth.

The Being moved very slowly; every flowing move riveted attention and compressed time. Its suns swam in currents, its outline flowed; petals shimmered. And reached. Touch?

Yearning. A warm sweet wave over the peoples of Ungruwarkh:

(One   Self)
(One Self) (nothing   other)
(nothing other)   (here   place)
(One/Self/here/place)

Ungruwarkh understood: *I am Universe,* says One/Self, over aeons reaching concept *Other.*

In all suns, no Other? ask Ungrukh. *In all Self/Universe?*
(life is)   (none   )
None aware! cry Ungrukh. *Ah . . .* their breath suspires.

Echo. The Being, dark and bright at once, pours love, longing, agony: one petal reaches, uncurls.

It holds a world.

Green-blue globe, a universe away, close enough to see each leaf, branch, tendril, wavelet, sand-grain—and Being, its gates of aching loneliness opened.

(come/love/learn/teach/know/ask/listen/hear   )

Ungruwarkh yearned toward it.

Oh, illusion! Kinnear bites his lips to stop his teeth.

But Ungrukh remember, beyond the barrier of awareness, their womb:

*   *   *

crouched on tree limb warm and rough under belly hair, each huge leaf hot green window of sun in burnt blue sky, draping tail flicks transparent-winged hummer about tawny spotted body mistaken for some giant flower, and below through branches turquoise water in its dish of white-hot sand where brown, striped, dappled shapes ripe for leaping upon flick brush tails and sip at the edge of the sweet ripple, while red-green, blue-yellow flying ones squawk their one-word cries, and beyond grasslands slope green-yellow into lavender valley shadow. . . .

"GalFed brings gifts," Kinnear whispers. "*Festuca durialis.* Does One/Self need that? There is no place here for me. . . ." Nor for that lump of barren rock and sluggish water, Ungruwarkh.

The current ran to and fro between Ungrukh and Being. Orbin remained still, waiting. Kriku might well have dissolved, shrunk, died. There was no sign of him.

The globe poised, reflecting jewelled light from an unknown sun.

"Slavery!" Kinnear screamed. "Damn you, you fools, it's slavery!"

Ungrukh about him stirred, and for a frantic moment he thought they would savage him. Or Orbin strike him down.

But they did not. He closed his eyes, clenched his fingers till he felt each knuckle, bit on his tongue with each pair of his sixteen pairs of teeth, tensed every muscle until it sent every nerve's message to his brain, bound his mind with every fact of his body, and waited for extinction as aware as life had made him.

Around him, Ungrukh closed and opened eyes, ran tongues over teeth, twitched tails, shook dust from their bodies; the center of movement expanded. And they began to hiss, the sound spread outward and over their mass.

Kinnear opened his own eyes and picked himself up, slowly, weakly.

Ungrukh hiss when they laugh. But there was nothing of joy or ridicule here, only a rueful sadness.

He looked upward. The Being waited, terribly black and fiercely bright; the globe shone; the Qumedni flickered.

Flickered and did nothing. Ungrukh laughed. By hundreds of thousands they had shaken off Qumedni, and in the presence of Being he did not dare hurt them.

Being, said Ungrukh, *your world is very beautiful, and you are the greatest marvel we know of and more than we can imagine. But we are not Other. That one who tells you of us and brings you to us is mistaken. We are small creatures who have nothing to give, and know nothing, and must learn for ourselves.*

Qumedni flamed, and if he wished the sky would fall upon Ungruwarkh it did not; the Colossus waited in patience before the microbes of a strange universe.

Ungrukh said: *Being, that world is magnificent, and it is an honor that you offer it to us, but if we live there we lose our awareness, because it is one we do not choose, and we become dull things, and you are as lonely as ever. No one in our universe knows what makes us aware, and no one can tell you, not even that one who makes such promises. Every one of us is One Self, and on our world we find the Other as well as we can. And often we die first. You know many places, and must look among them to find an Other who is as great as you are, and can comfort you.*

Where they found thoughts, they did not know, and what the Being understood of them they could not tell. They had absorbed ideas they had never conceived of and seen things they would never understand. They stood almost like cattle, but they were aware.

The globe dimmed; its light faded. It was becoming transparent when the dark petal lapped over it and it disappeared. The throats of the Ungrukh constricted, and they swallowed. For all the little they knew of beauty, they had recognized an example of it.

And the Being? Limb poised. To sweep away that insignificant life-form?

:Look there, Solthree! Look!: Kinnear recognized the crystalline mind of Emerald. He pulled himself away from the seductive brilliance of the great creature and turned to the southeastern sky.

Twenty spheres were drifting downward. A Qumedon fleet.

:*Solthree, why are they here?*:

Kinnear swallowed too. :*I called them. I didn't intend to at first, but when I was on the radio after I found Orbin had no back-up I told GalFed not to interfere on any account, even though there were renegade Qumedni here. As long as they knew that they were bound by agreement to report to Kwemedn....*: And Kriku must have known, must have realized...and allowed himself to be betrayed.

The Qumedon shuttles spat no fire, made no noise; color of lead sprinkled with soot they shone dully as they stopped to hover ten meters above ground while Ungrukh scrambled to escape their shadows. Kinnear thought Orbin must run now, but he did not, perhaps could not; his fires stilled and paled, pulsing faintly.

Twenty flickering Qumedni appeared skimming the ground beneath their shuttles, and the air they displaced whirled dust over the backs of the Ungrukh.

Fearful and awesome as they were they stood small before Being, and Kinnear wondered at their timing, if with their powers they had ever needed courage or known fear, in the way that Kriku, in his associations with organic life, had learned it. And he thought he caught a wave of something over and above the feelings of the Ungrukh, suggesting courage and determination: they had chosen their time.

For ten seconds the Qumedni probed, and they were not subtle: the massed mind of the Ungrukh opened like a wind tunnel and all their thoughts flared out of it.

The Qumedni withdrew their attention. It was impossible to tell from their demeanor what they were doing and thinking, for none moved in that uncolored cluster of shapes with writhing sparks; but it seemed they were concentrating on the far greater shape in the sky, whose limbs were now turned upward in what Kinnear would have considered a quizzical attitude if he were not terrified.

BEING, said the Qumedni in one joined resounding voice, THAT MEMBER OF OUR PEOPLE WHO MADE PROMISES TO YOU IS ONE WHO KNOWS NOTHING AND HAS NO ABILITY AND CANNOT DO ANYTHING...HE HAS NO POWER EXCEPT TO DESTROY HE IS AN OBJECT OF CONTEMPT AMONG HIS PEOPLE AND WE TREAT HIM THUS

Twenty white beams of light converged upon Orbin-Qumedni; he imploded in a tremendous reverberating thunder-clap with bursts of white lightning.

Without waiting for the dust to settle or the Ungrukh to stop trembling the Qumedni went on, ignoring the sudden swirl of limbs from the Being they faced:

DO NOT BE ANGRY BEING BECAUSE NOTHING HAS BEEN TAKEN FROM YOU IF YOU HAD ACCEPTED WHAT WAS OFFERED YOU WOULD HAVE BECOME VERY ANGRY BECAUSE IT IS WORTH NOTHING TO YOU . . . THERE ARE VERY MANY OF US AND WE HAVE MANY POWERS THOUGH THEY ARE NOT AS GREAT AS YOURS AND WE SAY

WE WILL TRY TO HELP YOU FIND WHAT YOU ARE LOOKING FOR WE CAN MAKE NO PROMISES BUT YOU HAVE ALL OF TIME TO SEARCH AND WE HAVE VERY NEARLY AS MUCH

BEING GO NOW THERE IS NOTHING FOR YOU HERE YET

Being hung suspended. Qumedni were still. The breaths of Ungrukh rasped in dust.

How can it believe them? Ungrukh asked.

It has no choice.

And it knows they can kill us before it can take us!

However Being reasoned, it sent one last faint wave of anguished longing that turned the hearts of the Ungrukh before it receded, diminished, allowed the curtain of the sky to close before it, and the moons to take their places.

The Ungrukh sighed and stirred. The Qumedni did not.

They moved northward in their cluster from under their massed ships.

NOW WHERE IS THAT OTHER ONE?

Silence.

IT IS TOO BAD THE SOLTHREE CANNOT TELL US

Kinnear cried out clearly, almost joyfully, "Thank God, I'm damned if I can!'

YOU MAY BE DAMNED BECAUSE YOU CANNOT

Khreng rose on hind legs, hands on the shoulders of those beside him. "Qumedni, do you kill all those you save to find one who also does his best to save us?" he roared. They had no eyes for him to stare down. He bared his teeth.

UNGRUKH THAT ONE IS ALSO CULPABLE

Khreng said, more calmly, "To both our peoples he is a sinner, Qumedni, but if we who are small and have few powers can forgive him, I believe Kwemedn can do the same." He looked about at his people. "I am not a leader here and I have no authority. Anyone who disagrees can say so and I shut up."

No one spoke; those who knew Kriku were grateful, and those who only knew of him were exhausted.

Only one Qumedni spoke now, and also in a more subdued manner. KHRENG THE ONE YOU CALL KRIKU MUST BE PUNISHED

Khreng dropped to fours, drew down his brows, and kept a stubborn silence.

I AM HERE. Kriku pushed his way through the crowd which had been shielding him and faced his people. Still in his cat shape, seven-toed, not quite without dignity.

"Why the hell don't *you* shut up!" Khreng snarled.

I WILL HIDE NO LONGER.

THAT IS A STRANGE SHAPE YOU HAVE CHOSEN COMPATRIOT

IT IS ONE THAT IS RESPECTED HERE, said Kriku. He changed, smoothly and quietly, into his burning self. IF YOU INTEND TO KILL ME I ASK ONLY THAT YOU DO NOT DO IT ON THIS WORLD

For the first time, Prandra cried out. "No!"

BE AT EASE PRANDA I SAID PUNISHMENT NOT EXTINCTION . . . KRIKU YOU DO NOT BELIEVE WE RESPECT YOUR WORK HERE . . . WE RESPECT IT . . . WE HAVE TOLD THAT CREATURE THAT WE WOULD TRY TO HELP IT . . . YOU WILL DO THAT . . . YOU WILL GO INTO ITS UNIVERSE AND DO FOR IT WHAT YOU HAVE DONE FOR THIS ONE IF YOU FAIL YOU WILL NOT BE KILLED BUT WE PREFER THAT YOU SUCCEED . . . THAT IS YOUR PUNISHMENT OR IF YOU LIKE YOUR REWARD

I ACCEPT THAT said Kriku. BUT I REQUEST THAT I MAY BE ALLOWED TO VISIT THIS WORLD AS I HAVE DONE IN THE PAST . . . AS LONG AS THE PEOPLE DO NOT OBJECT

"Oh, you are certainly welcome here," Khreng said. "Just don't come too often."

The Qumedni left, except for Kriku who needed time to call down his shuttle. The dust settled; the smoke drifted away; the volcanoes began to cool. The Ungrukh from the south turned homeward, tired and grumbling; the Spotted Pinks picked quarrels with the Scrublanders: both were too weary to keep them up. The Hillsmen gathered to go back to their home, but first Mundr sought out Kinnear. "Solthree, you tell us to separate or we die, and we keep together and stay alive. What do you say to that?"

"Tribesman, I say you are wiser than I, and if you ask Khreng he tells you the same." When he turned to look for Khreng and Prandra he found Khreng standing alone, head bowed and tail ruffled in dust: the blow of Tugrik's death had struck him. Kinnear could not bring himself to approach and went instead to see about disposing of the bodies. Orbin did not need to be disposed of: there was nothing left of him but a lump of glassy black rock fused into the ground.

In his mind's eye Khreng saw Prandra in their cave hunched down and buried deep inside herself. But there was no one in the cave, and its emptiness gave him another physical shock.

:*My-mother! Where is my woman!*:

Tengura's thought came in halting, quivering wisps. :*She is gone ... among the others ... so many ... I cannot tell where ...*:

"If *you* cannot tell where, that is far! Kinnear!"

:*No trace here—I thought she was with you!*:

He cried in anguish, "Why does she do this?"

:*Khreng, you know her better than I. I'll bring the landcar.*:

:*No! That blows away scent. Ask Emerald to bring Raanung.*:

He did not try to pick out a scent in an area trampled by thousands, but waited twitching near the cave mouth; presently two rangy shapes loped among the small fires of still fearful Ungrukh. "Mra'it stays with her grandmother. I bring my sister Nurunda," said Raanung.

"Good. My-son, Emerald says you are a great tracker. Can you help?"

"There is no need to ask."

It was mid-morning before they found the scent three kilometers beyond the river.

When they caught the first trace, Khreng paused and breathed deeply. Raanung looked at him and said with great care, "It does not occur to you that she may be dead?"

"Why? She wears no knife." He looked forward where the track led. "When my old woman dies she makes such a great fuss that half the world hears of it in a hurry."

Near the Eastern Plains settlement, Prandra's sister Ypra ran out to meet them in great distress. Prandra had passed at sunrise, running, and would not stop or speak; she had bared her fangs and growled even at the children she had played with when they were babies. "Tugrik is dead," said Khreng.

"Ah . . . my-brother, take food."

"Not yet."

By noon there were no hills except for a few humps among a chain of rivulets. The trackers splashed through these for an hour before they picked up scent again. They were aching and panting with exhaustion. None stopped.

Until the point at which Raanung paused to say, "There is blood here."

"I know," said Khreng and turned northward to follow it.

After half an hour Nurunda said, "Under an outcropping four kilometers north by east."

"Go back to Ypra and rest. Ask her to send for Kinnear."

"I fetch him myself," said Raanung.

Prandra was crouched beneath an overhanging lip of rock, bloody matter running between her legs. She did not, or would not, recognize Khreng, but spat and flashed her claws. Khreng did not try to touch her. Before he came within a meter of her, he heard the frantic thudding of her heart, felt the pain in her belly and the radiating heat of her body.

"Don't pretend you don't know me, old woman."

"Leave me alone." Her eyes were glassy.

"I tell others you cannot die without raising one hell of a fuss. Don't make me a liar."

"I lose . . ." she whimpered, "I lose two babies."

He crouched down alongside. "There is still time."

"No more . . . not ever."

Nurunda said, "My mother's sister dies of that fever." Khreng wrenched his head round to give her a murderous look. She added calmly, "That is before Galactic Federation comes with its medicines."

Prandra whispered, "Take the fire away from me."

"That comes from inside you and if we touch you we bring more infection," Nurunda said. "I am only a Hillswoman but I know that much. You get care soon."

"Thank the marvels of modern science," Kinnear said. "An ignoramus like me with clean hands and a pure heart and a hell of a lot of antibiotics can cure blood poisoning."

Prandra muttered, "You are an ignoramus. Nurunda is *only* a Hillswoman. We are nothing before great powers. How can we live this way?"

"Answer for yourself," Kinnear said. "You usually have a lot to tell others."

"I don't like this place. It is too bright and too white and has too many machines."

"And you're taking up too much space in the infirmary. Go home."

"I don't want to go home. That place I hate."

"Then where in damnation *do* you want to go, woman?" Khreng snarled.

"Where there is no one to remember what happens."

Khreng found for her a crevice in a split rock a few kilometers from the community where the busy minds reached her only in a faint hum and crackle. She lay there: the fever in her body was gone, but the one in her mind was turbulent with slivered images and aching memories. Her eyes were closed. She lost consciousness for a few minutes at a time.

Voices filtered:
I don't like this, said Kinnear.
It is only a great sulk, man. When she decides to get better she finds her senses ready for her again.

She did not care whether she took nourishment, but Khreng was merciless. He shoved her face in the water dish until she must drink or drown, pried her jaws open to cram in food, and clamped them shut so she must bolt it. Otherwise he left her alone and waited.

Sometimes through slitted lids she thought she saw Kriku's seven-toed feet, and sometimes the blind whites of her mother's eyes, or the long graceful neck of Emerald. *Mother?* That was not Emerald: she was running with cub-Emerald clutching the fur of her back; Tugrik chased the joyful young women, then diminished to a fuzz ball she rolled with in the dust, laughing.

Strange voice: *Do they always behave like this?*

Only when they feel like it, said Kinnear.

The great Shape hung in the sky, offering its world, *and oh, I know how it longs for—*

Some shift occurred as if a hand of creation had fitted parts that grew together. She fell shuddering into a vast warm hall of sleep.

On the branch among the leaves under the burning sky over the turquoise pool tawny and spotted among flowers and flying birds...

Was I wrong to deny them that?

:*No, Kinnear. A prison is a prison no matter how beautiful.*: She opened her eyes and saw Kinnear squatting before her in his blue cloth against the pink sky in the sunlight. She stretched, shot and retracted her claws. "You look well, Kinnear. I think this climate does you no harm after all."

His face was calm, his eyes steady. "I'm leaving, Prandra. There's a ship waiting for me."

"Good...we both have work to do."

"Yes...I hope I'll see you and Khreng again one day...I may not."

"You may not." She showed her teeth a little and raised her hand until it rested against his cheek; extended her claws so that they touched his skin, not to leave marks, but to remind him of what she was and what she wanted him to know. "One day you hear I am in the bottle, and then you do not try to see me again, ever, not even if I am in the next room."

He said gently, "Not even to watch the sunrise for you?"

"No, Kinnear, I am far too vain."

"No." He smiled. "I think that's pride." He took her hand from his face and kissed the pads. "Khreng, I expect to hear a report of peace among the tribes."

"Oh yes, and you can come see the statue they put up for me too!"

"It won't do you justice. Ungrukh, here are the new friends of your world."

He was gone in a flicker of blue, and Prandra crawled out from her shelter to catch the last mind-touch of his love and his own particular mixture of modesty and pride. Shadows fell on her and she looked up.

Small dark compact man—no, not quite like that memory. He had thick curly dark hair and beard, a wide snub nose, lively brown eyes. Beside him a slim young woman with straight black hair, light brown skin and eyes . . . a little like Yamashita's, and yet not quite. Looking somewhat anxious about these strange red cats.

"Jake Ekkart," the man said. "Only a little late. And here is Mei-lin Hsiu."

Prandra grinned, and made the young woman much more anxious as she rose and put her hands on Ekkart's shoulders. But Ekkart grinned back, in spite of the network of raw pink scars on his face from the ordeal he had endured to be freed of the parasitic disease. He knew she was testing and was not afraid at all. She hissed with laughter and dropped.

"Do I get to do that to the young lady?" Khreng asked.

"Not if you want to keep her here," said Prandra. "Jake . . . Jacob, not so?"

"Yes. Why?"

"It is the name of Diego Espinoza. But you are Ekkart, and that is enough."

"Not quite." He grinned again. "There are others."

He stepped aside for her to see, but she knew. Her legs were still weak and she lay down and watched Raanung coming across the plain with Emerald. On Emerald's back, held down tightly with her tail in firm defiance of tradition, was a male cub three days old.

Emerald did not hurry, and Prandra did not rise to meet her. No one spoke.

When Emerald's shadow touched her and the long tail plucked up the baby to settle it under Prandra's chin, she watched for a few moments while it kneaded its tiny paws against her teats where no milk would flow. It opened toothless jaws to roar a small creak of frustration. She folded an arm about it and licked the scrunched-up face a few laps.

"They are nothing much to begin with, but they grow." She laughed. "Here, give that old man there the son of his son and daughter and let us go home."

Science Fiction & Fantasy by the Best and the Boldest Women Writers From Berkley

Elizabeth A. Lynn
_____WATCHTOWER   04295-2–$1.95

Susy McKee Charnas
_____MOTHERLINES   04157-3–$1.95
_____WALK TO THE END OF
THE WORLD   04239-1–$1.95

Joanna Russ
_____AND CHAOS DIED   04135-2–$1.95
_____PICNIC ON PARADISE   04040-2–$1.75
_____THE TWO OF THEM   04106-9–$1.95

At your local bookstore or use this handy coupon for ordering: